Praise for *Girl Through Glass*

"A tragic depiction of a girl adored far too soon by a grown-up world. . . . Artfully rendered through the viewpoint of an adolescent dancer who performs with great maturity while remaining fatefully naïve. . . . So visceral, so real."   —*Washington Post*

"A haunting portrait of obsession, ambition, sacrifice, and the secrets one woman thought she left in the past."   —*BuzzFeed*

"Powerful. Gripping. Incandescent. These are only a few of the words circling my mind after reading *Girl Through Glass*. This beautifully written novel drew me into the rarified world of dance, filled with passion, glory, and heartbreak. As powerful storytelling kept me turning the pages, Wilson's extraordinary voice whispered to me about the things that both bind and divide us: desire, ambition, and love. This book will stay in my heart for a long time."

—Jean Kwok, *New York Times* bestselling
author of *Girl in Translation*

"A nimble, nuanced psychological drama that leaps through time and place with an appropriate and assured agility. . . . Wilson speaks with vibrant authority and acute vulnerability as she exposes the conflicted and competitive behind-the-scenes world of professional ballet."   —*Booklist* (starred review)

"In her lyrical debut novel, *Girl Through Glass,* Sari Wilson explores the beauty and complexity of time and the emergence of a woman's identity. This engrossing story, told with great artistry, captures the romance and rigor of art-making. Sari's prose is balletic: elegant, musical, and captivating."

—Ruth Ozeki, bestselling author of *A Tale for the
Time Being,* short-listed for the Booker Prize
and the National Book Critics Circle Award

"Intense and mesmerizing." —*People*

"The book's subject is less the ballet itself than the costs of early virtuosity—the feeling of being propelled by a force you don't understand and can't control—and the dangerous intoxication of the perfect, weightless moments when everything but 'air, motion, height' falls away." —*New York Times Book Review*

"Before now we almost knew that American ballet, after Balanchine, had—has—something savage and cruel at its heart; otherwise it would not be half so great as it is. But only a writer of very remarkable gifts could have the stylistic brilliance, the athletic daring, speed, power of ellipsis, the leap—to tell this dark story correctly, and to bring to life its principals: the crippled, romantic old man of a mentor figure and the beautiful, damaged young girl he shapes. In her stunning first novel, Sari Wilson has done just this." —Jaimy Gordon, author of *Lord of Misrule*, winner of the National Book Award

"Masterful. . . . Wilson's New York City imagery is applied exquisitely and dynamically. . . . In the end, the well-honed story line of *Girl Through Glass* is not unlike a certain kind of stylized psychological ballet, á la Antony Tudor, with heightened characters dancing along dire boundaries. Powerfully stark." —*Los Angeles Review of Books*

"While Sari Wilson's take on the New York City dance scene is pungent and vivid and slyly satirical, *Girl Through Glass* is not a novel about dance. For we never lose sight of the girl—eleven-year-old Mira Able, supremely gifted, mentored, and groomed and fêted . . . and desired. This novel of a girl who grows up way too soon is deftly plotted and beautifully written, and is about as suspenseful and affecting as a coming-of-age story can be." —Daniel Orozco, author of *Orientation and Other Stories*

"An astonishing debut. At once chilling and sensual, furious and tender, *Girl Through Glass* . . . will leave you haunted, mesmerized, and wanting more. I loved it."

—Elizabeth L. Silver, author of
The Execution of Noa P. Singleton

"An absorbing novel, rich with detail both about ballet and New York. Alongside the unusual setting of Mira's realm of dance are the . . . emotional struggles of a young woman dealing with adolescence, complicated by precocious talent. . . . For readers who appreciate complex characters and a carefully crafted style."

—*Library Journal*

"Few novels have affected me as deeply as Sari Wilson's *Girl Through Glass*. Wilson writes with an insider's authority of both the closed, cult-like world of ballet and the grim, crime-riddled New York of the 1970s, but this book's real pleasures lie in the depth of her characterizations. I loved, loved, loved this novel. So much so that I hid from my kids in the bathroom so I could read it!"

—Joanna Rakoff, author of *My Salinger Year*

"Uniformly engrossing. . . . Mira and Maurice's relationship has the fairy tale feel of *Beauty and the Beast*, but the pages brim with the realism of gritty, crime-riddled New York. . . . Surprising and bittersweet . . . elevates the coming-of-age story with a dark undercurrent about the cost of obsession."   —*Publishers Weekly*

"*Girl Through Glass* explores a lost New York through the eyes of a gifted young dancer struggling to harness the ecstatic power she wields—over her audience, her family, and the grown man who wants to make her his muse. Lush with the shame and exhilaration that lie at the lip of adolescence, Sari Wilson's debut novel bravely explores the risks of celebrating precocity."

—Miranda Beverly-Whittemore,
New York Times bestselling author of *Bittersweet*

"Wilson develops a compelling theme of loss and rebirth. Mira's story is fueled by a rage that burns intensely; the sacrifice, the dark side of her pursuit, will touch readers to the core. . . . This portrayal of a ballerina's transformation and sacrifice burns with the beauty of fire: it's powerful, it's destructive, and it dares you to try and look away." —*Kirkus Reviews*

"A debut novel of exceptional daring and verve, Sari Wilson's *Girl Through Glass* is a chilling, evocative portrait of the 1970s New York dance world and the young lives it consumed."
—Kate Walbert, author of *Our Kind*,
National Book Award finalist

"Sari Wilson has created a dark and beautiful world in these pages filled with complex and fascinating characters. *Girl Through Glass* is an impressive debut novel that will thrill readers with its steadily mounting tension, which builds, layer upon layer, to a surprising and satisfying conclusion."
—John Searles, bestselling author of
Help for the Haunted and *Strange but True*

"An intense, engrossing novel." —*National Review*

GIRL

THROUGH

GLASS

A Novel

SARI WILSON

HARPER ⬤ PERENNIAL

NEW YORK • LONDON • TORONTO • SYDNEY • NEW DELHI • AUCKLAND

A hardcover edition of this book was published in 2016 by HarperCollins Publishers.

P.S.™ is a trademark of HarperCollins Publishers.

GIRL THROUGH GLASS is a work of fiction. Any references to real people, historical events, or real places are used fictitiously. When dealing with actual people and locales, as much as possible I tried to conform to the historical record; all else is the product of my imagination.

HarperCollins books may be purchased for educational, business, or sales promotional use. For information, please e-mail the Special Markets Department at SPsales@harpercollins.com.

FIRST HARPER PERENNIAL EDITION PUBLISHED 2017.

Designed by Janet M. Evans

Library of Congress Cataloging-in-Publication Data has been applied for.

ISBN 978-0-06-232628-7 (pbk.)

17 18 19 20 21   LSC   10 9 8 7 6 5 4 3 2 1

For Josh,
from the beginning

The Beautiful is a manifestation of secret laws of nature, which, without its presence, would never have been revealed.

—JOHANN WOLFGANG VON GOETHE

(1749–1832)

GIRL THROUGH GLASS

GHOSTS

The garbage bags pile high on the sidewalks. The city shudders and heaves under the heat. The newspapers are filled with accounts of people being shot at night in darkened cars. Pride at New York City having its very own serial killer competes with the fear of going out after dark. At bus stops, children wearing keys around their necks— "latchkey" kids they are called—wait alone.

There is an infestation of bluebottle flies whose bug-out eyes see everything. They are poisoned to death in a citywide public health campaign, but barrelfuls of pigeons die too and their rotting corpses have to be stepped over while crossing the streets.

The sprinkler systems in the city parks break and, due to lack of funding, go unrepaired. Throughout Brooklyn the fire hydrants are decapitated and a barrage of water spouts forth. The children splash in the gutters with the pigeon corpses and dried Popsicle sticks and Twinkie wrappers, while the grown-ups stumble around, cursing and trying to drag them out.

Then there is the day in July when the lights go out. Block after block blinks off. Fans and air conditioners stall. Under the purple haze, people gather on street corners, in hallways, and in parks, around battery-powered boom boxes. A citywide blackout.

Thousands of ladybug eggs hatch in the Brooklyn Botanic Garden's suddenly warm storage freezer. In the days afterward, they blanket Brooklyn's parks and apartment windowsills. Then come the reports of looting and, up in the Bronx, of fierce fires in abandoned buildings. The people lock their doors and swear at the heat and pray for their city. The grown-ups are busy with the untenable state of their lives. Perhaps they feel relief at the darkness. It is the children who stand and watch their city extinguish like a dying flame.

When the ladybugs die, they fall to the grass, the floor, they crunch underfoot. They choke up vacuum cleaners. When the cool air comes, their husks are blown under piles of leaves, and, unheralded casualties of the ever-changing season, begin their descent into the earth.

Inside the world of asphalt and concrete, there is another world. Things that look like they are made by someone's hands: grosgrain ribbons and spiderweb-thin hairnets and soft leather slippers. Down the crumbling school corridors and cracked sidewalks, these delicate things can be carried like talismans in jeans pockets or book bags.

In this other world, the girls do not wear tight jeans, scuffed Keds, or stiff pleated skirts that come in cellophane wrappers. Instead, they wear tights that range in color from a soft pink to a bright salmon. They wear cap sleeve or tank top black leotards with bands of two-ply elastic around their waists. They wear ballet slippers: Capezios, which are a tawny, russet-pink, with soles that crack in the middle of the arch, making it look like their pointe is better than it is, or orange-pink Freeds, which are made in England—and have an aura of exoticness. The poor or oblivious girls wear Selba's, which are a flat pink that looks both prissy and cheap.

These girls—known to each other as "bunheads"—wear their hair braided or twisted and wrapped around to form a solid nub held in place with bobby pins and a hairnet. As bunheads, they each own a few prized hairnets of human hair, so soft and fine that they hold their breath while handling them; they pull the bobby pins out carefully, fold the nets into small balls of fur, and slip them back into their paper pouches. The mothers keep these pouches in their purse pockets—so expensive are they. Meanwhile, nylon hairnets from Woolworth's shift around the bottom of the girls' book bags while they are in the other world, catching on pens, the corner of books. The girls turn them round and round, searching for an unripped section.

In the whitewashed, cinder-block viewing room on the basement level of the new arts center, I take off my wool jacket. I smooth my black sweater dress, spray my hair to keep down the frizz, put on lipstick. I change into my heels. I load today's DVD behind the lectern and set up the viewing for the day. Today we're watching *Le Sacre du Printemps*. Of course they have already read all about it. They think they know it—Stravinsky's famous *Rite of Spring*—of course, *everyone* knows it. But few have actually *seen* it.

This is Dance History 101, first viewing section of the week. The students are a standard representation of the usual dance majors and minors, with a sprinkling of theater majors. Of the dance majors, there's two-thirds of the "dance cabal," the rotating group of students most devoted to dance at the moment, a showing from the contact improv crew, a few former bunheads who, despite their ripped jeans, piercings, and asymmetrical haircuts have not shed their romanticism or rigidity, and one kid who drives to Cleveland to take hip-hop class, since this department is modern-based, with a lineage that runs back to the 1960s.

They enter with a scuffle of backpacks and scrape of tin water bottles, these students whose style now resembles backwoods backpackers. They pull their laptops covered in stickers out of their rucksack-size bags. And, as an afterthought, their books, which they keep on their laps because there's no room on their desks. I've stopped trying to form chair circles. Whose idea was it to put wheels on these chairs? I wait for the chairs to settle into formation. Today it's a kind of a star-shaped cluster.

The DVD starts. Here is the opening of *Le Sacre*—fierce tableaus of people in bearskins and Roman sandals. A set of pointy trees, a round and ruthless sun. Their movements stab and jab and rush along with the thunder and jolt of Stravinsky's score. Halfway into the piece the group parts and reveals the shimmering awkward girl, the sacrificial lamb. She dances her strange stiff-limbed expressionless solo. Ostensibly it's the story of the ritual pagan sacrifice of a young woman who dances herself to death, but the choreography tells another story.

She strikes out, scours the stage with extended limbs, pushing back her attackers. She's not cowering, but filled with rage at her fate. She's not a lamb at all. At the final discordant climb of the shattering music, the group rushes toward her and raises her high above them, and it feels like a victorious moment. But a victory of what?

The students—I check their faces in the dimness—keep looking down or picking at the stickers on their laptops. When it's over I raise the lights. "Wow. Intense," they say. But how to unpack it, to *illuminate* it?

Michael, one of the cabal this year, jumps right in. "I mean *really*. Compare it to what we saw last week, all those tutus and girls in white and wailing violins"—the class laughs—"but if you think about it, it has the same, I mean the same *exact* themes as those Romantic ballets—*La Sylphide*. You know, the girl, the mad girl who loses her mind and dances herself to death . . . because she is too innocent or whatever—"

I nod. "Okay. But consider—you're used to seeing ballerinas in tutus, sylphs, fairy tales lit by oil lamps, and now you are going to the theater—it's 1913—and you are seeing *this*. How would it surprise you? Would it *astonish* you? Remember the title of our reading—'The Age of Astonishment.' "

We dig into the choreography—"jagged," "one-dimensional," "awkward" are the words they use. They note the turned-in legs and feet, the angular arms, the lack of plié. "Clearly a reaction to classical dance," says Jen, normally a quiet girl.

"Right," I say. I tell them that Nijinsky's dancers were often in open revolt at his choreography. "He made them use their bodies against every bit of training that they had ever received in the ballet academies of Russia and France. He asked them to betray everything they'd worked for."

"It's good Diaghilev's weight was behind him," says Michael.

"You mean on *top* of him," says Karl, the other gay guy in the group. The class titters.

"Private life aside, what is Nijinsky trying to do here?" I ask.

"I think he, Nijinksy, was just listening really, trying to fit the movement to the music. It's so fierce and so totally devoid of compassion. These are people who have been stripped down to *nothing* by the fear of the cosmos." Sioban's eyes open wide, as if she is just realizing the truth of what she is saying. "That's what he's trying to say in this dance. It's like *Heart of Darkness* by Joseph Conrad—it's about hate and fear and the savagery of the human heart, you know?"

They've been waiting for her to speak, passionate tawny-skinned Sioban who is just discovering modern dance, and is imbibing it with a missionary zeal. Classically trained, she danced professionally in the corps of a regional ballet company for a while. But she is also a neuroscience major and has an impressive bunch of scholarships, of the kind for "nontraditional students."

Michael jumps in. "It's camp! That girl's Godzilla stare—come on! It's totally over the top!"

Sioban stares at me, waiting. She has a long bony face and a constellation of acne scars across one cheek. She has curly black hair, which she wears in a high ponytail, and light blue eyes that look almost crystal. Her beauty is hard to find the source of. I remember she's a refugee from the world of ballet, that cult of beauty and perfection that I disappeared into for years of my life too.

My heart starts beating faster. I flush. I don't like to defend one student over another. But we're onto something here. "Well, let's not forget the audience's reaction, which was discussed in the article you read—near riots, remember? Can *camp* explain that powerful a reaction?" This is what I love about teaching—when some truth rises out of necessity, a truth that feels for a moment unshakable. Sioban's truth this time.

"This dance was deeply unsettling to a public still schooled in Romanticism. They wanted a fantasy of exoticism, not an encounter with our own deepest pathos." I'm walking around the edge of the star shape. Their heads crane to follow me. "Yes, it is a deeply unsettling piece of art. And it was very serious about its intent."

They—my students—bring me out, they bring me alive. I feel their eyes on me. They are waiting for something more. I drop my awareness down into my psoas muscles and envision energy into my legs. I feel my toes on the floor. For years the greatest challenge of the academic life for me was the lack of physical motion that went along with it. But I've learned that stillness has power too.

Then the words arise.

"Modernism wasn't just a response to what came before, but it was also a reorganization of self in relation to a changing world. So what is this world? A world that must confront the darkest parts of its own psyche without the aids of fantasy, of beauty, of escapism."

Before they leave, I remind them that spring break is coming up and that their take-home midterm will be available tonight, and due by Friday at midnight.

Now comes the deflation after class—the synapses have been firing, my temperature rising—and I'm back out in the March gloom, a shell of a person, my insides flayed and carted away. Teaching is an extension of my early performing.

The slushy ice crackles under my feet as I head toward my office on the top floor of Johnson, the looming stone and wood mastodon of a building built in the 1920s. I shudder, hurrying along the frozen sidewalk.

At Johnson, I stop by the program office to pick up my mail, then I swing by Bernadith Lissbloom's office. Bernadith is one of my supervisors, a history department head, a Russian history specialist, a lesbian, and a raiser of Rhodesian ridgeback dogs. She has been a supporter of me and my work, but she's old guard, comes at it from a social historian's angle, all materialist, Hegelian. No gender studies, no Lacan, no Derrida.

Her door is open, I poke my head in. "Any news?"

Her quiet, flush-cheeked bulldog self barely looks up. "Not yet. End of spring break we should have a decision."

Why do university administrators so much enjoy the power of withholding? I'm coming on the end of a one-year visiting professor appointment without a clear sense of where I'll be in the fall. Again. For the third year in a row.

Last November, when they announced the Pell, a new tenure-track cross-disciplinary position they were creating in performance studies, I thought, *Yes!* I feel a kinship with this small town, its frozen driveways, its bright gray lid of a sky, its timid attempts at downtown beautification, its inveterate army navy store, its cluster of local-food restaurants for the visiting parents. My self-destructive tendencies are in check here. In the past, my exacting nature has cost me popularity among my colleagues.

I hope I get the Pell. I pray for it.

Kate, I say to myself. *Do not fuck up now.* There's too much of me, or too much desire, or desire of the wrong kind. Whatever it is, when I *let go,* I ruin things. I need to keep myself contained, buttressed.

I've learned that the hard way.

At the end of the summer, Mira's mother takes her to Selba's. Selba's is in Manhattan, but all the way east, on a block of stores with names like Wetzel's Hosiery Outlet and Abraham and Son's Brassieres. Even if you go in the middle of the day, there are few people on the street.

They walk from the subway in the afternoon sun. Only the occasional car passes, stirring up the fetid water from the gutter. Men in tall black hats with curls of hair flowing from their ears peek out of the tiny storefronts. Above hang the black tentacles of rusted fire escapes.

And there is still the stench, the smoldering that's been in the air for weeks after the blackout. The smell of charred rubber and plastic hangs over the empty lots they pass. It makes Mira cough. The overgrown grass has been replaced by husks of bottles turned dark and cloudy from flames, scorched bricks, the flesh of tires. "The smell of the apocalypse!" her mother says, laughing. Mira holds her nose.

Inside the store, round women with stiff piles of hair guard the bins of cellophane-wrapped leotards and tights. They loudly tell customers to keep their underwear on, hand them stretched-out samples, and point to the dingy curtain. All the clothes in this store have something wrong with them—sleeves of slightly different sizes, crooked seams, or puckers in the fabric.

Her mother likes old things, used things. That is why Mira spends so much time at the dusty Salvation Army on Atlantic Avenue while her mother shops for plates, silverware, clothes. Selba's is one of those places where Mira's mother shops, not out of poverty but to prove a point to the world.

Her mother! Mira's mother is not like other mothers—and especially not like other ballet mothers.

Ballet mothers pack tiny, neatly wrapped sandwiches of sardines (good for the bones), little plastic bags of celery and carrot sticks, and yogurt with prunes. They name their daughters Danielle, Isabelle, Vanessa, something that sounds like a flower or a bell. They dress in one of two ways: in flats, Capris, and demure cable-knit sweaters—like grown-up versions of their daughters—or in fur and perfume, carrying shiny leather appointment books for their daughters. They wait in the dressing room for their daughters to finish class, crocheting or gossiping.

But Mira's mother makes Mira chickpea sandwiches on bread that crumbles when she touches it. Mira's mother wears orange jumpsuits and culottes, and *drops her off* and leaves *to do errands,* floating in at the end of class, smelling fresh and sour, like the ocean and a cloudy day. And instead of a name like a bell or a flower, she named her Mira because it is *unusual* and *different* and so now the Puerto Rican girls say *Mira Mira, is you red-haired Puerto Rican?*

No, she's just a white girl with a weird mother.

But now it scarcely matters anymore. Mira is eleven and can get herself to class. She travels with her friend Val who lives in her neighborhood but goes to a different school. They meet by the subway, their dance bags full, their hair already bound up in high ponytails, their hairnets and bobby pins in the outer pockets of their bags.

Mira's mother, in paint-splattered overalls and head kerchief, is conferring with a Selba's saleslady. The saleslady is rifling through a stack of leotards and her mother is nodding distractedly—Mira can tell she is still thinking about one of her half-finished paintings.

"Better to get them big," her mother agrees. The saleslady picks up a cap-sleeved leotard that has come loose from its packaging and lies on the bottom of the bin. She brushes off the lint.

"We're supposed to wear spaghetti strap," Mira says quickly. "Cap sleeve are for Level One and Two."

Mira's mother looks from her eleven-year-old daughter to the wigged saleslady; her forehead pinches together. "Excuse me," she says to the lady. Then, to Mira, "Outside!" On the sidewalk, they stand in a patch lit by the afternoon sun. The mica in the sidewalk glints all around Mira's sandals. A fat pigeon with a clubfoot pecks along the curb. Down the narrow street that intersects with this one, Mira can see the tower of a factory spewing smoke into the gray air.

Her mother puts her face right up to Mira's. But she doesn't yell. Instead, she leans against the wall and then slides down until she is sitting on the sidewalk. She drops her head in her hands. "Time for a break," she says. You can hear a bit of her Manhattan voice creeping in, a snipping of the vowels and a hardening of the consonants.

Mira sits down next to her. Her mother digs in her big suede shoulder bag.

"Mom, people are staring."

"Who are these theoretical people?" Rachel pulls out a bag of crushed nuts and smashed raisins and offers some to Mira. Mira looks down the long, narrow street. In the distance, she can see someone coming.

"Him." They stare as a man's form fills out with details. He has greasy hair and wears a plaid jacket. He is walking under a green and red awning. He is smoking a cigarette.

"You think you'll ever see him again?" her mother says loudly as the man lopes past.

The man steals a glance at her mother, then stops, as if he just remembered something. "Got a light?" he says.

Her mother scrounges around in her bag. Other mothers have purses, her mother has a *bag*—it is a big suede one made of colorful leather straps. She pulls out a dog-eared book of matches.

"Hey," he says, looking at the logo of the nightspot on the matchbook cover. "That's a good place. They've got a good piano bar."

"I know," she says. She pulls the kerchief off her hair, so that it falls down. It is long, wavy, and very red.

"That's some hair, lady," he says.

"Rachel," Mira says. "Her name's Rachel." Her mother lets her call her Rachel sometimes. Sometimes she insists on it. It's hard to say when she is Mira's mom and when she is Rachel.

He laughs. "Okay, kid. Okay." Something bright and bubbling passes between him and her mother. Abruptly, her mother puts the bag of nuts back in her purse and stands up. She shakes her head so that her hair moves over her shoulders. She moves her weight onto one hip. "We have to get on with our shopping mission."

He begins to move away. With a few furtive looks back, he moves into the shadow of the next building. Then her mother's hand is on the back of her head, pushing Mira inside. At the counter, her mother mumbles something. *An emergency . . . tow to the Bowery . . . Can you watch her for twenty minutes or so?* The ladies seem to understand something in her voice. Not quite her Manhattan voice. Not quite her Brooklyn voice. Something low and rolling behind the high, strained notes. The shop lady nods. As Mira climbs up on a rickety stool the shop lady has gestured toward, she knows there is no emergency. They took the subway here. Rachel's eyes brush over Mira with an unseeing look, and, cheeks blazing, she exits.

Mira sees through her sideways vision the man's plaid coat disappear and she feels the rise of the familiar loneliness of waiting, while the city rushes, clocks, and clatters all around her.

Ever since she was little, Mira remembers the feeling: her mother would be there, and then suddenly not. *Mom,* she would call. And then her mom would appear from another part of the house, or another part of a store, or even where she had vanished moments before from a crowded sidewalk.

Her mother always comes back from wherever she goes, her voice, no longer fraught and high, but low and Brooklyn, full of salt and tide. Mira's job is just to wait.

On the subway ride home, amid the rhythmic clatter of the train, Mira looks up at her mother. "Do you and Dad love each other?" she asks.

Her mother looks at her daughter, her daughter who, to her secret pride, is another version of her. Pale skin, freckles, hair the color of carrots simmered too long in broth.

"Of course."

"What's the difference between being in love and loving each other?" Mira's voice is becoming higher, more anxious.

Her mother sighs. "Being in love is like falling off a cliff. Being in love is like flying—or falling. All you feel is the wind around you." She adds: "Loving someone is something you can feel along with lots of other feelings."

"Can you hate and love someone at the same time?"

"Well, yes, I think you can. Yeah, I definitely think you can."

"Do you sometimes hate Dad?"

"Of course not. Why would you ask that?"

The train clatters and bangs in the tunnel under the water toward Brooklyn. When the train squeals into their station, they gather their bags and get off.

They turn down Clark Street. They pass stores whose front windows are still shattered. Tape covers the web of cracks at the florist shop. A board covers the front of the shoe repair shop. A lightning strike to a power generator, they said. Act of god, they called it. But the fires and broken windows were not caused by god.

They pass in front of the giant old hotel where old men gather pushing shopping carts stuffed with their belongings. Her father tells her to ignore these men, they are *tenants* who in time will be *replaced*, but her mother always greets them. "Evening, captains," she says in her Brooklyn voice. The men show grins of missing teeth.

A cool gust of wind blows in from the harbor. It is a clear evening, with darkness spreading across the sky.

"I hope Dad is home," Mira says. The shreds of a sunset hang over lower Manhattan, behind the lit-up jigsaw of buildings. An eerie silence comes over the city, as if it remembers how it is to be naked in the night.

But her father is not home.

"Maybe he's just late," says her mother, but her voice is low and unsure. Her Brooklyn voice. When Mira goes upstairs, she finds her father's dresser top cleaned of cuff links and his closet empty of suits.

In Johnson, I climb the creaking stairs to the overheated turret. Up past the college's alumni offices. Buttressed by a cup of coffee—black, no sugar—and the sweet smell of illicit cigarette smoke coming up from Dr. James's (emeritus professor in classics) office below me, I'll make it through office hours. Outside of the classroom, I'm not so easy with the students.

The office on the other side of the hall belongs to the other visiting professor in performance studies, Bill Krasdale. He'll be in later for office hours and then there will be a line of students waiting for him. That's Bill, the vulnerable, the well-loved by students—more shaman than teacher. I may have a few groupies, but he inspires love.

Sioban sits outside my office door. "Hola. Bonjour," I say. I fumble with the keys in the lock.

Inside my musty-smelling office, she flops into the metal folding chair. I squeeze by her, catching my dress on the edge of her chair, stuff myself behind my desk, and settle in. Behind me the ferns I brought up from seedlings have grown so thick they tickle my hair. They have flourished in the dim rafters here.

Still wide-eyed from her ideas, she hikes one leg over the other and bounces a green neon sneaker on her knee. She wears only workout clothes—pants so tight that they grip every muscle or so loose you can barely see her form.

"I just *love* your class so much, as you know." She gives me a wicked smile that makes her long face look fuller. She begins picking at a Buzz Lightyear Band-Aid on her finger.

I take in her nervous energy, her bitten nails half-stripped of their red nail polish, and it occurs to me that Sioban's headlong rush into academia is simply the animal's response to totally new terrain—fight or flight. It reminds me of myself in my twenties, when I was dancing modern in San Francisco, both fearful and willing to try anything. She is choosing to advance, to fight. I smile at her, a real smile.

I take a slug of my coffee. "I'm enjoying having you in this class. Your perspective"—I look out the window. It's started to rain lightly—"is invaluable."

"Thanks," she says too brightly. I wonder if I've betrayed something.

"So what can I help you with now?" I manage a warm, professional tone. To give myself something to do, I pull out my pile of mail and start sorting.

She pulls out the syllabus. "For our next research paper? On early modernist choreographers? I was just wondering—Can I do Nijinsky? I know we already did him in class, but I just don't feel as strongly about any of the others?"

Her eyes really are translucent. "I'd like you to do someone else, at least as a—a—comparison."

I've come across a single white envelope with my name on it. Something about the letter gives me pause. It's a plain envelope with my address in meticulous handwriting. I realize what's strange about it: there's no return address. I weigh the letter in my hand. It's extremely lightweight; I wonder whether anything is in it at all. I slip a finger in and rip it open. Inside the envelope is a folded sheet of Florentine-style parchment paper that falls open in my hand. I recognize the tight, cursive handwriting—from another era. My eyes hit the initial at the bottom: *M*. I snap it shut.

My head feels like it is buzzing with light; a crushing weight has landed in the back of my skull. Through all of this, I am apparently talking to Sioban about Nijinsky's sister, Bronislava Nijinska. I'm trying to convince her to write a paper on Nijinska using Nijinska's own memoirs, which is a terrible idea. "Bronislava was faithful to his modernist project. She wrote a memoir that's very illuminating. It tells the story of their youth in the Russian imperial ballet, it may shed new light on things. It's not authoritative but it gives insight—" I'm babbling. This tome will be hard to wade through. My fingers brush the shelves behind me and pull out the heavy book. I've actually been planning to read it through myself to see if there's anything there I can build an essay on. And this—my own possible scholar's find—I offer blithely to this girl for a term paper. She inspires a white streak of rashness in me.

Sioban is leaning over my desk, letting loose a smell of patchouli and sweat. "Thanks," she says taking the book. Her hand, the one with the Band-Aid, closes around my wrist. She's trembling slightly. I register the trembling hand. The tattered cartoon Band-Aid. Her strange, gentle touch. I register the fact that she's just violated the force field between professor and student. The door is open. I jerk my hand away. It's ridiculously bold what she's done. I've underestimated her. I shouldn't have picked her side today in class. She slips her folder back in her bag and smiles at me in a shy, mischievous way. Her wide excited eyes and long face, the bloom of the acne scars, dark red now, her cheekbones. *She thinks she's onstage. She lives her life as if she's onstage.*

I smooth my Ann Taylor sweater dress over my leggings, ignoring the snag that formed on her chair. She gives me another smile, this one coy and bright, maddening in its narcissism. She knows her power. I know that suddenly for certain. Despite everything, this makes me smile.

The most violent emotion comes over me—I have to look away. Now a draft comes rattling through the lead-paned windows, turning my coffee certifiably cold.

I stuff the folded Florentine paper back into the envelope and shove it under a stack of unclaimed student papers.

At that moment, Bill pokes his head in. "Hi—how's it going?" He's wearing a Russian winter hat, black and puffy, and his face beneath it shines. He's still handsome, but his opaque face is a toughened version of its younger self.

Sioban zips up her jacket. "I'm psyched to read the book," she says, her eyes gleaming. She thinks she has won. She thinks it's a game. Oh god. *God help me.* She makes her way to the doorway, squeezes past Bill.

Bill and I knew each other years ago when we overlapped at Berkeley. My last year of my PhD and in comes Bill the wunderkind first-year MA grad student, all loose-limbed from clown school in Europe. Over the course of that year, he sloughed off his clown exterior and studied his Laban and started focusing on *illusion* and a *practice*. He concentrated in theater arts instead of dance like me. I heard later that he started dating a hippie girl, Berkeley born and bred, who was *troubled*. This girl, Madeline, now his wife of thirteen years, and with whom he has two girls.

Bill steps into my office. "Kate," he says. "There's something I have to tell you." He takes his hat off. Some water drips from it. "I ended up putting in my application for the Pell." I stare at him. "Madeline's been happier—she's been working at the new co-op here and—I haven't been having much luck. The West Coast is all locked up."

The vibrations of Sioban leaving the room are still there. I stare at Bill, unable to speak. His face looks terribly smug. I've said nothing. He lowers his eyes. "I'm sorry, Kate. I know you were counting on this gig." He sighs and I know it's meant to evoke Madeline, his albatross.

With a mammoth effort, I ask, "Is she okay?"

He sighs. "She's been better."

"When did you put in your application?" I say finally.

"Last week."

"They took your application *last week*?" This is a bad sign. It means that it was probably an invitation. A buzz starts in my head.

A crush of fatigue crawls over me, which makes it easier to speak. "Thanks for letting me know, Bill." It comes out icier than I intended.

His eyes widen. He opens his mouth, closes it. "Okay, okay. I'll be seeing you."

"Bill—"

He turns.

"I didn't mean—"

"I know," he says. He looks tired, but I can see some damage has been done.

At home that evening, I put on a bathrobe, light a cigarette, and give in to my rage. Did Bill lie to me? Did he apply earlier? If so, he wouldn't be the first to keep a secret. It would only be karmic. The fact is, though, if the Pell doesn't come through I'm pretty much screwed. The only other thing I have out there is Alquinon, a third-rate university on the bleak border of Canada. I put in an application for a dance professor position (mostly technique, though) because it seemed a "safety school." But already a few other universities have passed on me.

I take a deep drag on my illicit smoke-stick saved for emergencies of this sort. I pick up a glass paperweight with a red flower embedded in it, a gift from my mentor in grad school, a woman who was part of the 1960s new wave of dancers and movement artists, and who passed away last fall. I run my hand gently over the smooth glass, then I pick it up and hurl it across the room. It hits the wall and shatters. A shiver runs down my spine.

After I clean up the shards of glass, I wander into my office and take a copy of my dissertation book—*Corporeality Subverted: The (Dis)embodied Feminine in the Aesthetic of George Balanchine, 1958–1982*—the minimalist gray and black cover, and hold it in my hands, looking out my back window toward campus. The sunset is starting up like some tired toy that keeps playing the same old tune. It is disturbingly bright—the clouds have opened a stream of luminous pink-yellow light the color of a scab on a baby's knee. The light has the brilliance of something having been saved up and now squandered all at once. Then the moment shifts: some tipping point of night has passed and I can only see myself, reflected in my window, surrounded by my office things, my big bright hair gleaming in all its hurrahs.

It's been two weeks since her father left. Classes at The Little Kirov have started again. In the girls' dressing room, Mira and her friends change. Mira loves this moment of transformation, when she gets to shed her jeans and emerges in her pink tights and black leotard—her second skin. Since her dad left, she has begun to wear her tights and leotards under her school clothes so she can skip the awkward moment of nakedness between her two selves.

She has been working hard, harder than she ever has before. This work—she had not known what it was to work before—comes as a relief. She clings to it, to the feeling of twisting her mind around a combination, the quivering in her legs when she stretches her dégagés until her toes cramp.

Val jumps up on a bench and begins singing the most recent hit song on the radio. Delia climbs up next to her, and Delia and Val sing together. Then Meaghan joins in. Standing on the bench behind her, they all sing together—the words are something about dreams, morning, kissing, and crying.

Mira can hear the song's orchestral crescendo in her head, but something stops her from joining in. She is too aware of the older girls—of Hannah turning toward them, of being caught in that smirking gaze.

The older girls are gathered in a pack over on the other side of the dressing room. They are half in their ballet outfits, and half still in their school clothes. You can still see their separateness, how in the outside world they would never speak to each other. Robin, a Level

5 girl, pulls on leg warmers and picks her way between open soda cans and unwound Ace bandages, toward the dressing room door. She has a little heart-shaped face and limpid eyes that blink a lot when she comes in from outside, and no matter what the weather, her skin is always white with the opaqueness of alabaster. She goes to a performing arts school and arrives with her hair already tightly wrapped in a bun, her tights visible beneath short denim shorts, the straps of her leotard poking out of a scoop-neck sweatshirt. With her far-off, liquid gaze, Robin focuses on a horizon visible only to her. Mira wants to see what Robin sees. They all do.

Hannah, another Level 5 girl, is changing too. Over her tights, she still wears a white oxford with a Catholic school emblem on the breast pocket. Her half-undone pointe shoe ribbons have edges dark with grime. (She has taken to walking around with them undone.)

Last spring, excitement over Hannah's discovery, her possible rise, spread through the hallways of the Kirov. Hannah had performed the Flower Princess in the Kirov's annual production of *The Wounded Prince* and a reviewer from the *Times* singled her out. He praised her for "a rare musicality" and "an extension that made her limbs appear to fly on their own." Mira had spent the rest of the spring huddled in the doorway of the older girls' class, dissecting Hannah's turnout, her arch, her anatomy, searching for clues, for understanding.

Then, in the spring, Hannah got to the final rounds of SAB auditions. Fewer than fifteen blocks north of Little Kirov is the newly renovated SAB, or School of American Ballet, boasting warehouse-size classrooms with industrial flooring and diffuse light. Here the mothers spend their time with their noses pressed to windows to catch glimpses of New York City Ballet dancers. A few blocks south of SAB is ABT, the American Ballet Theater's school, which fills an entire crumbling brick building with dark, sweaty, mysterious warrens of classrooms and rehearsal spaces.

SAB and ABT signify the community of the chosen. Getting into one of these schools means a shot at getting into one of these companies. All the other studios throughout the city, including The Little Kirov, are feeding ponds for SAB and ABT. Essentially, you go on to one of these two schools—or you go nowhere.

The long, hot summer has ended, classes have started up again, and Hannah remains at the Kirov, in the Level 5 class, with the other fourteen- and fifteen-year-olds. Hannah has missed her chance. Mothers whisper about "problems with her architecture." Was it her spine—or was it her hips? Or her feet?

Mira notices that Hannah no longer bothers to put her hair up in a bun for class but lets it swing loose in a ponytail. She has rounder thighs and now wears a bra that makes a lumpy shape in her leotard. As she comes down the hall, her ponytail swinging, all fresh air and unabashed anger, Mira avoids her "what's it to you?" stare. Mira pushes herself up against the wall and looks at her feet; she gets out of Hannah's way.

Too late. Hannah's gaze rests on her. Mira feels a wash of cold flood through her, which leaves her fingertips hurting. Behind her, Val and the others are still singing.

"You're good, right?" Now a smile is playing at both sides of Hannah's face.

Mira nods. She *is* good. That promise she has made to herself at the start of this year has bloomed into some beating, driving bird that pumps its strong, tiny wings in her chest during class. The harder she works, the higher the bird tries to fly.

"Leave her alone," Robin says.

"Oh yeah?" says Hannah.

"Yeah. Leave her alone."

Hannah laughs. "Or else?"

"Girls!" Laura's mother stands in the doorway with her hands on her hips. "Please!" Mira looks at Val and then down, fighting a smile. Laura's mother is the kind of ballet mother Mira and Val make fun of, the kind who goes up to the barre after recitals and tries to do some of the ballet moves herself, the kind who stands in the doorway and yells "We need a new nutritionist for Laura!"

Laura stands with her back to the wall, looking at her mother in dismay. Mira catches sight of Laura's prissy pink vinyl-shiny ballet shoes. Anger cleaves at her—who is this girl, who are any of them, to flout the sartorial rules of this world that can turn children into princesses and princes?

Hannah gives Laura's mother a stony stare. Laura's mother touches her hair self-consciously and turns. Laura's mother can't really yell at the older girls. They are the linchpins of this world.

"Come on," Hannah says.

The older girls brush by Mira and Val, Laura's mother, and the other girls and mothers, with a swish of their warm-up pants and the clunk clunk of pointe shoes against the floor, swaying under the weight of their giant dance bags. When they have passed through, a hush follows.

To Mira and Val, Laura's mother says, "Have some respect, would you? Go play outside in the hallway."

But even if Mira's mother were here, she wouldn't care. Her mother ties ribbons in Mira's hair when she remembers, and then they loosen, droop, and fall out, and her mother doesn't even notice. And now, with her father gone, she is even more distracted. In her red kimono or rotating sets of overalls, she is transforming the living room with stuff she carries down from the junk room.

"*One,*" her mother sings, "*singular sensation,*" as she walks upstairs with a beaded lamp shade she commandeered from somewhere in the house. The living room begins to fill up with big plants, throw pillows, and low soft-glow lamps that perch on the floor like sleepy cats. Ashtrays appear, too. Her father hates smoking.

If only her mother were wailing in the kitchen by the dim light of one bulb, red-faced, tragic and beautiful, Mira would understand. But her mother seems almost cheerful. She seems to have more energy. Her mother zips up and down the stairs, carrying objects from one part of the house to another, loudly humming show tunes Mira didn't know she knew.

_____

One night when Mira was much younger, she is awakened by her parents coming home giggling. In the morning, they stand with steaming coffee in their hands in their apartment's tiny kitchen, and with their faces flushed, they keep breaking up in laughter. Rachel's laugh is a skittering, uneven thing that can't seem to stop. Mira's father's is a full, throaty laugh that makes Mira nervous. He is normally reserved.

Her mother does most of the talking. "We've bought a house!" she says. "A Victorian house!" The house had been owned by the same family for generations. Some of the rooms upstairs have not been used for decades, Rachel says. They are filled with furniture— lamps, spinning wheels, moth-eaten couches. The elderly brothers who now live there are moving to a small condominium in Florida; what do they need with three floors' worth of dusty Victorian furniture? They've offered her parents all the furniture in the house for one dollar. One dollar! With some reupholstering and repairs, it is probably worth a fortune. How can they refuse? As they speak, her mother uses words she has never heard before: *parlor, foyer, banister, wrought iron, parquet.*

When her mother is finished, her father clears his throat and smiles his shiny-penny smile. "It's a good investment," he says finally.

The new house, a clapboard from the 1850s, is in a neighborhood that people describe by telling you about all the famous people who used to live there a hundred years ago. The old slate sidewalks crack and buckle. The rain gutters are full of Q-tips and cellophane. Plastic bags hang in the spindly trees. Sneakers garland the telephone wires. Chunks are missing from the stone stoops in front of the houses.

Their new house is on the edge of this neighborhood, in the middle of an especially cracked-pavement block. The block ends at an elevated overpass where you can feel the scrape and roar of the highway beneath you. It is a sad, old building with dark windows, sandwiched between two similar houses. An old ladder leans against the front, and, in the open pit behind the fence, there is a sawhorse, scrap wood, cement bags. The first time they pull up in front of the house, Mira feels something fall in her chest. "It smells gross," Mira says, when they are inside the dank front hallway. Neither Rachel nor her dad responds. The wallpaper in the hallway is coming loose in places and flops down in strips. From the ceiling, wires dangle from holes. The house needs stripping, painting, wiring, new plumbing.

In the beginning, they all live on the first floor, which is the only habitable one. Mira moves up to the second floor while it is still under construction, where her father, after work, still in his shirt and tie, attacks the imperfections of the old house's walls. For a time, Mira falls asleep at night to the swish and scrape of the planer, believing that this frantic, willful energy is enough to build a sturdy-walled version of reality, to keep the fairy tales at bay. In the dark, at night, in bed, Mira strains her eyes at the strange shapes the close moonlight makes against the walls half-scraped of their wallpaper. It is a form of prayer, this staring, this hoping, this squinting. She listens to the sounds of the house, the creaking and groaning, the words between her parents, high and angry, low and sweet. She imagines her parents singing a song she once heard at a Broadway play her grandmother took her to, their bright eager faces and open mouths. It makes her feel calmer to imagine this song, her parents singing it.

She has just started taking ballet at The Little Kirov, and she thinks often about the little room around the corner from the older girls' classroom, where the costumes are stored for the annual performance of *The Wounded Prince*. In early December the costume room will be opened and the dusty tutus hung by color, in descending size order, will be shaken off, their synthetic tulle fluffed, and the girls who were the Pink Girls last year will become the Blue Girls, the Blue Girls become the Yellow Girls, the Yellow Girls become the Flower Girls. She does not know what the Flower Girls become. And then there is the Flower Princess—there is only one Flower Princess. She wears a long dress and garlands of flowers pinned in her hair. She wears the most diaphanous white gown and tiara and, when all the action on the stage stops and turns to her, she must do the longest, slowest, most beautiful *penché,* and stretching out her arm, still deep in an arabesque, with her wand touch the Prince's lame leg. . . .

But time goes by and the house is not fixed. She doesn't know whom to blame for this—her mother, her father, or the house itself. Her parents still recline after dinner on chairs that creak and groan. They sip wine. When the caning finally snaps, the broken chairs are stacked in the corner, one on top of the other. These chairs can only be salvaged by certain old-time craftsmen—weavers, caners, upholsterers—whom Rachel hunts for by going in and out of antique shops, with a little notebook in which she has sketched the broken furniture. Soon, though, she has to take a break. They go to Chock full o'Nuts, where Rachel orders Mira a cream cheese on raisin bread sandwich, sips her coffee, and thumbs through her notebook, still blank of names. Her father pulls down another chair from the rooms upstairs. They still giggle as they look around the room, flush with their own bold visions. But, as the years go by, their efforts disappear into the house like the pennies and nickels thrown in a deep wishing fountain.

IRRECONCILABLE DIFFERENCES

It's over a month since her father left. In her red kimono, her mother plays game after game of solitaire at the table in the parlor. "He isn't coming back," she says. She doesn't take her eyes off the cards. "It doesn't mean he doesn't love you." Then she says some other words meant for Mira not to understand: *irreconcilable differences, separation by consent.* In response, Mira has her own words. "You said you loved him! You lied!" Rachel's face is set in stone. "This really has nothing to do with love."

Her mother reaches out and grabs Mira's arm. "The *only* reason we *got* married," she says, "is that we were in love." She turns back to her game of solitaire. Slap, slap. The cards continue.

Mira feels a jab of hate for her mother. She thinks about that loose snapshot in her parents' wedding album. How many times has she stopped when leafing through this album to stare at this snapshot, which is a different size and shape than the official wedding photos? Her mother, in her long white dress, is standing on top of a table full of young men. She's striking a pose, her head thrown back wildly, and she's laughing. The men have their bow ties loosened and the table is littered with corsages. It's late in the evening. Mira's father also sits at the table. Unlike the other men, her father is not laughing. His arms hang at his sides. He stares up at his wife, gaping, as if he is caught in a fire, burning alive.

"My mom is totally destroyed," she says to her friends who stand around her in the dressing room. "She wails all day and night. You can't even go near her. She wears this kimono and doesn't take it off. And she doesn't shower." Only the part about the kimono is true.

There is a part of Mira that has floated free with her father. The part that is left cares less about what others think and whether what she says is true or not. She often feels like laughing suddenly, for no reason.

"Maybe you should call Social Services," says Meaghan.

"Oh, come on," says Val, gnawing on her fingers. "You're exaggerating." Val's parents split when she was five and her sister was seven. When they'd met, Val was the one with tough luck, without a father, and with a shitty childhood. Mira, with her two parents, with her big house, couldn't *understand,* didn't *know.* Now Val is afraid of losing her trump card.

"Are you saying I'm lying?" says Mira, staring hard at Val. She never used to be able to stare at anyone without looking away before.

"Yes," says Val. She turns to Delia and whispers something in her ear. Meaghan titters, then whispers something to Delia.

"What?" says Mira. *"What?"*

When she gets off the train in Manhattan, she walks slowly down the streets, looking at each window of each apartment. A million people hiding behind curtains, her father in one of them. That you could lose your father in a city. That he can disappear into the streets, leaving only cuff links behind. It makes her stomach feel funny.

"Hurry up," says Val. "I'm sick of always waiting for you." Val rushes on ahead.

Mira goes up to a doorman standing in front of the giant apartment building on Fifty-sixth. It could be this very building. "Is Carl Able staying here?" she says to the doorman in his livery. "He's my dad."

The doorman steps inside and pulls out a clipboard from behind his desk. His chin doubles over as he pursues his list. "Sometimes they forget to update me. Did he just move in?" If a doorman, whose job it is to keep track of residents, can lose count, how would she ever find her father?

October turns cold. The old shutters knock against windowsills as a strong breeze buffets the house. Her mother sits cross-legged on a throw pillow on the floor, a blanket on her lap, papers spread out before her. "Look at me!" her mother says loudly. "I'm doing bills!"

Across the room, Mira sits in a chair and does her homework in the glow of a glass table lamp with a bordello shade. Mira's posture is unusually straight, as if she sits with her back to a wall. Only her head is tilted downward toward the ruled page of her notebook.

Her mother puts the bill in front of her to the side and looks at the one beneath it. It is from The Little Kirov, typed in heavy ink on onionskin paper. She holds it up.

"Agh," says her mother, shaking the paper. "What do you like so much about ballet?"

Mira does not look up. "It's beautiful?"

Her mother writes some numbers in her bank book. "It's 1977. Beauty? Where has it gotten us?"

Mira looks up. Her mother's red kimono, now wrinkled and dull; it hangs on her like a too-big sheet. Her mother looks small and pale. Dwarfed by the things in the room. The *junk*, her father would say. Her mother laughs her skittish laugh and covers her face with her hands. "Where has it gotten *me*?" She drops her hands and in a louder voice says, "Let it go down in flames!"

"Why don't you sit on the floor? You don't look comfortable," says her mother.

"I like this chair," says Mira.

"I am thinking of taking all the chairs out."

"No!" Mira says. When she sees her mother's expression, she wants to look back down. But she doesn't. Mother and daughter stare at each other for several moments; there is something between them, then nothing.

THE WOMAN
WHO BLED
IN HER SHOES

It's time. The letter. I hadn't forgotten, not exactly. The rage toward Bill had to be dealt with first, but now I go get the letter from my bag. In my ochre reading chair, under a gray-white Ohio sky, I spread the letter out on my lap.

I have gone away to a place where the dead go—no, not
Hades, a city that befits me. No ballet here, only early bird
specials and other sad people who have been banished to a
city with no reason for existing.

My mind treads water, eddies pull. That voice. It's his. How can it be? Can he still be alive? How old would he be now? I quickly do the math—eighty. Possible. But why *now*? Why contact me after so long?

I close my eyes. To leave the body. To abandon the body. I know this trick. It doesn't work. The body goes on. So I call myself back. To the Dutch Colonial that I fell in love with on my tour of the town late last spring. Its blue slate roof on the cupola (with pewter detailing) like ancient armor, and inside the hardwood floors and clean white walls, all of which felt vast after my last two small, linoleum-tiled (and ammonia-stink) faculty accommodations.

I open my eyes. Everything looks altered. The red ceramic vase my mother gave me for my doctoral ceremony, for which I have both an abiding revulsion and love. I've carried it with me from college town to college town over the past four years. I look over at my black office chair, my spindle-necked desk lamp, my modular desk to which I had attached an ergonomic keyboard. It's like peering through glass—everything looks altered, too big or too small in this space. Objects tossed together with no coherency. I remember only the compulsion, the desire and guilt in each item's acquisition. Only the rug under my feet feels familiar and recognizable, with its bold geometry of circles and triangles, a faux Mondrian pattern. These things—my chair, my rug, my desk—I'd chosen to create a work-space, now pulling apart.

I force myself to keep reading:

You killed me and I must thank you. I am one of the dead.
I do not deserve to have commerce with the living. I wanted
to tell you, my dear, because you too are one of the dead.
Do you know that yet? You will always be—no way to avoid
it. When you kill, you become one of the dead yourself.

I'm sure of it, suddenly! He is still alive. How raw, how familiar is his penchant for melodrama, for vitriol even. No one can hate like him—except me, perhaps. I have hated him with a passion that burns my scalp and palms, and stifles my voice. I have struggled with this hate, suffered it, abided it. At times it's been overpowering, at times it's ebbed; it's always been there, my whole adult life.

My legs are ready now; I stand; a burst of energy carries me into the bedroom and toward the closet. But I'm not heading to the closet anymore. Instead I'm reaching under the bed. Here, now, on the bed in front of me is an inlaid wood and enamel box. It was a long time ago, the last time I opened it. I open the box and take out one tiny pointe shoe that looks like it would only fit a child. It is the brownish color of a bruised nectarine. Barely larger than one of my hands—and worth at least twenty thousand dollars. Worn by Anna Pavlova in the second half of a performance of *Giselle,* in which the great ballerina had a rare tumble as she threw herself at the dying Albrecht. (Only one camp of balletomanes agrees that this was actually a fall. Another thinks it was a kind of seizure, a harbinger of the pneumonia that would eventually kill her.) At least, this was one of the several stories Maurice told me about the shoe over the years. You can no longer discern the bloodstain that Maurice pointed out to me. The fabric is worn away at the tip of the toe box, exposing the layers of binding underneath. The ribbons are brownish and shredded at the end but have held up better than the rest of the shoe.

I take out a tangled mess of grimy pink pointe shoe ribbons. Something a cat might have played with and discarded. Sometime after college, I found a giant tub of my old pointe shoes in the basement of my father's Connecticut house, where he and Judy were living before they finally divorced. I cut off all the satin ribbons, leaving the shoes, denuded, cracked, and bent but still startlingly pink in their satin skins. A childish gesture. Like cutting the hair off an old favorite doll. I threw the heap of limp ribbons in the garbage. Then on second thought, I went back and picked them out of the garbage can, balled them up, and put them at the bottom of my suitcase. Back in San Francisco, where I was getting my MFA, I stuffed them in this box. It was a maudlin gesture. Hyperridiculous. Bathetic, even.

Next, I finger a bent graying business card with NEW YORK LIBRARY OF THE PERFORMING ARTS on it. Not sure this one gets "exhibit" status. I put that aside and remove a perfume decanter top. Exhibit C. I never had the bottle. It has the telltale Victorian flourishes. The body of a swan is etched in the glass. The wings are open behind the swan so that it looks like it is exploding out of the glass in a Victorian fantasy of flight. I hold the top in my hand, roll it back and forth. When I was younger, when he gave me this, I thought it was huge. It still seems uncommonly heavy, from another era when beautification rituals required a different kind of attention and commitment. One's perfume. Like another limb. It's a perfume bottle stopper. I sniff it. It smells of some kind of adhesive and musk.

Then I pull out a little book with a curled black leather cover. The pages inside undulate. They are yellowed and brittle. Still, you can make out the writing. Even black cursive with uneven line breaks, punctuated by dates.

One entry:

10/15 Bella chosen for Angel—next year will it be Polichinelle? I want to see her as a Polichinelle.

She must work on adagio. Développé and ronde de jambe en l'air. The shaking in her thigh. I have seen it. The problem is core strength. Will it come with time?

The Polichinelle variation will require work on her jumps. I must watch carefully how she lands. She must stop that birdlike flutter of her hands. Annoying. I don't care what B. says to her.

There are a couple of other things in the box—odds and ends whose significance I don't try to recall because his face—the very last time I saw it—comes back to me. Maurice's face. He woke up before I left the room. I see him now as he lay on the floor looking up at me and laughed. *Bravo, bravo, my dear, your finest performance.* His face is gray, his hair yellowish white against the stain of dark red that grows from the side of his head, his grin monstrous. He wears his old smile that shows his teeth lined up. It is full of brilliance.

"Stop making fun of me," I say.

His smile fades. He looks stricken. "I have never made fun of you." Then the wild, bewildered look. Then he closes his eyes. I leave. I run out of the room.

In the middle of October, Mira comes home from school to find her mother and a strange man sitting on the living room cushions. Her mother has finally changed her clothes. She wears a pair of jeans and a black turtleneck, and her hair is tied back in a frizzy bunch with a bandanna. The man sits across from her, cross-legged. The bottoms of his jeans are frayed. He has taken his shoes off; his socks are all wrong—shiny and too new for the rest of him. Though he is a big man, his hands are bony. Mira dislikes them immediately. They are attached to bony wrists that stick out of the sleeves of a blue worker's jacket like the kind that men working at the gas pumps wear. Although he is inside, he wears the jacket zipped all the way up. When he takes a sip of tea, Mira wants to shout a "No!" that will make this man disappear from her living room. His eyes, under his taxi driver's cap, are bright and watchful. He reminds her of the men her mother draws and paints from her Court Street studio window—those lurking outside Club Wild Fyre, the strip club, who push things along the curb with the top of their broken-soled shoes. She has invited them into their house now.

Mira looks straight at him. He takes a sip and places the cup on the carpeted ottoman that serves as their makeshift table.

"This is Gary Rosen. He is going to rent a room upstairs for a studio. He's a writer."

He takes off his hat and looks down at his cup. Mira regards him with suspicion. Someone who sits in a room and puts words on a page. But for what? And whom for? And why would one need a special room to do it in?

"What room?" Mira says. She does not drop her backpack. She does not say "hi."

"The extra room," says her mother.

"The junk room?"

Her mother smiles sheepishly at the man. "We used to call it that because that's where we kept all the extra furniture and stuff."

"Extra furniture?" he says. "Wow, man. What a concept."

Her mother's cheeks grow red. "It's not like we bought it. It was here, it came with the house." Mira looks at her mother, for she has used her Manhattan voice in their house, in Brooklyn, with this raggedy stranger.

"Sure thing," he says, looking around. "This is a far-out place."

"You're going to live here?" Mira says.

"Mira!" says her mother. "Don't be rude!"

He shakes his head. "Don't worry. I'll be out of your hair. I'll mostly be here during the day when you're in school."

Mira turns and walks out of the room, up the creaky steps.

"Mira! Come back here!" But her mother's voice breaks into the beginning of laughter.

She hears the man say, "Well, I should be going."

She hears her mother laughing again—high-pitched, energetic—as if her daughter's rudeness has fueled something in her. "Red hair," she hears him say. She hears him say: *takes after her mother.*

Soon after, a boy from their neighborhood is kidnapped. He is, it is said, kidnapped in broad daylight, while waiting for the school bus. It happens down below Squibb Hill, where Mira and her friends never go. There is nothing there—only old deserted factories. But this boy *lived* down there. The thought of a boy living down there makes her squirm inside. It is like imagining living on the moon. His sticking-out ears and cloud of curly hair appear on posters everywhere, under the headline MISSING. The graininess of the photocopied paper makes it look like he is staring out from behind layers of static, of white noise. So the world has grown less safe, not just for her, but also for everyone. *Missing.* One might go missing, one's face staring out from telephone booths and street signs, covered by a static blanket. Sometimes she has to pinch herself just to be sure she is here—that she can be seen.

After school, on the way home, Mira stops at one of the MISSING posters. She rips down the faded and watermarked paper and takes it home. She carries it to her room and hangs it on the back of her closet door. Sometimes she will talk to this boy, sometimes she won't. She will tell him about her father. She will tell him she hopes he is okay. Just to hang in there. She will feel better looking at him, knowing that someone always leaves something behind, even if it is just a static-y smile.

The temperature drops again and the rats hide in garbage cans and make nests under the grease-stained hamburger. The leaves fall from the trees. The hanging sneakers blacken with soot. Sirens comb the streets, the lights raking across her ceiling. Her mother thinks they are still looking for the *looters,* the people who *broke in* stores and *stole.* Bulky men in blue loiter on street corners giving the stink eye to passersby. She knows they are looking for the boy. But they won't find the boy. He has disappeared, just like her father.

The cops wrap yellow tape around trees on Squibb Hill. It says DO NOT CROSS. No one ever removes it, though bottles and Band-Aids and Newport cigarette packs gather around so that by next spring, when Mira has moved to Manhattan, it looks like there's been a party.

Ms. Clement waves her hand in the air to start the class, slips a Chopin record out of its sleeve, and puts it on the turntable. The scratching needle starts up the tinkling piano tune and the girls begin the movements that by now are rote.

Mira holds the barre, the smooth, round wooden pole that draws a line around the room. She points her foot in a *tendu*. The air is bright with afternoon light, an elbow of shadow rests on the floor. Ms. Clement walks slowly along the barre, surveying her girls. Mira feels Ms. Clement's half-lidded eyes on her and then her dry, pointy fingertips rest gently on the small of Mira's back. "String through the top of the head," she says. Her other hand massages the air in time to the Chopin waltz.

Ms. Clement runs The Little Kirov. She's a dancer in her fifties with a vague past—a "European touring career" is how she puts it. Ms. Clement wears too much of the wrong kind of jewelry and chiffon to have really been a Russian dancer, even in her assumed prime. Mira thinks about something her mother said to her once—that Ms. Clement looks like something out of an Ingmar Bergman movie. She doesn't know who Ingmar Bergman is, but she pictures him like someone small and stooped with bright eyes. "A woman," Rachel said, "standing by the window, with the light a certain way. Not miserable, not happy, just *there*." What Mira knows is that Ms. Clement belongs with them more than in the world of adults. Mira has seen her talking to the parents after the recitals—her big eyes wandering around the room and her fingertips drumming restlessly on top of the piano. Unlike her classroom teachers, who stand in front of the blackboard in their starchy pantsuits and winged hair and gaze at them with malevolence, Ms. Clement looks at them with a gentle fatigue, like someone who has just drunk a glass of milk before bed.

Today Ms. Clement wears a knee-length black chiffon skirt and a long-sleeve black leotard gathered with an iridescent pin at the nadir of her sloping breasts. She moves on to Val, whose elbow has dropped again. "Arms round as a beach ball, Valerie," she says. She puts a hand on the back of Haijuan's head. "Don't forget," she says, and they know how she will finish: "A little magnet on the chin. Chin to collarbone."

In Ms. Clement's class, something secret blooms in her. Mira doesn't get this feeling anywhere else. She is learning that ballet makes a science out of the movements of living. She is learning how to walk in that special dancer way—like a bright, fearful bird. She is learning how to hold her fingers as if she has just let go of a dainty teacup, still feeling the pressure between her thumb and middle finger. She is learning how to smile and lift her chin as she pliés. She is learning that to be a girl is to be strong and tireless. She smiles and lifts her sternum, moves her arm from a first, to a second, to a fourth position, gathering up the air and redelivering it. She will be reborn, transformed. She can feel it.

Yes, she is a girl in pink tights and ballet slippers, a girl with a heart beating. Her body will move; it will take care of itself. Plié, plié, grande plié. Open her arms, close her arms. As if relearning the very rhythms of breathing. Outside, above the rusted fire escapes, the birds circle high above Seventh Avenue's canyon of buildings. *Relevé,* turn to the other side.

"Movement," her mother once said as she watched Mira practice, "is the thing that interests me now. How one thing changes into another."

Tondue, dégagé, *tondue,* dégagé. *Passé.* She rises on her standing leg, bends her other knee, and points her toes into the crook of her standing leg.

Ms. Clement, in her breathy monotone, says, "Lovely, Mira. Nice long legs. Yes, little ones."

As the girls are leaving the room, Ms. Clement calls out to Mira to stay behind. She drapes her long arm over the girl's shoulders, then dips her head and looks at Mira over her bifocals. The glasses are red and overly large. In them she looks like a regal fly, the dotage queen of some insect tribe. Mira stares at the nicely scuffed toes of her Capezio slippers. She has done her elastics in an X, the way she has seen the SAB dancers do in photographs in the books her father has given her.

"Please accompany me to my office," Ms. Clement says.

The small, cluttered office has a faded carpet and a gingery smell. A steady peck peck of a typewriter comes from one side of the room, where the office manager, Mr. Feltzer, a hunchbacked man in black-framed glasses, works on bills.

Ms. Clement positions herself on a battered office chair and covers her shoulders with a shawl. Mira sits on the hardwood school chair facing her teacher. Mira had never thought of Ms. Clement as old, but next to the piles of papers on her desk, flanked by two towering filing cabinets, Ms. Clement looks tiny and ancient.

"Dear," starts Ms. Clement. "We think you are doing very well here. You have good line and, even more, you have the je ne sais quoi."

The sound of the typewriter stops briefly. "For this year's *Little Prince,* we would like you to be the Flower Princess."

"But Robin is the Flower Princess," says Mira.

Ms. Clement laughs—a strange sound—like music from a rusty toy.

"The Flower Princess is a part, dear, a role, for each girl to step into as she will. Robin, yes, she is a lovely Flower Princess, but so will you be, and so will the girl after you. It is a part. . . ." Here she trails off, adjusting some papers.

Mira sits on the scratchy wood of the chair. She feels suddenly very hungry, a deep ache that comes not pleading and insistent as hunger from her stomach, but general and complete, from the farthest reaches of her body: her ears ache with this hunger, and her buttocks, and ankles, and toes. She sees herself as the Flower Princess, onstage, healing the Prince. But the image fades, leaving a darkness as if the sun blinked and never opened its eyes again.

CHAPTER 9

That night I dream of New York City. It's summer and heat radiates off the concrete. The trees billow with leaves and plastic bags. Light shimmers over the jagged tops of buildings, revealing the complex geometry of the skyline. I am a girl again, wandering the streets, and there are other kids wandering with me, each of us with large pockets for our hands and blimps for our heads that keep rising toward the sky. I begin floating up. The wind is so powerful. Night falls and the city is dark and cold, now hunkered down in ice. I am myself, but a child, floating along the rooftops. I see the darkened frozen canyons stretching out below me, all sandstone and brick. The wind is frigid and I wear only a thin jacket. Above me, beyond the balloon of a water tower, a shadow speaks with *his* voice. And there is his smell, sour and sweet, and his breath like ancient paper. I reach out to him, but he crumbles to dust, like rice paper. I try to pick up this dust, to save it, but it's too late. I am already falling into the darkness, into one of the canyons.

I've been to New York City several times for conferences in the last decade. It now has very little to do with the tumultuous, rioting city of my youth. The city I have seen as an adult, from the midtown hotels I've stayed at, is a sparkling, renovated version of my childhood city.

The last time I was in the city, I didn't go uptown or to Brooklyn. I didn't see, and didn't look for, the overflowing gutters, or the stone carvings of angels outside stately mansions. I kept my briefcase close and trod a narrow path to sushi restaurants with my colleagues. There was one late evening at a wine bar in the West Village. I told no one that I had lived in New York as a child. Even still, as the strange twilight hung over the buildings, I felt something buried rise to the surface, and I had to keep going to the bathroom to stare at my flushed, absent face in the mirror.

That evening I cook myself a rare steak and eat it in the dark. I read the letter over again and this time it seems oddly threatening. It's really a short letter, just a paragraph. It feels purposefully mysterious, even provocative. The style is ornate, his particular Old World way of talking. It offers no solid details, just evocative ones: *"Not Hades, a city that befits me," "early bird specials and other sad people," "banished to a city with no reason for existing."* But the letter also reveals anger and self-pity. Neither of these emotions fits with the Maurice I knew. The questions barrel toward me: Is it him? Is he alive? If he's alive, where is he? Is he still at his old apartment? Why now? Why try to contact me now?

His face drifts back to me again. This time it's from the beginning, the first time I ever saw him. We never discussed it. Did he too remember that we had met before, when I was just a child—a few years before he appeared in the doorway of the studio?

But the image that comes to me now is not of the end, but of the very beginning. A chance encounter before anything had happened that could be called secret. The images are raw and bright and fill up my mind.

Inside the opera house, the air was thick with light and heat, the buzz of excitement. The ballet was over—it was during curtain calls—I would have been nine or ten then, not eleven yet, the age when my father moved out, and so much changed—and I had run down the carpeted stairs, through the deserted lobby, and into a packed and thundering proscenium of carpeted walls blaring with lights. I had fought my way through the black stockinged legs and gold-clasped purses to within sight of the stage. But then it was too crowded. I couldn't move anymore—and I couldn't see more than a sliver of the stage. A face in the crowd turned toward me, a slight man—it was him. He reached down, said something like, "Poor thing. You can't see, can you?" He helped me up on the armrest of a seat and held me there while I balanced over the crowd. I remember the small face, the thin mustache, the oddness of his smell, like apples and something sour. I remember his face was bright with rapture, with reflected stage lights. With his help, I balanced feet away from the stage. The male dancer's face was orange with makeup, the female dancer's muscles stretched like rubber bands over bone. I shouted my *Bravos* at the dancers until I was hoarse.

A girl and a man meet. A girl and a man, too old for her, meet and are changed, though they don't know it yet.

Something is hardening in me—and something else is softening. I put on my running shoes and, despite the ice, take the path back across campus. I head to Baker. No one is usually using these studios now, what with the new Art Center. The Baker studios were never converted to a state-of-the-art facility. The floors are wood, the windows rattle, the rafters are strewn with old bits of rope and old props. But I like them, these old Baker studios. There's a dreaminess to them, like a stage set from long ago, and the air above you is vast.

I don't turn the lights on. It's easier to dance in the dark tonight. If I move, I keep my thoughts at bay. They are unproductive, tangled. They lead me back only to questions and an old pain. Coming through the high windows is a still, bright moon that casts long blue shadows across the floor.

I shuck off my coat. I skip a warm-up and just start moving. The shapes my body makes are interesting. At first I don't recognize them. My upper body is doing one thing and my lower body is doing another. My arms are beating a rhythm. Then the rhythm changes—I'm following it—and it becomes faster and more violent. In the midst of a series of contract and releases—a release fall to the floor, a roll, a pitch upward with a side extension—I realize I am actually threading ballet steps in. God love me, it's been years but my body remembers: pas de bourrée, glissade, jeté, the first sequence I learned as a girl and which we would do at the end of class and it would feel like we were flying. It's been ages since I've choreographed something original, but there is something interesting in these sequences. Now I'm close to the floor, locking in a plié, my arms shoot out, I tumble, I roll.

I'm not dancing for anyone. I'm just following the patterns. Then I am good and sweaty and everything is less precious, everything is flowing. My body is cooking. I am moving in space. There is the vastness of this once-gym, its 1920s bones, all you have to do is look up and see the steel poles and nets made of a kind of string no one uses anymore.

I'm moving in and out of the shadows, circling: fall, roll, jeté.

I am *dancing*.

And then the lights turn on. They thunder on across the rafters and the landscape of blue shadow is replaced by a false yellow sunshine that shows every decade of scuff and bang to the floors.

I'm left blinking, gasping for breath.

"Oh my God! Professor Randell! You scared me!" says a voice. And I look and then I see—I can't believe it, what are the chances— it's Sioban. Her hands, one of those on my wrist, the same hands, the color of ash in this light, flutter to her face and then drop at her side.

I open my mouth and close it again.

Then she laughs. "OMG, I didn't know you still did ballet!"

"I don't—that was just—" And I am deeply embarrassed.

"You still have mad skills! You were killing it!" Has she been watching me dance before she turned the lights on?

I stand, blinking in the harsh light. I finally have discovered my voice, remember who I am. "Sioban, did you sign this studio out?"

She nods. "I have it starting at eight, but I can take A. No one is in here."

"No, I'll move over to A," I say, walking over to get my things.

"Or—" she says. "We could share it. I've been working on my contact"—she drops and does a sudden roll and then springs up—"the act of trusting, like you said, or *letting go*—." She flushes. "Would you—could you—do some contact with me before you go?" Her face is deeply red now. She moves toward me.

I don't know why, but—and this is really inexcusable—I nod my head.

I think I'm grateful for the lack of speech between us. Our movements together are surprisingly seamless. But her body is too rigid and moves in parts, from the center outward. It avoids its own mass. For all her skill, she doesn't know how to flow and release into another body. She's using too much muscle and not enough bone. "It's not like partnering," I say. I bend again and she lays her spine along my spine. "Good," I say. Now she's allowing herself the help of gravity. "Follow the point of contact," I say. "Very good!" How grateful I am to be the teacher again.

"Oh!" she says, and I see that she has the feeling of doing *less*, how liberating this can be for bunheads. I'm pivoting and taking her weight and then she goes stiff again. "It's okay," I say. "Let yourself be heavy. Don't worry. I can take it."

"I can't," she says, and her voice catches. I turn and spiral up, still in the grip of the motion, and then I am facing her, she's breathing hard, and her face is pale. "I—" she says, and she kisses me boldly, sloppily in a rush, and I don't pull away. "Shit," I say. She doesn't move and neither do I. We're both just breathing. Then she kisses me again with more confidence this time. It's a strange sorrowful kiss, too old for her years, and it scares me.

Rehearsals for *The Wounded Prince* begin the first week of November. On Saturday morning, Mira has her first rehearsal with the boy who plays the prince. His name is Christopher, and he comes on loan from ABT, where they have whole classes full of boys. (At The Little Kirov, boys appear and quickly disappear from classes like supermarket circulars from apartment building vestibules.) The first time Mira saw Christopher walking down the hallway, she was eight, in just her first year of taking classes. In the dressing room, she heard mounting whispers. She listened. It seemed to have to do with a boy. The boy who played *the Prince*. He was coming to rehearse with the Flower Princess.

She ran out into the front hallway with the others. They practiced splits against the walls as they waited. For once Mr. Feltzer did not shoo them away. Every time the elevator door opened, they grew still. Finally, he arrived. He exited from the elevator wearing a green scarf, a black wool blazer, and a white untucked oxford. His hair was thick and honey-blond. She had never seen a boy so beautiful. Christopher's hard blue eyes reflected back all their gazes.

Now here is Christopher, leaning in the doorway of the rehearsal studio. A year since Christopher has last been at The Little Kirov. A year is a long time. He wears a loose sweater over corduroys, no coat, even though it's cold outside. His face is longer, his features more angular. Small red dots on his nose. *There is something wrong with him.* After all these years, this is the clearest thought she has coming face-to-face with the boy who plays the Prince.

Christopher puts on a smile that Mira has seen in kids who know how to act around grown-ups. He kisses Ms. Clement on both cheeks.

"Hey." He nods at Mira, who is hanging back. "So you're the new Flower Princess. How old are you?"

"Eleven. I'll be twelve in April."

Ms. Clement says, "Mira is quite good, if young. But, dear—you remember, you once were so young!"

"Ha-ha." Christopher laughs a grown-up laugh.

Up close—she is within a few feet of him now—his neck is long and taut. As he laughs, he does so with a girl's delicacy that makes her look down.

"Okay, dear, go and get changed. We have Mira for another half an hour. Then we can go over your part. You remember it, I hope?"

Christopher picks up his shoulder bag and moves toward the boys' dressing room, in some dim corner of the studio. "I never forget it," he says.

While Christopher changes, Mira and Ms. Clement go over the opening again. *Ronde de jambe*, port de bras, *développé*. These are the movements from the beginning of *The Wounded Prince,* in which the prince comes upon a girl dancing in a forest clearing. She is supposed to be gathering food for her mother but has forgotten her errand. And Mira does feel someone watching her—from the studio doorway. She instinctually raises her chin and doubles her effort. When she finally peeks, she is surprised to see it is not Christopher, but a small man with a neat mustache leaning against the doorjamb. He clears his throat.

"Maurice! What a surprise!" says Ms. Clement.

"Please," he says. He bows his head. "I heard there was a new Flower Princess. I had to come see her."

"Well, meet Miss Mira Able. Mira, this is Maurice Dupont . . . who is a very generous man."

The three of them in the doorway: Mira, her teacher, and the man. His suit is charcoal-colored and he wears a red folded handkerchief in his breast pocket. Mira walks over and holds out her hand. He takes it in his tangle of bony fingers. He gives off an odor of talcum powder and spicy cologne. He stares at her with very black pupils. Her face feels like it is burning.

"I enjoyed watching you."

"Thanks," she says.

"You understand movement."

Where has she seen this smile, these teeth, small and even, like little stones lined up on a ledge?

She remembers dimly, a face like this one. It comes back to her—the male dancer's feline face and the ballerina's sinewy arms. He was there that night at the ballet, when her father still lived with them. The cardboard shoulder that she leaned on, the pale face crossed with a black mustache, and the smell of something sweet and also something sour. Her mother had worn her hair long over a green dress. Her parents had held hands. That same night: holding this little man's shoulder and shouting *Bravo!* He had brought her closer to the dancers than she had ever been before.

Ms. Clement is looking at them.

"You helped me see—at *Giselle*—onto a chair—"

"Did I? Was it that most amazing performance? Kirkland and Baryshnikov? Never another like that."

Ms. Clement is watching Maurice.

"Well, of course, I like to be useful. To help the little ones."

Mira has no idea what is happening. She just knows she wants the little man to look at her again in that way he just did, the way that makes her feel more visible than she ever has.

Just then, Christopher brushes past the man and comes into the studio. He's in his rehearsal clothes—white T-shirt, black tights. His hair is carefully combed back off his face, and he wears a bandanna tied around his neck. In his dance clothes, he is more recognizable. As he makes his way into the studio, he stops. He says to the little man, "I've seen you at David Howard's, right?"

"You may have. I've been helping David with outreach—"

"What?" says Ms. Clement.

"Well," says the man. "I like to be useful. . . ."

Christopher begins rehearsing his solo from Act Three. Ms. Clement claps her hands. "Come, Mira!" she says, moving to the center of the studio. Mira runs toward her teacher and Christopher. When she turns back, the little man is gone.

It is Act Two and the moody prince has taken to gazing out his window. He spies the girl dancing in the palace garden. It is the same peasant girl he saw dancing by the river, who had so transfixed him. Their illicit dance had led to the terrible curse upon the land—and his own lameness. They perform a duet that is supposed to be his reverie.

Ms. Clement and Christopher mime the first lift. When she puts her hands on Christopher's shoulders to demonstrate, Ms. Clement lifts her chin high and her wrinkled lips pull back in a practiced stage smile.

Mira takes Ms. Clement's place. "Try, children." Ms. Clement steps away.

Christopher rests his hands on her waist; Mira pliés. Partnering lifts are brand-new to Mira; never in her life has she been so close to a boy. Up close, his face looks distorted—as if seen through a fisheye lens—his eyes big and staring, his pale forehead a wide plain of white. His smell is deep, like old fruit or metal shavings. His hands grip her waist tighter and she jumps, but it's too late. She's not ready. The force of his hands moves up her torso, rubbing her ribs raw. She coughs. He releases his grip.

"Shit," he says, rubbing his forehead with the end of the bandanna. "You okay?"

"Let's break, children," says Ms. Clement. "Let me speak to Christopher."

Mira goes to the bathroom in Middle Studio. While in there, she peers at herself in the mirror: a pale girl with a long face and a blast of freckles across her cheeks. They usually fade in the winter, but they haven't this year. A nimbus of hair has escaped from her bun, as usual, and floats in frizzy wisps above her head. Her hair looks burned, the color of embers at the end of a fire. She turns on the tap and drinks thirstily. She closes her eyes and imagines the little man's black eyes on her—burning through her like a sun. Slowly, the tickle in her throat recedes.

"We try again," says Ms. Clement, when she returns. This time Mira is ready. She stands in front of Christopher, her hands on his shoulders. "Plié, then jump. Do not wait to feel him lift. Then it will be too late. You must trust, then jump. Trust, jump." Ms. Clement counts out the three-four time. Mira pliés, then jumps blindly into the air. She closes her eyes as if jumping off a diving board. This time she feels a response halfway up. Christopher propels her farther into the air, pivots, and slowly returns her to the ground. As he is lowering her, he grimaces. Then his face returns to normal—a mask, staring but not seeing.

"Good, children," says Ms. Clement. "Mira, you are anticipating your partner." She pats the back of her untidy knot of hair and walks over to Christopher. "Christopher, dear, don't let her get away from you. Keep her straight above you. Then gravity will help you."

They repeat the lift again several more times. Now Mira concentrates only on the timing. Each time she leaps, she finds herself moving through the air with greater force than her jump should allow. She lifts her arms into a fifth position, high above her head. At the highest point of one of the lifts, she catches sight of herself in the mirror. A girl in a black leotard high in the air. For a moment, she forgets about how she got there; there is only—air, motion, height. Behind her is the face of the little man in the mirror, watching.

After rehearsal, Mira dresses quickly and leaves the studio. Clouds left over from a morning rain scuttle across the sky. She passes the pizza place, the restaurant with the fried clams, the corner bookstore. This part of Manhattan was hardly touched by the blackout. No boarded shop windows, no burned lots.

A small man in a suit exits a camera store and joins the flow down the street. It's *him*. Maurice. She knows it. He turns right onto Fifty-seventh. She is supposed to turn left toward the Columbus Circle subway station, but instead she follows him.

She pulls the strap on her bag tighter. She can easily keep pace because he walks in an odd, flapping way, as if his joints are too loose. Like a marionette who's not properly controlled.

The clouds break and a bank of lighter sky appears. It's a luminous, spooky white. Fifty-seventh Street's handsome facades briefly light up as she trails his coat down the middle of the sidewalk. Now the city comes alive around her. Shoes click by: high heels, loafers with tassels, some made of the shiny skin of an alligator. Legs in pants: checkered, bell-bottomed, brushing the concrete as they go. Skirts: denim and sleek leather. Shopping bags swing. Folded umbrellas tick by. Faces covered by sunglasses. Eyes drip with makeup, mouths open in laughter. A cup wrapped in folded cardboard jumps in front of her. It's attached to a man whose eyes are raised upward, an unseeing blue. She feels a new calmness settle over her: the power of her anonymity. She pushes past the cardboard cup, past this broken man.

The little man rounds the corner at Bergdorf's and she follows him up Fifth Avenue to the pillared gates of Central Park. There she loses sight of him in the crowd.

She pauses, but not for long. He's there, standing right in front of her. He holds an oversize black umbrella above his head despite the fact that it's not raining anymore.

He smiles broadly, as if he has just said "Bingo!" or "Lotto" or "Connect Four" or any of those words that mean I *win, you lose.* Only she doesn't feel like she has lost. She feels like she, too, has won a prize. She doesn't have time to be embarrassed.

"Are you following me?" he says.

She looks down.

"Can I ask you something, Mira? Do you want to be a ballerina?"

She blushes. "I take ballet."

"Hah!" he says. "And how long have you been doing that?"

"Five years."

"How many days a week?"

"Every day but Wednesday and Sunday."

He smiles. "And *why* do you do this?"

She doesn't have an answer.

"To *become* a dancer. You have to say what you want." She looks up. There are lines on the side of his mouth that she hasn't noticed before. They make him look even more puppetlike.

"Yes," she says, for suddenly she does know what she wants: to dance with the Russians. To dance with Baryshnikov as her partner. To dance with giant spotlight-like-eyes on her. She is giddy with anticipation. All the attention she will get, each piece given to her, each unwrapped to reveal a pair of eyes like his.

"I want to show you something, Mira," he says.

He raises his arm and a horse and carriage stops. She climbs in underneath the rain shield.

She isn't afraid. He's nothing like the "perverts" she's heard about—dirty men in trench coats who stalk playgrounds. She likes his neatness: his folded handkerchief, his trimmed mustache. She likes his gaze, which assesses her with some kind of special knowledge. He knows about dance—she can see it in his eyes, the way he looks at her. Christopher himself had said he was connected to David Howard's studio, and everyone knew David Howard's is like an annex to ABT. His gaze brings her closer to the city's glittering center of professional ballet.

The inside of the carriage smells like wet metal. As they ride through the park, she looks through the rain-splattered plastic at blurry forms—trees with dripping foliage and boulders in the shape of mythic animals. The carriage lets them out up by the museum with the dinosaurs, the polar bears, and the space rocks. Here the little man hails a yellow cab. They pass restaurants, shoe repair shops, a pet store. They are in another neighborhood now, one that she doesn't recognize. There are some big apartment buildings, but there are also smaller buildings with gloomy entryways. They get out in the middle of a block, in front of a squat brick apartment building. She follows him into the lobby, past a doorman's desk, which is vacant, and into an ammonia-smelling elevator.

Inside his apartment, he tosses his gloves on a side table and, without removing his coat, says, "This way, please." His apartment smells of old-lady perfume and the inside of a new car. As she walks through the dim rooms, the city recedes and is replaced with the soft clicks of invisible clocks and the eerie glances of tropical fish from a large tank in one of the room's corners. He leads her into yet another room and stops in front of a tiny, shriveled pinkish thing hovering inside a cube of glass.

"There," he says. At first Mira thinks it's someone's cut-off ear. She's heard about serial killers. Those who cut off body parts after they kill you. For the first time since she decided to follow him, she is afraid.

Then she sees that it is a shoe. A pointe shoe.

"Pavlova's," he says.

Pavlova. The tiny, beloved dancer who famously bled through her shoes. "Pavlova's, from her final performance. Do you see the blood?" He taps on the glass. "I saved it from them. There are some who would have cooked and eaten it! They would make soup out of it! Barbarians!"

He is staring at her in that way again. "She was the last of the great classical ballerinas. Trained by Petipa. She lived to see everything—the dissolution of it all—war, revolution, the birth of modern dance. The dear had such weak ankles. Her feet were disastrously arched. The agonies she suffered!"

"I know," says Mira. She did not know any of this.

She stares at the shoe hovering in space. The cracked flank, its ripped toe box, the flushed skin, the brownish bloodstains. An organ removed from a body.

Then he raises the lights and she can see it rests on a glass pedestal. Some almost-invisible strings hold the tiny, battered shoe in place. Beyond the shoe, she sees the far wall is covered with photos of dancers. A few are autographed studio portraits of ballerinas she recognizes: Patricia McBride squints her cat eyes. Gelsey Kirkland's doll-like face looks surprised. Merrill Ashley's strong jaw commands the room. Kay Mazzo's gamine gaze charms. But the majority of the pictures are black-and-white and faded. It is these that Mira finds herself drawn to. She wanders past this gallery of unknown ballerinas from times past. Strange unreadable writing is printed in the corners of some of the pictures.

"Where are these from?"

"All over the world. There's a rare one of Michel Fokine in *Harlequin*." He waves his hand at a picture of a muscular man dressed like a court jester. "Alicia Markova in a revival of *Pas de Quatre*. Here's Nureyev as Drosselmeyer. Pierina Legnani as Odette and Odile. My father saw Legnani dance once. He said it was like wind blowing around on a stormy day. She was pre-Pavlova—squat, muscular. And, here, Olga Spessivtseva in Diaghilev's *Sleeping Princess*."

More than anyplace Mira knows—more than her crumbling, fried-food-smelling school, or her cold room at home, with its walls still half-flayed of paper, more even than The Little Kirov studios—she has the feeling of belonging in this room.

He points out a photo that shows a lady with a little helmet-like hat and red lips, holding a swan on her lap. The bird's tiny face is nestled in her neck. "Here's Pavlova with her pet swan." Then he gestures to a photo right next to it of a woman on the ground in a white tutu bent over an extended leg.

"When she was dying, she said, 'Bring me my swan!' She died with her costume in her arms." He smiles, somehow satisfied.

"Come on," he says. She follows him back through the rooms. He stops in the living room, turns on the lights, and motions for her to sit on a couch that folds around the room. She perches on its edge. The walls are pastel green, the drapes yellow-gold. A portrait of a blond lady in a green dress hangs over the couch. Mira touches the cool leather of the couch. She loves the feeling of something so sleek and unmarked. So different from her own house's dusty throw pillows, chipped wood furniture, scratched mirrors. She realizes that she is still in her parka and that it smells like French fries.

She hears a clatter of dishes. Now he's back in the doorway holding a plate of cookies. He's taken off his coat, and as he makes his way across the room, she can see for the first time how thin and stooped he is. A complicated set of maneuvers precedes each step he takes. One of his shoes' soles is several inches higher than the other. The laces are thick. Shoes for a cripple! She feels something wild and green grow in her. Fear. Fear of a different sort.

At that moment, she thinks of her mother. She's never wanted her mother so much: the feel of a certain scratchy purple dress her mother used to wear often. She imagines her mother opening a can of Chef Boyardee. The meat paste at the center. The sweet, watery tomato sauce. She feels her Brooklyn self rushing back—the clatter of her Shrinky Dink necklaces, the pilled bottom of her two-year-old bunny slippers; the stack of dusty records on her bottom bookshelf.

She sees from the clock that it is six thirty. She is usually home by now.

"Can I go now?"

He pauses in front of her with his mouth twitching. "Of course you can go, Mira."

He goes to the phone on the wall, dials, and speaks into it. He is calling her a cab. Then he walks her to the front door. He pauses with his hand on the doorknob. Before he opens it, he turns to her. "It's a secret, you know. Don't tell anyone I let you see it. The shoe."

She is walking into the bright hallway when he says, "Wait—"

She turns. He stands half in the brightness of the hall, half in the gloom of his apartment. She can barely hear him when he speaks again. "Can I have something—to remember you by?"

A cab is waiting for her downstairs. She is on her way home; it's okay. She reaches in the pocket of her parka and pulls out a crumpled old hairnet with a bobby pin stuck in it and hands it to him. He takes the tangle of nylon and metal. Propping the door with his body, he examines it. He smiles. "Thank you," he says.

On her way home in the cab, Mira anticipates her arrival: her mother will be on the phone with Mira's father talking in low worried voices. The lights will be on, and the old TV in the corner of the living room will be blaring the evening news as her mother listens, in case there are reports about a child having been killed. When she finally walks in the door, her mother will grab her in her arms and say "I was so worried!" and Mira will allow herself to say "Mom."

But when the cab pulls up, her house is dark. The whole downstairs is quiet. When she reaches the third floor and sees a light underneath the door of the junk room, her heart sinks. Every instinct flares up in her body and she knows what she's not supposed to do. She does it anyway: she throws open the door.

Someone growls. Someone else shrieks.

Amid the chipped porcelain dishes and dusty piles of books, Gary is kissing her mother. Her mother's body on an old weathered table pushed up against the wall. The fabric of her mother's kimono spills around her and Gary is pressed up against her, his hand inside her robe.

Mira's stomach rises to meet her mouth, so she is surprised words can get through. Apparently, she is shouting at them. Something that sounds like "You! You! You!" Gary jumps off her mother; her mother pulls her robe around her, too slow to hide the pale, flushed skin. The rage Mira feels is immediate, swift, fortifying.

"I hate you." She doesn't know which of the two she is saying this to.

"Mira!" says her mother. "Oh, Mira. What are you doing in here?"

"You didn't even know I was gone!"

Her mother clutches her robe more tightly and stands up. "I—you were at rehearsal."

Gary is pulling his shirt back on. His thick man-arms are yellow and bruised-looking. "Weren't you even worried?"

"I have faith in you," says her mother. "I trust you."

Everything is moving too fast for her. Her mother's quivering floral smell and some other thing: like warm metal bleeding out into the air. Mira touches her lips, her nose. Her nose is bleeding. "Why? Why do you trust me?"

"Gary, go get some tissues," says her mother.

While Gary is gone, her mother puts her head down to Mira's. She says, "Your father called. He wants to see you."

Gary returns with a handful of toilet paper. As Mira cups the paper to her nose, she thinks of Maurice, the little crippled man who likes to watch her dance, whose quiet apartment is filled with pictures of dancers and Pavlova's tattered pointe shoe. She decides then and there that she will never tell her mother—or her father—about him. She'll never tell anyone about Maurice. He is *hers*. And she has the sense that this is another genuine secret, one that gives her power.

FLOWER PRINCESS

Sioban leads me to a ramshackle off-campus house, up some rickety wooden back stairs, whispering that she shares the house with five—or maybe six—others. She opens a back door that squeaks mightily in the cold. Then we are in her room. "My own entrance," she says in her rushed voice, energetic and sheepish at once. I stand in the doorway. She turns on the light: a mattress on the floor, covers askew, a chest with the lid propped open from which stream all sorts of fabrics, blank walls lit with nails from which hang beaded neck-laces and earrings, none of which I've ever seen her wear. There's a lamp on the floor and a heavy antique brocaded mirror, the only thing that looks to be of value, propped against the wall. The effect is of a medieval chamber, an idea of comfort and beauty from a more primitive civilization.

She takes me by the hand. This is my moment to back out, to say no, to defend my future against the present—but I do not.

Her hand is long-fingered and moist. "Come," she says. "Don't be scared." She takes off my coat and her own. The cheek with the acne scar is scarlet, from the cold or excitement, I don't know. Her eyes hum like oil behind glass. She sinks onto the bed. I sink down next to her, and in a second she is naked, and her flesh is so perfect.

She moves in her long-muscled limbs, all clavicles and hip and knee, and in her long sheath of that skin that now looks like dusky ash still glowing from a fire. Small breasts, dark nipples, no bra. She stretches out, full of confidence in her nakedness, and pulls me to her. I am overcome with a deep desire for her and, god forgive me, I kiss her breasts. She raises her hips up to meet me. She has not asked me to undress and I have not offered. We acknowledge her body is enough for both of us. Then I do something I never have before—not in those few times I have fallen into bed with a woman. In my twenties, my modern dancer days, gender mattered less than whose bed I could crash in that night. I put my tongue inside of her. She moves against me and I feel her whole body open up. She tastes of salt and ripe flowers. She squeezes my face with her thighs and shudders. When I raise my head, I catch sight of a crumpled sock on the floor next to the bed—a purple sock with red hearts. I stare at it, this fearsome thing, lying there with its careless vanity, then at the young woman before me in her medieval chamber, her body still possessing those long ballerina's muscles.

I pull away. "I have to go," I say.

Her face is surprised, even frightened. "No," she says. "Stay," she says. "It's okay. Really, it's okay."

The ridiculousness of her confidence sickens and exhilarates me. I am for the first time deeply afraid for myself and what I have done.

Back at my house, I shower and change out of my dance clothes, and call my mother. I catch her at work. "Mom?" I say. "Sorry to bother you."

"That's okay. What's up?" Her voice is generous. Something is going well.

She's an office manager at a nonprofit in SoMa and often works reception too. I picture her red hair, white roots, flat against her skull, still-attractive face knotted against the phones and computer screen. We talk every few weeks, but this call is off schedule. What do I want from her? I want to tell her about this girl, the terrible kiss, and what followed, and even more—the letter from Maurice. I want to tell her everything. Life has me by the throat, I want to say. I am choking. What if I could tell my mother my secrets? What if I could have told my mother my secrets? But our relationship has always been built on signals and codes sent from neighboring countries.

I take a deep breath. She says, "Hey, did you hear anything?"

"About the Pell?" I say. "Not yet. Bernie is saying after the break. But—" I'm about to tell her about Bill, but stop myself. "I won't keep you," I say. "Just tell me—what are you reading?"

Listening to her talk about her latest obsession has always, somehow, helped me, though I know it's maybe not in the healthiest ways. I can relax into gratitude for not being captive to the same endless desire to search.

"Jung," my mother says. "Hang on, that's the other line. It might be my boss." There's a click and the line goes hollow. She's gone and when she's back, she says, "Sorry—"

"Jung—still?" I say.

"*Again.* He says that the soul is mostly outside the body. Isn't that strange?" Her voice has the same tensile quality I'm so used to, a wire passing overhead, between herself and something or someplace else invisible to me.

No, it makes sense. I take a deep breath. "I don't know," I say at last. "I've often felt that the inside of me is hollow, waiting to be filled up with what the day brings to me. As if it's something *outside* of me that gives birth to whatever's inside of me. I've often been afraid that I'm nothing without these things, totally hollow. I wouldn't exist."

There's such a long pause on the other end that I say, "Hello?" and then she says, "Really? I never knew that. That's so odd and interesting."

Then it feels like there is nothing to say. The landline has that porous quality again, and none of the abrupt static of a cell line that could cut us off any minute. Suddenly I am desperate. "Hello? Hello? Mom?"

"I'm still here," she says.

In early November, Mira's father appears again. He says he's been staying with friends while he "figures things out." But he wants to see Mira. So the Sunday morning after Mira follows Maurice home, her father comes to pick her up. He wears a new long, stylish coat with a fur collar, and his cheeks are freshly shaved and raw-looking. His eyes are rimmed with red.

She climbs in his car—a new silver Toyota. Inside, it smells of leather and air freshener. It strikes Mira that her father is a very neat man. She had not known this about him, exactly, or had not thought it in those terms: *my father is a neat man.* How has she not known this about him? For how long has he been living in her mother's messy, upside-down world?

They drive through the silent early-morning Brooklyn streets. The city has slid into a cold late fall. Dead leaves clog the gutters, and the dog shit on the sidewalk has started to freeze into hockey pucks that the boys at school will kick at the girls. The air has finally shed the burned smell. Now it slaps your face and freezes your lungs. The plastic bags in the trees whip in the wind like banners on ghost ships. She watches as a newspaper blows down the street, catching a man in the face.

Her dad asks Mira if she has eaten. She shakes her head. She imagines that he will take her to a restaurant—maybe in Manhattan—where they will eat things she has never eaten before. Maybe quail eggs. Or snails.

Instead, only a few blocks away, on Court Street, he parks the car in front of a storefront restaurant sandwiched between two gated jewelry stores displaying giant gold earrings, necklaces, and bracelets. A battered blue-lettered sign reads: D UT PAV LION. Despite living ten blocks or so from this stretch of commerce, Mira has never noticed the Donut Pavilion, much less been inside of it.

They enter: a harmless-looking drugstore with a lunch counter. It is steamy inside, with smells of frying. Next to the counter is a rack of ancient greeting cards printed with salutations like "I Miss You!" and "From the Moment I Met You . . ." and pastel pictures of sunsets, flowers, and butterflies. As her dad climbs onto one of the ripped orange stools, Mira fingers their warped parchment paper and embossed covers. She lingers on a pretty card with a raised yellow sunset reading "Together Forever."

In a moment that moves past without a beat, Mira slides the card into the inside pocket of her jacket. The next moment, she is perched on the stool next to her father.

He leans toward her, as if he is telling her a secret. "*This* is a real diner. There was one like this where I grew up." Only once has Mira been to the town where her father grew up—it was cold and gray, with empty, windy streets. She remembers a white front porch and a quiet room with a crucifix hanging on the wall. This was the house he'd grown up in. She had been scared—of that crucifix, and of her stern grandmother whose face was as hard as a cement mixer. Her grandmother had died soon after that.

Without the coat, her father looks more like himself. He wears a corduroy button-down shirt, khakis, and the rubber shoes he calls "duck shoes": his weekend outfit. Behind the counter is a Hispanic man with a long, burnt-looking face and a white hat. He is constantly running an orange dishrag over the counter. Her father orders Mira a breakfast special—eggs and bacon and toast. He, himself, will eat nothing.

"How is your mom? How is the house?" he says.

"Okay."

He looks down and, with a thick finger, traces the grain in the counter. "Your mother will have to sell that house."

Mira's mouth is filled with the eggs and toast. "Really?" she says.

"We'll see," he says.

She pushes her plate away without finishing her breakfast. Her father motions to have a powdered sugar donut placed before her.

"I'm not coming back," he says.

Mira looks down at the donut, at her plate sprinkled with powdered sugar dust. When she looks up, she sees her father has an amazed, helpless look. His skin glows, as if a light is behind it, and his eyes are wide, as if he is seeing something wonderful in the distance. He is blinking a lot.

"At least for a while. We're going to see how it goes. Apart. This is something—your mother—we both have decided on."

They sit there for some time, then she says, "I hate you" in a low voice.

"I know," he says.

The counter guy sucks his teeth and wipes the counter aggressively with his dishcloth, veering very close to her father's coffee. Then he rips a check from the pad he keeps tied to his apron string and slaps the check down in front of them. Pale green, curled at the edges.

Her father shakes his head, as if that settles something.

Mira stares at two grease stains like small overlapping continents across the top of the check. Fingers, grease; it turns her stomach.

"I should have my own apartment soon."

"Where?"

"I'm thinking Murray Hill, maybe Chelsea, maybe Kips Bay." He laughs. *Manhattan.*

As her father pays, the long-faced counterman barks something out. Mira's heart skips.

The counter lady looks at her. "You have something, sweetheart?"

Mira pulls the greeting card from her pocket and puts it facedown on the counter. The lady clicks her tongue and smiles kindly—a luxury, since she knows she has won.

"It's for my mother," says Mira stupidly, the sallow impulse to lie springing up but fading.

"What's the matter?" says her father, who has walked back from the door.

"Your daughter almost shoplifted something," says the lady. "But Jimmy here"—she gestures toward the counterman —"he see her. Right, Jimmy?"

Mira reaches into her pocket, where she carries her saved-up change and drops it on the counter. "I was going to pay," she says.

The checkout lady, in one motion, gathers up the change and turns the card over with long beige fingernails as hard as pieces of sea glass. There is the glaring, gaudy sunset of turquoise and pink. And the horrible words. Her father looks at it, then at her, with a solemn face.

"It's my fault," he says. "I wouldn't get it for her."

"I don't really want it," says Mira as she gives her father what she hopes is an accusatory stare. And she doesn't. She looks at the picture with the silly words. She sees, as if it is written out in front of her, for the first time, that in the gap between what is hoped for and what is, you can find all sorts of silly, embarrassing things. She must be careful, she must watch herself.

The lady drums her long fingernails on the counter.

"Are you sure?" her father says. Mira nods as hard as she can, bouncing her head on her neck hurriedly so that it hurts.

The counter lady peels the card off the counter carefully like it is a wet dollar bill and puts it on the other side of the cash register where Mira can only see its edge sticking out. She returns Mira's change.

Her father looks at her with his red-rimmed eyes. "Oh, Mira," he says. "You must ask when you want something," he says. "Or you're going to turn into your mother. Always taking, never asking."

————————

One afternoon soon after this, Mira passes a bunch of older girls smoking under the awning of a camera store on the corner of Fifty-sixth and Seventh. When Mira nears the corner, she recognizes Hannah, her friend Portia, and two other girls she doesn't know by name. She is surprised to see that Val is among them.

After standing for a minute, Mira gets up her courage and walks up to the group. Hannah is wearing tight jeans and Frye boots. Her ponytail is gathered on one side of her head. Her eyelids shine with eye shadow. As she exhales, she closes her eyes halfway. Portia has her hair swept back with a toothed headband, and still wears some of her dance clothes: legwarmers over her sweats, leotard poking through her bomber jacket. The other girl, a small chunky girl whose name Mira knows is Noelle, barks out a laugh in agreement after Hannah says anything. They all hold cigarettes in their hands. Val raises the cigarette to her mouth and blows out a stream of smoke into the bright air. How does Val know how to do this?

"Hey," Hannah says, catching sight of her. "It's the Flower Princess."

Mira walks right up to them and tries to put her arm through Val's, but Val pulls hers away.

"I remember when I was the FP," says Hannah. She flips her hair back. "I thought it'd be better."

"It's for little girls," says Noelle.

"There's the *Prince*," says Portia, huskily.

"Yeah, the *Prince* . . . ," says Hannah.

Mira does not know what to do with her hands. She looks at her feet. The sidewalk is dotted with smashed cigarette butts and black, discarded gum. She tilts her head back. The sky above is an ominous gray.

"It might rain," she says.

Val looks at her with heavy eyelids. "So?"

"*It might rain.*" One of the other girls imitates her.

"Want a smoke?" Portia holds out an already lit cigarette.

Mira thinks about the quiet studio upstairs. Robin will be there practicing already.

Mira drags on the cigarette. The smoke catches in Mira's throat, and she coughs, once, then twice. Then she can't stop. The other girls laugh. "She didn't even inhale," says the freckled girl.

Val takes a step back. "God, Mira," she says, when Mira finally stops coughing.

Val looks at her like she has just given her a dare. Mira tries to pull her eyes away, but Val holds them. Now the blood is in her ears. It is as if her whole life is under attack. Mira's eyes fill with a strange water, and the girls recede like chips of colored glass in a kaleidoscope.

She runs. Their laughter comes from behind her. She hears someone say, "Shit"; someone else, "Damn"; someone else says, "Wait."

In Middle Studio, Robin is already warming up. She has one leg on the barre and is bent over the raised leg in a swan dive. She looks up briefly when Mira enters, nods imperceptibly, and lets her head flop over her leg again. Mira walks in and takes the barre against the other wall and begins to warm up.

During class, right before center, Ms. Clement stops the girls. She lifts the needle off the record. "Mira, come here." Mira walks out to the center of the room with her feet turned out. Standing in a first position, she brushes her right leg out along the floor. "Notice," Ms. Clement says, "the turnout begins at the hips, not at the knee." Mira extends her leg, lifts her chin, and makes her face blank. As blank as a desert. She has learned how to do this so that the others will not have something for their hate to attach itself to (for this is the third time this week she has been called to demonstrate).

They all move into the center. The first center combination is *allegro*—a series of glissades, a pas de bourrée, *changement*, and *soutenu.* Mira is quick, birdlike. Her feet obey her mind exactly, beating the air with the sure strokes of wings.

She has never felt her power so cleanly or decisively.

———————

The next Saturday when Mira leaves rehearsal, Maurice is waiting for her outside The Little Kirov. He's bundled in a fur coat. He invites her to the Russian Tea Room. Despite its proximity to the dance studio, Mira has never been to the Russian Tea Room. She has only seen it in movies.

He walks her around the corner and right through wooden doors festooned with lights. They sit in a puffy red booth. On the forest-green walls hang gold-framed paintings of jesters, clowns, and little girls. The room is a patchwork of colors and sounds: busy waiters wheeling clanking tea carts maneuver around a gold centerpiece clock whose wide, cheery face clicks and bongs. Beside their table is a giant silver pitcher with a spigot, which Maurice tells her is called a samovar. From it comes hot tea. Today Maurice wears all blue—dark blue trousers, a light blue sweater, and a red ascot. In this new guise, he reminds her of Jacques Cousteau. She is getting used to the fact that he appears in a different guise each time she sees him.

It is barely more than two weeks since their first meeting, but she already feels she's known him forever. When their cups are filled with the hot liquid from the samovar, he raises his glass and says, *"Nazdrovia!"* She tentatively lifts hers and he clinks his glass to hers. He smiles and points at the wooden dolls lined up on a shelf across the room. "This place is a hundred percent Russian. With a little kitsch. But who says kitsch isn't Russian? They are really quite *art brut.*"

She nods. For once she knows what he is talking about. Her grandmother had given her a Russian nesting doll for her tenth birthday. The dolls painted on oblong wooden eggs. The women get smaller as the eggs get smaller. Each woman rests inside another woman until the last tiny woman stands there wobbling on the table.

Maurice waves a waiter over and orders some things Mira can't pronounce. Then he smiles at her. The noises—the laughter, the tinkling silverware, the clatter of food carts—grow louder as she looks at him, her eyes burning.

"They used to be my friends."

"Who?"

"Val. And the other girls—"

He laughs. "They're not destined for greatness as you are."

Her eyes are filling up again. The room is collapsing into blurry shapes and streaks of light. She hasn't been able to get the girls out of her mind. "They whisper."

"Enough," he says. "Mira, I want to tell you a story. Imagine, dear, *before* electrical lights. No spotlights, no disco balls. This is how the first ballerinas danced—in theaters lit by gaslights, close to the fire. Now, these early ballerinas would sometimes get a little too far downstage, too close to the lamps, and their fragile tutus, which were longer in those days than they are now, well—they would catch fire, go up, *poof*! The ballerina engulfed in flames! Many ballerinas died this way. But they didn't stop the show. Poor Clara Webster burned in front of the audience and they carried her off and the show went on.

"One night a dancer named Rostova was performing *Swan Lake*—there it was, the fire. In the mirror, she saw her own wings in flames but rushed out onstage right on cue. Siegfried, without missing a beat, grabbed a blanket from backstage, pas de bourréed over to her and wrapped her in that blanket. He had second-degree burns on his hands from trying to tamp out the worst of the flames. But they were onstage for the next act, Siegfried doing lifts with a bandaged hand. And Rostova danced the rest of the evening beautifully."

Mira's head throbs.

"The audience, interviewed afterward, said that they thought the fire was part of the performance. The audience only knows what it is told."

He looks at her, his black eyes boring into her. "Now these girls. They are like your fire." She makes herself meet his eyes. "Mira, you must learn to dance with the fire."

There is a din inside her head that matches the one in the room. She looks around the room: everything glitters strangely. It's too bright, like a dollhouse come to life. She feels like she's seeing it all for the first time.

Suddenly, her gloom lifts.

A bow-tied waiter places a bowl of soup before her. It is a deep purple red, hot and salty, with bits of something like earth floating in it. Beneath the earth and salt, the tangy silver of the spoon. Then a plate of folded pancakes arrives on their table. A number of small dishes accompany them—sour cream, apples, jam. Her mouth waters at the tastes on display. She tries each one in succession—she has always been a good eater, with a taste for sweet and salty, sour and bitter.

Then Maurice leans over to her and whispers in her ear, "My dear, do you see that man over there?" Mira looks at the corner where Maurice is pointing and she sees an older man—a man with white hair and the small wizened face of a turtle—gazing at a young girl sitting across from him.

"That, my dear, is the great Balanchine."

There's not a girl who dances in New York City who doesn't know about Balanchine—Mr. B. He is synonymous with the great and the rare. He is father of the "pinhead ballerina"—that new variety—the waif with the strength of an ox. But to Mira, he is a confusing figure, more shadowy than the stars he has produced, more mysterious than Mikhail Baryshnikov and Natalia Makarova, the show-stoppers of ABT.

The great Balanchine wipes his mouth heartily. His twinkling eyes scan the room. They rest on her for a second before they continue on. Mira's eyes shift to the girl next to him. She sits with her hands in her lap, looking down. From her small ears hang strands of diamonds. When the girl looks up again, Mira sees that she's not a girl but a *woman*.

Balanchine and the young-but-old woman gather their things. They don't have much—he has no coat and she has only a tiny gold-clasped purse that hangs from one long-fingered hand. She puts her other arm through Balanchine's. Her eyes are trinkets—wide and bright. She doesn't smile. He steers her among the tables of the room as he makes his way toward their table. Then he and the glittering waif stand before them.

Balanchine nods at Maurice and turns to Mira. His eyes are small and almond shaped, and through his skin you can see the bones of his skull. His eyes crinkle as he takes her in.

"Is she one of mine?" he says.

"No," Maurice answers. "Not yet."

"Ah," he says.

"Her name is Mirabelle."

Mr. B nods. The woman blinks her startled eyes. They turn and make their way toward the door.

Sioban doesn't come to contact class on Tuesday. She doesn't show up to Dance History on Wednesday morning either. We are doing Léonide Massine and Balanchine, the early days of Ballet Russe de Monte Carlo, the years when Bronislava choreographed her masterpiece, *Les Noces*. I imagine Sioban back in class, her tightly pulled back hair and lean body, her eyes anodyne, her speech subdued. I will say, *Sioban, we need to talk*. But where should our talk be? A booth in the coffee shop in town? In the classroom after everyone's gone? My office? Each place rife with danger.

Then comes Friday afternoon. I'm in my office. Bill pokes his head in. I am *sure* he's going to tell me he's been given the Pell—delivering me into a year of deep income instability and insecurity, another overly educated, impoverished vagabond floating around the country. I am preparing the acrid congratulations, when he says. "Kate, are you okay?"

I'm caught off guard. Is my distress that obvious?

"You look like hell," he says, grinning.

I haven't been able to deal with my contact lenses, so I am wearing an old pair of glasses—tortoiseshell frames that leave an orange greasy smudge near my temples where the chemical coating is wearing off. The prescription is years old. But it's a relief in a way to see less well: if *I* can't see as well, perhaps others won't look so closely at me.

Bill disabuses me of that.

"Thanks," I say. "It's just a scratched cornea." I have no idea where I get this lie. "And my shower's been broken." *Lie, lie.* "But thanks for your concern." I am not able to keep the bitterness out of my voice. My disdain for him at that moment is pure and unadulterated.

He is saying something about his aunt rupturing her cornea but I'm not really listening. My worse vision helps me see the broader outlines of his face, the shape of it—I realize that the name Krasdale must be a shortened form of something more ethnic.

Then he claps his hands on his knees a few times and says, "Kate, the other night, I was driving home after coming back from dinner and I saw"—he looks away—"I saw you and that student—I saw her in your office the other day, just walking together." Then he looks right at me now. "You walked side by side without talking. *Exactly* in step together. Like you were going to an important meeting or something." He laughs.

"God, Bill. Don't you have anything better to do?"

"Listen," he says. "I've been there before—almost there." I wish I could see his expression better. Is he smiling or grimacing? I have the strange thought that he's flirting with me.

"I'm offended," I say, harsher than I intend.

"Be careful, Kate, be very careful. I am not the enemy."

"Leave me alone," I say. I am yelling. "Leave me the fuck alone!"

"Have it your way. Don't say I didn't warn you." His tone, dire and mean, is so out of keeping with his generally jovial demeanor we stare at each other in shock. Then he shakes his head. "It's your decision to self-destruct, not mine."

"Get out. You bigfooted me. You have no right—"

"You're a tough one, Kate." He shakes his head again and turns to leave. "I've tried to help. Don't say I didn't try."

Then comes the weekend. It's weekends like this that make me glad I live alone. I don't want to have to think about anyone else right now. I shop and cook, I make a stew, I start grading the midterm.

But my worry is constant—a ghost tic in my consciousness spouting new scenarios. What is going on with Sioban? Am I going to get a call from some parent somewhere, complaining of a crying, inconsolable girl? (I think of the trembling hand on my wrist, the crumpled sock on the floor.) Is she talking to friends? Does she *have* friends? She comes to class alone and leaves alone, quivering with ideas, rattling the others. I go so far as to look up her home address in the student register. It's a town a few hours away that looks from a map like it could be considered a suburb of Cincinnati.

Or what if she is vindictive? What if she goes to the administration instead of her parents? What if she says—Dr. Randell *put her tongue inside of me?*

By Sunday evening I've finished everything I need to do and, in this fallow time, I really start drowning. I try reading, but can't concentrate. I try researching, but my mind wanders, the pen droops, and I become fixated on hunting for splinters of glass on the floor.

That night I call my mother again. The phone rings and then her piqued voice answers. *Hello?* She always sounds like she's being interrupted. *Hello? Hello?* I imagine I'm catching her on her roof garden, at her mushroom breeding pots, her freckled knees reddening in the spring sun. Rainy season is almost over there in San Francisco. Things dry out quickly. The sun blankets and burns and chills the rooftops and soon the cool summer breeze will start up. The fog doesn't ever come this far inland.

It's enough just to think of her. I hang up, cutting off her annoyed *hellos.*

My phone is languid on the table now. It shows its dull off-line screen. The sky darkens outside of the curtains. Then my eyes rest on the knives I keep in a basket on the counter, a hodgepodge of well-used curiosities. Estate sale specials. I pick an old knife from the basket and run my palm along the edge of the blade. It surprises me when my hand comes away with a long cut. I watch the blood wind its way into the little wrinkles in my palm. I rip off a sheet of paper towel and wad it into my hand. Staunch the inevitable—but for how long? There is a universe of deception behind one secret. Not all secrets see the light of day. My life is a testament to that.

Why am I drawn to the illicit, the secretive? It's like a curse I can't shake, no matter how far I've come. What have these secrets cost me? A normal life, and intimacy of a typical kind. There is no doubt something still wrong with me, deep down, something that this letter has unearthed. Here I am, one secret at my heels, another blossoming before me. It's absurd. *I* am absurd.

Holding my hand, I head to the bathroom to look for gauze.

I have to go to New York. There may still be people there—people from long ago, another era—who can help me put the pieces back together. There's someone in particular I have to see—if he's still there. I hesitate, then go to Facebook and, with my throbbing, bandaged hand, poke around. I am looking for Felicia, one of the few girls I used to dance with whom I've kept in touch with (at least sort of). I find her page: there are some posed photos of her in exotic locales, sunglasses and smiles, her black hair pulled back. But no new posts for six months, the last one a "like" for a salon. Still, I message her and say I am coming to town. "Any interest," I ask, hoping I sound good-humored, wry in my own way, "in putting up an old friend?" (Was the word *friend* the right one?)

The performance will take place the weekend before Christmas: Saturday, December 17. There's only a month left of rehearsal time, and one weekend is lost because of Thanksgiving weekend. They've just finished another rehearsal, but there is still so much to do—especially on the lifts.

Christopher and Mira gather their things silently. Out of the corner of her eye, Mira watches him fold his leg warmers and pack them in his bag. His T-shirt is wet with sweat and his face pale with effort. He pulls on a blue sweatshirt and takes a comb out of his bag and runs it through his damp hair. Then he uncaps a stick of something and walks up to the mirror. He pulls his high bangs back again and gazes at his forehead, rubs his fingers lightly over the skin. Then, carefully, with quick, sure strokes, he draws a dark line beneath one eye.

"Nice job," Christopher says, without looking at her.

He has switched to the other eye.

"Thanks," she says, unable to look away. Again, those words: *there is something wrong with him.*

"But we still need to work on the lift," he says. "You're still holding back. You have to trust me, trust that I'll be there."

She pulls her leg warmers off, tosses them in her bag. The cooler air slides over her shins. She knows what he means. She hasn't been able to recapture that feeling of abandon that she had the first day they rehearsed the lift—to close her eyes and *just jump* as if she were launching herself from the diving board into the deep end of the pool. *Trust.* Yes, that is the operative word. But she's not sure that it *is* her fault. When Ms. Clement is not watching, he is cavalier, he is sloppy. He doesn't plié enough, so that when she runs and leaps into him, it feels for a moment like a collision rather than a lift. She can feel his effort but it comes with a hitch, too late. Once he almost dropped her, she knows it, though he pretended it was just his jockstrap that had come loose. But can she say this to him, to a boy, a prince from ABT?

The truth is that she is disappointed in the difficult work of partnering. It is nothing like it looks: two bodies seamlessly flowing into and away from each other. It is nothing like dancing on your own, feeling the power of your own body transporting you. No, partnering is all sweating and grunting and hard-edged bones, hip bones jabbing into finger bones and taut thighs ricocheting, straining against a heaving shoulder, slick with sweat. It is unseemly and difficult, without the reward of self-mastery.

She surprises herself. "Maybe it's not *me,* maybe it's *you,*" she says.

He looks at her. He looks tired, his face too long, his eyes too blurry, his skin sickly, his hair dank, too old and too young at once. *There is something wrong wrong wrong with him.* Then he steps back and regards himself. With the smudges beneath them, his eyes appear deeper set, his skin paler, his hair blonder. "It'll be fine," he says. "You'll figure it out. Just keep practicing."

She looks down—her turtleneck has hearts on it. How babyish!

She remembers Maurice's story of Rostova and her partner. How he looked out for her. How he saved her when she caught fire. To *trust* and then leap. She needs to find a way to leap, she needs to close her eyes, she needs to ignore the hitch of his knees buckling, the unstableness of his stance, and the soft grunts that he might not even know slip out from somewhere in his slick-with-sweat throat. That is the job of the ballerina.

"Sorry—" she says.

He pulls his bangs back, rubs his fingers lightly over the skin of his forehead, investigating his pimples. "Are you going to audition in the fall?" he says.

She and Val had said they would audition for SAB and ABT someday, but it had been far off, an idea. Now she sees that it's not far off at all. She must have nodded because he says, "SAB or ABT? Or both?"

For her only one shining, glittering acronym matters—the one owned by the wise, shadowy face she saw at the Russian Tea Room with Maurice. "SAB," she says. "I met Mr. Balanchine once."

He cocks his head and smiles, though it's really more of a smirk.

I will go there. Next year. But she has to wait for August when they famously line girls up along a barre and lift their legs and check their arches and say which ones have a chance before they even dance. They wait for the last minute, a minute before September classes start, to hold the audition.

He nods. "You should. You'll probably get in. You have the right line. No hips. They hate hips."

"I'm only eleven," she says.

"Yeah, well," he says. "When I was your age, I was already the *Nutcracker* prince."

"I know that." She smoothes her white turtleneck with the hearts on it.

He laughs. "Of course you do. Did you read that book about me?"

She looks down and feels her face fill with blood.

He smiles slowly. "That's all right," he says. He is enjoying himself. He rubs his eyes quickly, almost violently, and shakes his hair.

He is about to leave. Suddenly, she doesn't want him to go. She doesn't want to be alone in the studio in the fading afternoon. She doesn't want to go home on the train to her Brooklyn self, to her mother, to her absent father. She thinks about Gary, who, despite what he said, is over at the house all the time clattering away on a typewriter and lurking about, his hungry wolf's face saying hello to Mira so that before Mira has to pee, she sticks her head out into the hallway to see if he is there. She thinks of her father with his head in his hands at the steamy diner. Her father's new place: that bright apartment with the brown couch and squat black phone. She wants to say something to Christopher that will encompass all of this.

"My father skipped out." *Skipped out.* She's never said that before. She doesn't even know what it means, exactly. It makes her blush.

He zips up his bag. "I'm sorry." She can see he means it.

Now Christopher looks at her. His eyes look darker, deeper set, with the slight smudges beneath them. The old swooning feeling comes back to her. Only it is changed. She feels a vertiginous swell of something for this long-faced counterfeit prince. She knows now though that it is not love. What is it?

"That guy? Watching you that first day? I know him. I remember him. He comes around David Howard's." He begins lacing up his high-top sneakers. "Be careful of him. He's a creep." Now he doesn't smile. He looks at her with his bruised-looking eyes. "There are creeps everywhere. The perverts are the ones who get caught."

He pauses in the doorway and turns back around. "Ballet is not about me. It's about you. You'll see. *Ballet is woman.* That's what Balanchine said." He reaches in his pocket and holds out the eyeliner pencil. "Here," he says. "It's almost finished anyway. Try to get it right under your eye, otherwise it looks lame. It gives your eyes depth. If you burn it first, then let it cool for a minute, it's even darker."

She takes the pencil from him.

He turns and walks down the hallway to the elevator. She watches him go, her fist clenched around the little hard nub of a pencil.

She stops by the dressing room on the way out to get her coat. The room is deserted except for Robin, who has stayed after the older girls' class to practice, no doubt, and is changing into her street clothes. Robin is naked. She has never seen Robin naked before—she usually arrives from school already with leotard and tights on underneath her street clothes. Her body is long and extremely white, more substantive than it appears in leotard and tights. Her nipples, big as raspberries, sit directly on her ribs.

There are two bright red spots on her pale cheeks.

Robin nods at Mira and begins pulling on a pair of jeans without any underwear.

Mira stands awkwardly in the center of the room for a moment. Then she surprises herself by walking up to Robin. "Are you going to audition?" Mira asks. Robin hunches over a bit and peers at Mira as if she is surprised to find her there. Mira realizes she has made a big mistake: she has come too close to Robin. But she doesn't want to move back. If she moves back it will somehow be admitting she made a mistake to begin with. She and Robin are practically pressed up together. She can smell the certain combination of flowers and salt that she associates with those older than she is, with a next phase of life. She is dizzy with being so close to Robin's long flat body, milky skin, and raspberry nipples.

Robin's face looks beautiful in the weak, dusty light of the space—long and pale, big eyes, and a strange grimace. Her voice—which Mira realizes she has never heard—is a whisper. "In the fall? Sure. But just for SAB this time. I haven't heard such good things about the ABT school."

"Me, too," Mira says. She can't believe that she's speaking to Robin. She pictures the old man with the glittering woman on his arm.

Then another whisper from inside a see-through undershirt Mira has seen men but never women wear: "How many times have you tried before?"

"None," Mira says.

"Really? Most girls start auditioning at five or six. When I was your age, I had already auditioned four times."

Mira sees what her mother's lack of vigilance has cost her—all the missed opportunities. At the same time, she's amazed that Robin, perfect Robin who had played the Flower Princess for two years in a row, didn't get in. Her face fills with blood. She doesn't know where to look.

"Look," Robin says.

In her palm, Robin holds a purple plastic square the size of a Cracker Jack box prize. Robin is looking at her searchingly, but

Mira does not know what is expected of her. Is she supposed to touch it? It looks like a toy, but she knows it's not a toy. Printed on the puffy plastic is a silhouette of a helmeted head, like a Greek warrior's, and beneath it is the big word TROJAN. Mira looks up. Robin blows at the wisps of fine hair that have fallen around her eyes, hair so fine it looks like the thread of spiders. She still hasn't put her shirt on. "Well, anyway," Robin says. Robin closes her hand and the plastic square disappears with a crinkly sound. Robin begins to back up and Mira knows something has changed. Robin has shown her something she wanted to. Something important. But Mira doesn't know what.

That night, in her room, Mira strips naked and looks at her body in the mirror. She imagines Maurice looking at her. What would he see? A child? A woman? A girl? A dancer? The sticking-out ears, the too-wide mouth, the knobby knees are those of a girl. Her flat, muscular stomach and long, lithe arms belong to a dancer. On her long torso she sees the hard nipples like swollen insect bites that don't go away. But they are pale, not rosy. She sees they belong to a child.

She takes out the eyeliner and uncaps it. Using one of the cigarette lighters Gary left downstairs, she burns the tip like Christopher said to do. It softens and becomes gooey. She draws a line underneath each eye, but it comes off in too thick, liquid globs. When she tries to rub it off, it smears and streaks and she can't get it off with her hands, no matter how hard she rubs. After a while, she is just transferring the black smears back and forth from her fingers to her eyes.

She goes downstairs in her pajamas for a cup of milk before bed. Her mother and Gary are sitting at the kitchen table playing cards. As she passes, Gary tosses his cards down. "You're cheating again, Rachel," Gary says. Her mother laughs and says, "My way or the highway."

As Mira passes, carrying her milk back upstairs, her mother grabs her. "What's that on your eyes?"

"Nothing," says Mira.

"Little Cleopatra," says Gary.

Her mother pulls Mira closer. Her mother's expression is too small for her big features. Her mother's eyes settle on her in that rare way, really lock in. Mira's right up against a landscape of flushed, freckled skin. Gary laughs. "Shut up," her mother says. Her mother grabs a paper napkin lying on the table and wipes Mira's eyes hard with it. The black smudges are on the old balled-up napkin that her mother tosses on the table. Her mother looks at the napkin, then from her to Gary, tosses her cards into the center of the table next to the napkin, suddenly stands—the chair tilts back and forth before it rights itself—and says, "Game over."

Today her dad is taking Mira to the Thanksgiving Day Parade. Her mother gets up early and makes Mira some Cream of Wheat. She can hear Gary thumping around upstairs. She's grateful that he doesn't come down. The cereal is so thick that her spoon sticks up straight. There are lumps in it, so Mira does not eat much. She watches the sky lighten to a peevish gray and then stop.

Her father parks on Eighth. They walk over on Thirty-eighth to Broadway, where they find a crowd pressed against police barricades, spilling over, bundled in blankets and coats, with their own stepladders (her father's secret weapon!) and chairs and even giant ladders. A great crush of paper cups and thermoses. She and her father stand amid the throng. Everything in the damp, gray air.

They are pressed in next to a short, pretty lady and a boy a few years older than she is. The lady has short brown hair on which she wears a puffy pink hat.

"We're from uptown," the lady says to Mira's father.

Her father begins chatting with the lady. The wind blows, scraping Mira's bones with its teeth, through her jeans and jacket.

"We rarely get below Forty-second," the woman is saying. "It's such a treat for Sam." The boy looks at Mira doubtfully and turns his head back to the wide avenue. A giant cacophonous Snow White float has just passed. Now a single clown is walking by, waving tiredly. His red nose and floppy feet bounce up and down at the same time. Occasionally, little paper squares tumble from his spiky black hair.

Despite herself, Mira laughs.

The boy looks sharply at her.

"It looks like he was electrocuted."

"He's supposed to look like that. Some people think it's funny. Electricity is not really funny." She looks at him more closely to see if he is joking, but he doesn't appear to be.

She pulls on her dad's sleeve, but he doesn't turn. He's too involved with telling the lady something. The lady is laughing and he is waving his arms, and he knocks the lady's hat to the side and she laughs harder. "Best restaurant north of Forty-second Street," he's saying.

"I'm Judy," the lady says, reaching out a tiny gloved hand to Mira's dad. Her mother would hate this woman and her ready smile, her sparkly lip gloss, her pink fuzzy hat.

The boy leans closer. His flushed cheeks are bright with the cold, his eyes are clear and thick-lashed. His dirty blond hair is thick and tousled—also blond, but different from Christopher's honey-pale hair. Despite the cold air, his jacket is flung open, and his flannel shirt untucked. He looks like an athlete, someone who hits or kicks balls and someone who has lots of friends. She turns away.

"My mom is hitting on your dad," he whispers. "It's so sick."

"Mira is a ballet dancer," she hears her dad say. "She'll be performing in their school production this winter."

"Oh *really*?" says Judy. "*The Nutcracker*? I *love The Nutcracker*.

The tree, the party scene, the Dew Drop Fairy. I cry during her solo. I *love* ballet. It's so beautiful." She gives Mira another look. "Does she go to SAB?"

"The Little Kirov," says Mira.

"Sam has some girls at SAB in his class."

"They're snobs," says the boy.

"Sam, please, attitude . . ." She rolls her eyes. "My son is *très sportif.*"

"What's your sport of choice, son?" says her father. She's never heard him call anyone "son" before. The boy looks at her dad. "Lacrosse."

This boy is too old, too handsome for her. She doesn't know what to say. She says nothing. The clown has passed.

The lady points down the avenue. "Here comes Mickey Mouse!" She looks at Mira and the boy as if they are six years old.

"Mom, that's Mighty Mouse."

She smiles again. Her voice lowers a notch and she hisses, "Attitude, please."

It's true. Here is Mighty Mouse. His enormous smiling face comes toward them, and then stops. His ochre-colored, prosthetic-looking limbs, too thin for the gourd-shaped body, his giant smile. Now the balloon is right above her. The arms and legs wave and shudder. There are many creases in the fabric. Something is wrong, she knows it. The balloon handlers, men in beige space suits, have stopped. They twirl and spin their spools of string, their eyes raised to the sky.

"Dad," she says. "I think it's going to fall."

"No it's not, honey. It's just the wind."

She sees people high above, their heads out the window, waving handkerchiefs. The balloon lists sharply to the side. Some of the spacemen unwind the string as quickly as they can; others wind it as quickly as they can. People are pulling their heads inside the windows. The crowd around them begins to shuffle.

"Dad, it's really going to fall."

"It's okay, honey. They're just adjusting it."

Mira covers her head with her arms.

"Mira!" says her father.

The boy is laughing. "Combat zone! That thing is gonna combust!"

"Sam," says the lady.

She peeks out. The smiling moon face is now lurching over to the other side. She looks around: everyone is laughing. The black-haired, electrocuted clown is back again and he is pantomiming the serious spacemen, with their somber engineer's faces, their longshoreman's caps over their heads. He is cartwheeling, leaping, tugging on an invisible line, now he is falling. Like border guards that are trained not to see what is in front of them unless it violates the rules, the spacemen do not look at him, they do not blink.

They right their ship through some effort of physical and mental communication that astounds Mira. And then they are walking again in unison.

"See. It's just the way it is. It's constantly in motion. Don't you remember this is the way it is? You weren't scared last year."

Mira is amazed. It's true: the trajectory of the balloon is not straight ahead but side to side down the long avenue. The spacemen are constantly running and spinning and frantically twirling their spools of string, eyes raised on the swollen body above them. She suddenly feels very tired.

To Sam, she says, "Ha-ha." Then she turns to her dad. "I'm cold." Her father hands her the plaid blanket he has been carrying under his arm and she wraps it around herself. For the next two hours, the little children around her—a boy of five or six and his younger sister, both sneaker-clad and moon-faced—jump up and down and squeal. Do all children secretly feel, somewhere, what she does now? Has she always felt like this—and just not known what it was? Was there always this chug under her heart when her dad raises the camera and says "Smile"? Like that cloud of fatigue that descends over her eyes when she hears there'll be games—oh no, not apple bobbing or sack racing again? What does it mean? She is glad there are no balloons made of *The Wounded Prince*—of the Flower Princess, of the lame Prince, of the Sorcerer in her fiery red. She intuits that these are creatures of the imagination that would lose their power if blown up into great, unwieldy balloons knocking against the concrete world. She huddles against her father as she watches the floats and balloons going by.

When the parade is finally over, the pink-hatted lady turns to her dad and says, "All that fun and the cold air has really fired up my appetite. How about some lunch?" Her small eyes get smaller and focus on Mira, and her gloved fingers rest for a moment on Mira's dad's arm. She has sparkling diamonds in her ears and one gold ring over a gloved finger.

The next week, Mira finds Maurice waiting for her after rehearsal. He calls out to her from a parked car. At first she doesn't know where his voice is coming from. Then she sees—a shiny, maroon Mercedes parked on the corner of Fifty-seventh Street. She pokes her head through the open window. It smells deeply of new leather. The seats are a dusky maroon (a few shades darker than the outside) and the dashboard is black.

"It's new," he says. "My first car. They have all these devices now. It's amazing."

Inside it looks like an old-fashioned carriage, like the kind he took her in that first time. He sits at the wheel on some kind of box covered with sheepskin. There is a lever—he holds it with his hand—connected to the steering column. Attached to the rearview mirror hangs a chain with a tiny glass swan that spirals, its translucence lit by all the lights of passing cars.

"It's got a lot of power. It handles divinely. The classic and the modern converge." He laughs. "Do you like it, Mirabelle?"

"Why do you call me that?"

"I like to. Is it okay?"

"Yes," she says.

"Would you like to get in?"

She's been warned, of course, against getting into the car with a stranger. But he is hardly a stranger by now, Maurice—*her* Maurice. She looks at Maurice's pale hands, his delicate fingers. Gary, who now lives with them, more or less, is a stranger; Maurice, who owns such beautiful things, who cares only about beautiful things, is not. She feels she is learning something about the world.

She goes around to the street side and gets in. She runs her fingers along the smooth cool leather of the dashboard, the slick, stippled leather of the seat that squeaks softly beneath her. Under the car's soft skin, she can feel its metal body. She remembers the cool, strange quiet of his apartment, in which all noises of the city subsided and the past sprang up, rich and alive: the dim rooms, the inert smells of luxury, underneath it, an old familiar scent of apples and cinnamon, and beneath even that, something deeper and stranger. She recalls the gallery of black-and-white photos of famous dancers from the past, all of whose names he knew, and then, Pavlova's frayed tiny shoe. She could almost hear it, the shoe, lit from above, beating in the center. All sounds outside fade.

She feels a rush of good feeling for this man, Maurice, her friend.

A strange spell comes over her; she feels no need to speak. She feels like she and Maurice are in a bubble, present only as watchers. It is powerful. They sit in the dark in the miasma of chemicals and leather without talking for some time. People pass on one side, cars on the other. Being inside the car reminds her of his apartment.

"I'm scared," she says finally.

"Oh!" he says. "Of what?"

"I don't know." She watches the cars. The lights of the cars streak by. On her right, the ceaseless sidewalk parade continues.

Then the strange, now familiar laugh: a rusty laugh with high and low sounds, like an ancient language shouted in the hall of a mausoleum. She is growing to trust him; he appears, of all the adults in her life, to be the only one who tells her the truth—perhaps the only one who *knows* it.

"Let me tell you something. Do you know why my legs are like this?"

"No."

"I had polio. When I was about your age I had polio. I was in an iron lung for eight months. When I got out I couldn't walk right."

"Oh."

"Do you know what an iron lung is?"

She shakes her head. She does not look at him. She does not want reasons. She does not want him to explain anything about himself to her.

"It's a giant machine that breathes for you. There were others in my room in their own machines. They often left the lights out, even in the daytime. When I lay in that darkness in that hospital, in that machine, I felt scared at first. I felt panic. I felt like I was dying. I heard the breathing of others around me, but I couldn't see them. After a while, I realized I wasn't dying. I was afraid. I was afraid of the dark. After more time, I knew I wasn't going to die and I began to like the dark. I thought of it as my friend. It gave me cover, the cover of invisibility.

"You know, sometimes I sit in the dark and watch you dance in my mind's eye." He turns on the small overhead light above them. It lights one side of his face. He gives her his stones-on-a-ledge smile. "If you are not afraid of the dark, you will fear nothing and no one. Most people are afraid. You can take cover there. You can speak from it, move from it. They won't find you there. They won't even look there," he says. "Listen." He turns off the light again. The night envelops them.

"What?"

"Shhh."

"What?"

"Shhh."

"I can hear it," he says. "Something's coming. Something big."

She *does* hear it—a suspension of all noise. In the middle of the tumultuous city—beeps, blares, sirens—all recede. For a few seconds, there is in the midst of Seventh Avenue evening rush hour, a total, profound silence.

"I've felt it since I was your age. Do you hear it?"

"Yes."

And she did.

"The angels are passing," he says. He takes down the glittering swan ornament attached to the mirror. "You are going to be wonderful. I am so proud." He looks at her, feline, glowing. She wants to be held like a bird in his hands, eaten, loved, devoured. She closes her eyes.

"You will come to see me perform as Flower Princess, right? Are you coming with anyone?"

"Ah," he says. "Just my memories and my dreams." He hands her the heavy glass ornament. "This belonged to my mother. Beat your wings. Fly into the night. The dark will always get us. Make it your friend. Envelop *it*. Let it envelop *you*. If the dark is coming, make it your friend."

And then, just like that, suddenly, it's over. The crush of sounds returns: the flux of traffic, the wheezing of buses passing, the clatter of foot traffic. Just then, someone thumps the car's roof. A man gesturing at something they can't see. His face is twisted in anger. He shouts, "Move your car, bozo! You're in a no-standing zone!"

"Ah, yes," he says and smiles. "They are never far behind." He hands her a card that she puts in her pocket. "Keep this," he says. "It may come in handy."

Later, when she takes it out in the garish fluorescent lights of the subway, she'll read: FOR MY MIRABELLE—MAURICE DUPONT, BALLETOMANE, and a phone number.

"You must go." Maurice leans to one side and adjusts the lever that controls the pedal for his bad leg. Reluctantly, Mira climbs out.

"Mirabelle." He calls her back over to the window one more time. "You will be wonderful. I can't wait! A star is only a star because it burns brightly in the dark night. Against the dark night. *At home* in the dark night."

Then he turns the ignition and she steps back. She watches from the well-lit sidewalk as the sleek black car bucks and shoots down Seventh Avenue.

BLACKOUT

The next morning, I know what I have to do. I find Bernadith in her office, in Birkenstocks, her feet planted firmly on the floor, and a new bobbed haircut. She seems relaxed, pleased to see me. She assumes I've come about the Pell, and after she has me sit, she reaffirms that they will not have a decision until after spring break. I decide not to mention Bill and his application.

"What happened to your hand?" she asks.

"Just a cut." I examine my hand. My homemade bandage is already ratty-looking and stained, which gives me a strange satisfaction. "It's not as bad as it looks," I say. My voice wants to rise into the squeaky registers. I give her what I hope is a disarming smile.

"Ah," she says. I can't tell if her expression is bemused or concerned. "You have to take care of yourself. None of us are getting any younger."

"Yes, I know, Bernadith." I'm embarrassed to find myself slapping my knees a few times like Bill had done with me, a blunt-edged cudgel for a finesse moment if there ever was one. "Bernadith," I say. "Unfortunately—there's been an indiscretion."

She looks at me with what I can only say is—this is clear, even without my contacts—alarm. "Are you talking about yourself?"

I nod. "A student."

"How many times?"

"Once only."

She clicks something on her computer. Her face has grown more voluminous and is dangerously close to purple now. Something twitches near her eye. She sits back. "I know how to dig up something if it's there. There was nothing on your record. Not a smudge—"

I examine my hand. "I am disappointed in myself—beyond disappointed." As I say this, I realize how true it is. My hand throbs. Suddenly tears well up behind my glasses.

"I know this may affect my chances for the Pell—" I add.

"Forget the Pell. This is bigger than that." Her face has gone from beet-colored to pale. "I like you, Kate. But I don't understand you." Some timer goes off on her computer. She clicks the mouse a few times and waddles over to her window. Her office is on the ground floor and looks out into an underused courtyard. Concrete benches no one ever sits on, patches of sparse grass, and some spidery indistinct-looking bushes around the edges. Birds flit back and forth from bush to barren bush. On one of these bushes by her window some sort of creeping berries, like pox.

I have to twist around to see her. "I'm sorry," I say.

My vision is blurring even more. I take off my glasses. "I really, really want this job," I say, choking on my words. *How could I have fucked up like this?* I dab at my eyes with my bandaged hand.

She turns to me, her back against the window. Her face has resumed its normal color. Somehow I can see it better now, even through my tears. Her mouth softens. It's not a smile, far from it, but something has loosened. Then the ghost of a true smile emerges. I can't tell if its source is kindness, bemusement, or irony. This is by far the most intimate time I have ever spent with her. Previously, she had been like pretty much every boss I've ever had—friendly and remote in equal degrees—concerned most of all with efficiency and bureaucratic issues.

"Kate," she says. "I know the life of a visiting professor is not easy. I know the life of a woman alone is not easy. I know sometimes it's all just too much—the loneliness, the work, the keeping up. . . ."

"I make no excuses for my behavior."

"Do you like teaching?" she asks suddenly.

I remember the time, after I followed him through the streets of New York City, when Maurice asked me if I *wanted to be a dancer.* I remember the energy of that moment, the knowing that I was at a crossroads. That what I answered meant something. Meant everything. Then the *yes* had rushed out of me, the force of it surprising myself. I hadn't known the force of my own desire. Now I know I will say yes again, but I tell myself to wait a beat. I think of walking through a circle of students, their faces on me, pulling ideas out of them, their faces opening at the dawning of their own knowledge. *Building castles in the air.* I let the "yes" out slowly, almost reluctantly, as if saying this truth will bring some new curse on me.

Something quizzical and sly comes into her face. She glances over at her office door, which I closed on entering. "You know, there are procedures for these things." She looks away. "But it's a tenuous situation. As you know, this is not perhaps the best time to be telling me this—officially."

I understand that in the midst of my truth telling, she is giving me a chance to preserve my secret. She is offering me a way out. "Your evaluations are excellent, your scholarship is the kind that I really want to support. . . ." She rubs her hands and claps suddenly. "Will he report it?"

"She," I say.

She gives me a long look. "*She* then."

"She hasn't been back to class."

"Talk to her. You have the chance to—to—make it right." Now she looks fierce and satisfied. As if we've concluded a difficult business meeting.

I try out a smile, and she returns it. "I'm hoping to go to New York for spring break," I say. "I'm thinking of doing an article about Bronislava Nijinska."

"By all means," she says, and smiles more brightly. I see that she feels good, condemning me to further attempts at self-mastery.

She has gone back to her computer now, its blue radius pulling her in. "Just make sure you come back."

I'm up now, about to open the door, when she stops me again. Her hands are on the keyboard. "Why—her? I'm curious."

I look at the floor, stupidly say the only thing that is in my mind, which she has somehow wiped clean of artifice. "I don't know." Then I say, "She's beautiful."

She frowns. "Really? I know everyone has a secret—I wondered about yours—but I didn't think it would be this ordinary."

I have to say something in my defense. "The Vikings before they jumped off the cliff? The samurais before they commit hara-kiri? What the suicide bombers say before they detonate? Their heads are all filled with visions of beauty."

"I won't speak as director. I will speak as your friend." She leans forward and squints at me. "What I see is a woman who is *becoming*. What you are becoming I really don't know." She shakes her head. "And, truthfully, Kate, I don't know if you can do it here."

Felicia Facebooks me that afternoon—a message saying she has an extra room and that as long as I can be, as she knows I am, "discreet," she is happy to put me up. *Discreet?* Discreet how? *Discreet* like don't leave underwear in the bathroom? *Discreet* like don't bring heroin addicts you meet in Times Square into your room to shoot up? *Discreet* like don't have sex with your students and if you do, certainly don't get caught?

I honestly don't know if I can be discreet anymore, but I don't mention that. I buy a plane ticket for Wednesday, two days from now, which gives me a good five days in New York before I need to be back.

Dance is exploding onto TV and into the movies. Baryshnikov's *Nutcracker,* with the cast of ABT, is broadcast to millions, a prime-time holiday special. In the theaters, the blockbuster movie is *Saturday Night Fever,* which celebrates the disco craze. Along with Mira, all of America has fallen under the spell of dance.

In New York City, that winter, the holidays come. Uptown, at Lincoln Center, there is New York City Ballet's *The Nutcracker,* where out-of-towners and New Yorkers alike, in a rare moment of solidarity, watch the tree grow while their daughters stare wide-eyed as Marie and Fritz enter the land of the synthetic snowflakes. Downtown, in Greenwich Village, at Judson Memorial and St. Marks, purposefully pagan performances feature dancers in cutoff sweats standing on chairs and rolling around on the floor to the sounds of an out-of-tune guitar. Even farther downtown, in the lofts of SoHo and Tribeca, glazed-eyed people gather to dance in altogether different ways into the early morning hours.

It is in the windy stretch of Seventh Avenue in the twenties in a lower midtown uncolonized by dance that The Little Kirov rents the musty basement theater of the Fashion Institute of Technology for their annual performance of *The Wounded Prince.*

Mira waits backstage for her entrance. It's the opening of Act One. The Prokofiev score dips and rises cheerily. The prince's hunting party is passing though the clearing. Between Mira and the world onstage, the motes of dust swirl like bugs on a warm spring night.

When Christopher finishes his solo, he will glide offstage with his attendant (Enrique, joyous, hair wild despite the Polish dressing ladies' best efforts, a gold-painted cardboard horn clutched in his right hand, eyes shining as if *he* were the prince). Then, it will be *her* turn, *her* cue. She must listen for the hill the music climbs, then the beginning of the fall into the valley, the long loose valley where there is sunlight and playful animals, and the flute calls back and forth from one end of the valley to the other. Her torso is itchy from the body suit she is wearing—a stiff pink thing made of mesh and a strong elastic material—under the Flower Princess's yellow calf-length dress.

Christopher plays hide-and-seek with Enrique. He wears a sleeveless hunting shirt, brown britches, and moccasins. He carries a bow and arrow. He does a series of small leaps and draws his right hand back to pluck an invisible bowstring. His face is pasty white, white-white, as white as the palest rock beneath the river water, staring up at you. But the rock has a layer of garish paint on top of it.

She remembers earlier, seeing his face and hers in the mirror, side by side. The music rises, hovers, and then begins to fall. No, not this valley, she remembers, the next one.

She and Christopher sat in front of the long greasy mirror with the plastic Christmas-size bulbs trumpeting all around it, announcing their ghost faces being made into painted marionettes. Pink for lips and cheeks. Eyelids green as the brightest Crayola.

She feels a prick of heat at her knees. Her head is tight with the bind of hairspray holding her hair back into the many braids that it took the dressing lady—the black-haired one with the mole on her chin and the cigarette-smelling hands—so long to do that her scalp began to burn and she began to feel dizzy. The lady pulled and tugged and clutched at Mira. The bobby pins the lady gripped in her teeth moved up and down like insect antennae trying to communicate something dire.

The larger woman with the stomach making a ledge for her breasts worked on Christopher. She said, "It looks like much much, but it's not much much. Onstage, you must be seen. Onstage, lights take away, so you must put back."

Christopher looked down at a textbook he cradled in his lap while the blond one adjusted his costume. The other one's hands worked on Mira's shoulders, smoothing and gathering material under her arms where an opaque sleeve hangs too loosely.

"You know this, Christopher? Of course, he knows. You are big star, dancing at Metropolitan Opera House."

She stepped back and touched up something on his cheeks.

The black-haired one said of Mira, "This one is so small. Last year's was big, then bigger." She clucked as she braided Mira's hair. The blond one laughed.

Mira stared at her pale painted face and at Christopher's in the blaring mirror. The prince of her nine-year-old self who could cause her to feel woozy. And now her own bright eleven-year-old self in a diaphanous yellow dress and a body suit made of flesh-like armor. Here are their faces side by side in the mirror.

His green tunic was being sprayed with fresh brown splotches of spray paint. He looked up from his textbook and caught her eyes in the mirror. His eyes were outlined in black and were bright and watchful. His long, narrow face was stately and remote and confident. He was important. He was the Prince. His fingers drummed softly against his green thigh. A hard, artificial smell floated out from her hair. She smiled and her hair crackled.

Now Christopher, in his green and brown tunic, has exited stage right. Enrique, whose darker skin seems to hold the stage lights better, raises the horn to his lips and arches his back in a series of fake blasts. *This* is her cue. The music hovers again, then begins to fall. She adjusts the wooden basket she carries on her arm, lifts herself up on her toes, raises her arms, and runs forward. This is all she can think: *run forward, keep running, stop center stage, at the little blue X marked on the floor. Ronde de jambe.* She picks the mushrooms. Glissade, bend and arch, glissade, bend and arch. She puts them in the basket that she carries on her arm. She is the flower girl. But she is also another girl. She is the girl watching the flower girl and she is judging this girl. Is she carefree enough? Is she smiling enough? Are her battements fast enough? Is her jeté high enough? She is behind the music, then in front of it. But then she is just the one girl, the carefree girl dancing, with movements so natural to her it's as if they are her own. Beyond the lights like too many suns in the sky, she can see only darkness. She relaxes and moves easily in the music as if a fish in water.

"Wonderful," the voices say as she runs into the wings. Then back onstage for the second dance with the Lavender Girls. Val, Haijuan, and two other girls doing a pas de quatre. "Lovely," says Mr. Feltzer, standing in the corner, his eyes bulging and liquid. And she knows it was lovely. Like a fisherman with a rod in the water, she feels the audience tugging on that line—and she reels it in, just a little tighter—and the line between her and the audience is taut. When she pulls, they tug; when they tug, she pulls. She imagines Maurice out there. When she rises up and can almost touch one of the suns, a girl flying high in the air, smiling, and she feels like she can touch Pavlova's shoes. She and the Prince finally gaze at each other from across the stage, and they begin running toward each other, when the Sorcerer in red, played by Hannah this year (it was the only costume she could fit into, Mira had overheard the ladies saying), moves from upstage down between them, doing her flashy cancan kicks and tossing her head back, like she does when she barrels down the hall with her loose limbs and her big bouncing chest clamped down with an ace bandage, as the music booms and grinds cacophonously. Then, sure enough, the Prince's horse (Enrique again, now sporting a canvas and papier-mâché horse's head) rears up and tumbles to the ground with Christopher's legs beneath him, and Mira too collapses (her head hits the floor dustily) under the Sorcerer's spell. Hannah in her red jumpsuit does a deep grand plié and shakes with a vengeful anger, and the curtains jerk closed.

Intermission. Fifteen minutes. Costume changes. Makeup touch-ups.
Everyone darting this way and that. Some sitting and playing cards.
On her way to the changing room, she passes a group outside the
stage door. Val and Haijuan are there, squatting in their Lavender
Girl tutus, their faces smeared with the assembly line makeup: a
crude dab of eye shadow across their lids and a smear of blush along
their cheeks. The jester is sitting with them. He is a squat, muscular
man in his early twenties in white face paint (black diamonds around
his eyes), a shiny white unitard, black leg warmers, and a black
beret. Val whispers something to the jester and he turns to look at
Mira with his cool eyes. He rises from where he sits in the midst of
the group and says, "Flower girl, little flower girl, I have some medi-
cine for you." Wearing a tiny smile on his face, he holds out his flask.

"I have to change," she says and slips into the bunker-like makeup
room to complete her costume change. Actually, she knows, and
they know that she knows, that she could have stopped for a minute
and laughed and drunk the sweet-smelling stuff the jester carries
with him in his painted flask. (She'd tried it once and it set her throat
on fire.)

Having completed her costume change, she pushes back into the
wings to take her place for Act Two. In the little cubbyhole between
the lighting booth and the backstage wall, underneath the scaffold-
ing and wires, through a cloud of stage-lit dust, she sees the man in
the white unitard pressing the flask to Christopher's mouth like he is
feeding a baby. Christopher is in his gray tights and blue velvet tunic,
opened to show a white T-shirt. As she watches (they do not notice
her), Christopher drinks from the jester's hand the way the sparrows
in the park eat from the fingers of decrepit old men. The man watches
Christopher drink, his eyes glassy. Suddenly, he pulls the flask away
and kisses Christopher hard on the mouth. Christopher does not
fight him, does not sway, does not kick; in fact his whole body seems
to relax.

Meanwhile, the curtains have opened, the music has started up, and the audience is swimming like hungry fish just beyond the suns that burn high in the sky and applauding, for Act Two is beginning and Mr. Feltzer is whispering, "Christopher, where are you? It is time. It is time." Christopher's eyes are opened already, but they look like they have just opened. Mira stands, still staring at Christopher and the jester with the wet smirking lips. Her face, under its painted-white mask, feels red hot.

"You—" she says. The pink girls, the littlest girls, are coming into the wings now, and the thrumming of their feet and their quick, startled breathing is all around them. In the midst of this commotion, neither she, nor Christopher, nor the jester moves. They are locked in a complex web of stares, the reverberations of which maintain the architecture of the moment even as it has passed and she has begun to disbelieve what she just saw.

"You said—I—I could *trust* you," she says in a hushed, spasmodic whisper (she is still trying to observe, perhaps unconsciously, the rule of silence when backstage).

Christopher laughs as he buttons up his tunic. "I said *should*, not *could*." The jester laughs, too. Mira notices he has a red striped candy cane painted on the front of his unitard. How did she not notice this before? Had he hidden it somehow? If so, how?

"You're drunk," she says. This word has the effect she wants.

Christopher straightens up and looks at her. "I'm fine. I can do this part in my sleep."

"Christopher, you are late," says Mr. Feltzer, who has appeared next to her. Christopher pushes past Mira and past Mr. Feltzer, and launches himself onto the stage, dragging one of his feet and hunching his back, for the prince is lame in the second act.

As if she is dislodging something from her throat, Mira says, "He was kissing." She points at the jester. "Kissing."

Then the jester comes toward her. She takes a step back. The veins are pulsing underneath his white face makeup. The black diamonds around his eyes quiver. Now there is the gathering of the music into a rattle-like force that means it is the jester's turn. He bellows, "Do not," he says, spitting the words in her face. "Puts your nose away from where it belongs." The jester takes his beret and throws it on the ground. Then he screams in his other language, in which she hears the name of her country—"America." He pushes through the crowd that has gathered around him, past Mira and Mr. Feltzer, and he leaps out into the false sunshine, where the Prince is waiting for him.

But Mira cannot let it go. She cannot let it pass. She feels this with certainty. It is a feeling, a *knowledge,* that trumps all other feelings. She has an obligation, somehow—to herself, to the Prince, to Christopher—to remember this moment. But she has no time to figure it all out as she too propels herself forward for her entrance.

*She closes her eyes and leaps. The stretch in her legs, the rising feel-*ing under the breastbone, the white space of flame in her head. She imagines Maurice saying, "Ah, yes, this is a leap. She leaps with her whole body."

"I *hate* her," she hears someone whisper in the wings.

Under her sternum, the fist of her heart releases, opening up its palm.

The force of her blind leap almost knocks Christopher over. She smells his sour, ragged breath. His arms buckle. He lunges to try to gain his balance. She lists to the right. She feels a cool breeze from the empty orchestra pit below. She realizes that she will fall; *she is falling.* She hears a grunt as he pulls her over to the left and with another heave she is above him, his hands on her hip bones, her back arched, her leg suspended. He has righted himself. At that moment, she realizes her dream of becoming the Flower Princess—there is an unbearable fullness in this, and then, as soon as she is aware of it, it is gone, this fullness, and in its spot, a strange new empty spot, a death at the center, a nothingness, of a star imploding. In its absence is a falling away of the girl who cares too much, who wants too much, who hopes too much, the girl who thrums with too much life, who needs too much. The spotlights blare down on her and she smiles, *falling falling* into the velvety darkness—victorious.

Maurice holds her in his arms. She does not recognize him at first because his black hair has turned completely white, total soft shocking white. It is shining like an orb around his head. His mustache is still ink black.

"Your hair," she says.

"What?" he says.

"It's all white," she says.

"Really?" he says with a strange smile. "Isn't that wonderful?"

Mira has her own room at the hospital. They wash the bigger face off her smaller face and substitute a white gown with a green diamond pattern on it for her yellow dress. They put her in a beige room in a white bed that grumbles and slides upward with a lever that she can press so that her legs go up, then down, and her head goes up, then down. The machine above her clicks and bleeps softly. They have put her here for "observation" after taking so many X-rays that she loses count. They are most worried about the concussion that she has sustained. They tell her that, except for a hairline fracture to her wrist, she is fine inside.

Her mother sits beside her bed. Ms. Clement arrives with Mr. Feltzer and she comes in and lays her hands on Mira's shoulders and smiles while Mr. Feltzer stands by the door. A bunch of red flowers arrive, bouncing on their stems, without a card. She knows they're from Maurice. The nurse puts the flowers in a plastic vase by the bed. The red-hooded things, as ripe and curious as fruit, crane their slender necks to look at Mira in her movable bed.

Her mother laughs when she sees them. "Did your father send those ridiculous things?"

Her father doesn't notice them at all. He comes in, all rush and concern, pulls the chair right up to her bed, scraping the floor, blocking her view of the flowers. "How's my princess?" He smiles his distracted smile, kisses her, and ignores her mother, who now hovers by the door.

After everyone leaves, the nurses wheel in a big brown-skinned girl with a gap-toothed smile and frizzy hair sticking up all around her head. The girl talks to Mira about what she likes to watch on TV (*Little House on the Prairie, Sanford and Son, CHiPs*) until Mira can't keep her eyes open anymore and she sleeps. She is awakened by the sound of squeaky shoes running into the room and the talkative girl is coughing loudly and hard and gagging, as if she has eaten something terrible. But she has not eaten anything. People are running and shouting all around the girl, and then someone wheels in a big silver machine and takes black Ping-Pong paddles and puts them on her chest and flicks a switch and with a thump her body dances but her arms lie still. They wheel that gap-toothed talkative girl out into the hall, with the nurse's squeaky shoes running alongside her, and the gurney with an IV wire flailing and the silver machine silent.

Somehow Mira sleeps again but the memory of the girl's singsong voice will not fade, and she wakes every so often and looks over at the green curtain they have pulled across the space between their beds. Her cheeks sting with some secret shame as she eats her morning Jell-O like a good girl, and she thinks about the girl and about how the girl would ask Mira a question but wouldn't wait for her to answer but would continue talking with a new subject of her own. They pull the curtain back again and the bed is now empty and remade.

When she asks about the girl, the nurse makes a pucker face and says, "It was her heart. No one expected it." She knows this, then: she will never forget watching the jester kiss Christopher like he was smothering a bird. That this is a world in which a girl can be almost dead, almost crippled, and yet not. A world in which trust is the hardest thing. A world in which she is never safe except when she is leaping with her eyes closed. She thinks of Maurice, of the girl with her flaming tutu. The flowers, now a day old, smell of their watery stems, plant matter, algae.

She closes her eyes.

The nurse catches herself and frowns. "I don't think I was supposed to tell you."

When her parents come that morning to pick her up, they come in together, their faces flushed from the cold and talking about the snow that is coming. It is supposed to come tonight or tomorrow. Two feet of snow, they say. They each carry bags of bottled juice, more than she can drink. Mira starts to tell them about the girl who was wheeled in, talked her to sleep, then coughed and would not stop coughing and was wheeled away and never brought back, but she does not finish, she cannot finish.

CHAPTER 18

The day before I leave for New York, I finally drive over to Sioban's house. It's been almost a week since I fled from her room. I park across the street in my professor's car and, in broad daylight, climb the same rickety wooden stairs I climbed that night. It's been warmer, though, and the steps are swollen and covered with dark stains where the ice has melted. When I get to the top, I don't even pause. I knock boldly on the door—the sound reverberates in the crisp afternoon air. A student with a backpack walking on the other side of the street turns to look at me. Before I can worry about what will happen if Sioban is not there, the curtain behind the panes moves and Sioban's long, articulated face peers out. The curtain is replaced, and then the door bursts open. The hot air blast of her smell—sweat and essential oils (rose? patchouli?) surrounds me. I think of Bernie saying "Make it right." I smile. "Hello," I say.

Sioban lets me in and then turns away, without saying a thing. She walks back to her desk. I hadn't even noticed this desk before. It's tucked in the corner. On it is a large, heavy textbook of graphs and charts, and an open laptop.

"Physics?" I say.

"Actually, neurobiology," she says, folding herself into the desk chair with her back to me. She crosses her legs underneath her. There is nowhere else for me to sit except on the bed, so I stand.

I realize with dismay that I'm still attracted to her. I take my coat off and fold it over my arm, covering my bandaged hand. "You haven't been back to class," I say. "You didn't do the midterm."

"You noticed?" she says.

"Sioban," I say. "We must talk."

She crosses her arms and turns to look at me. She looks different. Just this morning I was able to get my contacts back in, and it's strange to have things delineated so sharply. Is it just that I can see again? How complicated it is to really look at a person. The particularities are overwhelming. Her lips look thinner, her skin more uniform. The acne scars on her cheek are small pale puckers, barely noticeable. She wears leggings and a striped boatneck shirt. She's also wearing glasses, which I have never seen her in before. They are metal and round, the opposite of stylish. Her dark curly hair is actually the only thing that looks the same about her—it's pulled back into the high ponytail I'm used to. No scarves or jewelry, nothing extraneous. The only exception is a complicated timepiece on her wrist, which looks like a scuba diving watch. The expression *neat as a pin* comes to mind. A clean, efficient girl, not an artist of any type. Her scientist side?

"Sioban," I say again, trying to get my bearings. She has gone back to reading. "It's too late to drop my class. If you don't complete it, I will have to give you a grade commensurate with that. You don't want that. Your sponsors don't want that."

She is skimming the textbook, highlighting everything she reads.

"I see you are upset," I say. Even in this clarified, reduced state, how much space in a room she can take up shocks me. I'm starting to sweat now.

She slams down the highlighter. "Upset? Yes, I am upset." She gives me a ferocious stare. "In your class, with you, I felt like something mattered, for my *ideas*—my *mind*. You were so important for me." She flings her head down on her book. "You just left—you just *left*. How *could* you?" I'm shocked to realize she's crying. "You just left me—alone." She pauses and wails. "*Naked.*"

What had I expected? Not this level of anger and self-righteousness. I say, "Sioban, what we did was wrong. I take full responsibility. But it can never happen again."

She scoffs in the midst of her great, heavy gulps. "Love is never wrong."

Oh dear god, I think.

When I don't respond quickly enough—my brain is whirring too fast to speak—she says "Don't you love me?" There is nothing good I can say here. I look down at her beige carpet, where there are no longer any errant socks.

Love? That had—truly—never occurred to me. What does this say about me? *This is a professional situation,* I think. *Make it right.*

I go to her and reach out my hand. My hand hovers over her head. "I care about you, Sioban," I say. I *see* the pain I've caused the girl. I can *see* her. Not just because of my contacts. Her face, overwhelmed, but unafraid. My early performing made me into a weathervane for others—I don't want that for her.

"You are too gifted, too young to lose your way," I say. I want to touch her face. "You have your life ahead of you. And I mean it. I don't want to get in your way. Dance. Be a scientist. Show the world what can be done. I've made rules for myself that I maybe didn't have to. But it's too late for me to fix that." I laugh and my laughter sounds strange to me. "But maybe I can fix some of it. We'll see."

She stands, turns into me, and then my arms are around her and it is a hug but it is a strange hug. There is nothing sexual in it. Her thin body seems thinner. It's like hugging myself, her bones and muscles are my own. I feel incredible tenderness. I am amazed that I have managed more kindness toward her than I have toward myself. I feel relief and something else, maybe something like hope.

"Listen, I am going to take a trip—" I say. "We'll talk when I get back."

She clings to me. She grabs my arm, the one with my injured hand. Though it's wrapped in my jacket, a pain shoots up my arm. Then I notice that Sioban's science textbook is propped up by another book, a thick one. I can just catch the brown cover and the ornate font, a generic title treatment in those days. It's Bronislava's memoirs. She's been using it to prop up her textbook. She catches me staring at the book. I pull away and bury my face in my bag as I search for one of my cards. I pull one out. It's actually from my previous college, but that doesn't stop me. I scrawl my cell number on the back of it and tack it to her wall with one of the push pins sticking there. "I'm going to New York," I say. "Call if you need to."

"Fuck you," she says, but her voice is lighter. Something has shifted again. She is letting me go. She has reclaimed something. She knows it. My heart is racing and my stomach sinks. This will be harder than I thought. It's almost impossible to maintain my boundaries with this girl. The tidal pull toward her is too strong.

She turns back to her desk like a snail into its shell, to her graphs and charts, to her highlighter, to her young rage and pain, and as much as I want her, I want *that*, even that, with a burning heart, I want all of that.

Maurice is right. The dark does come.

A few days after she's out of the hospital, Mira is back at home, sitting on her scratchy blue flowered comforter in her unpainted room. She's listening to *Don Giovanni*. She wears her terry cloth robe and dangles her feet in her puffy bunny slippers over the side of the bed. She finished her homework early and then alphabetized her bookshelf, which is filled with old books, many of which originally belonged to her mother. She fiddles with her beige adhesive wrist guard. Underneath this device, which she must wear for another week (but thank God it will be off in time for the SAB auditions), her skin itches as the tiny fracture heals. The itch has settled under the flesh-colored fabric. It is always there, rummaging about in the kitchen, doing its homework. Sometimes it jumps up, startled, and yells, and that brings tears to her eyes. She never knew an itch could poke you with the hot end of a poker. She never knew an itch could make you cry. She wants to tear off the wrist guard and rip the itch off, but she can't. She is not allowed. If she plays the opera loud enough, the itch is quiet and she can't hear her mother or Gary laughing or doing whatever they do downstairs.

Her eyes run over the Nancy Drew and Hardy Boys mysteries, with their cracking cardboard covers and gingery smell, and her four old records, *The Osmonds Greatest Hits*, *Free to Be You and Me*, Burl Ives, and one called *English Songs of Old*, stacked on the lower shelf, dusty now. In her closet, her shirts and dresses hang neatly, a sight that gives her pleasure even now that she is almost twelve. On the desk against the wall, her cat mug with pens and pencils in it sits on an old leather blotter that had belonged to her father. The two posters on her walls half-scraped of their wallpaper: one black-and-white of Baryshnikov as Albrecht in *Giselle* leaping like a pouncing cat, and one of Makarova—she had wanted Kirkland but the message to her mother had gotten garbled—in a *penché* in front of a dusky sunset studio backdrop.

She is listening to one of the records she recently found in the corner of her parents' closet. Her father's opera records that he didn't take with him—*Die Fledermaus* and *Don Giovanni. Don Giovanni*'s opening aria begins. She braces herself against the thundering orchestra and the trills and vibrato of exalted, expelled emotion. Something cracks inside her, and then flows like liquid. She doesn't know the story—doesn't care to—but she understands it is a drama of impending doom and revenge. The itch pokes its head up. She rubs at the outside of the hideous wrist guard. She imagines Giselle with a meat cleaver, thundering in among the Wilis, hefting it toward Albrecht's head, his head rolling off his neck, blood on the Wilis' white tutus.

There is a knock on her door. Louder now. She can't ignore it. She opens the door wide as the aria blares behind her. Gary stands before her in his ripped T-shirt and black engineer boots. She glowers at him.

"Can I read you a poem?" he says. "I just wrote it." He comes into her room and sits on her bed. He holds a piece of paper. He reads to her:

> *Killer black house flam flap flapper eyes cold flat palm*
> *   greenbacks*
> *mother, daughter flypaper hooters stuck down pinned*
> *   beneath the viaduct*
> *I live in darkness shout out I can hear only—hold me.*

"What do you think?"
"I hate it," she says.

He smiles. "I thought you would," he says. He reaches out and touches her wrist.

"Does it hurt?"

She shakes her head.

He doesn't take his hand away. "I can't believe that guy didn't catch you. What an asshole. Your mother thinks ballet is reductive claptrap, but you know, I thought you were great. You were *really* pretty. Beautiful." He is close enough that she can smell the coffee on his breath. She can see pores on his nose like little holes in cheese. She doesn't pull her hand away.

"She says, 'Who defines what is beautiful? Whose definition is it?' She can't stand that you are getting sucked into some old dead guy's idea of beauty, I guess." He laughs. "Maybe I'm just an old guy." He smiles and she notices his eyes are gray. They look sad. For a second, she doesn't hate him. "Or maybe," he says, pulling her closer, "she's just jealous."

A hand brushes against her wrist and grabs. She holds this hand, dry and calloused, but firm. On the other side of her she can feel a bony shoulder against hers. He pulls her to him. It is a bony chest full of need, a scratchy feeling on her neck, his scratchy lips eating her skin, and to her surprise she does not cry out. The mouth finds its way to her chin and wrestles upward, fighting for her mouth, finds it, and rests there. It recoils at first in surprise, then presses harder against her. She closes her eyes. She imagines it is Maurice. She kisses the mouth back. It is her first real kiss. Mira thinks: *This is real. This is real.* She does not know what this means, but it comes to her in a swift fall of words, like a curtain descending.

Just then, with a sputtering flicker and a snap, the lights go out. Her record player whirs to a stop. Gary pulls away from her. She hears him walking into the hallway. "What's happened, Rachel?" The first thing Mira thinks is: the world is ending. Mira feels her way out to the dark hallway. She hears her mother in the hallway below. "What now?" says her mother with a burst of glee in her voice. She loves it, thinks Mira. The world is ending and she loves it.

"Is everyone okay? Is it just us?" says her mother, reaching the third-floor landing.

They open the door of the junk room, and the streetlights are blaring inside the windows like a set of binoculars—two eyes burning down on them. Far to the right, if she squints her eyes she can just make out the digital clock on top of the Watchtower building blinking the time on and off: *7:15*.

"It's not the neighborhood," says Gary. "It is just us."

Then her mother is downstairs on the phone for a long time, yelling and cursing. "Process difficult to reverse," she says, repeating something being said to her. Finally, she hangs up. "They say the electricity bill hasn't been paid," she says. She blames it on Mira's dad, who she says was supposed to take care of it.

"It's your fault," says Mira, knowing that it is; everything is, will always be, her mother's fault.

For the next two days, the house remains cold. The curtains billow with the air that leaks in through the splintered windowpanes. Mira walks around with blankets draped over her, as does Gary. Her mother won't resort to blankets, but she wears a terry cloth robe over her kimono. All the parts of Mira's body outside of the blanket grow purplish with cold. In the early morning, when she gets up, she can see her breath come out of her body. Sitting at her desk at school, her teeth chatter and her feet are numb for the first few hours of each day. She rubs them against the metal prongs of her chair to get the feeling to return to them. Everything hardens in the cold: her mattress grows into a slab of stone, the old oranges in the fruit bowl become bowling balls, her sheets crackling slivers of ice. Her pointe shoes are especially brittle. She, her mother, and Gary use candles and gas lanterns that her mother buys at a hardware store on Court Street. She places candles all around the parlor. Mira sits on the floor of the living room, the TV dark beside her, doing homework by candlelight. They carry the camping lanterns when they go up or down the stairs. With mincing steps, wrapped in a blanket, Mira *bourrées* her way over to her dresser. She draws lines under her eyes. In the oily light of the lamp, she gazes at her pale face. Gary's eyes brush over her as she walks by in her long white nightgown, carrying a lantern. She lowers the light so that dark envelops her. Her mother comes into the room and says, "Oh! Our house is haunted!" Then she laughs her slipped-on-a-banana-peel kind of a laugh. . . . "Our house has ghosts! Whoo hooo . . ." She rushes at her daughter the way she sometimes did at her studio when her work was going well and would grab Mira and spin her around. Mira smells her sharp flowery smell. Her mother stops and picks up a cold-withered orange from the buffet table next to her. Holding it, she walks through the flickering of the parlor to the window. "A generator. That's what we need. A generator. We don't need those Con Ed fuckers," she says.

Mira dreams of Maurice. He is driving her in his car down the snake of the highway—it's the East River at night, over the bridge. He parks on a side street. He takes her through the streets, looking for something. He takes her hand. There is a delinquent hush over these Brooklyn streets. He stops at a dented steel door in the alley behind a large building. She stands beside him, wearing her winter coats and mittens. He fiddles with the handle on the door and then pushes against it hard, then harder, against the dented metal. They go through the door into a cinder block hallway, which winds around until it leads to a big subterranean room. This room looks like it belongs at the bottom of an ocean. There's a weird bluish light. In the middle of the floor is a cone of light, and in the middle of the light is a table and three chairs. In the room, there are at least a dozen kids from her age and up. A blond boy and two girls sit playing cards. The boy has very red eyes, reddish skin, and, when he smiles, red teeth. Maurice takes her hand and walks to the edge of the pool.

"Children, this was once the largest swimming pool in all of New York. They filled it with salt water. All the ladies came to bathe. My dear mother came. She said it was marvelous. That is why I decided to buy it."

Yes, Mira now sees it is not just a hole in the ground but something built with an intention. All things at one time had a purpose, however difficult it might be to understand later.

Just then a girl with brown hair in tight braids that stick out from her head approaches them. She wears a smock and has the largest eyes Mira has ever seen. She wears no shoes.

She looks down and hands Maurice a bunch of wilted yellow flowers. "I saved them for you. We didn't know if you would ever come back." He laughs his bell-like laugh. She turns and runs back to a shadowed corner, from which Mira hears some whispers and shuffling.

Something inside Mira relaxes. She knows that girl somehow.

"Do they have homes?"

"No," he says. "Or no longer."

"Why?"

He laughs.

"Attention, caution," says Maurice.

"Find me," she says and runs off. Despite the fact that it is so cold in the house, she wakes in a sweat, with her heart pounding, shaking. She cries, not out of sadness but because, for a time, a few moments in this dream, she felt happy and complete.

In the middle of the fifty-sixth hour of their lights-out period, Mira reads in the cracked bathtub by the window in the junk room by the pale winter light. She's covered herself with three blankets. There is no wind and the tree outside the window shimmers in the startled air. Now she is turning the final pages of *The Black Stallion*—the midnight thoroughbred is heading into the last furlong with victory in his stride—when she hears a deep voice echoing in the hallway downstairs, a male voice. "Helloowwww," it says. "Anybody home?"

She stands. "Dad!"

Her father stands in the dim hallway. He looks huge-shouldered, giant.

"Carl!" her mother says, appearing.

"You could have called," her mother says.

"I wanted to see how you were faring—" He looks at Mira. "What's on your eyes? Why's it so dark and cold in here?" Then he sees Gary, who appears in the doorway behind her mother. He stares at him for a long second. "Who is that rodent and why isn't he wearing any shoes?"

All the attention focuses on Gary's feet. Despite the cold, he doesn't have any shoes on. A map of blue veins runs under the skin.

"I'm Gary." He uses a strange, polite voice. He extends a hand. Her dad does not shake it.

"He rents a room for writing. A writing studio," her mother says.

"Which room?"

Her mother looks down at her legs and smoothes the robe over them.

"Which room?"

"Your study."

"Oh my God, Rachel."

"Carl," her mother says. "Carl. What was I supposed to do? You left me alone here. You hadn't even paid the electric bill. What was I supposed to do?"

"Don't play the victim, Rachel. I gave you the money to pay the bill."

He gestures to the living room. "I want to talk to you." Her mother begins to follow him out into the living room. When they leave, she and Gary will be alone in the shadowed hallway, with the beaten and broken furniture, her parents' voices colliding in the parlor. She remembers Gary's mouth on hers, scratchy, searching. The dark, she remembers, with a strange excitement, is coming again soon. What will happen?

"He kissed me," she says loudly.

Gary looks at her like he has forgotten something important.

Her parents stop at the threshold, in the doorway. Her father turns back to her.

Gary smiles a strange smile and holds up his hands. "Arrest me."

"What do you mean? When? Where?" her mother says.

"I—shoot—" Gary drops his hands. The strange smile is stuck on his face.

"Gary, I think you should leave," says her mother.

Then her father rushes at Gary and hits him straight in the face so that Gary bangs against the wall and clasps his hands to his nose, which explodes into something bright red. Mira has never seen her father hit someone, her father of two modes: homecoming joy and worried absence. She does not associate her father with violence at all. Thus, she does not recognize what she sees as violence, but as a strange dance of color and motion, somewhat beautiful, in slow motion, out of time.

"Carl!" her mother says now with more solid confidence.

"My stuff," Gary mumbles as he sinks to the floor.

Her dad says, "Mira, pack a bag."

"You can't," says her mother. "He'll leave. I'll make him leave."

"I can and I will."

"You don't get to take the moral high ground."

"Yes I do," says her father, grabbing Mira a little too hard by the elbow. "Forget that bag. We're leaving."

Less than five minutes later, she has her jacket on, her school bag is packed with a nightgown and change of clothes, and her father ushers her out the door, his hands like a guided missile on her back.

"Mira!" her mother calls as they pass. "Mira!"

Gary is outside too in front of the house, gathering his things off the ground that her mother has been throwing out the door in batches. He wears his boots now, unlaced, and his nose is swollen and is growing purplish.

As Mira passes Gary, he gives her a sad grin. She likes him at that moment, she really does. He didn't try to lie. Her father's voice is low, a growl. "Come on," he says. The slate of the sidewalk rises and falls in great slabs like shifting tectonic plates. Mira walks down the uneven block, her heels and toes rocking up and down, stepping carefully to avoid the cracks, which are everywhere. From behind them, she hears her mother's rangy Brooklyn voice shouting, "I am not an unfit mother."

Mira looks back at the stoop, at the peeling wrought iron and the weather-stained clapboard, and then she turns back to face the street ahead. Her father is taking her to Manhattan, where the lights, she imagines, will never again go out.

———

For the "time being," Mira lives with her father while her mother "gets a grip." She loves her father's new apartment. It is small but it is very high. It has only three colors—black, beige, and white. It's in a new building on Second Avenue in *Kips Bay*, a neighborhood she's never known before. It's very tall and made of glass and steel. From the windows you can see in all directions. To the south, red brick columns swell from the earth like primitive golems of clay. To the west, rise the Park Avenue fortresses of yellow sandstone. To the north, the midtown skyscrapers shine like monoliths glinting golden in the sun. Up here, she is elemental, protected.

But there is a third father, it turns out. He is not the whiskey-peppermint preoccupied father of the mornings, nor the cheery, doting shiny-faced father of after-dinner wine. This father brings back piles of dry cleaning and hangs them over the back of the kitchen chairs so that whenever you walk by you can hear the whisper of the plastic. He washes his underwear in the sink and hangs it over the towel rack. This father is always going off, in his ironed suits, to see lawyers to "argue for his rights." He wants to keep her; he doesn't want to send her back to her mother. When her mother calls she says, "The only reason I let him take you was that I didn't want to fight over you."

Her father's new apartment is filled with sounds. The operatic blast of his new, digital clock radio. A tiny Pavarotti pours forth from the box you can hear from the kitchen. These are all sounds she has not known since the old sad gray house, when she was upstairs and he was down. The razor buzzes, the kettle he uses to make Sanka bleats, the spoon clinks as he carries his cup to the bathroom. Hollow drone of the coffee grinder, the lawn mower growl of the juicer; she has never known there are so many gadgets. They gather in the kitchen like costumed partygoers eager to show off—their sleek white and black plastic and invisible machine parts. Voice of the radio: traffic report heard through the hustle of static. There is the familiar bright, sharp, shattering whiskey-peppermint smell, which now she understands comes from a can of shaving cream with bold green swirls on it and a corroded metal bottom that she avoids looking at whenever she is in the bathroom brushing her teeth. But there is also a new bottle on his dresser. It's a blue bottle in the shape of a ship. From it comes a deep, woodsy smell, dank and primitive, that she doesn't like. It's this smell that shatters her sleep if none of the sounds do first.

She and her father go back to the sad, gray house with the broken stoop to "get more of her things" for her. Gary is gone, his studio cleared out. Gone is the picture of the skinny man and the poster of Al Pacino. The walls have been spackled with a white as white as her hospital sheets had been. In the living room, the beaded lamps, the giant cushions, and the low table are all gone. There is a multicolored woven rug in the center with a brand-new sofa.

Her mother acts differently. She wears a pair of corduroys and a turtleneck with a scarf tied in her hair. She grips onto a coffee cup the whole time they are there. She holds it up to her chest as she follows her daughter around, watching her pack.

Nightgown, pants, shirts, socks, toothbrush, ballet tights, leotards. "Enough for two weeks," her father says, but it will, she knows, be more than that. She takes the faded poster of the missing rat-faced boy from behind her door. She takes Maurice's card—she'll put it by her new bed.

"Where's Gary?"

"He won't be back," her mother says. "I'm sorry about him, Mira. Did he hurt you? Tell me, did he?"

Mira shakes her head. "No. He didn't hurt me."

Her mother takes a sip of coffee and looks quickly at her father. Their eyes meet and there is something that passes between them. Her eyes are red and full of water.

"He won't ever do that again. I'm so sorry, I'm sorry, sorry." She begins crying.

If Gary had been here, he would roll his eyes and she would laugh at her mother's tears. He might say "Oh, Rachel—watering the lilies again?" Then her mother would laugh. In honor of Gary, Mira laughs. Both her parents look at her.

Her mother offers them pumpkin bread that she's just baked. Mira is surprised that her father accepts. They all stand in the old kitchen on some new linoleum her mother has just put down. It is white with brown designs and it makes her feel strange. In the kitchen, everything is clean and orderly and shiny. Outside, it is getting dark and the squirrels chirp.

Her mother looks down at her clogs while her father eats. Her father hums a tune. He looks happy, like he has just won a prize. He looks like he is enjoying the bread very much. He glows with a proprietary shine.

Mira, looking at her mother looking at her clogs, feels bad for her. She sees that telling on Gary has cost her mother something. It has given her father something.

Her father puts the bread down and says, "We got rid of him, didn't we?" And he chuckles.

"Carl!" her mother says, without looking up from her feet. She says nothing more. Her parents are now in the grip of something new between them. She does not understand why they are being nice to each other now, her shiny-faced father and her red-faced, shy mother.

No one mentions Mira's own performance, in which she fell, and Christopher did not catch her. Is there nobody but Maurice whom she can trust? Christopher had said "trust me," but he couldn't be trusted. Maurice who never asked for anything. *She* had followed him, had brought him forth from the city, and he had magically shown up.

Maybe the people who tell you to trust them can't be trusted, and the people who ask nothing are the ones who are there when you need them.

That night she goes to her father while he is washing dishes in the kitchen.

"Did they ever find that boy?"

"Huh?" he says turning to her.

She says his name, pronouncing it the way that she's pronounced it in her head—two long words with too many consonants—but it sounds strange in the air.

"Who?" he says.

She goes into her room, gets the poster, and presents the worn, crinkled sign to him as if it is an X-ray of her insides. "The boy," she says, "the one they lost."

He grabs the paper and before she can stop him, crinkles it up, and throws it into the garbage under the sink. "Mira, why do you keep stuff like this?"

Now she is yelling. "Did they find him? Did they? Tell me. Did they?"

He wipes his hands on the dishrag and reaches for her. "No, Mira. I don't believe they ever found him."

"Fuck you! Fuck you!" she yells. She's said it once to her mother. Now she says it again to her father.

He slaps her then—a quick, hard slap to her face. He has never hit her before. His face is beet red and his jaw shakes. He holds his hand as if he has hurt it. Her cheeks burn as she stares at him. This third father is one who hits her, is the one who punched Gary. But then his violence was directed at a man she despised and there had been the giddiness to cover the fear—fear of her own father.

The slap stings more than hurts. But like the hand-washed underwear, Pavarotti radio, the cologne in the shape of a ship, it's the strangeness of the slap that she hates.

Some shirts in their dry cleaner bags are piled on the back of a chair. She backs up into them, slips to the floor. "Fuck you! Fuck you!" Her father grabs his coat and says, "I am going to be late." He pauses at the doorway to tell her that a babysitter will be there shortly. He locks the door behind him. *Take care of yourself,* he says.

An hour later, the babysitter still has not come and the snow has started. Mira goes to the heavy black phone, hard and thick as a giant beetle, and picks up the receiver. The dial tone, a low even moan, rushes out at her like the language of another species—and she giggles. She giggles again and again. She can't stop. Then she dials the number on the card. The phone rings and rings, and on the fifth ring, a faint, sleepy man's voice says, "Hello?"

She giggles.

"May I help you?"

"Can I please speak to Maurice . . ."

"Mirabelle?"

"Yes."

"Where are you?"

"At my dad's." She stops giggling.

"Who is there with you?"

"Nobody."

"You're all alone, then?"

"Yes," she says. And now, instead of giggling, she begins crying.

"Okay," he says.

"I'm scared," she says.

"Turn out the lights. Look out the window," he says. Her sobs slow down.

She is quiet.

"Do you see?"

She flicks the living room switch and stretches the phone cord as far as it will reach. "Yes." Against the brick of the old building across the yard, the snowflakes are visible individually—puffy, like cotton balls, drifting slowly, joyfully. She tips her head back and stares up at the snow spinning downward in a crazy swirling vortex.

When she returns to The Little Kirov, Mira dances like a demon. She dances with a wildness that makes the other girls gape, and then snicker when she is out of sight. It isn't that her breasts have grown or her toe shoe ribbons are grimy, but something in her far-off expression, the seriousness of her too-pale face, the flush of her cheeks as she works over and over again on her pirouettes and battements. She dances as if she is the only one in the room. She dances as if it's Mr. B himself standing in the doorway watching her, and not a little studio on the seventh floor of a crumbling office building.

Even the little girls push themselves up against the walls as she passes.

Now Mira understands Hannah's impulse to fling her head back and kick up her leg, and laugh like a tornado. She understands Robin's blank face and scarlet cheeks. It is terrible to be singled out, to feel eyes on you all the time. It is *wonderful,* and terrible too. But more than that it does something to your insides: they don't feel like they belong to you anymore. Your seams come loose and parts of you start coming out. It makes normal things—like walking or talking—feel hard, and things that are hard—like holding an extension until your leg shakes—feel easy.

She wears the wrist guard for a week more until the fracture heals. When she was young and fell down and scraped her knee, grown-ups were kind to her; they bent down and investigated her cuts and bruises, applying a Band-Aid and Mercurochrome. But no one is kind to her about this injury. It seems a dancer's injury is different—it is to be treated with suspicion and avoided at all costs.

At the end of that week, she finds Maurice waiting for her outside The Little Kirov. She smiles and her smile is too big. She can't help it. His newly white hair floats up from his head in a shimmering lawn. It makes his pointed chin and arched, still-black eyebrows look even more elfin. His brown eyes, with their large pupils, confront her with their amused gaze. It makes her laugh. Only he can make the coil of tension inside her subside.

"I like your hair," she says.

"I've heard of that happening. Going white overnight."

"Thank you for the flowers," she says. She looks down. "I'm sorry." She is surprised to find that she is about to cry.

His hand is on a new walking stick made of marbled wood, with a silver tip. "You were wonderful." He says this word *wonderful* as if it's never been said before. "You *fell* wonderfully."

"I trusted him. It was his fault."

"No, dear, this is not true. You closed your eyes." He leans toward her. "No matter, you fell beautifully."

MANUFACTURING BEAUTY

CHAPTER 20

PRESENT

That first building where I lived on my own in San Francisco was a real tenement. Bathrooms in the halls. It was young women who lived there—wannabe dancers, actors, models. I was there a year before I got my own rattletrap studio in the Tenderloin, the kind with the toilet two feet from the stove. I would be there for seven more years. Sometime in those years Felicia and I got together a few times. She was still in L.A. working at acting and getting some gigs. We tried to be friends for a while. Her apartment in Los Feliz was cheerful: Chinatown gauzy curtains, plush sample sale linens, Oscar de la Renta shirts and slacks hanging in her closet, sorted by Easter eggs colors. Her fingers twirled and her hands fluttered as she spoke. She was singing, cocktail waitressing, and working the perfume counter at Nordstrom. I admit it: I tried to drum up some marvelous pity for her—she'd not even gotten a BA—as someone who represented what I was leaving behind, but I couldn't. She seemed too cheerful, and too charming. At her apartment, we drank coffee from Viennese cups and ate linzer tortes off Bloomingdale's china. On the surface we had a lot in common—single ex-dancers living in apartments with antiquated plumbing. Were we really that different? Yes, we were. After a few moments together, any fool could see we were different animals.

The last time we saw each other was at an L.A. costume party. I was dating a sound technician whom I'd first met years earlier during one of my modern dance performances, and then later at a café I was working at while getting my BA. The sound technician still thought of me as a dancer, though it had been several years since I'd actually danced professionally. I was keeping him company on one of his business trips. Felicia was on the arm of a slim man with an earring in each ear who introduced himself as "Madame Tussauds' boy-toy." She was singing then. I'd seen her name up on some Fillmore clubs. I asked her about it. She laughed wildly. She wasn't cute anymore, but she was still beautiful. Her lips were red and perfectly outlined. When we were young, I could see the effort it involved, but now it was invisible; it had seeped into her pores. Maurice had hated the young Felicia's beauty, her mother's hand still obvious, but would he have hated this one? Her beauty was now so vibrant, so integrated. It wasn't a face on top of a face.

Felicia wore a black-and-white-striped jumpsuit with a cape thrown around her shoulders, high-heeled boots, a giant silver bangle, her dark hair in a blunt pixie cut. She was carelessly, languidly, unavoidably gorgeous. I felt like an ink-stained wretch.

I thought about that time her mother did our hair, having to sit still while her mother held a steaming hot curling iron to my scalp, how if I moved too much I would get burned. "*Scalded*," her mother had said. "*Don't wiggle or you'll get scalded.*"

"What are you?" I said.

"A crook." Felicia laughed.

The man with her laughed, too. "She's a jailbird, can't you see?" He held up two feathers attached to her sleeve.

My date—Ryan was his name, I think—was a Plague of Locusts. He wore a lamp shade with paper cutouts of locusts we'd made together. I was Alice in Wonderland with a forty-ounce bottle of Colt .45 malt liquor (really apple juice). We were stoned; they were drunk.

When I realized Felicia was drunk, some of her beauty wore off. But a lot was still left.

"Still dancing?" She poked my chest.

"No," I said. It was the first time my heart didn't sink when I said it. I just said it and then felt relief. After all, it was true. I was twenty-eight years old, a nothing career as a modern dancer in San Francisco behind me, but a BA finally under my belt, and just starting a master's in performance studies at Berkeley. I was newly focused on the life of the mind, this bright space before me; I wanted to move into that.

"No shit? I thought you'd ride that train till the very end."

"Well—" I said. I would have said *I did,* but Ryan didn't like negativity. "I'm at school. Berkeley."

"School?" She said this with genuine surprise.

"Going for a PhD in dance studies."

"Wow," she said, straightening up a bit and trying to hold herself in check. "Good luck," she said, and fell languidly against the man.

Now it's with a kind of anthropological interest that I cross Seventh heading west on Fifty-eighth. Past Eighth Avenue, I don't recognize this as New York. I feel like I'm in Cincinnati. A parking garage. Blocks of condos unmarked by graffiti. A chain drugstore, a garage, a sparsely populated outdoor plaza jutting out from one of the recessed condo buildings. As I walk, I clench and unclench my hand. It's finally healing. In the airport bathroom, I took off the big gauze bandage and substituted for it a flexible oversize Band-Aid. The gash has faded to a reddened line with a not-terrible-looking cut at its center. The innocuous-looking Band-Aid takes a lot of drama away. It's drama that I don't need on this trip. It's important that I can at least sustain the appearance of normality.

At Tenth Avenue, the street begins to slope down toward the Hudson. In my high (too high? I've forgotten this is a walking city) boots, I pass the bones of scrawny trees, some of them not more than saplings. It's unseasonably warm. This weather is predicted to last the whole five days I'm here. I've left frostbitten Ohio and come to a place that is trying to be spring. My body, inside my coat, expands a little. My heels click on the hard, new concrete.

Felicia's apartment is in one of the new condo buildings. Sparkling, cavernous lobby. The doorman calls upstairs and announces me. "Miss Kate," he says into the speaker. The bronze-plated elevator doors slide open, and the elevator silently speeds me up to the fourteenth floor, where hotel carpeting pads my footsteps. I squint to read the tiny gold numbers on the identical beige doors lining the hallway.

Felicia holds the door open for me. We stand there, me gripping my little black conference suitcase, in my black travel outfit, my coat over my arm. My closed hand hiding the Band-Aid. She looks at me—takes it all in—with a smile on her face. What is she thinking? She wears a sparkling turquoise blue dress, high strappy heels of the same color, and bright red lipstick. Her hair is cut pageboy style and her body is toned in an I-have-a-rooftop-gym kind of way. I make a series of unkind judgments: she's trying too hard, she's lonely, she's putting a good face on it. Too old to be "done up" like this. The fact is, though—and this comes to me incrementally—she is still beautiful. Her skin is clear, her cheeks taut and pleasing, her eyes inviting. In her large, bright eyes, swathed in blue eye shadow, there is something vulnerable, even innocent. There is still the little girl with big eyes who always looked on the verge of speaking but didn't.

"Isn't Facebook amazing?" she says. She'd contacted me when I first signed up. We'd had a few brief exchanges but, really, my request to stay with her had come out of the blue.

I wheel my suitcase into her large living room. Floor-to-ceiling windows look westward toward the Hudson. The carpet has the marks of having been recently vacuumed.

My eye catches on a few sparsely placed, expensive-looking knickknacks—one of an elephant in sleek black granite and the other a silver orb sitting on a polished wooden chest.

"It's been forever and a year," she says. This brings me back. Felicia always loved phrases, quotes, sayings, clichés. I turn.

"Do you still like horses?" I say suddenly. "And pearls?"

She stares at me. "Horses?" Then she smiles. "Yeah, I saw some amazing racing in Europe last year. . . ." Her voice changes, grows softer, fumbles. "And pearls? Pearls? God, no."

Her hands flutter toward the kitchen. The kitchen: Williams Sonoma apron and chef's hat, unused, and some kitchen appliances—weighty and purposeful. "Coffee's in the freezer. Espresso machine on the counter—you know how, right? Eat anything you can find," she says. "Except my secret stash of Lucky Charms—just kidding—those too. . . . Please." She gestures to her waistline.

"You look fabulous," I say.

She smiles and looks at ease for the first time.

"Tell me," she says. "Why are you in town—I didn't get it, exactly?"

I'd been vague—a professional trip, I'd said. "A paper," I say. "Have you ever heard of Bronislava Nijinska? Nijinsky's sister, a choreographer, editor of her brother's papers, collaborator, mother. A woman in a man's world. Her professional journey coincided with the birth of modernism and feminism. She's been largely sidelined because she didn't fit into any movement."

She's leading me down a hallway. We pass a bedroom—spartan, elegant—a black duvet that glints like onyx in the track lighting of the hallways, shiny green decorative pillows, and a hanging tapestry, a bold design of black and white shapes intermingled.

"I'd like to resurrect her," I say.

Felicia stops at the open doorway to a dim, cool room. "Bronislava," she says. "No wonder, with that name. Well, professor, here're your digs. Hope you like 'em."

The blinds are pulled down. The air smells of perfumed air freshener.

"Okay," she says, giving me an air kiss. "I'm off. I'm working a show at the Javits. I'll be back later," she says. "But don't wait up for me. You know how it is—single gals."

"Thanks, Felicia," I say. "I really appreciate—everything."

She gives me a quick hug and holds me at arm's length. "Look at you—a professor. You've done everything right."

"Well, not exactly." I think of Sioban's tearful embrace—*you left me* naked. And the folded letter, creased from all my handling, in an envelope in my bag. I enter the room. "Not everything."

After Felicia leaves, I lie down on the bed. It is impersonal, surprisingly firm, like a hotel bed. When I open my eyes again it's nearly dark outside. I shiver, get up, stretch, and pad into the living room and go over to the windows. How must it be to live like Felicia? It's unclear to me what she does—and there have been a few things that make me know not to ask. The photos on her Facebook page, always taken by an invisible other person—her posing alone, stylish with her head cocked in an inviting way, in various foreign locations. Is she happy?

The sky to the west above New Jersey is pink and fierce. I pull a crocheted cashmere blanket from the couch, so soft it barely can be felt, over my shoulders. I watch the boats ply the water on the Hudson. The sunset is truly spectacular.

Maybe Maurice was wrong. Beauty is not about suffering. It is about being fulfilled, drinking in as much as one can; it is about life, not death. I think of Bernadith's face, her kind bulldog face, and her words: *What I see is a woman who is becoming. What you are becoming I really don't know.*

I watch a giant white cruise ship slip soundlessly out toward the Atlantic. I'm waiting for something. And then it comes: a calm falls over me. I go back to Felicia's guest bedroom, the undertow pulling me under. I can sleep now. If I'm lucky, I will dream. And my dreams will prepare me for whatever is to come.

Manhattan is in love with ballet. Every ten blocks there is a store selling tutus and ballet memorabilia. People leave clutching signed programs and worn pointe shoes wrapped in tissue paper. Not just girls and their mothers shopping for leotards and tights and pointe shoes, but also middle-aged people, respectable people, carrying briefcases stuffed with office papers.

Ballet dancers are celebrities. Their faces gaze out from bus stops and from billboards next to gold watches or diamonds. Their limpid eyes melt the barren concrete. Their names spring from grown-ups' lips in excited whispers. *Baryshnikov. Kirkland. Makarova. Nureyev.* On buses, sidewalks, subways, on TV you can hear impassioned discussions about which female dancer's *Swan Lake* Act Three is most powerful, and which male dancer's Act Two *Giselle* jumps achieve the greatest ballon.

The Russians, especially, are everywhere. Documentaries about them play over and over again, telling the same dramatic story of escape. Pictures of them bundled on tarmacs surrounded by men in trench coats and sunglasses, moments after they utter surely the most powerful words in the world: *I defect.*

These cold war princes and princesses had come over the past two decades, some before Mira was born. First Nureyev, his Tartar cheekbones turning from the cameras and mics, too-stiff, like the cold war had chilled him. Then Makarova came, bringing her tiny birdlike body, head wrapped in a gypsy scarf, her *Swan Lake* still intact, her back muscles famously rippling like feathers, they said.

Baryshnikov came, while Mira's dad lived with her mom, in a hail of photos, running to a getaway car. Godunov came last of all, his long hair and Thor face, and he became an actor in bad movies, and for this bunheads never forgave him.

Manhattan loves Balanchine, who is Russian, too. And Manhattan loves his academy, the School of American Ballet. To have a daughter accepted to SAB is to be chosen by the finest, harshest arbiters of beauty in the old doomed Soviet state. And to be accepted into SAB is the final stamp of approval in a world that is based on an ancient hierarchy. These Russians had abandoned their dying world to remake ours. So these girls offered themselves to the old Russians— and perhaps to save themselves from their own land of broken marriages and smog.

Their faces stare out from bus posters, taunting Mira, calling to her. Wait, she has to say. She has to wait a few more months, though she is ready now.

She can't wait to leave this small studio with the thimbleful of light spilling across it. She *has to* get into SAB. She can't stand another year here. Ms. Clement's face seems to have shrunk and folded up into even more creases since the night Mira fell, and though her teacher's hands still correct kindly, she senses something new in Ms. Clement's attitude toward her—something that if she didn't know better she would think was anger.

As for Val and the other girls, they now treat her differently. They are no longer mean to her. They speak to her with polite words and stony faces. She thinks about the girls she has known who got this treatment: they are the ones who have such badly broken homes or terrible skin conditions or such recklessness in their play that you cannot afford to be mean. You hate those girls with a hate that is based on fear. Your weapon against them—instead of meanness—is niceness. It is an effective weapon.

So she is one of those girls now.

She realizes that the more potent the gazes around her grow, the stronger her need to dance with a wildness no one can match. She feels a new violence at her core—a desire to do physical harm to someone, something. She imagines crushing her teacher's gentle hands, punching Val. Her pirouettes have a new briskness to them; suddenly, she can do more than five fouettés in a row.

She just has to make it through the spring. In the summer, The Little Kirov suspends classes and she can go to David Howard's studio or Steps, and her dad will pay for it, especially if she tells him it's so she can get into SAB, the *best* ballet school in the city. He loves anything that is best.

———

Maurice takes her to the Metropolitan Museum. They enter the great facade, with its drooping eyes and stern mouth, and then the vast, dim, and cacophonous main hall. Even in the din of the crowd in the atrium, she hears the low timeless, hollow echo of the sea, like from a conch shell pressed to the ear. Warrens of rooms swim off into the catacomb-like recesses of the building. The sandy-hued marble stones and tomb-like echoes are foreign to her.

Upstairs she claps and skips alongside him as they enter a room filled with Degas paintings. There is one of two girls at a barre practicing their port de bras. Here is one of a couple of girls behind a curtain, waiting their turn in the wings, the sliver of a shadowed figure in a top hat watching them. There is one of a naked girl bending over her chair massaging her feet. Her discarded costume lies on the floor, a puddle of tulle. Another one of a soloist, dancing in a long tutu on pointe, surrounded by the faces of other dancers watching her. The *chosen* girl. Though Mira can only see their heads from behind, in shadow, she is sure they are locked in frozen smiles. But they hurry through—Maurice won't stop.

Maurice leads her to a sculpture in the middle of the next room. It's Degas's *Little Dancer Aged Fourteen*. It doesn't look as good in real life, a midsize black statue of a girl. The statue is not shiny and sleek like the reproductions, but dull, rough-hewn. The dress she wears is old and faded pink, with too many pleats (her teachers would never allow a skirt like that). Mira takes in the girl's sagging tights, her too-loose ribbons in her hair, her poor posture. Her hips are too wide, her turnout comes from the knee, not the hip. Her eyes are closed and her face tilts upward toward an invisible sun.

Mira reaches out and grabs Maurice's hand, which is cool and dry. He lets her hold his hand. It is the first time.

"Here it is," Maurice says. "*Little Dancer.* She was a dancer named Marie van Goethem. She posed for Degas to earn money for her family. They were very poor. It caused a sensation when he exhibited it."

"Why?"

"No one wanted to think about the lives of these poor, hardworking dancers."

But Mira doesn't like this girl; she doesn't like anything about her. "She is daydreaming, not practicing. She's not beautiful."

He laughs. "There is no beauty without suffering. She is not beautiful but she moves toward beauty. See? *He* made her beautiful. That is *his* power. Someday you'll understand."

"She should open her eyes," Mira says.

He looks at her and raises his eyebrows. "Yes, indeed. She should."

That next evening, she comes home to find her dad on the couch with his too-loose grin. His gold buttons on a purple velvet vest glint. The TV is on a sitcom. Canned laughter floats out. He lowers a big book he's reading—*The Revolution in Marketing.*

"How was it last night then?" he asks. She wonders if he knows. He never lets on. For better or worse, Maurice is still her secret. She looks away, looks down at her dance bag, hides a smile. She feels how easy it is now to see Maurice whenever she wants. Her mother, for all her distractedness, could sometimes, all of a sudden, turn her attention on Mira and stare at her daughter like a drill trying to reach the center of the earth. But she can tell her dad anything she wants— "I'm babysitting" or "I'm going with my friend to a movie" or "I'm going roller-skating" (though she hasn't done this in years) or even the old "I'm doing homework at someone's house." He looks at her and she sees he knows he is supposed to ask her something else, but he doesn't know what it is. In the gap, she will say, like she does now—she sees his glass is empty—"Want another drink?" She goes to the little bar that has appeared in the corner of the living room and mixes him—he has shown her how to do this—a gin and tonic. In the gap, she gets the freedom to have her secrets, to know herself in a wider way, to ask him about the news of the day, all these things that make his face shine and him say, "Oh thank you, that's nice of you," vaguely, as if she were a stranger. She adds lime. *Another drink?*

But now, strangely, unaccountably, she struggles with the tears that are filling her eyes. She struggles to get control over her face. It seems to be doing something on its own. She drops her dance bag and covers her face with a hand.

"Are you okay?" her dad says. He hands her his drink napkin. It smells of lime.

She has a sudden painful burst of longing for her mother—not the mother she wishes Rachel was—but actually her mother, her big, strange-smelling self, her weird books, her too-long hair, everything about her that is wrong and out of control. She longs for that. Especially that gutsy cauldron of a laugh that sometimes erupts from her mother. When she left her mother's house, Mira told herself she did not care—she was *getting out of there*—out of her mother's life, of Brooklyn, of public school. She was moving to Manhattan, going to SAB, breaching two great walls. Her mother had felt like empty baggage she was putting on the curb.

But nothing has turned out how it was supposed to. Mira wipes her eyes, gains control over herself. Her dad pats her head distractedly. He makes her some frozen pizza, and they stand at the counter in the kitchen eating it.

"Honey, do you remember that woman Judy we met at the Thanksgiving Day parade?"

Mira nods.

"Well, she and I have become friends. She'd like to come over to make us dinner. Would you like that?"

"No," she says.

"Mira," he says, "I think it would be a good thing. For both of us."

She looks at her father. She looks away. When she looks back, his gaze has not wavered. This surprises her. "Okay," she says. "Yes."

A few weeks later, Judy comes over to make them dinner. Her dad isn't back from work yet. Judy makes several trips to her car, bringing in more kitchen devices than Mira has ever seen—a blender, a Cuisinart in a metal armature, a pizza pan, an electric juicer. She plays Elton John tapes in the kitchen while Mira ignores her, doing her homework in the living room. "One nice thing about a small kitchen," she yells cheerily, but doesn't finish her sentence.

By the time her dad finally comes home, Judy has covered the glass coffee table in the living room with a tablecloth. They sit on the floor around the coffee table for dinner. Their plates are piled high with some black sauce over what looks like rolled-up balls of hay. It tastes salty, chewy.

"This tastes gross," Mira says.

Judy stops eating, looks down at her plate.

"Mira," says her father.

"No, Carl," says Judy. "I know this is hard for you, Mira. It's a lot of change. Your mother leaving and your dad meeting me so quick." She hates that Judy says "quick," not "quickly." "It was hard when my husband and I split—and Sam, he had a lot of trouble."

"I don't care. I don't care about you or Sam. I wish you'd leave us alone."

Judy sighs, wipes her mouth with a napkin. "Well, honey."

"Don't call me honey," says Mira.

"Mira!" says her father.

Mira gets up and goes to her room.

Through her door, she hears Judy sigh and say, "Maybe—if you had made it back from work earlier—" Her room, cold, white, ridiculous. In the corner, she sees: someone has hung a silver-framed Pierrot, a smiling clown with tears flowing down his face.

She screams as loud as she can.

Over the next few months, her dad and Judy spend more time to-gether. Every week they go out to dinner. Every week, new things appear in Mira's dad's apartment. "She gets all this free stuff. They send it to her. So she can figure out how to sell it. She's really amazing that way. And this isn't junk like your mother brought in, you know. This is up-to-the-minute stuff. Modern. State-of-the-art." He holds up a big bowl made of metal with gold stripes across the rim. It is so shiny Mira can see her face staring at it. "If you bought this in a store, it would cost at least two hundred bucks. They sell it at museums."

"What is it for?" Mira says.

He puts it on the coffee table, looks at her annoyed, then laughs. "That is not the right question."

The other things that appear: purple velvet pillows, a giant sec-tional mirror, linked by a geometric gold filigree design. Are these things any different from the ripped furniture and chipped dishes her mother brought home? The fireplace bellows when they had no fire-place? The cracked umbrella stand that leaked rainwater. How is a bowl with no real use different from these things? Are Judy's things any more of a solution than are her mother's broken macramé and ripped pillows? Is it any more real than the stuff her mother brought home, sitting inert, lonely and desperate and wanting? She doubts it. Mira asked for the crying Pierrot picture to be removed, and her dad took it away. "Just don't bring any more of that stuff into my room." She thinks of Maurice saying you can't have beauty without suffering.

"Don't touch my room," she says. She likes it clean, white, like an empty box.

Finally school ends and so do The Little Kirov dance classes. On Judy's recommendation, her dad enrolls her in an Upper East Side summer day camp. Here, instead of the familiar curriculum of macramé pot holders and noodle collages, she has a choice among fencing, horseback riding, and bridge. She tries each of these things. Ballet helps with fencing but there are no other girls who choose it, so she drops that. Horseback riding is incredibly difficult and fills her with a sense of fear at loss of control. When she sits on the horse, she is painfully aware that she can't control it, and she knows it knows that. Still, she likes the stables and the types of tasks that you have to do before getting on the horse, the grooming and the feeding, the wooden-handled brush, and the clanking metal pails. In the end, she resorts to bridge, which is where the popular girls gather, and while they have a teacher walk them through the strategies, they exchange glances in a way that Mira recognizes from Judy's—confident glances filled with ownership. These are Judy's people, confident in their ownership of the world.

The trees burst with leaves. On the East River, little sailboats and tugboats dot the water's edge with sunbathers on them. In Manhattan, people sit on park benches instead of stoops, into the warm evenings, eating ice cream. On the hottest days, a few fire hydrants lose their covers (just like in Brooklyn) and water streams along the curbs, just as they did the previous summer, and the one before that, all the summers of her childhood.

In the afternoons and evenings, she takes class at David Howard's with other SAB and ABT girls and girls from lesser studios. To prepare for the audition she makes sure she works harder than any of the other girls. As summer lethargy falls over everyone else, she does not succumb to it, she does not let herself. She cannot. There is too much at stake.

In early June, her mother decides to move to California. She packs up her things and drives the old station wagon out of town. She hands Mira a jade plant that she tells her to look after, gets in the packed-to-the-brim car, and shuts the door. Mira's dad has been right: he is charged with selling the old, broken house.

A few weeks later, she gets a letter from her mother.

> *Mira, you wouldn't believe this giant country. How big it is! I pass in twilight through Battle Mountain, Nevada. Between two exposed mountain ranges, there's a long strip of light. It is the BIGGEST gas station I ever saw. You wouldn't believe how big they make them out here. The trucks that fuel up are immense beasts sucking the earth dry. There's an old town up in the mountains that some hippies have taken over. It's a ghost town! Should I go check it out? What do I have to lose? Everything in my life is gone, dissolved.*

In July, another letter comes from her mother. She has arrived in California. She writes that she "drove until she couldn't drive any-more." She says that she stopped when she got to the ocean—*the Pacific Ocean*—and she knew the whole continent was behind her. She took a job at an art supply store in a place called Market Street. She lives in a house on Guerrero Street, which means "the Street of the Warrior." However, her mother does not own this house. She lives in it with four other people, none of whom have children. She writes:

> *Talking to the other people in my house, I am beginning to realize how valuable you are to me. I know that I will return at some point, perhaps sooner than I think. This place is a Time out of Time. It is a place disconnected*

*from other Places. I have no history here. I am truly an
atom floating in space, as we all are, really. Someday
you too might see things and understand. I am trying to
capture this in my art—the sense of floating free. I have
finally broken free.*

*But I miss you, Mira, you are the only thing that
anchors me to Time and Place.*

Soon after, Judy invites Mira and her dad to a "special" dinner at her apartment. Judy has a large apartment on the Upper East Side—about twenty blocks from Maurice. This far uptown the apartments are roomy, with views that dwarf much of the city downtown. At night the lights shimmer below. During the day, you can see the high-up secret rooftop decks and gardens where the wealthy retreat during the summer. Judy has one herself: a wraparound terrace with little trees and white wrought-iron tables and chairs, and a bar on wheels.

The dining room: a long, wooden table, marble busts, shellacked parquet floors, heavy drapery, chintz flowered chairs. At the table, her father has his suit jacket over the back of the stool, his tie loosened, his top shirt button unbuttoned. He is rattling the ice in a cup. Since March, they've been doing dinner at Judy's. It's going better. It's becoming a regular thing.

Mira wears a new black velvet dress her dad bought her at Bloomingdale's. Sam is wearing lacrosse clothes—a dirt-stained jersey and shorts. His hair has grown longer since she first met him. It hangs in his eyes. He does not look up at her, at any of them, very often, but when he does, his baby face—nothing at all like Judy's, though his brown eyes are hers—is flushed, smug, cocky. Annoyingly handsome in a way that she is careful to ignore.

Judy compliments her on her dress. When they are all seated and served by Irma, the cook, Judy looks at Mira. "So she was taking class down at the Joffrey. But I hear it's just so uneven, so it's great that you are auditioning for SAB."

"Mira, Judy is talking to you," says her dad.

"What?" says Mira.

"I was just saying I was telling my friend about you and you know, her daughter goes to ABT—she's so impressed with that school—and anyway, just like you, she's going to audition for SAB and is taking class this summer at David Howard's."

"What's her name?"

"Kelly." A tall girl with bitten fingernails whom she has heard other girls calling in the dressing room.

Mira nods.

Judy is staring at her. "I just know you are going to get into SAB. To be at that studio would be an amazing thing."

Sam looks up from his meal. Is he one of the best at what he does?

Despite herself, Mira feels a soaring in her chest. Her mother has never taken such an interest in ballet.

Just then, her dad clears his throat and makes a clatter with his silverware. He reaches over and squeezes Judy's arm. "Mira, Sam—kids—" They exchange another look. "Sam—your mother and I—Judy and I—have decided to move in together, to join our families and make a new family."

"Sam—you will be brother and sister now. Carl and Mira will move in with us."

"When?" she asks.

Her dad and Judy look at each other. "Soon," her dad says. "This fall," Judy says.

"What room will she be in?" says Sam.

"The guest room will become Mira's room. Is that all you have to say?"

"I just wanted to know."

"Sam, you'll treat Mira like a sister."

"Fat chance."

"We'll talk about that, buster."

He gets up and leaves. "Sam—"

"This is so not a democracy. Don't she and I get a vote?"

"No, you don't."

"I hate being a kid."

Mira looks at her father and Judy—two old people who are happy or trying hard to be. She breathes in the lemony smell of the furniture polish. She listens for the beep of the new microwave in the kitchen. She waits for anger, but it does not come. Instead, something like hunger, something like the understanding of what you have to give up to be beautiful. She understands that her father and Judy are working hard to be happy, the way she is working hard to be beautiful. Maybe this will be okay. Judy looks at Mira and crinkles her nose. Her lip gloss glitters and her plastic chunky earrings shine in the chandelier's light.

"He'll just need a little time," she says.

Mira's desire to be a dancer has become synonymous with being *seen*—with being *chosen*. But looking at Judy right now, she has a thought, almost rebellious in its insistence. The thought goes like this: maybe Judy can see something neither her father, nor her mother, could see? Judy gathers them for dinner under chandeliers, while Mira sleeps in her white room and dances. Judy puts people together the way Mira is learning to put steps together. Judy raises her glass and smiles, and Mira returns the smile.

CHAPTER 23

I wake up in Felicia's guest room feeling weirdly great. I stare at the burnished wood ceiling fan, at the desk across from me. I roll over and stretch. I take the envelope, finger the letter inside, then tuck it back into my bag.

I hear voices next door, a door closing. I look at the clock: 9:03, late for me. Time to get going.

In the bathroom, I brush my teeth and wash my face and do the ritual with creams. In the light of Felicia's mirror, my freckles stick out. They make me look, I think, not younger, just preposterous. I've often thought of my face as existing on two planes: the under-plane, pale as the palest river rock, and the top layer, gravel or silt washing over it. The top layer floats over the bottom layer. Which one is more visible, I never know.

A man's travel bag—black, leather—is open on the sink.

The hallway carpet is plush on my bare feet and a shock of plea-sure goes through me. How must it feel to live surrounded by such luxury? What permissions does Felicia give herself that I can only imagine?

Back in my room, looking through my suitcase, I realize I've brought mostly black things. A few brown, and beige, and one taupe cardigan sweater. Middle-age colors. At the bottom of the suitcase, I find a bright scarf that a married lover once gave me as a gift. I've never worn it. I lay the scarf out on the bed. It feels soft in my hands, generous. My old lover's bearded face comes into my mind. I hold it there for a second. It was good for a while, wasn't it? I remember his face, his eyes—they were kind, sometimes. *I treasure you, Kat. You are my secret treasure. I hoard you.* I pull on a pair of black Banana Republic pedal pushers and a black long-sleeved button-down top, the black suit jacket, and a pair of green leather flats. I put on some simple pearl earrings and then tie the scarf on.

I take the old business card with me, as well as Maurice's letter. I put everything in my backpack and leave the room, shutting the door quietly behind me.

In the living room, Felicia sits on the couch next to a man. They sit side by side, comfortably, as if they are a married couple. The man—a handsome, very dark-skinned man—reads a paper, his coffee in front of him. They both wear white robes, bright white, and their feet are bare. On the table is a pot of espresso and a set of black china cups and a box of Italian biscotti. A newspaper in French called *Il Est Midi* is folded in quarters, well creased, belonging to someone used to traveling. Light spills into the spotless living room.

Felicia turns to me. "Good morning."

"Morning," I say, suddenly shy as a girl.

The man looks up over his spectacles and smiles.

"Kate, Alain. Alain, Kate. Kate is an old friend."

"Ah," he says. He stands and offers me a warm, dry hand. "Old friends are gifts." His voice is deep and resonant. He has a strong French accent, with a rolling undertow of humor.

"She's a professor now. A professor of dance. Here on academic assignment."

"Ah," he says again, sitting again.

Alain, I learn, is Senegalese. He went to school in Wisconsin. He is a diplomat who works for much of the year at the United Nations. He has two wives in Senegal and a place in New York near the U.N. However, he prefers to stay with Felicia. He finds it "utterly satisfactory." Felicia smiles and doesn't miss a beat.

"Felicia and I saw the recent Mark Morris at BAM. I found it somewhat disappointing."

"He's incredibly talented," I say, "but spread thin."

"I agree," he says.

"His operas are best."

"*Dido and Aeneas* is an accomplishment."

"When in doubt," I say, "turn to the Greeks."

"The African myths rival those of the Greeks, you know." He is smiling.

"My great Western ignorance." I smile.

"I will fill you in." He winks at me, picks up his newspaper.

Felicia has gotten up and is pouring more coffee; a cup has appeared for me and then I am sitting with them, engulfed in their casual intimacy. Felicia goes to the kitchen and comes back with a plate. "Please, join us."

"No thanks," I say. "I'm off on assignment." I try a smile.

"Kate is researching—a woman choreographer—who exactly is it again?"

"Bronislava Nijinska."

He smiles and lowers the newspaper. "The great Nijinksy's sister? And likely the true genius?"

"If I can sufficiently resurrect her." I strap on my backpack. "The Performing Arts Library has a great selection of archived works by Bronislava. And a state-of-the-art screening room. Great footage of her early pieces, which I've been teaching." This much is true at least. What would they say if they knew? Bronislava is a red herring, a ruse.

*The streets, the canyons of buildings, are less cavernous than I remem*ber them. The temperature is in the fifties, the sky a slate blue and cool, but underneath there is a softness to the air, the same harbinger of spring I felt yesterday. People are in overly optimistic fashion choices—shirtsleeves, light jackets, hatless. They look vulnerable, unadorned.

There is something in the air in New York that makes my blood pound the way it did when I was a child. At Columbus Circle, the explosion of people excites me after the mostly unbroken quiet of Ohio streets. I head up Broadway, then cross over to Lincoln Center.

Before I realize it, I'm standing in front of the New York Public Library for the Performing Arts, another building of glass and steel, this one built in the 1960s. I do something strange: I wave the business card around in the spring air, as if to summon something. But what? There is nothing. There is only the past, my past, the detritus of it all around me. What can I do except wade through it, picking up pieces and examining them? I stare at the card, and the name on it. Suddenly, now, it all seems too real: this half-baked plan of mine to find out if he is still alive and how much guilt I should bear for his life—and my own.

CHAPTER 24

On the morning of the SAB auditions, Mira wakes early to a city that spits and shines like jewels. Outside her window, the sky is bright with early white light.

She pulls on her favorite pair of tights—Capezios, three washings—and a black tank top leotard. Then she pulls off the tank leotard and puts on a new spaghetti strap one that Judy had bought for her just for the audition.

It's a warm day, late summer. She pulls on a cotton dress and packs her dance bag. She looks around. Her room feels smaller. She sits in the squat brown living room chair that smells of shampoo, waiting. She can hear her father snoring through his half-closed door.

Leaving her father sleeping, she gets up from the chair and lets herself out of the apartment.

Outside the city explodes with light. She sinks into the light, not running from awning to awning for the shade but taking the middle of the sidewalk.

She walks to the Lincoln Center fountain, bright, parched concrete. Maurice is waiting by the fountain. He wears the same black cape and a black top hat, which he removes when she arrives. Girls in buns with their mothers file by. He says, "Remember the Russian Tea Room when we saw Mr. Balanchine?"

How could she forget? The blood soup that tasted like dirt, the pale woman with the glittering ears, the golden clock that churned in the middle of the room.

"The Russians are scientists of the body. They have studied these things. The legs must not be too short, the head not too big, the instep pliant. It has taken them a hundred years to get the proportions right. I hear they do X-rays in the Soviet Union, but here parents wouldn't like that. But why not? It's better to know before serious training begins. Otherwise, it's a waste of everyone's time.

"Aside from this, they will be looking for one thing: that you know the steps. Don't worry about holding your pretty arabesques, just be quick, and clever, and to the point."

She looks at him. Her face grows hot as the morning sun. She imagines him kissing her the way that Christopher was kissed by the jester, smothering her, taking all of the anger out of her, draining her of everything.

She nods. Her blood in her ears. She understands.

The SAB hallways are packed, filled with hive-like activity. Girls in leotards and tights, mothers stiff-backed, like generals before a march, sitting on benches. Each girl wears a number pinned to the front of her leotard.

She passes a plumpish girl. A girl who smells of a strong flower perfume. A girl whose mother is straightening the seams on her tights, a girl who wears her bun high on her head like a geisha, one girl, an older girl, Robin's age—where is Robin?—whose feet poke out of her cut tights showing reddened, calloused, and bent toes, another older girl whose spine is so bony that you could play the xylophone on it. She passes a girl wearing a monogrammed robe and another whose father hugs his daughter to his chest, saying, "Do it for me, please." One girl's mother—a skinny woman with giant glasses—stands over her daughter while the girl does sit-ups.

Here she is not a girl who trusts too much, a girl who closes her eyes, a girl who lies in the hospital bed while they wash her big face off her little one. Last night, on the mattress at her dad's apartment, staring at the ceiling, freshly painted white, she went over the steps as if going over multiplication tables. She gave each step a numerical value and added and subtracted until she arrived at a number she assigned herself. Now she feels a bolt of confidence, the kind you feel when you open your blue booklet and realize the test question is the one you studied for. *Quick, and clever, and to the point,* Maurice said.

In the office, a woman has Mira write her name in a book. Then she gives her a piece of paper with a red number on it—146—and a safety pin.

Mira goes to the end of the long padded bench, peels off her street clothes. Next to her stands a girl with an amazing turnout. This girl's mother wears a white leather vest, white rhinestone-studded pants, and heels. She says to Mira, "I had a hell of a time getting here. An hour and a half on the Queensboro. If Felicia gets in, we'll have to move to Manhattan. She'll *need* a chaperone. And, I mean"— she leans toward Mira, so she *is* talking to her—"there are worse things for mothers to do, right?" The lady's red lips part in a smile. For a moment, Mira wishes that this glamorous woman was her mother.

"I live with my father." Mira uses a new, clipped voice, a Manhattan voice. She does not mention Judy or Sam.

The woman looks down at her hands. "Every situation is different, of course. But for Felicia, I *would definitely* need to be here."

Felicia's mother keeps talking, and her voice blends with the clomp of girls walking down the hallway in their pointe shoes, and the call-outs from the ballet masters in the audition studios, and the piano swelling up and then crashing to a stop. The girls five or six numbers ahead of her have begun to disappear. Mira catches Felicia's gaze, and the other girl smiles, humble and sweet, a smile that so belies her well-trained body and pixie-cute face that Mira, despite her best effort, smiles back.

A brief barre and then they move to the center. The steps are not difficult, but they are done faster than she is used to.

The old Russian teacher speaks little English. Her English, when it emerges, is almost impossible to understand. Mira stops trying to understand. Instead, she just watches the old woman's hands. Though veined and gnarled as old tree branches, they are quick and expressive. Watch them carefully and you can see the footwork. This woman was once, Mira sees from her hands, a very good dancer.

She follows this wordless direction, the old Russian teacher's fast-moving hands. Then she is warm and not thinking anymore. Her regular mind is asleep; her snake mind is awake. She is dancing. But the other girls haven't figured it out. There are girls with too-pointy faces and girls with too-round faces. When she sees them lined up in the mirror, her in their midst, she can see each one's imperfections; it's like an extra-special super power she has. Felicia of the perfect turnout is also managing to follow along. Some of the others are just standing and watching her and Felicia. A few of the girls have begun crying, softly. Others are flailing, turning blindly this way and that, beating their legs haphazardly, in their lovely leotards and their perfect buns. A girl runs out of the room. Another girl stands still without blinking, a stunned look on her face. They must avoid this girl—sometimes knocking against her.

The teacher adds yet another movement phrase, and now the combination is full of twists and turns, two allegro parts and one adagio, followed by another allegro. The only way she can keep going is to follow those hands, which, perhaps without her teacher's knowledge, mold and shape, dropping clues.

The teacher smiles at her and Felicia and the one other girl who is keeping up. She is a tall girl with stick-straight brown hair that has escaped from her bun, legs like stilts. No. 152.

"Okay, girls. Yes? We begin."

She understands that she has beaten these other girls. What is easy for her is hard for others! In this controlled competition, un-muddied by kindness or the pretense of equality, she has won. Mira lifts her chest, raises her arms, beats her feet in time to the old Russian's gnarled hands. She hears Felicia's ragged breath beside her;

she hears herself gasping for breath like someone who has been sub-
merged too long.

The woman in this office has a helmet of tightly curled hair, hard,
painted nails, and a strange accent. She wears a heavy gold pin held
on a bright, geometric-patterned jacket. Behind her is a framed series of old-fashioned-looking prints and an orderly bookshelf of
bound books. Even the light from the shutters falls in disciplined
strips across her body. Suddenly Ms. Clement's flyaway hair and watery bug-eyes seem *wrong* to Mira. Horribly wrong.

The lady asks her one question: "Do you want to be a dancer?"

"Yes," says Mira. *But*, she imagines her mother saying, *she used
to want to be in the circus too. And before that a veterinarian.*

Her stone-gray eyes have the slightest smile to them, and in her
manner, Mira understands, this woman is inviting her to embrace
the gold pins, the quick short words, to enter the land of wanting, of
becoming. There is no place in this world for Mira's mother. The
woman flicks her eyes away and adjusts a gold watch. There's nothing her mother can do. She's not here.

"Yes. Yes. Yes."

The lady smiles quickly at Mira.

"I was the Flower Princess," Mira says. The woman nods, but it
is already over, their moment of connection. "Congratulations and
welcome to the School of American Ballet. You will be in Second
Intermediate Level. This paper has your schedule on it. You will be
expected to come to all classes. If you stay, and if you advance, you
will need to come to daytime classes. This may require that you go
to a special school. Many of our children go to Professional Children's School." The woman makes marks on a piece of paper and
hands it to Mira. "You have some parents—some mother? Some father?"

Mira nods.

"Ask them to inquire into it."

Back outside, she stops in the middle of Lincoln Center. Her mother's voice is back. *What a bitch,* Rachel would have said. *What a total bitch.*

That evening, she and Maurice dine at Café des Artistes. He wears the same black cape and a black top hat, which he removes when she arrives.

He assesses her with his special glance.

"They checked your extension?"

"Yes," she says, remembering the woman's strong hands pulling her leg to her ear.

He nods. "They want to make sure they are loose enough—the tendons."

The arch? The femur? Those old, alive hands feeling through her skin for her bones. The audition studio, cold as a refrigerator. Barres against the bare walls. The gray floor, a veneer like wax paper. The old woman came around and lifted their legs one by one. Another woman followed, making marks in a ledger. Mira's leg went up; the old woman asked her to point her foot. She said something and the other woman wrote something down. They spoke in Russian. It sounded both gravelly and fluid.

Her bones are the right size, the right length; she has been measured, vetted.

Overcome by hunger, Mira reaches for the bread and the butter knife. Her roast chicken dinner arrives as she is buttering her bread, and she cuts the flesh and the juices flow. Mira swallows, the cool taste of chicken dimming in her mouth. It is exotic, delicious, like something dug up from the earth. Yes, her mother is gone—but, like a girl in a fairy tale, she has been given a substitute. An admirer: as rich as her father, as doting and attentive as a mother should be. She gets up to go to the buffet and returns with a pile of stuffed mushrooms. How she loves stuffed mushrooms.

Mira nods. She is going to be a ballet dancer, she feels it. Her bones will knit together in new ways. Her torso will lengthen. Her hands will grow strong, her fingers blunt, and her feet rough and calloused as tree bark. You will see the tendons in her neck, and her elbows and her knees easily hyperextend. Her hip ligaments will become so loose that whenever she sits on the floor, her legs will roll outward and her heels will touch. Her breasts, when she grows them, will remain as small foothills with no real valleys. She feels Maurice's eyes on her, pricking her skin, buttressing her. How simple it all seems! She will stay this way forever. Her head is shining, she is buzzing with light.

He says to her: "I will call you Bella. You are not Mirabelle anymore. You are *Bella*."

MR. B'S GIRLS

CHAPTER 25

PRESENT

"Does a Robert McAllister work here?" I say to a tall man wearing poodle cuff links and a badge around his neck. I'm inside the library now, at the information desk.

"Rob?" he says, and for a moment I think he will laugh at me. "He's in Special Collections. End of the hall, turn right. Elevator to the third floor."

I pass a photo of Mikhail Baryshnikov in his prime, and a bunch of framed Playbills from 1980s dance and theater, and a large glassed-off display of *Sesame Street* muppets. I get on an elevator.

On the third floor, I check my bag and coat, go through a metal detector, and enter a large, featureless room where a few people are hunched over old-looking books and sitting at AV machines. I follow signs to Special Collections, a far outpost. Here is a desk where an older man in a plaid shirt and badge sits. I take a deep breath and head toward him. He looks up from a computer. He has a close-cropped beard and dim watery eyes. He is very old.

"Excuse me," I say. "Hello. Are you Robert McAllister?"

I can recognize little of the man I met one night thirty years ago. The chiseled line of the jaw is gone, the face is now ovalish. I think of that younger version of this man saying, "I'll leave you two alone," and how those words have echoed through my life. I finger the envelope in my pocket. I almost turn to go. He's looking up at me, this old man, waiting.

"Yes," he says. "How can I help you?"

I take a deep breath. "My name—I—I'm Kate Randell."

He's looking at me with confusion.

I look down. "I'm working on a paper on Nijinsky's sister."

"Oh, well, we have some great resources from that period." He turns toward the computer screen.

"Wait," I say, pressing myself against the desk. In a hurried whisper, I say, "That's not why I'm really here. I think I met you once, a long time ago, one night, at someone's house, his name was—is?—Maurice. I was just a girl then, really a little girl, well, not so little—fourteen—you might not have thought I was little—maybe I looked older—"

Rob looks at me. Our faces are very close. "My god," he says. "I always wondered—" Then the deep lines in his face smooth out. He sits back in his chair. "Are you hungry?" he says.

We go to an overpriced coffee shop across the street. When we're settled at a table with menus, he looks right at me.

"My god," he says again. "How did you find me?"

"I have the business card you left for him that night. For this library," I say. I hand him the card. "I actually can't believe you're still here."

He laughs. "Yes," he says, fingering the card. "They wanted us to be anonymous. But I begged to differ." He hands the card back to me. "They never gave us business cards in those days, so I had one made for myself. That's how much I wanted to impress him. There are very few of us left from back in the day. I'm semiretired. I'm in only two days a week these days."

A waitress comes by. He orders a salad and I order a soup, but there's no way I can eat.

He says, "You know, I was the one who found him."

I try to hold his gaze but can't. I look outside. A van drives by with a sign that reads GUM REMOVAL SPECIALISTS!

I look back at him. "Did you get—in trouble?" *In trouble?* A child's words.

"They questioned me."

I blurt it out. "Did he die? Is he dead?"

He looks at me carefully. "Those are two separate questions. I know the answer to one, but not the other."

He looks away for a second, then back at me. "He did not die—not that night."

I wait for it to sink in. The pain of not knowing and the fear of knowing all wound up together have apparently made a knot under my ribs, because now I feel that knot loosen and something flow out of me. It's physically painful. It pools out of my rib cage, down my arms.

"Are you okay?" says Rob.

I nod. "Go on. Please."

"He was in the hospital for a while. They had to make sure. He had a seizure and there was some paralysis on his left side—which was, as you know, his bad side."

"The polio."

He nods, takes another bite. "But, no, he did not die. Slowly, with a lot of physical therapy, he recovered use of his arm, but not much of his leg. He never was able to get around very well after that. He had to be under supervision. Constant care."

The pain—or whatever it was—is gone, and I feel a hollowness under my ribs. Cripple to invalid! I search my mind for legal terms that might apply: *battery, assault?* But not: *murderer.* Into that space rises a pure sweet relief.

I look at Rob, searching for more. "I just need to—to know."

"It's complicated," he says finally. "He was not a bad man. But his relationship with you was not right."

He looks at me then, really looks at me. His once-chiseled face, sagging with age, the roots of white bristles showing, those kind blue eyes. His eyes look beneath the freckles, beneath the skin, into the deeper rivers of my being. It's like he is seeing into what I was before Maurice came along, before so much was decided. And in looking that far, he touches on something that reminds me of what I was, what I could have been, before I knew so certainly what I wanted, before Maurice had said to me, "You have to say it, say what you want." And in seeing me that way, seeing into me before *I* was me, I feel something returning, something even sweeter than relief.

"I never felt like a child."

"No, I don't suppose children like you do." I look away, dab my eyes with my napkin. I try a sip of the coffee.

"Walking was very hard for him. After a while, he moved to a facility that could care for him."

I think about the postmark on the blank envelope. "Do you know the name of the—place—the home?"

"It's been some years. About an hour north of here. Armonk? Yes, that's right. A very nice place. He was receiving excellent care." He turns his eyes to the street outside. Two men with large handheld metal tools scour the sidewalk with blasts of water. *Gum removal specialists.* "So, to answer your second question . . . I don't know if he is dead."

The waitress brings my soup and his salad. The soup is way too complicated. It has lots of things floating in it. A minestrone. I push it away. Then I bring out the letter and slide it across the table to him.

He runs his hand over the envelope, opens it gingerly, unfolds the light parchment paper, reads it. "Yes, this is his handwriting. . . . But this letter, it doesn't sound like him. He wasn't angry with you when I knew him."

I take the letter back. I fold it and put it back in the envelope.

"When was the last time you saw him?"

He looks troubled. "For a long time, I visited him regularly. It meant something, I think. To both of us. But then, several years ago, well, I stopped."

"Why?"

"The boy."

"What boy?"

"This boy. He was—not a boy, a young man." He wipes his mouth with his napkin, and pushes the half-finished salad aside. Now he orders coffee. "He started to come visit every few months. He was, I thought, a bit strange. Intense. He flew all the way from California to visit Maurice."

My skin goes cold. All the new good feelings dissipate. *A boy? A young man?* I square my shoulders, raise my chin.

He looks down at his plate and then up. His face is very sad. "Maybe I was jealous. I felt he didn't need me anymore. Some of us—for better or worse—like to be needed."

I brace myself. "What was his name—the boy?"

He shakes his head. "I don't remember." He smiles sheepishly. "He was a lawyer."

He looks at me for several long moments while we sip our coffee. "Every year, Maurice gave a lot of money to SAB. They might have his contact information."

He gestures for the bill. "There's something else—I don't know if—but, well, one more thing," he says. "The young man who showed up, well, Maurice introduced him as his son."

"His son?"

Rob stands to leave. "The old fool. Surprised everyone."

So Mira becomes one of the three hundred girls who attend SAB. She is put into B1, Intermediate Level, where the color of leotards is midnight blue. She is one of the four routinely selected by call-outs to demonstrate the steps. *Mira, Felicia, Natasha, Bryce.*

She feels that thing that was set loose by her fall—the part of her that wants to laugh and fling back her head and twist Ms. Clement's kind hands until they break—brought her here. Under the stares of the Russians, this thing rears up, animated. The Russians hate her and she respects them for it. It makes her dance better. It is now these women, with their faulty English, their imperious attitudes, their quick jabs to her flesh, their movement tics and flourishes—it is this that she craves. It is this that makes her feel she has arrived.

Maurice shows her a documentary called *The Children of Theater Street.* It is about the making of ballet dancers in the Soviet Union, the same great ballet factories that produced Baryshnikov and Makarova. She learns that in this other land the boys and girls come from all over—hundreds, even thousands, of miles—to audition. They are measured, and their natural gifts are tested, the way they tested Mira. The documentary follows the lives of the chosen few girls and boys who have been taken from their homes in the provinces and brought to Leningrad to train. One girl sleeps on a cot in the kitchen of her host family's apartment. It is rolled out every evening and rolled away at five in the morning when the girl rises, and after a breakfast of beets and bread by flashlight (her host family still sleeping), she begins her hours-long journey to the Kirov studios, where she will have a long day of grueling classes. She is eleven years old.

And now Mira is studying with these Russians, who had trained in those *very same* ballet factories; Mr. B—Balanchine—had gathered them together: Alexandra Danilova, one of his earliest partners. Kiev's State Theater's Tumkovsky and Hélène Dudin who emigrated after World War II. Felia Doubrovska, who danced at the legendary Mariinski Theater before the Russian Revolution. Former Bolshoi principals Nikolai Tarasov and Andrei Kramarevsky.

Mr. B is both familiar father figure, warm and human, and as remote as a god. Each girl lives for the day he will visit her class, run his eyes over the lot of them, stop at *her*, and magically elevate her to the likes of one of his muses. Suzanne Farrell is his most revered. The newest of his muses, Darci Kistler, is scarcely two years older than Mira.

Like a family, bound by its own mythology. One can hardly switch parents; one makes do, adapts. In family life, in a family of good children, each one strains to be the best.

Mr. B's girls. They are being molded into the stick-thin hipless Balanchine ballerinas, known far and wide as Balanchine's "pinheads." *Pinheads*. If there is a fairy tale at work here, it is not really *Cinderella*, but something more like *Hansel and Gretel*. A brittle finger bone, a threat of fire and oblivion, a trail of receding crumbs disappearing in the woods of a vanishing child-self.

The SAB changing rooms are like a gym, with metal lockers, long wooden benches, and a back room with showers. The only thing that sets it apart from a gym changing room is the big cat litter–size box of rosin in the corner by the door, where the hard yellow rock sits chipped and battered amid a powder of its own skin.

One afternoon after Mira has been at SAB a few weeks, she is in the changing room before class. She takes out her pointe shoes and bends to unroll the ribbons. The shoes are new. Capezios. Just this morning she closed her bedroom door on the toe box several times to break them in. (Judy shouting from the kitchen, "Mira, what are you doing? Stop making that racket!") She shakes them out and runs her hand along the lining just to make sure. She heard about a girl who had to go to the hospital because someone put glass in her pointe shoes and it chewed up her feet so badly that she was out for several months. Or that was the story. You hear things, lots of things. You never know what is true.

As she is slipping on her shoes, two girls come in from some class in sweat-drenched leotards. They both have brown hair, but one looks wispy and the other more solid. Yet another brown-haired girl comes in behind them, thinner than the other two.

"How much do you have to lose?"

"They want five pounds by the summer."

Mira thinks of Adele, a girl she's heard stories of, who was supposed to have been great. Mr. B has picked her out during a class, once. But after Adele was *talked to* about her weight, she began peeling the skin from the bottom of her feet and the wounds caused an infection that finally put her out of class for a month. By the time she came back to class, she had gained more weight. She was not invited back after the summer. Though Mira has never met Adele, she is a present figure, ghostly, in her life.

Mira watches the third girl. She reminds Mira of Robin from The Little Kirov. This thin girl is not B Level—she's C Level, marked by black leotards. She has Robin's dark hair, heart-shaped elfin face, and bow-shaped lips. She has Robin's untroubled translucent skin. But Robin's thinness is an ethereal slightness, whereas this girl's thinness is one of will: her collarbones and ribs stick out like bony fingers. Only her calves and ankles are substantial. There is something about this not-Robin that, despite—or maybe because of—her anorexia, makes her look older, almost like a lady, a grown-up.

Mr. B does not like anorectics. Thin is good, yes, but the anorectics end up getting sidelined and leave. Still, the line is fuzzy. A girl can be delicately thin and then, only a few pounds less, she can have the tell-tale gaunt rigidity of the anorectic. Anorectics are not reliable. They stick around for a while, all bone, no muscle, downy hair growing on their backs, until they can't dance anymore. Then they disappear. Mira does not know where they go.

Not-Robin sits on the bench and pulls her leotard down so that you can see her pinprick nipples that barely rise from her ribs. She looks at Mira with some kind of raw emotion, and for a second Mira has to look away.

Mira looks down at her new Capezios, with their barely cracked toe box. She feels some wall coming down, that she is growing less complicated, some jewellike part of her beginning to shine again. Her mouth opens to say something.

Not-Robin turns to her locker, and when she turns back her face has changed. It is shut tight and strangely blurry. A closed window streaked with rain.

Then Mira comes crashing into her ridiculous childhood self— and she is humiliated at the sight of her. Here again is the girl who dreams about being a princess, who loves the prince above all else, who thought saying "Fuck you" would solve all her problems, who accosts a jester because he kisses the prince (as if most ballet boys didn't prefer boys). She has to look down.

All at once, the other girls laugh.

The taller girl snorts and says, "I hate when they get boners! I hate when they get them and stick them in your back."

"Oh yeah," says the wispy girl. "Like when you're partnering, like for pirouettes? They have to hold you around the waist and they get a boner and it's sticking you in the back."

How many times has Mira come to this moment? She sees herself in the wings watching the jester kiss Christopher, his head back and broken-looking, the fierceness rising in her. How many times has she been asked to hate that ridiculous girl? Still, she can't. She can ridicule her, but she cannot hate her. She is like a younger sister, stupid, fresh, naïve, ridiculous, but hers—*her* sister. But she thinks now of that night in the terms Maurice has laid out for her: she *fell. You fell wonderfully.*

Everything will change—is changing. She will no longer be Mira, but "Bella": someone new and better and braver.

———————

In October, Mira and her dad move into Judy's big apartment off Park Avenue. Park Avenue from Sixtieth Street to Eightieth Street is its own world, a twenty-block island of determined wealth and privilege that abruptly ends with a stretch on Madison of public institutions—a big red brick school tagged long ago as a bomb shelter and a bedraggled public park. On this island, things are as they've been for a long time, or at least everyone has agreed to pretend so. Mothers in heels, wall portraits of family members, maids in uniforms in the kitchens, dining rooms with sideboards of weekly polished silver. Kids leave this world only to walk a few blocks to their private schools or climb into their family's Mercedes to drive to the Hamptons.

Brooklyn is an excuse for sitcoms, the Bronx shorthand for urban desolation and fear, but Park Avenue floats untouched, insulated. This is Judy's world—and now her dad's and hers.

Judy enrolls her in an all-girls private school. Mira walks a few blocks to her new school, tucked in a town house off Fifth Avenue, built of marble and wood, nodding at the doormen on her way, who stand in the dimly lit antechambers in stiff hats and brocaded lapels, protecting what is left of her innocence.

The difference between Brooklyn public school and Manhattan private school: *everything*. No cafeteria workers. No hot lunch. No Tater Tots. No bouncing baloney. In private school, kids *buy*—not bring—their lunch. Overpriced salads from the Madison Avenue deli. A steak sandwich from the deli two blocks away. Mineral water. At public school, no one got more than a dollar a week in allowance. Here, they get twenty-five dollars a week! "Recess" in a pebbled concrete yard is replaced by "gym" in a shiny wood-floored room of skylights and the squeak of sneakers and balls hitting the floor. In this shiny gym, she plays volleyball. The girls' voices lower an octave and become hard and urge her on and if she hits the ball they thump her on the back and if she misses they turn away from her and clap their hands quickly to dismiss her failure. "Keep the energy up," they say, clapping again.

In public school, the teachers are decades older and have pock-marked skin, circles under their eyes. Their eyes skate over her in relief whenever she is silent. In private school, shiny-haired young teachers call on her when she doesn't speak enough. The other girls look at her expectantly as she tries in her new voice to get her ideas across. The ideas flow up as if from nowhere: she sees wind as a symbol in *Wuthering Heights*. She sees the Chinese Confucian system as an enviable moral code and in one paper compares foot binding to wearing pointe shoes. Her mother lets her go to this school because her father is paying for the tuition. But having gone to a private school herself, her mother warns her daughter of "the snobs, fruitcakes, and counterfeits" who are at these kinds of schools.

But the girls are nice to her for some reason, maybe because she is a bunhead, or maybe because she is Sam's sister. Sam is popular for being a good lacrosse player. He goes to an all-boys private school—her school's "brother school"—about ten blocks away.

Or maybe it's because she tells these girls that she has a rich, old boyfriend who is going to marry her when she graduates high school.

Maurice gives her money on Friday nights—"the babysitting money" she would be making if she were really babysitting. With this money, she buys jewelry from Bloomingdale's that she tells them is from her boyfriend. They gather around and their makeup-less faces—no makeup is allowed—press in to see her latest acquisition. They believe her, or appear to.

After school, she climbs on the crosstown bus to SAB. It cuts through the park at Sixty-sixth Street and then travels west on Sixty-fifth. She gets out on the corner of Sixty-fifth and Amsterdam on the north side of Lincoln Center. The bus is often strangely empty. For some reason, not many people make the journey at this time of day from the East Side to the West Side.

Mira takes her place at the barre. She nods at the other girls whose names are called most regularly. They nod back curtly, sergeants who offer passing acknowledgment of the heavy responsibilities the others carry. And that is a bond of some sort—not friendship—but it is a bond.

The best girls—there are two of them besides Mira in this class—hold a careful alliance. Her two competitors are Felicia and Bryce. Felicia, in her Princess Leia buns, has the air of waiting. Bryce's long limbs twitch as she warms up. They stand together along the far wall where the view of the mirror is most direct, and after class they gather in the hallway or dressing room to compare notes. Unlike at The Little Kirov, they do not envy each other, or not in the same way, not raw on the surface like children. They are already chosen—each of them—so they tolerate, they hate, one another as professionals.

Felicia has perfect turnout, perfect arches, perfect extension, and perfect balance. She dances with an easy precision. Nevertheless, there is something vacant about it. Her face looks like she is watching TV. She shines at adagio.

Bryce is long and gangly and a bit spastic. She moves constantly, even between combinations. She is loose-limbed like Hannah: her limbs fly up like she has no joints. In fact, she is double jointed.

When she marshals her energy well, you can't take your eyes off her. Her specialty is allegro.

What Mira has that neither of them has is allegro *and* adagio together. But she worries that when Mr. B finally comes to their class, on that day Bryce will be wild and perfect, or Felicia will be a little less perfect and pay attention, and then it won't matter what Mira can do. She will not be chosen.

She tries to follow Felicia's steps and duplicate Bryce's energy— and to copy neither.

Then the old Russians' attention turns to her. "Mira! What do you do? What you make?" yells Ms. Tumkovsky, stamping her foot in her dusty funereal outfit.

Then Mira can snap her eyes away from the out-of-the-ordinary thing. Mira feels the challenge of hate rising, some force of will, energizing. She can relax into it. And Ms. Tumkovsky's critiques are a taut rope that Mira can clutch onto as she descends deeper into the class, into her body and its needs, and the needs of the steps. Her mind, in the hands of another, grows pliant, as she keeps moving, her body leading. She is following a path into the forest, one stone, then another, and soon she is deep in the forest and doesn't care that there is no light, no sound of birds, no mother, no house, no prince. Then there is no mind, just her body moving in space. There is just this and Tumkovsky's voice that is around her.

At the same time, she knows it is not enough to be small and have no hips. It is not enough to be one of the best. It is even not enough to be the best in the class, hated the most by the Russian teachers. You must be singled out by Mr. B during one of his random classroom visits. He might ask you to point your foot. He might ask to see an arabesque. It doesn't really matter. It is his eyes that matter. They have chosen *you*. You are now one of "Mr. B's girls."

And from there? You will be chosen for *The Nutcracker*—a child in the party scene, or a Hoop Girl, or a Polichinelle if you are older. From there, you will be put on the fast track. You will be invited to take company classes. Apprenticeship is within reach. He might give you your own perfume—he gave Karin *L'Origan*. *Réplique* is what he gives Suzanne (so that he knows who has been in the elevator and hallways). If you are very lucky, he will invite you to his apartment during summer season in Saratoga Springs and cook you his borscht and you will eat it (though it will be the only thing you eat all day) because he hates anorectics. Then you will dance on the stage at Lincoln Center, on the same stage as Suzanne Farrell and Peter Martins, you will wade through a carpet of rose stems that have been thrown at you during curtain calls. You will have an apartment near the theater with a small mattress and China tea set (but you will need nothing else). You will travel the world on tour, dancing on the stages of the great European capitals. You will be *seen*, you will be *adored*. You will be a ballerina in the greatest ballet company in the world.

But she knows—they all know—that Mr. B only invites one or two girls a year into the company—and that's on a good year. But despite these terrible odds, this is the only way to go from an SAB student to a New York City Ballet dancer.

After I say good-bye to Rob, I wander for a while until I end up in a café packed by tourists and decorated with cellophane-wrapped sandwiches. I pick up a turkey wrap and sit at a table to eat it. This food is just right—unobtrusive, barely food. I didn't manage any soup and my head is pounding from the coffee.

I finish half the wrap and toss the rest away. My cell buzzes. A number I don't recognize snakes across the screen. I turn off my phone and let it go to voice mail. Probably a wrong number.

I have to get out of here. I have to move because I have to think. I start walking east, toward Central Park.

Yes, there is a part of me that wants to believe I am blameless— like Rob suggested. I was only a child. I was not responsible for our relationship.

But some lines from the letter run through my head: *I am one of the dead. I do not deserve to have commerce with the living. I wanted to tell you, my dear, because you too are one of the dead. Do you know that yet?* Something hardens inside of me. *This* is Maurice. Maurice of the exotic fish, of the too-salty capers and arugula, the Cordon Bleu, of the Indonesian silk ties and New Zealand wool scarves. Not an old man in a convalescent home. In a relationship like ours that was based on aesthetics, perception is everything. If he saw himself as dead, did I in fact not kill him?

My assault on him caused him to become an invalid for the rest of his days. I did not kill his body, but did I kill his spirit? Perhaps. But maybe even as I destroyed one Maurice, I gave birth to another?

Because he destroyed me that night. That girl always searching for the spotlight. And gave birth to another girl. This girl became the woman I am now.

That girl took her mother's last name. Symbolic? Yes, of course. But it made paperwork easier. Our insurance was through the small law office off Market Street where my mother worked part-time, later full-time, still doing her art in the evenings and on weekends, and having the same last name made everything easier.

Kate Randell is one who, instead of seeking out the spotlight—hungry for eyes to fill her up with their gaze—looks for the dark. Her eyes go to the peripheries where she can hide, her mind moves away from bright conversation—laughter, gaiety—to the murmured subterfuge among discontents. She seeks the cubbyhole at the library in the back away from the window, books with black-and-white photographs, creaky microfiche machines in the basements where she watches tiny decades-old dancers in black and white skitter and jump, and then, under the weight of her heavy spirit, she rears herself into battle for some words to put on the page. Each sentence, each page, each article, each lecture, a dim victory against him and what he has wrought.

I became a child who could sink into the blue sky, bottlebrush trees, Point Reyes, who knew what parasailing was. I watched my mother struggle from one artistic obsession to the next. I stopped dancing for a time, became a punk girl hanging out in video stores, on stoops, at Fillmore District clubs. A new sense of self bloomed: the watcher. *I* could watch. *Others* would do. Clearly, it was safer to watch than be watched. And out of the watching, grew the thinking, and out of that grew writing.

But I didn't stop dancing forever. My body didn't let me. By my senior year of high school, I had begun to dance again. Not ballet, though. I took modern and contact improv classes, which were held in raw spaces where there were raves at night and contact jams during the day. This was a dance world inverse to SAB's, whose stars had not started dancing until college, whose bones had not been bred to turn out, whose ribs did not rise automatically at the opening bars of a familiar classical piece. Their feet were flat, their hamstrings tight, their torsos too thin or too thick, but they had vision. They didn't care about beauty, but about art.

I went to some of their performances. They were held in cavernous lofts that smelled of ketchup and alcohol, and lights burning through cheap filters. These dancers moved in the half-darkness, across a bed of Styrofoam nails. They stood on their heads and stacked their bodies one on top of the other until the bottom person emerged gasping and red-faced. Sometimes someone onstage spoke a string of words. A grainy video popped up overhead and dancers moved in front of it as if it weren't there. I looked around the room at all the people who sat there watching these shows and thought: they like this; they choose to see this; it is *something*. But what? What would Mr. B think? What would Tumkovsky think? What would Maurice think? They would hate it, of course—it wasn't beautiful and it wasn't tragic. There was nothing about it that made you want to cry, or leap with joy, or dance for a stranger in a dark apartment, or put on a swan's costume and pas de bourrée in the moonlight. Nevertheless, it held a power, and it fascinated me.

For the next five years, I drifted in and out of small modern troupes and contact improv groups. It was the 1990s in San Francisco. The dance scene was dispersed, experimental, allergic to hierarchy. The watchword was "experimental." This meant everything that ballet was not: release technique, contact improv, choreography collectives, multimedia, performance-based, "personality." Dancers were praised for their quirks, their clothes (or lack of them). In my first post-ballet piece, I came onstage topless in leather pasties. My mom applauded loudest of all.

During these years, I worked many jobs just to get by. I tried catering, bookkeeping, waitressing, all demanding. The life of the struggling dancer is like that of an addict. Classes are like dope: life is driven by the need to get enough cash to take class. Even then classes were twelve dollars a pop. Food work is good because, though it doesn't pay a lot, you get free meals and the free meals add up. Tossed onto my own resources, living with a roommate in a Tenderloin apartment (by twenty, at last on my own, no longer with my mother), I could not afford *not* to eat. The stuff of my life then: my earplugs next to my bed (from my roommate's midnight visitors), my scale, my laundry rack of drying tights and leotard, my crumpled Ex-Lax packages at the bottom of my bag, my split ends (couldn't afford a haircut), the card from the man who offered me free cocaine to sleep with him, which I hadn't thrown away. My fingertips permanently smelled of the garlic from the hummus that I mixed in batches for the catering company, so that when I fell asleep, I felt like I was still mixing great tubs of it.

One night in rehearsal a choreographer named Elso, who was from Norway, asked me to Ace-bandage two miniflashlights to my chest, above my breasts. They reflected beams on the ceiling as I danced and flickered as I moved my arms in the way Elso showed me. He said, "Your breasts are like the stop lights." I realized then that no matter how long I danced now, I would never again get back to the place where I was a princess who gazed at the prince's face in the mirror and he smiled a secret smile at me.

But then I remembered: when I fell, *Christopher* did not catch me. *Maurice* did. Who was the real prince of my childhood?

The mirror lies. We know this. Its secret smiles are the images that match our own dreams. But it persists, categorical and seductive. How often have I learned this? Still, the desire to trust the image persists. And persists.

It was during my period of being a poor modern dancer that I saw Christopher again. I'd heard he was with the San Francisco Ballet, partnering the sensation of that year, some soloist whose name I can't remember. Then I heard he'd left the company, that he was "sick"—which in dancer lingo was a euphemism for something terrible, if it was bad enough to keep you offstage. Soon after, I heard that he was strung out, living in the Tenderloin too. Someone had seen him panhandling on BART, this prince of my youth. I heard from another dancer friend who'd danced with him at ABT—he was a junior soloist there in the late 1980s—that Christopher was in the hospital. She said we could visit him—that he'd opened up his room to anyone who wanted to come.

He lay in a very white bed. He had tubes sticking out of every part of the body. His head looked enormous on his shrunken limbs. His lips and fingertips were blue. His hair scanty, his skin mottled, a web of veins rising to the surface like some flourishing underwater growth. The body! The dancer's crucible. Giant purple circles bloomed under his eyes; the scars from Kaposi's sarcoma dotted his yellow skin; his clavicles and knees protruded. Even in the hospital bed, his legs rotated outward at the hips, and his feet lay in a perfect fifth position. Such a bunhead thing to notice.

In the corner, by the window, some ridiculously young ballerina was doing her short nails. The smell of nail polish was thick in the room. By now, I had cut my hair off. I no longer considered myself a bunhead. Still, how well I knew their scornful stares, their crazy-long hair, their Cleopatra eyeliner, their too-proud duck walks. Ballerina girl didn't even look up when we came in.

My friend kissed Christopher on the cheek and hugged him gingerly. He winced at the contact. Then he looked at me. "Hey, it's Flower Girl," he said. I couldn't believe he recognized me. "Thanks for coming to my wake."

"How's it going?" I said. "It's been a while." It'd actually been years since I'd seen him, since our Little Kirov duet. At SAB, we'd rarely crossed paths, he was an apprentice and in company classes while I was only in intermediate classes. When we did, he'd only acknowledge me with the briefest nod. I'm not even sure why I decided to go see him, except out of some morbid curiosity, I guess.

He started laughing. I remembered that laugh: it always made me think he knew more than I did. "You were such a serious girl," he said. Then he started to cough.

"I'm sorry," I said. I meant it.

"It's been better." Then he looked right at me and didn't pretend. I saw how bad it was. I saw he was going to die. I put my hand out and he took it. My friend looked at us. I felt time close in on us. *The demise.* "Well, I won't miss this," he said, waving his hand vaguely around. "But I'll miss—"

"What?"

"You know."

I nodded. I understood. He meant dancing. I felt a terrible wave of sadness. What happens when I feel compassion is that it opens something in me so wide it hurts. It lets so much life in that I don't know what to do. I am flooded, I shut down. I get angry. I've never known what else to do in the face of beautiful, monstrous life baring its teeth, death in its mouth. I'm not proud of it, but I turn my face away.

I gently pulled my hand back.

"My last will and testament, you know, was to go to my own wake," he said. He turned his face to the wall. When he turned back, he was smiling. "Thanks for coming." It wasn't till I was in college, a few years later, that I heard he died.

At the old age of twenty-four, I went back to school to get my college degree. I strung classes together from community colleges, and when I had enough credits, I transferred to San Francisco State. Did I fall under the spell of school in the same way I had with ballet? The rigor of it, the logic of it, the step-by-step of it? The specter of a greater good hovering over all of it. The promise—in the form of degrees—of mastery. It was like crack to me, to my burned and buried ego. The illusion of getting ever closer to a perfect. The illusion of mastering a subject through knowledge, of going so deeply into something that it opens up and spreads its secrets wide.

This was another happy, dark period of my life when my quest for knowledge colored everything. The walls of my cubicle at the library were my home. I spent hours in bed with books and wine.

With my notebooks and books, I could move through time now. Becoming an historian, I believed I could master the people who had schooled me as a child, used me, taught me, possessed me.

At one point, I saw a therapist. All my friends were seeing therapists. But my therapist's patient listening, her books, her entreaties, her couch were not enough. There was something wild about my pain that I couldn't put into words and that, finally, I couldn't part with. Maybe at the bottom I knew that if I went too deeply into it, I would be admitting something terrifying.

The day has turned sallow. I've been walking along the border of the park.

Suddenly, I just want to sleep, nothing more, nothing less. I only want to lie down in Felicia's hermetically sealed apartment across from another sunset of fire. I don't want to think anymore. I don't want to remember. I want to sink into a deep sleep, an empty forgetting sleep. *A boy. A young man.*

I remember Maurice's eyes burning into me, as if he owned me. I remember the inside of his car, its plush silence, like the inside of a theater before a show. My broken wrist, his broken legs. Two broken things. But I had *wanted* that too, to be owned by him.

I turn around and head away from the park, back toward Felicia's apartment.

The smell from the dank hallways seeps into the classroom. A rainstorm has moved overhead. Steady rain pounds on the high studio windows. Outside, the sky is green. A leak has begun near the window and has made a small puddle. An industrial rubber bucket has appeared. Every twenty minutes or so, Danilova carries the bucket herself to the doorway, where it is carried away by one of the male scholarship students, all the while calling out instructions to their class. For the minute she is gone, the water leaks onto the floor.

They are in the middle of Variations with Danilova. "Remind me of days of Russian Revolution," Danilova says in her accented singsong voice. "No bread, no toilets, no heat! Ah, we are so lucky here to only have some small, silly leaks." Her English is much better than Tumkovsky's. Her body is still recognizable as a dancer's. Even in her ballroom shoes—an American affectation they all forgive her for because she is Danilova—her high arches pop. Her legs are still long, muscled—a dancer's. She wears dark eyeliner. Her hair is dyed blond, short and swept back. Along with her trademark brightly colored scarf—she favors blues and greens—Danilova gives the impression that she is on a yacht in the middle of a high wind. She holds her nose up high. Her chin quivers with dignity.

"*Tondue* finish, girls. Now *ronde de jambe*. Yes, girls," Danilova is saying. "Make the body sing."

Mira can feel the shift in the room. The air pressure drops. She turns. Mr. B is teetering into the room on the arm of Karin von Aroldingen. They all turn to stare, then try to pretend they are not staring. She hadn't even heard he was out of the hospital. But here he is now. His turtle-like head is tilted at a strange angle, but he doesn't look sick. Though he is not a tall man, he does not seem short either. He is taller than Maurice.

"Hello, dears," he says. "Hello!"

Mr. B lets go of Karin's arm and cocks his head to take each of them in. He walks over and looks in the bucket.

He says something to Danilova in Russian and they laugh. "Girls," he says. "If the sky is falling, make it beautiful."

Then he turns to the pianist. "Play nothing," he says softly. "I want to hear them." Since she saw him last at the Russian Tea Room his face has grown longer and his skin more papery. Maurice looks like a boy compared to him. But she recognizes the eyes that touch on each of them brightly, merrily. She remembers the question he asked Maurice: *Is she one of mine?* What had Maurice said? "No. No," he had said. She widens her second position. Danilova has them line up in a row in back of the room. They will do their across-the-floor for Mr. B. They will parade one at a time.

He wants to hear them, he wants to see them. They do not meet one another's eyes as they unwrap their chiffon skirts and hang them from the barre. Now they stand in just their white tights and pink leotards.

"Just walk," Mr. B says. "Just walk." *Just walk?* The great Mr. B wants them to walk across the room?

"Like waiter at Russian Tea Room. Just walk, carrying tray. You want to do Plisetskaya head-kick? First you must be waiter."

What Mr. B is asking from her is something no one has asked from her before in all her years of ballet. Why couldn't they do an arabesque, a million-dollar pose, flash a smile? Why couldn't she show him how she could be beautiful—how nicely she danced— how well she had learned? *I know how to walk. I want to learn how to be a ballerina.* She imagines saying it, the words dropping out of her mouth like heavy drops into a bucket. Would they shock everyone? No, all the girls must feel as she does.

But she does not say this. No one does. They are dancers—they do not talk, they move. Of course they do what Mr. B asks. They walk past him. One by one, Mr. B stops them as they walk across the room to correct them. He watches Felicia go, head held high, her arms in first position. "No, no," he says. "Too pretty." Then Bryce goes, walking too fast, skittering like a mouse, slipping on the little puddle by the bucket and, arms flailing, catching herself before she hits the ground. "Yes." He gives a dry giggle. "Better."

It's her turn. She feels something: cold, shivery, then hot. Her skin prickles. She feels a wildness growing in her, something like a panther about to spring. *How has a walk, just a walk, set this free in her?*

"Yes," Mr. B says. He is pointing at her. "Fast, no thinking. Don't think. Do."

He stops Mira in the center of the room. He stands before her. "*Bourrées*. Same feeling. Very simple step, right? But very difficult. Must feel wind at back. Very fast. Never catch up to yourself." The music has started again. She is moving, now running, her *bourrées* are too rushed but he doesn't chide her like Ms. Clement would. "Yes," he says. Then she has forgotten him. She is moving across the floor and over the floor and cannot see him watching; she is just moving and feeling. The music has stopped but she has kept going, her eyelids at half-mast. When she finally stops, breathing hard and looking around, she sees that he is gone and everyone is looking at her, their eyes burning with hatred, and she knows without anyone telling her that she is a Mr. B girl.

After class, she rushes out to the fountain to meet Maurice. He's there, his shimmering white lawn of hair, his black cape. Wearing a top hat, the gentleman from the storybooks—her prince—waiting for her in the lamplights outside by the fountain, like Drosselmeyer in *The Nutcracker*, holding out something to her, this thing, a gift—the nutcracker!—but in this case the gift is his hungry, adoring eyes that alight on her, burn her into being, and now she is here: *a Mr. B girl*.

"He came to our class today. He asked me to demonstrate."

"Ah." He takes her hands in his. "He chose you?"

The one thing in her tilting world, her scattered life, the one who held her to the side of the pool, told her to jump. She'd jumped. She looks at him. "Yes." He smiles.

Back at Maurice's house, in his living room, he has not turned on the overhead light, and the streetlight shines in from outside, illuminating the space in front of the couch like a spotlight. He stares at Mira. He takes a few awkward steps toward her. His face is whiter than ever before.

"Bella," he says. He whispers: "Show me what Mr. B saw." Behind his gold clocks, without his velvet, his chandelier, his exotic fish, his candelabras, he needs her.

She dances on pointe, which is hard on his carpet. She does an extension in *relevé*. She *bourrées* from one end of the room to the other, thinking about what Mr. B said, feeling the same wind at her back, the shivery hot-cold feeling.

When she is finished, she stands panting in the middle of the room. His eyes are shining.

He leans forward. "I see it," he says. "It's a cold wind on a winter's night that cuts the cheek, it's that last breath in the body that does not want to leave, it is earth and sky. I have not seen that before. How did he get that?"

"He told me to walk like a waiter at the Russian Tea Room."

He stares at her, then laughs.

She laughs too. Her laughter sounds strange to her own ears.

"If only my father could see this . . . ," he says. His eyes are half closed.

She moves closer. Then she takes another step toward him. They are nose to nose, about the same size. When did that happen? Did he shrink? Did she grow?

"Can I see it?" She points to his bad leg.

He bends down and shimmies his pants up his leg. The leg is withered, skin over bone held in by the crisscrossing leather straps of a giant metal brace. The skin is like a baby's—raw, pink, unused but dented in furrows where the leather has cut into it.

"A ballerina's leg, it is said, is skin over steel. Mine is steel over skin."

"I want to touch it." She reaches out, feels tenderness—and what she calls that feeling is *love*.

Suddenly, he grabs her hand with one of his. Stops it in midair.

"*You* are beautiful. *This*"—he hits his leg savagely—"is ugly."

He lets go of her arm, bends over, and rolls down his pants.

He is backlit and she can see only his eyes gleam yellow in the glow of the streetlamp. He grips her shoulders. "Who invented the pointe shoe?" he whispers hoarsely.

"Master Taglioni," she says. "He invented it for his daughter." She can smell the sweet-apples and sour-cinnamon smell.

She can see him smile, even in the dimness, his white teeth lined up, rocks on the ledge.

She relaxes. She can play this game. He has told her this story already a few times. It is so important to him. "Premier of *La Sylphide*," she says.

"Paris Opera House in 1832. He whispers in his daughter's ear, 'If you make a noise, I will kill you.'"

"She does it. She dances silently," she says.

"The audience gasps! How?"

"The pointe shoe," she says.

"Yes, and the Romantic ballerina was born."

PEARLS

"Whoa. Are you okay, professor?" Felicia opens the door, an orange feather duster in hand, a novelty item that she holds without any evidence of a joke. She's wearing sweats and a workout shirt.

I can no longer help it, can no longer help anything. I can't hold it in any longer. "Something has happened, Felicia," I say.

She leads me to the living room and sits me down on the couch. There's no sign of Alain now. I take the envelope out and put it on the coffee table.

She sits across from me and lays the duster on the floor.

She looks at me quizzically. I let it all spill out. "He wrote to me. I didn't know if he was alive—didn't want to know . . . I tried to forget. But I couldn't. Then this—" I push the envelope toward her.

"Hold on," she says. She crosses her legs. "Who wrote to you? Please explain."

I take a deep breath. "Someone I knew a long time ago. When we were kids. At SAB. It was so long ago. But—"

"Wait—oh my god—was it that weird guy with the limp? He used to wait for you after class, by the fountain?"

"*What?*"

She laughs. "Oh, Kate. We *all* knew about him. Sometimes we called him 'the creepy guy.' Bryce called you two Beauty and the Beast.

He was a bizarre character." She's smiling now, not at me but with a secret that she's preoccupied with. Something more in my chest drops away, and I'm overcome with tears. The room looks momentarily brighter and bigger. Felicia's pale face glints through this new light. She has no lipstick on today.

"Can I tell you a secret?" I take a deep breath. "It's like this. Imagine if you've lived all these years thinking you were someone, but now you see you were wrong."

"Well, we all have lots of different selves."

"No, not like *that*. It's like—you're still a *child* and everyone else is a *grown-up*."

"But you're a *professor*."

Attempts to describe an inner life, always doomed to fail. She wants to help, I see. I'm struck by the fact that somewhere, against the odds, she's learned kindness. My focus splits and I see both this Felicia, this adult of the mysterious jobs and fluttering hands and crystalline skin, and also *at the same time* the girl whose earnest, pleading eyes and careful ringlets I admired so much until I understood the effort involved in creating them. I remember her mother, the strange quiet of their sequestered life.

But these—I catch myself—are childish thoughts, childish categories of being: good, bad. Smart, stupid. But I can't help it, I can no longer help anything. I am becoming that child again.

It's clear, I am out of the habit of trust. As an adult, my friendships have been practical, mutable, and not lasting. There were some grad student friends, others who were popping pills to stay up all night and show off their cerebral gymnastics. We traded tips on academic journals submissions policies and grants, and then retreated to our studio apartments where we tripped over our decades-long research projects and, in lieu of camaraderie, ferociously updated our blogs. But I was drawn mostly to the troubled or crazy ones who ended up dropping out. The others were competition, and the ambiguous childhood state that allows for friendship with natural enemies had dissolved by then.

Felicia pours me a gin and tonic. A green lime that sparkles in the strange distilled light. I close my eyes. I take a sip of the drink. It's sweet and bitter at the same time. I can taste both flavors. They bloom side by side in my mouth.

When I open my eyes again, I ask her, "Do you believe in fate?"

She looks out her large windows. The sky is brushed white, cloudless, and sullen. From where we sit, you can see just the tops and sides of buildings.

Felicia examines her manicure. "I've wanted lots of things in my life—to be a dancer—a singer—an actor. I've wanted them with what I thought is the strength of desire that would deliver those things. But wanting something doesn't make it real." She says this cleanly, without self-pity. "I never thought I would be—whatever I am."

She stirs her drink, as if she'll unearth something at the bottom. "I don't know what you think you've done wrong, but it can't be that bad. You walked in here with that grim professor face and that chilly voice. But now I see that you're just like the rest of us. You're human. Hu-man. That means—fucked-up."

By the time we finish our drinks, I'm completely exhausted. I tell Felicia I'm heading to sleep early. As I get ready for bed, I try to go over what I learned from Rob. Maurice is alive—probably. Armonk. Westchester. He is—could be—close. So close.

I listen to the water run in the pipes in the walls. Felicia, flushing the toilet, or taking a shower? My face fills with blood at overhearing someone else's habits, this small intimacy,

Maurice's face drifts back to me. I want to smash it, to pulverize it, this face that has stayed with me. He is, apparently, still alive and has kept changing. This is perhaps what I am most angry about: that he has gone on changing.

As I am climbing in bed, I see there's a new voice mail on my cell. It's from this afternoon, and it's Sioban, who I gave my number to, in a moment of stupidity (or, possibly, compassion, it's hard to know which). I listen with trepidation. Her voice is low, and soft. There is none of the anger from the last time I saw her. It's hard to make out what she's saying—her voice is garbled and there are long pauses between her words—but I catch "can't stop thinking about you," "please call," "I'm scared," and, finally, "I'm sorry." The "I'm sorry" sends a cold shiver through me. Then the line goes dead. I turn it off. Anger I can handle, but sadness really scares me.

About a month into the semester, Felicia invites Mira over for a sleepover. On Friday after class, she, Felicia, and Felicia's mother, Rita, take the F train to Queens. Felicia lives in one of a row of tightly packed brick bungalows. Inside the apartment, everything is very puffy. The couch is puffy. The curtains are puffy. A white shag carpet covers the floors. In the kitchen is a chart on the wall, and next to it a stack of stickers with gold stars and smiley faces. In Felicia's bedroom, the carpet is pink. There is a bed in her room covered with a puffy bedspread and canopy. In her room are also laminated placards taped to the wall that read: *BREATHE! PROJECT! SMILE!*

The girls sit on Felicia's bed. Her friend turns to her. "I can't believe you're a Mr. B girl now. It's so amazing. I have one of Mr. B's girls in my home right now. You are *so* lucky, Mira."

"I'm sure he'll choose you next."

"Really?"

"I *know* so." Mira didn't, in fact, know anything of the sort. But it felt good to say it, to have this moment of intimacy, of sharing something—purely, simply—with another girl.

"I want to give you something." Felicia gets up and places a jewelry box between them on the bed. She opens it for Mira to examine. "Take anything. Anything you want."

Mira touches the things inside one by one: a macramé friendship bracelet; a feather brooch with half the feather broken off and exposed, its stem ragged; a diamond necklace that talks. It says, *I am a beautiful princess!* A haphazard, slightly grimy collection, a typical girl's.

At the very bottom is a pearl necklace and pearl earrings. They are very white and round and shiny. Mira pulls these out, holds them up to her neck. "What do you think?"

"They're real. Bite them. That's how you can tell."

Mira looks at her friend, quickly bites the round balls, and pushes them down to the bottom of her pocket.

Then Felicia is at the closet, pushing one of the wood-paneled doors back and pulling out a dented shoe box. She motions Mira over to where she squats. Felicia takes the lid off the shoe box to reveal an assortment of candy bars. They have soft, worn, creased wrappers, as if they've been handled too many times. Mira and Felicia huddle in the dark corner and finger them.

"Where's your dad?" says Mira.

"He lives on Long Island. He owns a store, so he can't come very often. But it's okay. My mom and I are like a team. We understand each other. My dad doesn't really get it."

"My mom's in California," Mira says.

"Do you miss her?"

"No," says Mira.

Rita serves dinner on a table set with glazed black-and-white ceramic plates and black-and-white zebra-striped napkins. Loud bangs of metal utensils on ceramic. On their plates, Rita piles some kind of grain and then carrots in a thin, oily sauce.

"Am I on a diet again?" asks Felicia.

"Felicia's frame, unfortunately, she gets from her father," says Rita. She looks at Mira. "*You* have a thin frame."

Mira blushes. A cozy, puffy world, just the three of them. What would that be like? Rita's red lips glisten with canola oil. She looks at Felicia as if to say "I told you so."

After dinner, Rita takes just Mira into her bedroom, where she does Mira's hair in pigtail ringlets like Felicia's, with the brush attachment to a hot curling iron, something Mira has never seen before. While she works, she tells Mira to close her eyes. But Rita is not happy with the results of her efforts and has to start all over: she brushes the curls out of Mira's hair, then braids it into two very tight French braids. Now Rita is satisfied with the results.

Then Rita takes out a giant makeup kit that opens accordion-like into different levels, like a house with many rooms. She puts rouge on Mira's cheeks and green eye shadow over her eyes. Rita applies the makeup with firm, confident strokes. Mira feels a pleasant, animallike warmth come over her. When Rita finishes, Mira looks at herself in the mirror. She looks feline—a thin face and big staring eyes.

"Do you think I could be in a commercial?"

Rita nods, smiles. "With your red hair and freckles? Of *course* you could!"

Rita puts her hand on Mira's back and leads her into the living room, where Felicia is watching TV. Felicia squeals when she sees Mira.

"Mom, do me, do me!" Felicia says. Rita laughs. Then she takes Felicia into the bedroom and does her hair and makeup too: pink cheeks and blue, instead of green, over her eyes.

The three of them drive to a giant supermarket. Inside, people turn to stare—two made-up girls, and Rita. Mira imagines that they are both Rita's children, both going to be stars. What would that be like, rushing around from audition to audition, always ready to go to a casting call, always beautiful with big eyes? She feels how the makeup makes her stronger. How the world turns a brighter face back to her. People smile at her. She smiles back. She is part of something. She is initiated—how strange, to make oneself stick out and then to feel that you belong. She sees that, too. It's a raw kind of joy that rises from her collarbones into a blush.

They walk back to the car across the giant parking lot, carrying things they don't need, in a light, cold rain, talking loudly. It smells like steel and fish, the inside of a star.

*Later, when she is on the verge of falling asleep under that wood-*tiled ceiling in Felicia's puffy room, she feels a sharp pang, and as obliterating darkness falls, she doesn't think of her father or of her mother—but of Maurice. Maurice in his green and gold living room, Maurice in his maroon car with his special box of a seat and special levers; Maurice showing her the poor *Little Dancer* statue, blackened with age, her tired face turned up to a hopeful sun. Mira shivers with a new kind of guilt, with the knowledge that she has somehow betrayed someone—or something.

———————

The next afternoon after classes, Maurice is waiting by the Lincoln Center fountain. Mira walks up to him. He stares at her. Her eye shadow and eyeliner got smudged, so she tried to replicate what Rita did with some drugstore supplies.

He turns from her and walks his marionette walk up Broadway. For a moment, she considers not following him. It would be easy not to, to just get on the crosstown bus, head to her dad and Judy's apartment. But who would she be then? Just a girl, one girl among many, without a mother, with a father who, she now knows, dries his underwear on the backs of kitchen chairs, and whose aftershave smells too strongly of peppermint, a father who she knows can hit her.

The crowd begins to swallow up Maurice's diminishing form. She runs to catch up with him. When she reaches his side, he does not turn. He keeps going, shoving the gum wrappers aside with his walking stick.

He hails a cab and she climbs in beside him. "Where are we going?"

At first, he doesn't answer. Then he says, "Home."

When they pull up in front of his building, he turns to her. "Get out."

In his apartment, he pulls her into the bathroom. He thrusts her towards the sink, grabs soap, and rubs it over her face. She starts coughing. He turns on the water and pushes her face under it. It's too hot. She screams. He turns on the cold. Now he throws that on her face—she's sputtering.

"That hurts," she says.

"Who put that on your face?" he says.

"Rita did it."

"Who's Rita?"

"Felicia's mom."

"This is not what a *dancer* wants. This is what a *whore* wants."

"It looks special."

He doesn't seem to hear her. He grips her harder. "This is beauty you can buy for ten dollars, twenty dollars. No one can give you the beauty ballet gives you."

"Stop," she says again.

He grabs her by the shoulders again. Then he yanks the string of pearls from around her neck and pulls hard. "These are fake." They snap and spill all over the floor. They roll around in the hallway outside the bathroom and clink on the tile in the bathroom like pebbles against a window.

In the living room, he takes down a photo in a silver frame from a shelf. She's never noticed it before. It's a black-and-white photo of a large-bellied man in shirt and tie and funny, balloon-like pants. Through his pince-nez glasses, he stares out at the camera. His eyes are far apart, giving him a broad, fierce look. He holds the photo right up to her face. "*This* is the photo I've really wanted to show you. This is—was—my father. My mother always blamed ballet. And my father. For the polio. You know why?"

She shakes her head.

"Because I got sick right after seeing my first live ballet performance." He leans in toward her. "I think she was just jealous because she didn't come with us. He only had two tickets and he took *me*.

"It was 1947. I was eleven. My father was home from one of his maritime adventures. And he had managed to get tickets to see Toumanova dance at the Paris Opera. Dancers were coming back from all over. Balanchine was in France again. Toumanova! Toumanova— she was no longer so young, it didn't matter. We loved her anyway. The baby Russians were now grown up. We'd seen them before the war as girls—now they were women. We loved them, too. And there were new ones. Ulanova. We could only hear stories of her. It wasn't for ten more years that we would see her. Still, she was all the rage.

"My father took me even though there was a polio outbreak in Europe then. People were sleeping on roofs, avoiding public places. But Toumanova was dancing, so my father was going. And he took me." Now he is grinning at her, his eyes are moist and soft.

"About half of my father's comrades from the Balletomane Society were there, though they sat far apart. Some of them wore face masks to protect themselves. Not my father, though. And not me. I remember you could hear sounds reverberating off the empty boxes.

"I don't know why my mother let me go. She was very protective of me. I was not allowed to swim in public pools, for instance." He gets up and hobbles to a shelf and pulls off a little tin box, brings it over. He opens it to show some ash. "But, at intermission, Father gave me a cigar at the café. The only cigar I ever smoked. He said to me, 'Son, you may never go to war. The only other thing that teaches the same is ballet. When I watch the dancers, I see my fallen comrades. I see blood and bullets. I get the same feeling as right before a battle. That weird quiet—like angels passing. *Someone will die in a few minutes,* I would think. I never thought it would be me. Isn't that strange?'

"As we traveled home through the wet, cold streets, all I could think of was Toumanova as she did her port de bras and arabesques. She was so brave and clever, so beautiful! My mother had me soak in peroxide, put me to bed, and gave me onion soup for a week. But it didn't matter. At the end of the week, I got sick."

There is something new and self-mocking about his smile. "My father disappeared after that. He couldn't deal with me, an invalid son."

Mira has begun to tremble. Her face is sore.

"Well, that is all in the past. But you see—I cannot escape your Mr. Balanchine—it was he who choreographed the piece for Toumanova I saw that night, *Palais de Cristal*." He looks at her. His face clouds over again. Now he looks strange, sad. "I am a pale shadow of him. I am a shadow of my father."

Mira is standing right in front of him. They are so close. She can smell him. His pale face hovers before her. "No, you're not." She looks down, then up again. "You're not—a shadow."

She reaches up and kisses him. His lips are dry. He does not stop her. Later on, she will wonder if she imagined it, but at the time she knows it is true: he responds. His lips move.

He pulls away and wipes his mouth, looks up at the ceiling. In a different voice, he says, "The wise child." Who is he speaking to? He is speaking to the ceiling? Then she knows—*his father*.

"I don't regret it," he says as she draws back, the strange feel of his dusty mouth on hers. "He only had two tickets. But, at intermission, Father gave me a cigar at the café. The only cigar I ever smoked. *I* got to go with him."

They stand in the room, not talking, just breathing. What has happened? Something has changed, some line crossed. But he is quiet now. He seems calmer.

He waves his hand and smiles his little stones-on-a-ledge smile. "Do you still have that swan I gave you?" Afraid to speak, she nods. The heavy glass thing lolls about on her bedside table—it once got chewing gum on it, which left a sticky residue. It sits next to her other trophies: a fully-autographed SAB company catalog, Maurice's calling card.

"Good," he says. He pulls her, now more gently, through the kitchen—a clean, yellow-tiled room that smells of old oranges—into a back room that smells of the perfumed flowers she noticed when she first came into the apartment. He flicks on the lights. A bed with a white crocheted cover, a tightly shorn wool rug of jade green, and Chinese porcelain lamps on the two bedside tables, also painted with delicate flowers: the room of a lady who worked at being a lady. He flings open a mahogany box on one of the bedside tables and pulls out a string of beads. He holds them in his papery hands, an offering.

She stares at them. He shoves the string of pearls into her hand, closes her hand. "These pearls were my mother's." He sits on the bed. It groans. "They're real. They're for you."

"They're yellow."

He laughs. "Each one was once a grain of sand. The oyster grinds the sand, grinds and grinds. The fake ones are white. Your Mr. B understands that." He looks toward the window.

"Don't worry," she says, clasping the pearls hard in her fist. "It'll be okay."

He looks at her hopefully, then down again. Then more pointedly. "Really, Bella. Will it?"

Outside there are sounds: people whistle for cabs, ladies' heels click on the pavement, horns blare then fade.

Lying in bed that night, she thinks about what has happened with Maurice. There are no words for it. Something has happened between them that can never be forgotten. She gets up and looks out her window. A tall woman in a long white coat walks her dog. The trees along the sidewalk rustle in the breeze. She stares outside for a long time.

I wake, cloudy headed, to a sweet, pungent odor. Someone has put some flowers at my bedside—lilies, harbingers of spring—mixed in with baby's breath. Indeed Felicia has learned kindness. How to thank her?

I let the layers of consciousness come to me: they press on me— one by one: it's Friday, the end of a work week. I need to be back by next Wednesday, so I have to make this day count. Sioban's voice on my phone last night, austere in her sadness. I listen to her message again, noticing the way she stops and pauses between her words. The pauses make it seem like she's creating—or at least managing— her emotional output. *She lives her life as if she's onstage.* I will need to respond today, but what can I say? What can I possibly say?

I'm out of the apartment by ten thirty. There's no sign of Felicia. I leave her a hastily scrawled note on a notepad in her kitchen. It has silver bells in the corner and Latinate lettering across the top. I rip off the sheet of paper, and write *Thanks for the flowers,* underlining *thanks.* Then add a fragment—*beautiful.* I leave the note on her immaculate kitchen counter, and tuck the pad into my purse. Leaving my backpack, I grab my coat and rush out, closing the door softly behind me.

Outside, it's still unseasonably warm. The sky the same blinding white, the breeze as balmy as yesterday afternoon. A spooky gentleness to the air. Like after a catastrophe. I duck into a diner on Ninth Avenue and order a giant breakfast of eggs, toast, home fries, and coffee. I eat the whole thing, even the pile of blackened home fries. I sip my coffee, wait for the check. The bill arrives, I pay up.

I'm going back to Lincoln Center. It's my only option. Rob told me that Maurice gave money to SAB. He was giving me a clue. Maybe he wants me to find something? As I retrace my steps from yesterday, I try to order my thoughts. Rob also told me that there was a young man, someone who Maurice introduced as his son, who was a lawyer. I just want to know if Maurice is living or dead and if he sent that letter or not. I am here for information and information only, I remind myself. The past, while critical, is also just incidental.

If he wrote it but did not send it, that would be one thing. If he wrote it and sent it, that would be more worrisome. He would then want something from me. But what can he want? I gave him everything a long time ago. What I have managed to salvage for myself—my career, my students, my ideas—suddenly seem like nothing more than crumbs. It seems on this trip all roads lead back to Lincoln Center, that citadel of my childhood. Is it guarded as fiercely now as it was then? Will they give me a donor's contact info? I know some institutions are on a more secretive relationship than others when it comes to the source of their funding.

I need a plan, I think as I walk across Columbus Circle and turn up Broadway.

The SAB studios are on the fifth floor of the new Juilliard building, a spacious glass and steel building just to the north of the plaza. I take the skybridge, cross the gray stone plaza, and join a group entering the lobby. The lobby, long and narrow, of a golden tomblike marble, is divided by a line of turnstiles. Against the back wall, a line of security guards sits behind what look like old-fashioned bank teller windows. The group ahead of me files through the turnstiles and heads to the security guard windows. They are being asked to show their IDs. To the left of us, through a little gate, passes a steady stream of long-necked girls with their hair coiled up on their heads—

ballet girls. We inch forward toward the guards. I watch the river of girls flow through.

Now it's my turn. I slide my ID under the grate and tell the tired-looking guard that I am here to pick up my daughter. "Where's your family pass?" she says without looking up. She's making notes. "I'm sorry, I left it at home," I say. "Shoot. But if I go back and get it, I'll miss her. She's waiting for me." My heart is pounding. The guard raises her eyes and gives me her full attention, then nods. "Don't forget it next time." I thank her and follow the bunheads to the elevators before anyone can stop me.

When I get off the elevator, I'm overwhelmed by the diffuse light and by the minimalist, corporate chic of the decor. The entrance to the school is filled with a white marble boat of a desk flanked by bronze busts of Balanchine and Kirstein. Gone are the glass doors to the School of American Ballet of my era. Gone are the architectural prints on the walls. Gone are the studious faces of musicians you would pass in the hallways outside the dance studios.

Then the busts of Balanchine and Kirstein pull me back in. They watch me warily, like heads of Cerberus. *I must know the password. I have forgotten the password.*

Just being here makes my palms sweat. I rub them on my pants. An odd, dizzy feeling—of unreality—moves to my knees. I am blinking too much.

I approach the desk. I smile.

"What can I do for you?" says the woman behind the desk. She is a thin and heavily lipsticked woman of indeterminate age. She has an air of intense politeness that promises nothing. My eyes snap into focus. Desperation makes me bold.

"I'm here because of my . . . daughter," I say. "I'm visiting from Ohio and . . . well, it's her dream, really. To study here."

She gives me a professional smile. "Our Web site has everything," she says. "We really don't accept general queries like this. We do offer occasional tours. They should have stopped you downstairs. . . ."

"Oh, I am sorry," I say. "Yes, they were kind enough to let me upstairs. I'm just in town for a few days—"

A small smile appears on the gatekeeper's mouth. "Oh, heck," she says. "How old is she?"

"She's eight."

"We start at six."

"Oh! How does it work?" A woman wearing ponderous shoes and a thick utility belt—a security guard?—has appeared behind me, by the elevators. I'd better hurry. Into my mind springs an image of the girl I've been speaking of—this pretend child—a girl with dark hair and sparkling eyes, braids with ribbons in her hair. Cute, energetic, boyish. No hips, high instep, long flexible legs that shoot up and take a long time coming down. She would—I judge the apparition through the receptionist's eyes—get in.

The gatekeeper goes back to paper clipping what appear to be letters. "Well, as you must know, we are extremely selective. Admission to any of our courses is only by audition. There are separate auditions for winter term and summer course. Students may audition specifically for winter term in September. Auditions for summer course are held in April and May."

I slow my breathing, wipe my palms on my skirt again. "I know that *many, many* girls want to come here."

The receptionist puts aside the stack of papers and takes off her glasses. She leans forward, as if to tell me a secret. I bend over the partition to catch whatever she will tell me.

"We accept only one in a hundred." A smile cracks open her face. She's older than she first appeared, this gatekeeper. "But perhaps your daughter is that one in a hundred?"

At that moment I see something. Her ramrod-straight posture, her tight smile, her too-red lipstick, her overly sinewed neck and big-knuckled, short-nailed hands, which she articulates with unusual care; she's a former dancer. Of course. A bunhead! They live on after their dance careers are over.

I nod. A phalanx of chattering girls enters. Their bodies are just on the cusp of change—long legs and tiny torsos filling out ever so slightly. They look about the same age I was when I started coming here. Bunheads here haven't changed much. They still wear buns high on their heads, they walk like ducks, carry themselves like little queens—with a grim regalness that still startles.

A woman with a short, stylish haircut stops at the desk. I step back to make room for her.

"Excuse me, Ms. Harrington," she says to the gatekeeper. "We'll have our form in on Monday." A genteel southern accent. So the mothers still come with their girls, making the pilgrimage, setting up house close to the citadel of beauty, biding their time, training their sights. *Where are the fathers in all of this?* Hasn't that changed either?

Harrington? This might be the bit of luck I need. When the hubbub passes, I lean over the counter. The security guard stalks the lobby behind me. "Please. I'm sorry." I lean farther in and whisper, "Can I tell you something? I used to dance here. I was a student here, back in the day, you know? Oh, of course it was ages ago. But you know you never forget being a student here."

My eyes are still blinking too rapidly. The gatekeeper puts on her glasses and looks at me, this time taking me in in a different way. Finally, she whispers back, "What years?"

"Umm . . . 1978 to 1981."

"Wait, I was here then too."

"Are you—*Bryce* Harrington?"

"Yes," she says. "And you?"

"I'm . . . I was . . . Mira Able."

"Mira Able?" She pulls off her glasses and tosses them on the desk with a clatter. She stands. "What the hell?" I recognize the flashing eyes, the quick, stabbing words of my old classmate. "What the hell happened to you? You just left and . . . after that day. Everyone was talking about it. You just disappeared. No one could find you. I always thought you'd call me, or write me, or something, you know." She leans back on her heels and crosses her arms. "We were friends, right?"

I'm on the other side of something now. My breath comes more regularly. This *is* a stroke of luck. I smile a genuine smile. "We were enemies."

Bryce smiles big and wide. "We were *frenemies*!" Her eyes sparkle. I can see a cap on her front tooth.

"Yes, we were!" I say. "We were the best in the class!"

With Bryce's glasses off, her eyes look smaller, her face softer. She's speaking loudly now as another group, this one older, slides by us, with curious stares. "Remember how Tumkovsky would yell—'Catch your breasts! Catch your breasts!' And how Danilova would"—she begins to warble like her—"'not so fast. You do not take train, take stagecoach, take horse.'"

A girl runs up to Bryce and says, "I have a new maker. My feet are much better!"

"Who is it?" Bryce says.

"It's Castle Maker!"

"That's great, hon," Bryce says. "They say he's excellent for narrow feet."

As the girl runs off down the hallway, I say, "Her *maker*?" In our day, only professionals had makers. Individual makers of pointe shoes—craftsmen who still handcraft pointe shoes.

Bryce says to me, "They all have their own makers now. They even have a Web site for the makers, so the girls can 'meet' them."

"Wow, even at their age?"

"Yep."

"With *pictures* of their makers?"

"Yep."

Through this barrage of words and images from my past, through my rapid blinks and sweaty palms, I bring myself back. I refocus: I have to. I am here for one reason only. *Who sent the letter? Is he alive?* "Yes," I say. "We were *totally* frenemies. But . . ." I pause. "Listen, Bryce." I lower my voice. "We really need to catch up, but I'm here for a specific reason today and . . . I need your help."

"My help?"

I take a deep breath. *Don't think. Do.* "I need to find out about a donor to SAB."

"Who?"

"Someone who I knew a long time ago."

She stares at me. Her mouth purses. "That creepy guy?"

I laugh. "Beauty and the Beast," I say. "Felicia told me."

"Felicia?" She wipes her mouth with the back of her veined hand. "What is she doing now?"

"She's—ah, between things."

She nods. "Yes," she says. "It's our age." She waves her arms at something invisible. "But what're you, like a private eye?"

"Actually, I'm a dance historian. But this is something—extracurricular," I say. "Apparently, he donated a lot to SAB over the years. I'm trying to find out—if he is still alive. I thought, well, you might have access to that information." I pause. "It's important."

Bryce shakes her head and grins. She places a hand on my shoulder. She is all verve and no-consequence now. She asks a woman walking by with a blinking Bluetooth to watch the desk and leads me down several long hallways. She waves to people as we pass. She lowers her voice. "It's been much too tame around here. It's like a factory now—everything is a factory now. But I love good gossip, and I can smell some here." She is full of a brisk, youthful energy. Bryce pulls me into an office, and shuts the door.

It's a small room with a few empty workstations. Bryce leads me to one, and says, "I have access to the donor database. I have even managed it. . . ." I hear the old pride in her voice. She jiggles a mouse on the keyboard and a monitor lights up.

I look over Bryce's shoulder. I can smell her soap—lavender?—and something bitter and straw-like, coffee or loofah. I remember her in a sweat-drenched leotard. We never smelled then, I don't think. Our sweat was pure, stainless, the sweat of angels, of demons.

"I want to hear the backstory sometime. Okay, Sherlock?"

He took my childhood. He stole from me what was most precious. He gave me a gift I could not keep.

"Deal," I say.

"Now give me the name."

"Maurice. Maurice Dupont."

She bangs away at the keyboard.

"Yes, here it is. Right here."

Blinking on the screen is his name.

"Every year he gave in the thousand-dollar range, starting in 1980. Twenty thousand dollars in all. Considerable. Not Inner Circle. But solid Dress Circle."

I look at her.

"Those are our names for it." She squints at the screen. "But then, he stopped about ten years ago. Nothing."

"From Dress Circle to nothing?"

"Wait! But then, a year ago, he gave a million dollars!"

"A million? That's Inner Circle, right?"

"Sure is."

"Is there anything else?"

"There's a name, the name of a lawyer, Kevin Fox, and an address on Park Avenue." Now it's my turn to squint at the screen. I pull out Felicia's pad—the one with Latinate lettering at the top—and scribble down the name and address. I notice, for some reason it's clear now, that the lettering reads *CARPE DIEM*.

In early November, Mira stands in front of the hallway bulletin board. Her eyes rest on a single sheet of white paper, the typed cast list for *The Nutcracker*. At first, she doesn't see her name anywhere on the list. Her heart beats too fast. Then she sees, yes, it is there.

Party Scene
Angels
Hot Chocolate
Candy Canes
Polichinelles
Hoop Girls

At the very bottom, *Marie*. And next to *Marie*—Mira Able! When she tells Maurice, his glittering smile falls into place, like it was he who had gotten the part. He says, "Of course."

She doesn't see Mr. B again until a Friday afternoon Nutcracker *re-*hearsal. Mr. B is there, wearing a cowboy shirt and a string tie. His turtle face looks handsome. He's whispering with the New York City Ballet children's ballet master, who is scarier to her than anyone. He's legendary for his yelling and berating, his blow-dried hair. When they put the Nutcracker doll in her hand, it's lighter than she could have imagined, and she pantomimes the steps she knows by heart now. As she cradles the doll, gazing at its big Easter Island face, she imagines Maurice. She imagines dancing for Maurice, the silence and the splendor of that.

Mr. B walks forward, stops the pianist. "I know this one," he says. Then he's beside her, playing Drosselmeyer. He swings a pretend cape, takes out the doll, offers it to her. He smells of straw and coffee. "This Marie," he says, "has the energy of my Tanny."

Tanny, he called her Tanny! the girls in the dressing room will whisper with envy. Tanny—short for Tanaquil—Mr. B's fifth wife. An exceedingly beautiful girl with an incredible extension, tragically crippled by polio in the prime of her career. Mr. B nursed her for years. The other girls' whispers will be loud with envy and hate, but they are also far away and can't reach her.

Mira's fame is growing at SAB. First a girl who Tumkovsky is mean to, then a Mr. B girl—and now a Marie. There are lots of girls Tumkovksy is mean to, a handful of Mr. B girls, but a finite number of Maries. Only one a year.

The other girls, and their imperfections, fade away as Mira runs ahead on a stream of energy and light. Her body tells her what to do and she just goes along with it. The steps are second nature. Her body turns, folds, extends, all on its own. It's a song in her body. The high notes are sometimes so high and long that she is left wide-eyed in amazement along with everyone else. Something great is growing in her, unrolling its tendrils, sprouting buds in all directions. Sometimes the song in her body is almost too loud; it fills her eyes, makes them tear up in something like gratitude.

Mira misses a total of two weeks of school for her Nutcracker *per-*formances. In the party scene, Marie and her brother, Fritz, chase each other underneath hors d'oeuvres serving trays. Apart from the Sugar Plum Fairy in Act Two, they get the loudest applause. The music is spongy and bright and they bounce like bubbles in it. Then comes her favorite part. With a drumroll, Drosselmeyer appears, swishing his black cape, smelling of dusty oranges. Mr. B himself used to play Drosselmeyer, they all know that and still, his presence is there, in the cape, in the mask, in the staff. When she is offered the nutcracker, she grabs the doll and twirls, arms outstretched, showing off their secret—the great urn of a toy that steals the show. The cymbals crash and the drums pound, and the audience erupts. A thunder of clapping breaks in her ears.

Her dad and Judy come to see her every weekend. Judy brings a client to each performance and takes them backstage to meet her. Her mother flies in to see her, too, without anyone else, and wears a loose flowered dress. Maurice is there for every single performance—he doesn't come backstage to see her, but he often sends flowers, and while she is surrounded by her dumb broken family, she senses him lurking, waiting just around each corner, behind some stage door. (Though when she peeks, she never sees him.) Then, he is there, waiting for her by the fountain at their time. He drinks her in and drinks in her success, and everything falls into place. He is with her, even when he is not.

Throughout the spring of 1979, Mira performs more than any other girl in her division. She is chosen for the premiere of *Le Bourgeois Gentilhomme* with the great Rudolph Nureyev and Patricia McBride. Because she's an SAB girl, one of Mr. B's, she's valuable outside the company, too. She appears in children's roles with the Maurice Béjart and Maya Plisetskaya companies when they are in town on their American tours.

And the needle on the scale doesn't budge for her, even as for others it swings upward. It seems she will never get bigger.

In April, Mira turns thirteen! Maurice takes her to an Afghan restaurant where the people are dressed colorfully and blankets are on the walls. She smiles so much her face hurts. Other girls have boyfriends who go around with shoes untied and braces with egg in them, but she has Maurice. She is the luckiest girl in the world.

The school year ends. Classes end. Summer comes. Mira's invited to go to Saratoga with the entire NYC Ballet company for SAB's elite summer session. One day that summer, Heather Watts turns to her in the hallway and says, "You're Mira, right? I know he likes you."

Her mother invites her out to San Francisco to stay with her in her new group house, but Mira doesn't go. She's working too hard, there's too much at stake, and her mother wouldn't understand that.

One night before classes end for the summer, Judy comes into Mira's room and sits on her bed. She spreads a magazine across her lap. The front cover shows a gaunt-looking girl staring at the camera. The headline reads: Anorexia: The Epidemic Sweeping Our Nation. Judy is looking at her through squinted eyes, as she always does when she seizes on something she thinks is important.

"Of course, I had heard of anorexia nervosa, but I didn't know the depths of it, the severity of it . . . I mean the possible severity of it." She taps the magazine cover. "I mean, there is a girl in the hospital now, a ballet dancer, who refuses to eat though she is dying. She's at death's door and was caught jogging by her bed. She has to be restrained so that she would not burn off the meager amount of food that she does consume. It's just . . . horrible!"

Mira says nothing. She wants to laugh. When she hears grown-ups talk about anorexia and bulimia, she has a curious detachment. How misplaced their worry always is! Her secret will always be safe because grown-ups look in the wrong places.

"Now, Mira, I want you to tell me if you recognize any of these symptoms in yourself or in others you know: reluctance to eat, creating rituals around food, severe hunger pains, distorted body image, a feeling of dislocation—that means, I don't know what it means."

"I know girls who are anorexic, Judy," Mira says. "And believe me, I am not one of them. These girls are so skinny they are disgusting. They can't even dance."

Judy stares at her through wide eyes, perhaps hearing a tone she hasn't heard before in Mira's voice. But Mira knows Judy can't say anything really because she herself is so invested in Mira as a dancer. She always loves to show Mira off to her friends at dinner parties.

She finds out that Felicia was not invited to return to SAB. Felicia's stomach has begun to stick out more and more—Mira thinks of the candy bars in the closet, shorn of their skins.

They sit on Felicia's bed in her puffy room. "What will you do?" says Mira. "Are you going to another studio?"

Felicia slides her eyes away, then looks right at her. "My mom and I are moving to L.A. to try our luck in Hollywood."

In the fall, Mira is moved up another level at SAB. She's in B2 now. She still wears a midnight blue leotard, she begins partnering. For Variations, she has the famous Danilova, who is teaching her the first scene of *La Sylphide,* the girl who enters a window at night to a sleeping house, a sprite come to visit the earthbound. *Bourrée, bourrée, bourrée,* head cocked, listen. *Bourrée, bourrée,* listen.

Mira switches to the Professional Children's School, where students with her talent and schedule go. She loves it there. There are others like her there. There are a number of other SAB girls. And many actors, who leave in the middle of class for auditions. She sits next to kids she has seen on TV. They talk a lot in class and have holes in their jeans, which makes them different from the bunheads like her. Like the other dancers, she dresses neatly and doesn't talk much in class, but always does her homework. The teachers are very nice and even try to be friends with the kids, because it is the kids' lives that are the most important thing. They are what everything else must be arranged around. Some of these teachers even come see her perform and say things outside of class that they shouldn't, about how great she is, how much better than anyone else.

In November, Nutcracker *time comes again and she's chosen for the* Head Angel, which is a very good part. She wears a golden tiara and leads the other girls into tapestries of shiny gold shapes. Again, her mother comes into town, and her dad and Judy come every weekend with friends and clients, and even Sam comes twice with a new friend named Oliver.

There's talk of her being chosen for a workshop performance next year. They pick only a few girls. Mainly C level. Then she could be offered a company apprenticeship. In two years, she could even be in *Swan Lake,* dancing in the corps, onstage with her idols. Maybe then she'd be down to a high school correspondence course. But who would care about that if she were sixteen and dancing with New York City Ballet?

*Her mother has been calling her regularly. She comes to visit in Jan-*uary and suggests that they go to places she *never* would have before—museums and even a Broadway show. She invites Mira out to San Francisco for a few weeks in the summer. She's in another group house. She tries to make it sound fun—*dance classes nearby*! Mira has to explain that there are no classes like SAB classes, and if she's chosen again to go up to Saratoga for summer session, she'll have to go, since this is her chance to show she's company material. But maybe, she adds, crinkling her eyes the way Judy does, she could spare a week at the very end of August? Her mother gets red between her freckles and says, "Your room will be there for whenever you want to come." Then, as if to reassure herself more than Mira, "I've got a good job now. It pays the bills." Her mother looks so proud of herself, which makes Mira feel both happy and sad. Mira doesn't know what to do with her face, so she smiles and says, "That's great, Mom!"

Soon after, she dreams that she stands in the dark, watching Maurice sleep. She feels strong, brave, and beautiful. Then he rises from his sleeping position—but it is like he is still asleep—and his hair has grown so that it is long and silver-white, down his back all the way to the floor, hanging like a veil. And then he takes out a wand—yes, she knows, it's cheesy—and he hands her an apple to eat. It is shiny and red and looks delicious, but there is a wormhole in it and she can't take her eyes off of it and the longer she looks at it, the bigger and rounder it grows until she feels like she is looking into a dark tunnel to the center of the earth. And then she hears Maurice's voice—but it is changed, like a woman's voice, like her mother's voice from a long time ago. (She used to tell those stories, really long involved stories.) "Who are you?" she says, but the woman doesn't respond. She just looks at Mira and smiles. And she doesn't know what to say. Then she realizes that she has no shoes on and her feet are bare and there are leaves under them that crunch when she walks. It is like walking on old brittle bones. And then she has this amazing feeling of power move though her. It feels like she is being lifted up off the ground, like she is floating out of her body, and it feels so good. Then the lady with the veil is gone and the hole to the center of the earth is gone and it is Maurice again.

She knows what the dream is about, she knows what she has to do: it is a sign telling her to do what she has wanted to do since she turned thirteen and knew about the birds and the bees. She wants to have him touch her, to touch her in a way he never has before, with warm hands. She wants him to whisper in her ear "I love you, Mira."

Walking home from the bus, Mira passes the bar Dorrian's, that famed outpost of debauchery, where Sam and his friends have started to gather. Even early in the evening, it's going full swing. She purposefully crosses to the other side of the street, evading the bar's overflow onto the sidewalk. She and her sister SAB bunheads don't talk about boys, sex, clothes, hair, drinking—the courtship rituals that occupy most girls' time. As a bunhead, she is exempt—barred?—from all that. For one thing, there isn't even time. They have Technique twice a day—morning and evening. In the early afternoon they have Variations or Partnering. Then all day Saturday they are in class, with a break for Music Theory. As her life has turned to maintaining an elite routine, the routine and focus of a professional athlete, her nighttime dreams have exploded into strangeness and mystery. Sometimes, as she goes through her day, she has the sense of being a sleepwalker. But her dreams are wild and vivid. Only when she is dancing does she feel as alive as she does when she is dreaming.

At SAB, she'll soon be in Level C, the Advanced division. There's no doubt. For Variations, Danilova is now teaching her a sequence from *Coppelia*. Ms. Tumkovsky continues to be mean to her, and now she shines under this meanness because it shows she is good; she is a Mr. B girl. For Variations, they wear white leotards, so thin they look see-through. No elastics, no leg warmers, no warm-up pants allowed. It's as if their bodies, now edging toward complete, are owned by SAB, as if the results of all their efforts are to become less substantial—ghosts, rays of light, permeable. On some girls, you can see small breasts sprouting and hips spreading. These girls are placed in the back rows, off to the side, at the end of the line. A lot of the girls complain about the see-through leotards, but she likes them. Her body is small and strong, her legs fly on their own, she turns and turns in her spot, whipping her head around to her internal song. She hears the song all the time now. She has become a body in space that can read Danilova's, and Tumkovsky's, and most of all Mr. B's mind. When he calmly walks into the room and his eyes rest on her, she knows without him speaking what he wants. There is no need for words anymore.

At one point she finds herself onstage with Merrill Ashley, whose eyes are as big and bright as ancient coins. She is so close she can smell the sweat on Merrill's skin and watch the ribbons of muscle in her back quiver as she arabesques.

There's no longer any need to tell Maurice what she's learning— she simply shows him, dancing longer and longer in his parlor room, into the night in her private display for him. Sometimes she does a whole class for him. He watches, eyes glistening. Their dinners grow shorter, then nonexistent. They come to his place, eat cookies and guzzle Coke, and she dances, the sweat light on her skin. She's never felt more beautiful.

She loves him. She does. Their relationship is special. She could never have it with a boy her age. She loves his fine delicate fingers, his pale skin withered like a faint crust over milk that moves with her hand when she touches it. She loves his hair smelling of something strong and stern, she loves his bony back with the shoulder blades like wings and the fine sinewy forearms and the bent leg. She loves the stone on his finger, blue in a gold setting. Most of all she loves his bones, his joints, the places where they come together—he is an animated skeleton. She sees his young face in his older face, so that she thinks he looks younger than people her own age. What she sees is raw desire—and love.

The spring of 1980 comes, cold and wet. The rain gutters overflow. Discarded umbrellas lie in heaps against garbage cans. The hallways of SAB smell of ragg wool and rubber, but aside from that, the school is immune to the weather—to everything outside. Like a humidor, it's kept on the cool side so that sweat dries easily, but not too cool to get in the way of a good warming-up of muscles.

Mira's hurtling toward her fourteenth birthday.

I spend the rest of the afternoon wandering and mulling things over. *Kevin,* a name Maurice would not have approved of. Is this lawyer the son Rob mentioned? But his last name is not *Dupont*, so maybe he's not the one Rob mentioned. I don't plan on going back to Felicia's. Not until I try to meet Kevin.

The walking is good for my body, which is sore from lack of movement. Usually a day doesn't go by without me getting in the studio or working out. The haziness has burned off now and the sky is a tepid blue.

While I am waiting for a light, I call my mother, but then hang up before she can answer. Did she not get my message that I'm in New York? I left it on her cell before I left Ohio. It's weird that she hasn't returned the call. I think about texting her, but she has an old clamshell cell and limited texting. She says she doesn't see texts. Sometimes I worry about all the communication she misses.

It's midafternoon when I arrive at the law office address, a tall glass and steel building on Park Avenue, at the center of New York corporate power. The computerized kiosk in the lobby lists a Kevin Fox with a multiname firm on the thirty-ninth floor. My amateur sleuthing has proved worthy. I am absurdly proud. I am going to meet Maurice's lawyer and I will find out once and for all where Maurice is, if he is still alive. If Kevin is, in fact, Maurice's son.

But I am not ready yet. I leave the lobby and retreat to the low stone steps of a church across the street. The afternoon is slipping away. The sky has solidified into an iron-clad blue, a brilliant color that accosts the eyes. I bought a pack of cigarettes and allow myself a few. To the south, in a store window, is a big Easter display—all bright pastels and fake green grass.

Next week I'll be back in Ohio, picking up where I left off. But back to what? The smoke claws at my throat. A car's tires screech. The stone steps are scratchy through my pants.

I check my e-mail on my phone and find one from Bernadith. I hear Bernadith's tired, authoritative voice in it.

Kate, I'm sorry to tell you that there has been a report filed against you by a student. For inappropriate behavior. You will shortly be receiving an official e-mail. Let's discuss when you return.

I turn off my phone, push it deep into my bag, and watch the sky begin to change, shadows lengthen, until the street is cast in a glow from the descending sun. The sky is now purplish, ripe. How long have I sat here? I've spent fifteen years of my life studying dance history. What are my options besides the academy? Limited, to say the least. Have I just been traveling in circles? And here I am, right back where I started? A girl lost in the grandeur of tall buildings.

Perhaps I have always waited for this moment. Maybe I allowed myself not to know what happened to him. His continued presence in the world was the best bet for keeping in touch with the self I missed and mourned, a self I had never been able to say good-bye to. If he was alive somewhere, then somewhere my beautiful and perfect past self survived, too, and that was an equation that I didn't want to disturb.

Maybe.

I wanted to tell you because you my dear are one, one of the dead, you will always be—

It's time. I get up and brush myself off—somehow a layer of soot has formed on me—and cross the street. In the florid glare of a late afternoon sun, I enter the building.

SLEEPWALKER

I take the elevator up to the thirty-ninth floor. The atrium is black granite. Orb-like lights reflect on the floor like miniature suns. A mahogany desk, solid, unimpeachable (such a contrast to the all-light-and-air SAB studios) dominates the entrance to the office, but it is unstaffed and I move unimpeded into a carpeted hallway. A few young lawyers scurry by without giving me a glance. I hold my purse tighter, walk the hallways, glancing at the names on the doors. The assistants' desks are mostly vacant on this late Friday afternoon, stacked folders and pictures of smiling children.

I keep walking, fewer and fewer people pass me. Finally, among a row of offices, I see his name on a gold-plated nameplate on the door: KEVIN FOX, ESQ. A pool of light shines from the open door, the second to last on the hall. Will he have answers for me?

I fight the urge to run back down the hall.

I open the door and enter.

I look around the large office. The mahogany desk, the diploma, the potted plant, the giant plate-glass window, the glittering city against a sherbet sky. A computer station off to the side of the desk, a moonscape screen saver. Next to the desk are several piles of file boxes and stacks of legal folders. At the desk sits a young man reading papers in the light of a lamp; he looks up when I enter. He is a small man and his delicate features are dominated by severe wire frame glasses. The body is the product of many hours at the gym. The face makes my heart pound.

I stare at him without knowing what to say.

"Can I help you?" he says.

"Are you the executor of Maurice Dupont's will?" I ask. "He was a donor. To the School of American Ballet. They referred me to you."

"That's confidential." His tone drops an octave. "And you are?"

I move a few feet into the room. The smell in this office is strange—potent, fertile. I think of trees, of rain, until I realize it is the smell of coffee. There are coffee mugs all over the office.

"Kate."

I'm only a few feet away from him. I can see he wears a heavy gold signet ring set with a blue stone.

"That ring," I say. "It was *his*."

I pull out the envelope with Maurice's letter in it and lay it on his desk.

A funny look crosses his face. He sticks his hands in the envelope and pulls out the letter, opens it and reads. His face turns a strange color. He doesn't seem able to look at me.

"It came to my address. My home address," I say. "Which also is confidential."

Finally, he looks up. His face has changed and softened. His eyes look wet behind his glasses, but I wonder if it's a trick of the light.

"It's our curiosity. It's so human, really, the most human thing," he says, stepping around the desk toward me. His eyes are strangely wild, and for a moment I'm afraid. What if he is crazy—or violent? If I had never followed Maurice that day to his apartment when I was eleven, everything would be different. Have I learned nothing? I take a step backward.

But he isn't coming toward me. He's bending over and opening the drawer of his desk. From it, he pulls a packet of letters bound with a rubber band. "He gave me these—'Here,' he said, 'these are for her. If you find her.'"

I reach out to take the letters. There are about twenty or so, some written on Florentine paper like the one that I received in the mail. These look the oldest. But there are many others, written on other kinds of paper—pastels, crisper designs, perky retro colors. It feels like the weight of a stone has landed in my hand. All these words Maurice had written. To me. Over all these years.

I take the top letter out and unfold it. It's dated September 4, 2014. A year and a half ago. Fifteen years after I went to grad school. Thirty years after the last time I saw him. Thirty years after I moved in with my mother. I skim the letter, then begin shaking.

This, then, is my life waiting for me. Like some savings I had held in abeyance, all being spent now, at this moment.

> Dear Mira,
>
> Before I die, I want you to know that I'm sorry for what I did to you. I'm sorry for ruining a young life, for tying it in knots that you'll probably never be able to undo. I taught you to harden your heart as you strove. I taught you to prize only your value to others.
>
> I have lived a long life, much to everyone's (my own especially) surprise. Old age has taught me humility. I am able now to see things I couldn't before. How much damage I've done. I am sorry for what I did to you.
>
> I harassed you with my wishes, my dreams, my desires. I wanted the perfection of steps, a vision of loveliness. I hungered for beauty like only the dying can hunger for it. I wanted to continue living, although I myself was half dead. I wanted these things out of a terrible need and they made me who I was—who I am. I am sorry. I hope you can forgive me.

I look up. "Is he dead?"

"He passed away six months ago," Kevin says.

I fold the letter, tuck it back into the pile. I look for a place to rest my eyes—they find the moonscape screen saver, undulating.

I try to take this in: the monster-prince of my childhood is gone. Maurice is gone from this world.

After a moment I say, "If he was already dead in March, who sent the letter to me?"

Kevin fiddles with something on his desk. He doesn't—or can't—answer. When he looks up at me, I see the furrows in his brow. Behind the mask of the young professional I see the pain, the attempt to relieve it in work.

"Let me explain." His eyes dart to the window, then back. "I was engaged. To a great person. We had planned everything—our whole lives. Then on the train back from a client's meeting . . ." He looks right at me. "A heart attack. At twenty-six. They said it was a congenital heart defect, undetected." His eyes are brimming. "At first, I *couldn't*. Then I realized I could bear it. I would just have to be a different person living a different life."

I feel something inside trying to stem his words, to shut down. But another part of me is opening up.

"So two years ago—after my fiancée died—I began to search," he continues. "It took me a bit, but I found him. *Maurice*. I found my father." He continues to stare directly at me. "The papers had his name. When my mother signed them, she added his name. That was unusual—for the situation."

His gaze is disconcerting. I haven't felt this visible since I was on-stage as a child. His eyes are bright—unbearably, ridiculously bright—behind his glasses. My old purse has become very interesting to me. I slip the stack of letters I've been holding into my purse. "And your mother?" I mutter.

"That was much harder. My mother was very young. She changed her name when she had me."

I don't dare look up. The office feels like it has shrunk around me.

"But after he died, I finally got a name—"

I'm making strange sounds, low, and wounded. I realize that I'm crying, that's the sound I'm making. I hear someone knock on the door. Kevin walks out from behind his desk, tells them to come back later, and shuts his office door. He goes back to his desk. When I finally look up, he is staring at me so simply.

"You can't bury the past," he says.

"But *my* name—"

"There's a record. There's always a record."

I wipe my eyes with a tissue from my purse. "Rob said—but I didn't think. I couldn't. It wasn't possible." I nod, blow my nose, even give a little laugh. How shoddy, how childish, my attempts at not being found, at changing my life. How bold they seemed at the time. That dusty room at the courthouse. The line of divorce-seekers, of name-changers. That adult land of mistakes that one has to pay dearly for in paperwork and in emotional toil. The bleak but steady wind outside the courthouse. It was something, it was the beginning of something else.

I look at the wall and see an incongruous thing in the room: a photo of Pavlova bent over her leg. The same one Maurice had in his gallery of ballerinas past.

"So *you* sent the letter," I say. I'm trying to order things.

"Yes, I sent it," he says. "He wrote it, but I sent it. When he died, he left me the execution of his remaining estate. But the most difficult thing for me to adjudicate"—he adjusts his glasses and gives an awkward laugh—"was these letters. He had left them for you—my mother." He takes off his glasses, cleans them with a cloth from his pocket. He puts them back on and blinks at me. His eyes look clearer, as if the cleaning of the glass polished his actual eyes. "One night, sitting in this office here—after he was gone, I sat with the letters in my hand, feeling—well, sorry for myself. I took one of the letters from the pile, without even reading it—and put it in an envelope and sent it to the address I was given. I sent the letter to you. It's his, but I sent it."

"But—" I say, stupidly—"how—if he was already dead?"

"I took the train to Armonk and then a cab to town, and dropped it in the mailbox. Then I took the train back." He has pantomimed these actions with precision and grace. I watch his hands, pale and manicured, but muscled and precise. too. The very exact and intelligent way he moved had an almost mechanical affect that I recognize from Maurice. I always thought that was the result of Maurice's illness, but maybe it was just him.

"He was forty-something. I was fourteen."

"I know," he says. "He said, 'If you find her, be kind to her. She was—a child.'" He paces in front of his desk, shaking his head. "I'm sorry. He was so hobbled, so compromised—I can't imagine. The polio and then the stroke. He couldn't move around much at the end. He was confined to his bed. Tremors wracked his body. He'd had them for years, but they'd gotten worse after I found him. They came every few minutes and left him exhausted. This was only a few months before he died. Every time I visited, he'd say something mysterious. I didn't know what he was getting at."

He stands in the middle of his office, his arms hanging at his sides. "I was so angry when I started to search, so ready for a fight. Somehow I blamed him—and you. I thought my whole future was gone. In the months after my fiancée's death I thought that if you hadn't given me up, if I hadn't been adopted, somewhere I would have been spared the pain." He laughs huskily, adjusts his glasses. "Anyway, when I began to search, I never thought I'd find such an old man. Or someone in such a feeble state in a state hospital. I never imagined any of it."

I look away, but I'm listening.

"After he gave all his money to SAB, they moved him to a state hospital, and it was a pit. He wasn't well cared for. They didn't even change his bedclothes for days," he says. "Anyway, I moved him to a nice place. I could do that for him."

"Wait." I hold the top letter up. "Why did he give his money to SAB—if he felt like this?"

"I don't know exactly, but I could guess. He was a complicated man." Kevin walks closer to me. Standing in front of me, he looks smaller, lost, like he's just wandered into this office. "He gave his money to the archives. There is a stipulation that said it has to be used to preserve their records of the past."

That is something I will have to think through. What has been lost to me, he devoted himself to preserving. History is steeped in irony, and here it is. I am drowning in irony now.

Kevin is still talking. "I had him hooked up to five different machines. And I kept him alive—I did—for a time. He stabilized. I would go after work and on holidays and the weekends. I would sit by him and listen to the machines buzz and whir and beep. I was keeping him alive. That gave me peace."

I've been standing this whole time, but now I brave the edge of a leather chair.

"He began to have moments of lucidity. He recognized me. He wanted to talk. He told me about his ballerinas. He had saved all these old photos. He wouldn't let me touch them, and he handled them with protective gloves of some sort. He would take them out one by one and he would school me in why each ballerina through history was so great." He gives a little laugh.

"Trefilova was so athletic that she could do fifty fouettés before her first coffee," I say.

He laughs again. "Karsavina was a great pantomime artist."

"Ulanova was the greatest actress of them all," I say.

"Markova's powerful classical lines," he says.

"Taglioni—" I say.

"The pointe shoe of course."

We smile, an old cripple in common.

I am sitting, he's standing, we're just a few feet apart. "I just wanted to hear the stories about his life—and you. But he had to talk about his ballerinas."

Despite myself, I nod.

"Gradually, I got curious. I began to go to the ballet. He couldn't leave his bed, but I went and described what I'd seen to him and he closed his eyes and drank it in. I fed him ballet and he grew stronger."

I'm envious of all these words Kevin has to describe his relationship with Maurice. I have so few. My own self when I first met Maurice—an anxious wide-eyed girl.

Kevin's gazing out at the gathering dark in the East. He turns back to look at me. His glasses are off again. His eyes looks smaller and deeper-set. Actually, there is a lot of Maurice in him. The small stature. And the coiled energy, an intensity of gaze, a precision of expression. The way his eyes can settle into a pinprick of attention like his father's.

"One day he said, 'your mother was the greatest dancer of all' and I said 'who was she?' And then he told me. He told me everything. He told me how you followed him home and stood there in his living room as if you owned him. He said he fell in love with you then. He said you were the bravest girl he knew. He said, 'she could have been famous, but because of me she was not.' He told me how I was conceived. By then, he was very sick, he was dying. It was very difficult for me to hear."

"Ha!" I shake my head.

"He had a picture of you. He showed me. Here, I saved it for you." He goes back to his desk and pulls a photo from his drawer and hands it to me. It's browned around the edges, and small. Against the dim stage set of a castle, a blurry figure in yellow leaps high off the ground. An off-kilter figure in blue—a boy in a prince's tunic—stands with arm raised like in a strange salute. It's a strange, spooky picture, a moment in a play, not quite real. "It looks like you're flying."

"I was falling," I say. "I fractured my wrist that day." I hold it up to show him.

My son moves toward me. "I'm glad I sent Maurice's letter to you. I'm glad you found me." He's so close I can smell him, old coffee and the sweet smell of new photocopies. "I wasn't sure after what Maurice—my father—told me that you'd want to see me. Or how you'd react."

Secrets can make more secrets. My affair with Sioban, for instance. But I stopped that one. And Sioban, I remember, has reported me. No more secrets. Staring at this young man behind his enormous desk who was trying to stop the secrets by sending me the letter. A sneaky, imperfect way, I know.

"You need some time." He hands me a business card, writes something on the back. His hand is shaking. "It's my cell, my personal number."

"What do you want from me?" I say, taking the card.

The night sky is settling over the city and the room grows dimmer. Kevin makes an unsure noise. He stretches one hand out at me uncertainly. Then he drops it. He says, "Just to know you." But he looks unsure. His gaze has shifted, has become something else. Desperate? Angry?

The office has become unbearable, claustrophobic. It is pressing around me, smothering me in its fertile, deep stink, the pressing darkness, his too-bright eyes, his outstretched hand offering the card.

I grab his card, turn abruptly, push the door, and then am out. I am in the brightly lit hallway and then at the bank of elevators. When the elevator arrives, I step into it, and, for a moment as I watch the little numbers light up in descending order—27, 26, 25, 24— I hang in the balance, falling, suspended.

CHAPTER 36

It's the morning of Mira's fourteenth birthday. She wakes feeling strong, her body taut. She is one of the chosen girls, gathering from all around the city, waking on a Saturday and preparing themselves before their sleeping families even stir. These families rise at ten or later and, still in bathrobes, eat bagels and fish and cheese and fruit salad. They just *sit* and *eat*. It is astonishing. They begin their day as she is finishing her first class. Sometimes—as she launches into her second barre for the day, she imagines her dad, Judy, and Sam in robes and cloth napkins sitting before all that food on the little patio with a view of the East River, and she smiles to herself. Her virtue in counterpoint to their sloth.

In the new bathroom—Judy just had it redone—Mira pulls her washed, wrinkled tights down from where they hang on the shower stall from when she rinsed them out the night before. Over her tights and leotard, she pulls on a pair of tight jeans and her favorite boat-neck shirt.

She marches by her dad and Judy's room, then Sam's room, with her duffel bag loaded, shoulders squared against the weight.

It is eight fifteen. She enters the diner across from Lincoln Center and orders her regular: blueberry muffin, toasted, no butter. She will eat half the muffin before Technique, then a quarter between Variations and Pointe, the rest after her classes are over. And coffee— black. She has recently begun, like the other SAB girls her age, to drink coffee. They actually don't drink much, but they bring it to the dressing room, the hallway, and take tiny sips, leaving the blue and white cups floating around them like little buoys, marking their territory.

Mira stands in front of the bulletin board. More than two years have gone by since she became an SAB student. She shifts her dance bag onto the other shoulder. It's now a big girl's dance bag—filled with all the equipment required of pointe shoe maintenance: lamb's wool, first-aid tape and gauze, rags, hairspray (to stiffen the toe box), four pairs of pointe shoes from different classes—new ones to break in during floor, a worn-in pair for Variations, and a medium pair for Wednesday Technique class.

She scours the bulletin board while sipping her coffee. The coffee is sludge. It scorches her throat.

Her eyes move over the notices for rehearsal space, past Alexander Technique teachers advertising discounted lessons, to the Xeroxed green and pink notices from last week's audition calls. The notices specify age groups. "Ages fourteen and up." *Fourteen.* The magical divide between trainee and professional. She's fourteen today!

It might have been different if it were in the old days—begin performing at thirteen, travel the trains like gypsies, and disembark every night in a new town. But now, soon, at fifteen or sixteen, it will happen for them—or not. Boys have more leeway. For Advanced girls, especially those who reach D and who are not taken into the company, there are real questions: If they are not accepted into the New York City Ballet—and few are (only one girl last year made it in)—where will they go? Will they be accepted to a regional dance company? Say, in Phoenix? In Tampa? They will have to buy their own pointe shoes on a corps dancer's stingy salary. They are beautiful, rare specimens, but is there a place for them? Are they just to be placed on a shelf like Pavlova's pointe shoe and stared at? Will they become princesses with no kingdoms, concubines with no masters?

She takes her time, as befits one of the best girls in her division. A girl with Mr. B's imprimatur. A former Marie.

A little girl in a powder blue leotard, the youngest of those who can perform, pulls at her bag. She turns to the little girl and smiles. The girl pulls out a *Nutcracker* program from her bag. "Can you sign?" she says.

Yes, when she is accepted into a professional company, wherever it is, Maurice will follow her. He *must*. He will come see her dance every night. Then, they can be together, in the open, no longer hidden. "What's your name?"

"Kate," says the girl. She's tiny, dark-eyed. Mira fingers her pack of cigarettes, checks her bun. She takes the pen and signs. After the girl is gone, she takes another big swig from the coffee cup, finishing it. Then she tosses it in the bin. She stops at the water fountain, gets a drink. The mysterious innards of the fountain thunk and the spurt of icy water hits her cheeks.

The evening of her birthday, Mira and Maurice sit at a table in the back of Chez Luis. She doesn't like this restaurant, its out-of-the-way location, the curly-haired host who smirks at them, and the wine lists longer than the menu. The place shines of lacquered wood. Maurice's father, of the fierce predator stare, might have come here, she imagines, in his pantaloons and pince-nez, to smoke a cigar. The only thing she wants here is the hamburger, which is way too fatty for her. She ends up with couscous and vegetables.

The waiter ejects himself from the shadows and waits to take their order. Though she orders the same every time, he never assumes. His face, blank, as she says, "The couscous." Maurice orders the duck à l'orange with escarole. Her stomach lurches under her ribs so that she has to touch that spot with her hands, ease it open again. She smiles.

Usually, she can feel Maurice's eyes moving over her, taking her in, her arms as she lifts her fork, the curve of her neck, the length of her back. But today there is a wall. Because he is not seeing her, she cannot picture herself. She lights another cigarette. He waves the smoke away.

She brushes her hand against his wrist, in that space above his cuff link.

"Bella," Maurice says. "You know the rules." He sighs, his eyes on his silverware. He is wearing that new bolo tie and a shiny silk shirt. Recently his way of dressing has changed. She doesn't like it. In addition to the bolo tie and shiny shirts, he wears black turtlenecks. And he shaved his mustache off and got a modern haircut. He looks like someone from these times rather than from the black-and-white photographs on his wall, which are now bolder to her than the colors on TV.

"Even on my birthday?"

"Especially on your birthday."

Yes, there were his rules. When they are walking in the park, hands just brushing lightly, and they see a boy and a girl, not a few years older than her, sitting with their hands up each other's shirts or in each other's pants, he says, "Disgusting."

"Why?" she says. "Kissing is nice, so why not—? Why not that?"

"It is something," he says, "that is not for dancers."

She is a Mr. B girl, in Level B at SAB, and has a rich boyfriend with a fancy apartment who loves to watch her dance, *lives* to watch her dance. Well, how many girls have that?

Yet she sometimes wonders why she doesn't feel happier. It might have to do with Mr. B, who has been absent from the school for the past month after a health crisis. No one knows what is wrong exactly. Some words are whispered—cancer, multiple sclerosis—but they are too terrifying. Mostly, they just whisper that he is *sick*. That is all they need to know. That the god of their universe is sick is a terrible blow. It is just not the same without the knowledge of his presence lurking somewhere in those halls and classrooms, the possibility that you will turn the corner and see him coming toward you on Suzanne's or Karin's arm, his ascot knotted neatly, his eyes suddenly—possibly—alighting on you and seeing you, bringing you out of yourself and into a new existence. Sometimes, as she stands at her metal locker in the clean dressing room before or after yet another class, a terrible word flies into her brain: *why?* At these moments, she chastises herself. Maurice would say, as Mr. B himself would: *don't ask, just do.* They are dancers, after all. They are vehicles, instruments.

Maurice would scoff at the very desire to question her mission, the chance she has that he never had. Compared to transcendence, what is happiness? He is right about that. He is always right. What would she do without him to keep her on the track of the beautiful, the true dancer?

Maurice. Dancing for Maurice. Her mother—gone, then back, then gone, with her turban and big shell earrings. Her sagging father. Judy. Sam. Only Maurice does not change. He is—must be—constant. Maurice is one of the constellations in the sky she reads about (but can never see from the city).

The maître d' brings the food. Mira trembles with hunger but she makes herself wait to taste it. How warm and salty it is. Fearful of the complex anatomy of the "normal" meal, she has trained herself to taste only the primary and the elemental—warm, cold, sweet, salty.

She stubs out the cigarette in the ashtray that has appeared.

Mira may be the shy schoolgirl in her Jackie O. wool jumpers Judy chooses for her, and her slim Fiorruci jeans and boatneck shirts and penny loafers, but Bella is more of a creature than a girl. Bella feels what it is dangerous to feel. It is Bella who slips her foot out of her loafer—she still has her tights on from class—and props her heel on the edge of Maurice's chair and nestles it into the place where his thigh meets his hips. She moves her toes around. (Bryce calls it a snail, and when it is ready, it "swims.")

Now he claps his eyes to her. "What?"—he spits—"are you doing?" He pushes her foot to the ground. Hard. As quickly as the universe can expand under his gaze, it now contracts. What *has* she done? She is filled with a burning thought: *I hate him.* She lists the things she hates about him: She hates his perfectly arrayed lawn of white hair. She hates the turtlenecks and jeans he has begun wearing, hates his cream-colored snakeskin belt and the way his turtleneck looks tucked into his jeans. She hates his new calfskin fedora. She hates his twitchy pale hands with the manicured nails and signet ring.

She shoves her foot back into her loafer.

Studying her quarter-eaten plate of food, right then she even hates Pavlova's dried-apricot pointe shoe waiting in the humidor for them to pay their ritual homage. She can't stand it.

Fine, she thinks, fine. "Then you won't have it." The only power she has. To take all of herself away from him. "I hate you," she whispers, looking down.

The book is on the table when she looks up. It's open, its small lines of cramped handwriting filling each page. Next to the gold-edge paper of the book is a profiterole with a candle in it.

"Happy Birthday, Bella," says Maurice, smiling his stones-on-a-ledge smile.

They know each other's bodies. He knows every tendon and bone of her form and how flexible and how strong each is. She knows his curved back, his pale, well-groomed hands. *His father didn't want him, but I will take him.* She looks at his legs, one white but normal—with faint muscles and man-hair. She doesn't like this one. It is not hers. He has let her look at the polio leg without pants: it is like a baby's, this leg, the skin very white and new-looking, knee strangely swollen, deep indentations in the skin. The white, dry skin through which you can see bones. She loves this leg. Without it, he wouldn't be hers. This foot is a tender, warped white thing, almost bloodless in appearance, that reminds her of something on display, under glass. This foot is highly arched. It fascinates her. The "drop foot" is a friend: a foot in *relevé,* a foot balanced on nothing, on air. The ball of the foot pushes forward and the heel comes up, a consequence of a shortened tendon. He wears a special shoe. Thick soled with laces, a shell hard as a beetle's, heavily laced. This shoe holds his heel down. Drop foot? *Drop* foot? She thinks it should be called *raised foot*. His leg rests in a long cradle of the brace made of metal and leather. He lets her put his shoe back on, lace it up, gently, severely.

The more she excels at SAB, the more her own powers expand, the more she understands, in some deeper way, his physical weakness and limitations. She has a feeling of careful ownership of him.

Their relationship, this young girl and this man, is one based on infirmities. Together they worry about the popping sound in her hip joint when she does adagio extensions. He found a trainer who worked with her on hip placement. Like many teenage dancers with grueling schedules, she experiences the ailments of the middle-aged. He knows best the medications: Tylenol for tendonitis, aspirin for shin splints, Excedrin for joint pain. Epsom salts, valerian, and vitamin B.

So of course she wonders—the normal girl in her wonders—what it would be like to be kissed, not measured or judged, just kissed. Since Gary, she has had no physical contact with any man other than Maurice.

She wonders how it would feel to have a boy's hand creeping up her shirt and, not finding much there, prying at the waistband of her pants, at her zipper. She is sure that there would be something of interest for him, something even ballet had not touched. Sometimes at night, the song in her body stops long enough that she can hear, not her bright strong limbs, but other parts of her body—her stomach with hunger, and other, deeper parts. Then she grabs her pillow between her legs and squeezes hard and bites its corners, gnashing her teeth like a wild animal.

In his apartment, she dances for him. She strips out of her street clothes, down to her leotard and tights. She does the combination from Danilova's class. The one with the three pirouettes. And wouldn't you know it—she does all three pirouettes out into the arabesque perfectly. There, across from her, he sits on his wrap-around leather couch in the furrows of light carved by the Third Avenue streetlamps (he doesn't turn the lights on).

She stops and stands there in the dark, listening to his shallow, even breaths. She has gone through the whole thing—once, then twice—hearing the sounds of the accompanist, hearing Danilova's high, warbly entreaties and commands—*yes dharlinks, dharlinks, this, not this, yes this but not this*—and then she has moved through a thin layer of sweat in the stuffy room. She feels strangely light-headed, probably from not eating enough. In the end, she ate almost nothing at dinner.

She peers over Maurice. *He is asleep!* He has never fallen asleep before.

Why has she begun to cry, silent tears that flatten out along her cheeks? Her face is wet, her mouth open with the silent sound. *He is asleep!*

Maurice sleeps, his face tilted upward. She bends over, kisses his pale lips lightly, just grazes them. He doesn't stir. It amazes her. His breathing doesn't change. In her tights and leotard, she curls her body next to him and closes her own eyes. Garbage cans rattle in a breeze, sirens wail far away.

Her eyes do not close; she doesn't let them. She imagines her mother passing through the mountains to arrive at the Street of the Warrior. She pictures how her mother looked last time Mira saw her—before the trees lost their leaves. She looked bigger, more solid, in a broad colorful shirt, her hair wound up in a white turban, wearing heavy clanking shell earrings. Mira had not wanted to hug her. Her mother smelled of incense and something like tar, but when Mira hugged her anyway, she embarrassed herself by crying into her mother's many necklaces.

They lie there—the girl and the man—without moving for a long time. Outside, people whistle for cabs, high heels click on the pavement, horns blare then fade. When the sounds change to slamming car doors, rushed, barked words, the sudden curls of laughter, and the down-the-street swoosh of taxis dropping people home from parties, some alarm goes off inside her and she moves. She rubs her arms, which have fallen asleep.

She gets up and pulls her pants and her shirt over her ballet clothes. Then she leans over Maurice's sleeping form and says, "It's time."

He wakes suddenly, as if he just closed his eyes for a second. He opens his eyes and stares at her—startled, fearful. "What did you do to me?"

"Nothing," she says. "You fell asleep."

He rubs his eyes, pushes her away. He sits up. Grabs his cane. Takes in her appearance but does not move. "You are beautiful," he says conclusively. His voice is unkind, full of blame.

"I know," she says.

Later that night, Maurice drives her uptown—*twenty blocks* north—past humming streetlamps. His car after all these years still smells of new leather. She looks at him, maneuvering the lever that allows him to make up for his bad leg, the grim paleness of his face and something new about him, something that reminds her of her mother in her studio when she was much younger, a distracted quality, like he is straining to hear music from a long way off. She reaches over and turns on the radio.

"Mozart?" she says.

"Mendelssohn."

He parks the car across the street from her dad and Judy's place. After she gets out, he rolls down his window and turns to her.

"Bella . . ."

"What?" she says, her heart pounding.

He looks at her, his old face troubled, but says nothing. It's almost spring, and a smell of something blooming wafts into the car.

"I think . . . maybe . . ."

"What?"

He looks out the window. He pauses and gives her a strange look. "Do you enjoy dancing?"

She stares at him. No one has ever asked her this question that she can remember. As a girl, she would have answered *Yes! Yes! Yes!* without thinking about it. But she is not a girl now. She knows that suddenly.

He lowers the volume on the radio but the music still simmers. He hands her some bills.

At first she liked the money because it could be turned into something—jewelry that she chose carefully because she imagined it was from him. It felt like a gift and she accepted it as such. But now it feels different. The money sits in her dresser drawer and collects there. She spends it on cigarettes, nail polish, but can't think of enough things to buy. It makes her heart hurt that she can't think of what to buy with it.

In the narrow strips of gardens along the sidewalk, things are blooming—things that smell.

Is it Mira who wants to cry? Or is it Bella?

Or—is it someone else entirely?

After Maurice leaves, she enters her dad and Judy's building and nods at Felix, the night doorman. The elevator is too far away. She won't make it, she knows suddenly. Her face crumples like a used dinner napkin. She drops her dance bag and covers her face with a hand.

"Are you okay?" the doorman says nervously.

"I have been lying," she says. "There are no kids."

This is Judy's world of nice-but-mean doormen, elevators to views of the city below, well-oiled furniture that feels dry and brittle. It is a world of fakes and phonies.

She wipes her eyes, goes right up to Felix's desk. Imagining that she is her mother, she says, "Do you think I'm pretty?"

He looks at her then. "Sure, you're a pretty girl."

She smiles. "Would you like to kiss me?"

He stares at her for a long moment. He is maybe fifty years old. His chin is droopy. His eyes have receded into papery folds. His posture is strangely good and he never sits. Now he stands, as stiff as a sharpened pencil, and looks at her, his eyes flash something she can't read. He opens his mouth to say something, then he closes it again.

"I think it is time for you to go upstairs." He looks at her as a grown-up would a child.

She looks down. She is ashamed. She is not her mother. She will never have her mother's power.

Now she truly begins to cry, babyish, trusting tears that pour out of her as if there is no end. Felix comes out from behind the desk and walks her to the elevator, a careful hand on her elbow as if she is an old woman.

Judy's apartment is filled with heavy shellacked furniture and puffy couches. This is furniture left behind by a previous life of Judy's that she's replacing slowly, since some of it still has *sentimental value.* Spilling out to the hall from the kitchen is a bright light, her father's deep arguing voice. She pauses in the dark living room, trying to gain control over herself. Her skin burns, her throat is raw; her eyes feel full. The way Maurice looked at her when he called her "beautiful"—like a curse word. He has told her that beauty is the highest thing in the world. (Not the magazine kind, but another kind, a kind only he can see when she dances in the dark for him.) Bella must exist not just for him but also for others. He must have taught her *something* she can use. Slowly, she straightens up and lets her breathing return to normal. She wipes her eyes. She tries out a smile.

Entering the kitchen, she finds Judy and her father standing at the breakfast bar. Her father has his suit jacket over the back of the stool, his tie is loosened. He is holding a rattling cup. Judy wears a long black dress with sparkling things hanging off of it. Her father's cheeks lift up in a smile and Judy gives her a quick birdlike grin behind which lie a thousand questions.

"Mira, your father's judgment is really—" They like to argue but they have little smirks on their faces the whole time.

"Judy, leave her out of this. Hi, darling," he says going over to Mira and giving her a hug. He is too warm and smells thickly of alcohol. She recalls Maurice's dry, powdery scent and feels an internal bolt of something—fear?—move through her.

"Honey, your hair needs a trim," says Judy, moving toward her and giving her arm a squeeze. "The ends look tired."

"She doesn't need anything." Her father pats Mira awkwardly on the back. "Her hair is beautiful," says her father. A pie, waiting on the breakfast bar covered by plastic wrap, quivers and molts before her like an oasis. She feels the lurch of her whole body toward it. She allows herself an apple from the fruit bin, which she slices in half carefully on a napkin.

"A *trim,* I said." Judy snatches up the other half of the apple. "Can I?" she says as she takes it. She puts her hands on her hips and stares at Mira. Tiny beating veins stand out on her temples. "So, Mira. Listen to this. The congressman says, 'I don't think I can get involved in that discussion.' And your father says 'Well, that doesn't hold City Hall back from getting involved!' Even if he didn't know that the congressman is backing the mayor's zoning plans—which I don't buy—he could have listened—"

"I didn't have a chance—"

"Oh, come on! You could have *guessed.*"

Her father sighs and turns to face Mira. "How was babysitting?"

"Fine."

He turns back to Judy. "And you shouldn't be so quick to judge—"

"They are going to come into their own soon," Mira says.

"Hmm?" her father says.

"The kids. They are going to be coming into their own soon."

"Oh, honey, they're still little, right?" says Judy.

"They're getting bigger," says Mira.

"Well, believe me anyway, it takes a long time." Judy and her father exchange a long look. Mira turns away, her face burns as if it has been slapped. She gets down off the stool, ready to leave.

"It's my birthday," Mira says.

"Oh, darling!" says Judy. "Of course it is!"

"Right-o," says her dad. "Happy birthday, honey," says her dad.

"Happy birthday. Happy birthday," sings her dad. "Tomorrow we will celebrate." He gives her another awkward pat.

"We have reservations at Le Cirque for tomorrow night—*our* birthday celebration for you," says Judy. "Sam is coming.

"Mira, you must be hungry," says Judy. "Please have some." Judy whips off the plastic wrap and pushes the whole pie toward Mira. Mira's stomach lurches again and the light-headedness she felt earlier comes back. Judy cuts a piece of the pie and wraps it in tinfoil and shoves it in the oven. She looks at the silver bowl of shellacked-looking lemons on the enormous black-topped stove, at Judy's wrinkled-but-still-pretty frog face, and at her father's starched-white middle straining against his tuxedo shirt. She is about to give in to the desire when Judy says it: "I'd like to know what you think." That means it is a client's pie.

"No, thanks," Mira says.

Judy squints her eyes at Mira. "You may be a gorgeous little ballet dancer, and it may be your birthday, but you still need to eat to survive. Have you eaten anything all day?"

"Yes," Mira says.

"What?" says Judy.

"Things."

"What things?"

"*Things.*" Mira pushes the warm pie away. She could eat it to satisfy Judy but she doesn't feel like it. She still has a core of roiling energy cycling around, hitting all her organs like a pinball machine on tilt.

"Not hungry. Where's Sam?" Mira says as she turns to go.

"In his room. Not out for once," says her father. "Get some rest, darling. Tomorrow'll be a good night. We have a lot to celebrate." It is one of his sloppy, drunken late-night "darlings" that she distrusts because they disappear in the morning.

"Good night, Dad." She stands in the doorway for a moment.

"You look tired," Judy says, looking at Mira as if for the first time that night. "Oh, and the Egremonts are coming for dinner next weekend and they want to meet a genuine New York City Ballet dancer."

"That's the *company*, Judy, and I'm—"

"I know, I know—you're in the school. Close enough."

Mira turns down the hallway, already leaving the complicated architecture of the kitchen behind. Her own hunger disappears strangely as she turns into the hallway.

Mira has gotten in the habit of stopping outside Sam's room. Tonight there's a light under his door. Sometimes there is a low thrum of music, but tonight it's quiet. She stares at the sign on his door that reads in bold red letters *IF YOU CAN'T PLAY NICE, PLAY LACROSSE.* The door flings open and Sam stands there.

She screams.

He laughs.

"Idiot," she says.

His baby face—his brown eyes are Judy's—is flushed, cocky. He wears a robe that hangs open loosely and some kind of athletic pants tied with a drawstring. He has Judy's practical competence—and cruel streak, too. His bare feet are big and bony and soft-looking. He is always bigger than she remembers. Behind him she can see his desk lamp spraying light on a loose-leaf binder.

"Want to come in?" he says. He holds the door wide open. From inside the room comes a warm moist draft, like someone exhaling.

She and Sam get along better now that they live together. He can say *whatever* he wants to Judy. Mira admires that.

"Shut up," she says, and walks straight in and sits on the floor. Now here, she doesn't know what to do with herself. She notices the tracks worn into the rug where the grain has been pushed down in one direction to his desk, another to his bed, and still another to the spot under his basketball hoop on the wall, where there is a worn circle. Sam pads back to his desk. She considers getting up and leaving—he has left the door partway open—but something holds her to the spot. She tangles her fingers in his beige shag rug.

She looks at his records lined up on the bottom shelf, his trophies and banners on the next highest one, his orphaned sports equipment spilling out of the closet and piled in the corner. She feels a funny feeling in her stomach, something sour. So many props to play his sports! In Sam's tropical-aired room, the neat clutter of his popular boy's life lies unconfirmed by anyone but him. She has only her body, this cruel, fallible, and perfect thing. For a moment, she hates herself deeply. She points her foot and flexes it—it curves like a banana and straightens into a ruler—and she feels momentarily better.

Her own efforts at being a bunhead, in comparison, for the moment, seem like nothing. Mirages. Dreams. She begins to breathe quickly. Ever since that day when Ms. Clement said "Yes, we have something here," and her father called her his little princess and she began to use that part of her that moved all the time, even when she was sitting still. Now: the way Judy introduces her to her most important clients even before she introduces her own son. The way her father looks at her after a performance and then quickly around the room with saucer eyes to see who else has seen that she belongs to him. And most of all, Maurice, who has, for three years now, secured her dancing in a fog of a dream.

"You're coming to dinner tomorrow night?" she says.

"Yeah, they told me I had to," Sam says. He's turned around in his chair and looks at her. "Hey, I have to ask you something. I promised I would. You know my friend Oliver?"

"Oliver?"

"Yeah, he's an attacker on the team."

Who doesn't know Oliver Corbitt? He's a dark-haired boy in the tenth grade. He speaks with one side of his mouth down, says "gnarly" to everything, wears his blue blazer opened, wears moccasins without socks, and has one of those haircuts with the front left long.

She has seen Oliver on the field, all grass stains and ruddy face and clapping his teammates on the back. How must it be to feel the wind in your hair and root around in the dirt and try to hit a ball with a stick and scream about winning but in the end not care that much?

"So?"

"So what?"

"You are so retarded. So do you like him?"

She recalls once seeing Oliver's muscular legs and flushed cheeks and thin face and green eyes with black lashes.

"Yes or no?"

"Yes," she says. "No."

Sam smiles and she watches his sixteen-year-old dimples grow. Her body flushes with a dark fear. She remembers Maurice, his announcement, his conviction: *you are beautiful*.

She looks down at her hand clutching at the long hair of the rug. She has pulled some strands out of their loops and left a messy patch. She is shocked that Oliver could see her as something concrete enough in the world to have an opinion about. She thinks of herself as a ghost, invisible when she isn't dancing or with Maurice. She bites her lip. She imagines going out with Oliver. What do others her age do? Could he ever understand what twilight world she lives in?

"What did he say to you—exactly?"

He sighs. "He said, 'Your sister is cute. She looks shy.' I said, 'She's a ballerina.'"

She begins laughing.

"What's so funny?"

"Fuck you," she says. She's on the verge of tears.

Sam shrugs. His face in the skewed light of the desk. "All right, have it your way."

Famous dancers are not known for their cooking, their houses. They are famous for sleeping on hard mattresses on the floor and owning no furniture. Mira fought with Judy until Judy relented and let her get rid of her bed. Now she sleeps on a mattress on the floor. She got rid of the TV, too, and the cushioned chair, and kept only her desk, a trunk for her dance things, and a small white bureau—leotards in one drawer, tights in another. In her closet, her Fiorucci striped boatneck shirts in six colors, her suede boots, her white oxfords, and her blue pleated skirts.

In her spartan room, Mira curls up on her mattress and closes her eyes. She takes her nightly inventory:

Breakfast: one hard-boiled egg, a glass of orange juice, muffin.

Lunch: 4 saltines, 1 Yoplait, three Cheez Doodles.

Snack: 8 pieces of Bubble Yum.

Dinner: eight bites of couscous, five bites of peas, some rice.

Now she thinks about the old sad brownstone in Brooklyn. She remembers the house as the repository of all that was lost: the cold turned to adventure, the three of them at a distant impossible time in one place. She once overheard her father telling her mother, "The city works on me. It works on me." And it never left her. At Judy's place, everything, from salt and pepper shakers to stove, is the "best modern option." Black and heavy, metal and steel, big and plastic. Why is life supposed to lead to more and more? In ballet, it is different: one becomes less and less, lighter and lighter.

———————

A week later, she waits at the Lincoln Center fountain for Maurice. She hasn't seen him since the previous Friday night—her unhappy birthday. He hasn't shown up all week after class, but he would never miss Friday night dinner. Or would he?

It's a cool spring evening, but at first it's not cold. She's still warm from her class. A long adagio sequence sings through her head and she mimes it with her feet as she waits. The last bit of purple sunset hangs over New Jersey. She watches it fade as Tumkovsky's commands echo in her head. Now it's just past gloaming. The wind picks up, it's brisk, the smells of someone's perfume.

Half an hour later, she's still waiting. She lights a cigarette and pulls her peacoat against her chest. She's said good-bye to Bryce, who is all dressed up because she's going to meet her mom and her mom's new boyfriend for dinner at Le Cirque. They pecked at each other's cheeks the way they've seen their Russian teachers do. She's watched the girls who are boarding together wander off in twos and threes comparing notes on pointe shoe ribbon sewing techniques. She watched from the corner as Tumkovsky, huddled in a black shawl, boarded a bus. The last of the bunheads—and their teachers—have been disgorged from the Juilliard building and disappeared into the city. Only she is left.

Where is he? Her face flushes as she remembers the last time she saw him. His pale face sunk in some kind of strange sleep, the sting of her solitary tears, and his pronouncement, so full of blame: *you are beautiful.* Her foot in his crotch. It had angered him—it was against the rules. What demon had caused her to act out? She feels it in her still, clawing just below the surface—neither Mira nor Bella— scratching at her skin. Her face retracts into her peacoat, hiding from the memory. A brutal wind scours in from the Hudson. Isn't that what he wanted? A beautiful dancing girl to look at? She has been that to him. And he has been—what? Something else just as necessary to her.

Another fifteen minutes passes. She begins walking. The traffic lights mock her. Hot dog vendors behind clouds of steam. Cars glide by like sharks licking at her heels. He is somewhere in this city, but not with her.

Walking toward the park, her dance bag swinging, a girl lost in the chaos of a crowd. She raises her hand, hails a cab, and gives Maurice's address.

When the cab pulls up to Maurice's building, she gets out. Just as she stands outside the door, wondering if she should ring, someone— man or woman she can't recall, as many times as she's played the scene in her head—pushes the door open and, head down, slips by her without even looking at her. The city is full of people hiding their faces. But if this person had looked up and stared at Mira, seen her, she might not have gone in. If this person had taken her in—a pale girl with a strange stare and grimace (but don't those ballet girls always look so grave and serious?)—everything might have been different.

Mira catches the door on the backswing. Her overburdened dance bag on her bony shoulder, she avoids the elevator, climbs the stairs.

She stands at the door to his apartment. She has never had to ring the bell before. She does so now. She hears it chime inside. Soon she hears voices—Maurice's high, peevish voice that makes her tremble, and another voice, lower and ready to chuckle.

Maurice stands in front of her in a black-and-white striped button-down shirt and matching string tie. His hair is slicked back. Behind him is another man.

"Mira!" says Maurice. He does not invite her in. The other man appears at his side. He has a cropped beard on his long face.

"Hello," he says. "I'm Rob." He holds out his hand. His eyes are glittery and kind. She looks down. He wears no shoes, only socks.

"I—" she says.

The man turns to Maurice. "I assume you know this young lady."

Maurice looks like he has come out of a dream. He lowers his chin, and his eyebrows pinch together. This is the Maurice she recognizes. "Of course," he says. "Mira. I'm sorry. I should have called."

Called? she thinks. When did he ever call? She called him once— years ago—the night it snowed. But *never* has he called her. And where would he call her, at her father and Judy's? Impossible. She's never even given him her number there.

As they all walk to the living room, Rob rests a hand on Maurice's arm. *Who is this man?*

The living room is brightly lit and smells of cigar smoke. There are two glasses of wine on the glass coffee table and a game of Monopoly in progress.

Maurice disappears into the kitchen.

Rob sits on the brown leather sofa. "You're a dancer?" His laugh is big and warm. It makes her want to like him, though she knows her only real option is to hate him.

She nods.

"Maurice and I have overlapping interests." He smiles. "Opera, dance. Anything that was around during Louis XIV's court."

Maurice comes back with a bowl of cookies. He places the margarine-colored bowl on the coffee table with the same collection of cookies that Mira has not touched in a year.

"Cookies!" says Rob. "Maury!" *Maury! Maury?*

Maurice retreats to the kitchen.

"I think Maurice hates me," she whispers to Rob.

"Oh, no," he says. "He's not the type. He's a pussycat. . . ."

She smiles as Judy would when you're saying something she doesn't believe. "He was supposed to meet me tonight. For dinner."

Maurice reappears with a plate of sliced apples and celery and a small, metal tin of soft cheese that immediately stinks up the room. He puts the plate down but does not sit down. He stands gazing down at them, his face greenish, and working. Some of his slicked-back hair has come undone and stands up on his head like tufts of grass. Mira has a violent surge of hate for him. Or is it love? She feels like crying. Why does he hate her so much?

Rob seems to be chewing something over. He looks back and forth at Maurice and Mira. "Well," he says. He stands. "I think I have interrupted something—"

"No!" says Maurice.

Rob puts down a Monopoly piece he holds in his hand. It's the tiny, rearing stallion that gleams metallic. "Maybe you can continue for me, Mira. I own all the railroads." He takes a card from his wallet and places it on the coffee table next to the gleaming horse. "In case—" he begins.

But he doesn't finish. Instead, he smiles, slips on his loafers and sports jacket and walks toward the door.

Maurice follows him. Mira can hear low voices in the hallway. She can't make out what they are saying.

Mira reaches out and picks up a piece of an apple, already browning around the edges, and takes a bite. It is waxy, too soft. She has a weird sense of hovering above herself and the room, staring down at it. She sees herself holding the apple, the piles of paper money, an ashtray ripe with ashes, and the beaten-up end of a well-used cigar. She has never really thought of this apartment as a place Maurice lives. No, she thinks of it as their place they inhabit together, where she dances for him in dark and silence and so becomes again the only dancing girl in the world.

She takes the card Rob left on the table and, without even looking at it, slips it into her pocket. Then she picks up the little horse and examines it. It's heavier in her hand than she would have thought for something so small. She studies it—the tiny piece is well fashioned. The features of the horse are distinct, but those of the rider are vague, only hollows in the metal that suggest eyes, nose. She shivers, clutches the thing so tightly in her hand, its sharp edges dig into her skin, making her eyes burn.

After too many moments, Maurice comes back into the room. He stares at her with a ghostly paleness. His eyes burn with something new. She doesn't care. He is hers again. She will do what he says. She will dance for him. It will all be okay. After all, she's still a Mr. B girl. She'll still be in *The Nutcracker*—if not Marie, and not Head Angel, at least a Polichinelle. Then she'll dance in Workshop, maybe Aurora from *Sleeping Beauty*. Then she'll be a company apprentice. She opens her hand to show the figurine, then slips it into her back pocket. "Your turn," she says.

He lunges at her, grabs for her pocket. "Give that to me," he says. He's shouting. His mouth is open.

"You'll have to get it," she says, turning to run across the room. He grabs at her pocket, circling her body with his arm. He smells different, not like oranges and cinnamon, but like moist air, like a wild animal. He tries again, but she squirms away and runs, squealing, to the other side of the room, then onward, through the dim rooms until she gets to Pavlova's pointe shoe. He's breathing behind her. She hears herself laugh as he catches her and then, in the next instant, he's yanking at her pants. She has no leotard and tights on today; what emerges is just skin, the skin of her belly, her thighs. She's on the floor. She grabs his shirt, saying, "I am afraid." But it's too late.

"Is this what you want?" he says. She is quiet now. He bends her knees up to her armpits and shoves himself inside her. It is a stiff tent in there. He pushes himself into her again and again, destroying everything he has built.

She sleeps, or something like it. They are on the floor of the room with the old photos of dancers. Like two trees' branches tangled up together. A forest. Together they make a forest of limbs. She is trembling like dry leaves in a heavy wind. He is bony, ancient, gray, and powdery. She is young, white, and sinewy. Her legs like steel covered in flesh. The corners of her mouth curve upward in a smile, but it is not a smile. She is like a thing falling—in space falling—to the ground. A dried leaf, a twig, a piece of dried skin, discarded, passed over even by the street sweeper's brush.

MY REMEMBERING SELF

After leaving Kevin's office, I walk, a particle in the bloodstream of the city. I let myself drift. Something comes to the surface in me. It is sadness, a deeper sadness than I can ever remember feeling.

I am carried over east, past brick buildings, a flag, stained glass. These side streets that are always full of surprises. I'd forgotten that about New York. Between the fortresses of Park Avenue and the helter-skelter of Lexington, anything is possible. Maurice lived on a side street, farther east, past Lexington.

What is Felicia doing now? Is she just coming home from some event? How many Lucky Charms would she have to eat to take in this news? I imagine telling her, her vicarious excitement. Drama!

I want to know you, Kevin said.

Have I *known* anyone my whole life?

The past is swimming all around me. My father is not a bitter, twice-divorced teetotaler on an Exercycle in Connecticut, but a robust alcoholic in the middle of destroying one family and creating another. My mother, not a glorified secretary with a storage unit full of paintings, but instead a beautiful young woman, angry and searching.

Maurice wanted my forgiveness. Can I give it to him? No. I can't. I am angry. The stack of letters Kevin gave me are burning a hole in my bag.

A bunhead passes me. Strange she would be so far east. She wears a leopard-skin hoodie, tight bright blue skirt, tights, espadrilles. Even through the Old Navy colors, I see her studio-pale legs, the battle between teenage softness and muscular power. Which one will win? She picks her way through the stream of people without looking at anyone. I must have looked like her, wandering through the city, devotee of a far-off god.

When I see these bunheads roaming the New York streets, I want to kneel and kiss them. I want to punch them, break them.

It's the gloaming now. The West Side is still in sherbet colors, but here it's night already. I reach Maurice's old building, an inconspicuous six-story brick apartment building, similar to others around it. Still, I know it immediately. It now has an awning, but I recognize the glass doors and the tarnished gold handles. I peer into the windows closest to the ground. In one, a forest of plants, in another what looks like a piano, curtains in another. Who lives in Maurice's sprawling (or do I just remember it as large?) second floor apartment now? Was it sold to pay for his care—all those years of care that I made necessary?

As I stand there in front of this unobtrusive Manhattan apartment building, my mind lurches. It's strange. Like some liquid that loosens concrete, turns it back into sand, one image dislodges another. And the images at first seem disassociated—as if they belonged to someone else. But then they heat up and my body responds. This is my memory. It belongs to me. It *is* me.

I remember everything now.

Maurice is there again, lit strangely by the light from Pavlova's case, which is broken. Glass all around. There is still the old meanness and mischief around his mouth, but there is something new in his eyes. He says something, peevish, victorious, and I can hear it. "You shouldn't have looked at me like that. You shouldn't have always been saying, *Touch me, Touch me.* You should never have asked that."

I raise the fireplace poker, step closer, and then *let it fall,* and it lands on his back, I feel him curve beneath it. He raises his hand and sinks to the ground like something without bones. He moves in stubborn slow motion. He's on the floor now. His mouth changes to a surprised smile.

That wild, bewildered look crosses his face. "Beautiful," he says. Then he closes his eyes.

It all surges back into the center of my mind and explodes outward. All the pieces are fitting together, but I don't really like the puzzle. I *smashed* the glass, I *broke* the humidor, I *stole* the shoe, I *attacked* him. But then there is the relief: I did not *kill* him. I am no murderer. But behind the relief there is something else, too.

My memory of that night, of what I did—and the feeling of that in my body. I remember so clearly now, the cool metal, so uncompromising in my hand, the weight as I pulled it back against the air, and the relief as I *let it drop.* No, I don't believe that, I *swung* it at him. He was a fire I wanted to put out.

I *could* have killed him. I know that is true. I *wanted* to kill him. And—I wish—I watch this wish—that I *had* killed him that night.

I shiver, though the breeze is strangely warm.

I head back west. Then I'm on Park, going uptown, nodding at the doormen as I go. A new breeze, this one colder, comes up. I wrap my jacket tighter. I walk in and out, light and shadow under the awnings that stretch all the way curbside to waiting taxis.

I have never been rid of him, not really, all these years.

Flotillas of taxis move unceasingly toward, then past me. One stops to let an old man out. It takes an eternity for him to unfold his body.

I see myself at Dad and Judy's, a bunhead sleeping on a mattress on the floor, counting her calories to help her fall asleep. I thought I owned the world. What a fool is the girl who desires to be a princess, trapped in the tower of her own making.

And now Kevin, his son. *My* son. *Our* son.

Other parts of the city forget themselves again and again. Where Felicia is, for example. Warehouses, then bars, now condos. And the new people who come to live in them.

Except Park Avenue perhaps.

I end up in front of Dad and Judy's old building on Seventy-ninth. Through the glass doors, I watch the doorman touch his hat as an elderly woman walks out of the elevator. He looks like a younger version of Felix, who would be retired by now. The uniform hasn't changed either, green with gold buttons, like an old-fashioned elevator operator. An anachronistic world. The doorman tips his hat to a woman walking out into the night.

Another piece of that night, a bit of memory, floats back to me. This one eases in gently, so at first I don't even know I'm remembering. It feels just like thinking. I'm at Dad and Judy's, I let myself in quietly; everyone asleep—down the hall to my room. There is blood on my shirt, and I take off my clothes, search my body for the wound that caused this blood—I can't see it, but I can feel it. It's my own wrongness, badness.

I sit on my bed and let the vertigo take me. I remember being on the floor, on his scratchy ancient carpet, his broken body on top of me. I walk—slowly—to the bathroom, wash the blood from my shirt with freezing cold water, ball up the wet fabric and put it in the hamper. I open my dance bag and find inside Pavlova's pointe shoe and Maurice's little black book.

I know there is never only one version of the past. We resurrect the past to suit the needs of the present. As I leave the fortresses of Park Avenue behind me and head to the boutiques of Madison, I understand something. Maurice didn't belong to this world any more than I did. We were both pursuing something that we didn't have a name for. We ended up calling it beauty.

And what is beauty? A whiff of smoke. But felt with the force of a cannonball. When you see it, it pierces your eyes, the heart over-flows, contracts.

I have told myself that life inevitably ends in tragedy. Don't the old ballet stories tell us so? *Giselle, Swan Lake*—those stories of betrayal, lost love, and untimely sacrifice.

But I don't know if that is true anymore.

I gave up my innocence. But I went on living. Maybe this was the greatest crime—against him—and against myself.

It is, maybe, neither of our faults. Where does outgrown anger go? Will it fade away?

On a corner of Madison, here's a photocopied LOST CAT sign on the lamppost. A fluffy white cat sitting on a brown leather couch. *Have you seen her?* Someone has scrawled over the sign in marker I FOUND HER! I touch the metal of lamppost on the corner and it's still warm from the sun. I'm filled with strange good cheer. A lost cat. Found. Bravo!

What should I have said to Kevin? I should have said, "I remember when I was pregnant with you. I remember feeling full for the first time in my life, I think. Then you were gone, and I missed you. The dream was over and another started."

I feel like I would die if I said that.

I head south down Fifth and then west on Fifty-ninth, skirting the edge of the park. Little pools of streetlights follow the dark paths into the park. A horse and carriage clomps by, jangling its belled harness. I smell manure, leather, and perfume. Does the horse care about this performance? It has a job to do. It gets treats. Or is it whipped? Balanchine escaped the Russian Revolution, way before Stalinism set in. If he had stayed, he might have been killed. Instead, he came to America. He started a school. I was born in America. I went to his school. The accidents of history are everywhere. The carnage all around us.

I pause in front of the Plaza, its big, subdued bluster lighting up the night, a quaint idea of itself for tourists, and also, still itself. I remember Dad and Judy going off to the Plaza one anniversary weekend. Sam and I avoided each other as much as possible, but one night we met in the dark kitchen and neither of us turned on the light, but instead we just stood in front of the refrigerator and ate straight from it without forks.

I have never truly, entirely, felt what was done to me was "rape." "Rape" suggests a finite act. What was done to me kept happening, went on and on. It is still happening to me. That one *time* produced a child that I was too young to carry. That time has never been over for me. The therapist I saw in my twenties wanted me to say "rape" because she was sure that my problem was I couldn't admit what had happened to me. But I didn't want to admit it. Because the word took away something too precious.

After I stopped seeing the therapist, I studied harder and danced more. The incessant movement, and the academic work, did its job. They kept the pain muted but still present. That was optimal. A reminder of a part of me.

A version of the past I could live with.

*I arrive at the Columbus Circle mall, which gleams upward in mir-*rored glass. When I lived in New York, all this would have been unthinkably tacky, but now it feels right. At the head of the circle, in front of one of Trump's hotels, is a giant metal statue of the earth spinning on its axis.

I am crying, the kind of tears no one can see, that can be dismissed as watery eyes or an allergy.

How does a city go on and on, remaking itself, losing itself?

This city is a mirage, a dream. A world spilling out, too small for itself. My past is always alive, is always being made. I bend again and again to that humidor, that glass tube of light, and I smash it to the ground. In the moment when the glass shatters but before it hits the ground, I have broken what I am. I am in the state of becoming something else.

I know where I will go tomorrow. The house that started it all.

CHAPTER 38

MAY 1980

Mira's body finally begins to change. Her breasts begin to show and her hips round slightly. It has taken her body a long time, but now it rushes to catch up.

She's hungry all the time. Her stomach lurches under her ribs. She eats some apple, some chips, some pie. She eats and eats. Something secret is growing inside of her. It is like a wild, unruly garden. It is something hungry and thirsty.

She sits bolt upright in bed in the middle of the night, covered with sweat. Her body is limp, foggy, wet, wrung-out; in contrast, her mind is buzzing and razor sharp. She feels bad, really bad, a different kind of badness she does not even have the words for. It's the opposite of how she feels when she is dancing.

A month and a half after Mira's birthday, one of the women of the pulled-back hair and buttoned blouses and gold pins—the one who met with her after the SAB audition—appears in front of Mira in the hallway. Her eyebrows are drawn together. Her face is strange and unseeing. "Mira," she says. "Please come here." Mira steps into the woman's office. On her desk are the ledgers, the big books she sees her walking around with and consulting. A heavy green sky out her window makes Mira blink.

Mira grips her bag tightly against her hip. She has never been called into an office before—is this being *talked to*? Usually, in a room full of girls all moving, she rises, bigger and stronger, out from under the blanket of *tondues* and pliés. She knows how to rise to be noticed within a line of girls, to stand straighter and command her legs to beat faster, to obey more quickly than the others. But, standing alone, in this blank office and faced with the woman's face, some other face she does not know—not kind, not mean, and not anchored by any movement—she feels herself disappearing.

"Mira," the woman says, taking a sip of her coffee. Mira keeps her eyes on a far roof through the window. "Your body—"

The woman says something in Russian as she puts down her coffee, then picks it up again. "No one say you are fat. No girl here is fat. For ballet dancer, is not question of *fat*." Her face smoothes out. "I remember one season at the Kiev, I eat only chicken and turnip. We are not allowed bread." She smiles.

"Some is made to be ballerina. You can do, do, do! Like ballerina. But some girls is not. We must find out this. Is better to know than not know. If not ballerina, something else."

Mira is so invisible now that she cannot move. She has turned into vapor at the same moment she is being told she has too much substance. "No!" she says suddenly. Then corrects herself. "I mean, okay. Okay."

The woman laughs. Mira has never heard this woman, whom she has seen in the hallways and classrooms so often, laugh before. It is a low, then high, unpredictable sound, like an animal skittering from corner to corner. "Mr. Balanchine likes you—you are a former Marie. But many girls change and we cannot do anything. Material is good but it—collapses." She is talking about Mira's body as if it were separate from Mira, a disappointment that has befallen them both. Her brows draw together—yes, sympathetic. "Dear, sometimes there is change. What can we do? No where to put girls then."

Mira's head pounds. Tears spring to her eyes. Sympathy, immeasurably worse that cruelty. Mira feels the ground unsteady beneath her.

In the moment before she turns, Mira notices, hanging on the wall a studio shot of a woman. It is a black-and-white publicity photo with that timeless look that means it could be from twenty or a hundred years ago. She is a smooth-cheeked young woman, in a black leotard on her pointes. Her expression is soft, her features delicate, well-spaced, exquisite. She has a serenity and generosity to her expression that Mira has never seen on her teacher Tumkovsky. But, yes, here at the bottom of the photo in embossed letters is her teacher's name: Antonia Tumkovsky.

In the distance, Mira hears clapping somewhere and the splat of water from the fountain outside.

Mira walks blindly down the hallway. Her shoes squeak. She locks the door on a bathroom stall. She sits on the toilet with her bag on her lap. Her breath comes jaggedly. There are shuffles and clangs from outside the stall. A strong odor of rubbing alcohol. More girls are starting to arrive. Of course everyone will know. There is a line between the girls who have been *talked to* and the girls who have not, as visible as a road divider. On one side the traffic flows freely; on the other side, it crawls along, snarled.

Breathing more regularly, she exits the bathroom and nods to the other girls, a few of whom are in her class. She opens her locker and begins to search for her morning classes' leotard. She doesn't dare investigate her body for its betrayal. For now, she treats it gingerly, like something broken that might have sharp edges she could cut herself on. Terrifying: she does not know how to fix it.

Airy and indefatigable, a Tchaikovsky serenade floats out from the studios.

Mira lies awake all that night. The next morning, she is strangely calm. It's a Saturday, perfect. She pulls on underwear, her tightest jeans, a polo shirt and a long green sweater with a belt around the waist. She dumps out her giant dance bag onto her bed—the tangle of leotards and tights fall out into a twisted mass—then she pulls the items from under her bed—Maurice's book and Pavlova's shoe— and shoves them into the bottom of the bag. She packs an extra pair of jeans, her favorite boatneck shirt, two pairs of underwear.

She climbs on the crosstown bus. At this time of the morning, the bus is mostly empty. There are no other bunheads. The streets are still quiet of the clatter of cars and horns and trucks. There are two old ladies who could be traveling together but don't speak. One is frail, with a bent spine and a tacky raincoat and a plastic kerchief over her head. The other one is round, has a direct stare and pink saggy cheeks, and carries a cane. She fixes on Mira with a conspiratorial smile. The ladies get off at Fifth. A middle-aged man with a briefcase and untied shoes gets on. He opens the briefcase and begins shuffling his papers.

Then it's her stop. She stands, in her light windbreaker, belted green sweater, and penny loafers, in front of a diner on Sixty-sixth and Broadway. It is eight fifteen. She enters and orders a blueberry muffin, toasted, no butter. The boy behind the counter stares at her for a moment too long before he turns to make her food. Already, the clean early-morning air grows muddy with the regular people who are rising, demanding their coffee, their donuts.

"Hey, Dimitri, doncha just stand there, get the girl her muffin. What's wrong with you?" A burly man with the same hair as the boy claps him on the back.

The counter boy hands over a warm ball of tinfoil. For a moment, both of their hands touch the pulsing mass of heat.

Standing there in that diner, with this boy, she feels like she is turning back into a girl—not Bella, not Mirabelle, but *Mira*—a normal girl. Everything in her carefully constructed life is splintering. She can feel it happening: and in the spaces, those moments of weakness, like when she went into Sam's room and he told her about Oliver.

"Are you okay?" the counter boy says. She quickly looks away and flees back outside to class.

The next week, she does something very difficult—she calls her mother and says she wants to come visit.

"When?" her mother says. She had imagined her mother would be more excited.

Mira begins to cry, heavy sobs that hurt her head. "Soon. Now."

"Whoa. Of course you can come soon. I'll talk to your dad."

"They think I'm fat," Mira says, breaking down.

"Those Russian pricks?" says her mother. "Screw them."

As soon as school ends for the year, Mira is on the plane to San Francisco. Her mother hugs her and says how good she looks, how healthy. Rachel's hair is long and she's wearing the same shell earrings that Mira saw back in New York.

Back at Felicia's, everything is quiet. She's still out. I take the stack of letters out of my purse. At the bistro table, I spread them out and count them—twenty in all. I sit for a while with my hand on them and watch the lights crawl along the other side of the river. I'm not ready to read them yet. I'll always have these now, to add to my collection, my exhibit of my past. But they are words, not objects. Evidence of someone's heart, someone's mind, someone's soul. When I've read them all, I will know his secrets, too, what was inside his mind all these years. This knowledge keeps exploding in my head. That old feeling of being onstage and having the lights on me comes rushing back—the excitement and energy of that—even as I sit in Felicia's silent living room. But that feeling fades and in its space is something softer.

I call my mother again, and this time she picks up. I jump right in.

"Mom, I met him."

"Who?"

"My son."

"Oh my god. How?"

"He found *me*. He's been looking for me."

She's very quiet.

"He's a man now. A lawyer. He wants a relationship with me." My voice spirals up at the end like a girl's.

"Oh, Kate."

"But it's okay, Mom. It's okay. I know it will be."

"Well, that's fucking wonderful then," Rachel says after a long pause. Her voice is thick. I wonder if she is going to cry. Maybe she's

thinking about me as a pregnant teenager beached on my bed, cling-
ing to my secrets.

"You're a fucking grandma." I laugh.

"A fucking grandma," she says. And she laughs, too. "I need a
cigarette."

But I will never tell her who is Kevin's father. I will never tell her
about Maurice. That is a secret I will take to my grave. Me, Maurice,
and Kevin (and Rob? I wonder suddenly) are the only ones who can
know that. But then I have this thought: *this is something I may no
longer get to decide.* Maurice was Kevin's father. This information
belongs to Kevin as much as it belongs to me. If he ever meets my
mother, *he can tell her who his father is.*

I start to dance. On Felicia's clean carpet, I'm doing the same moves
I was that night in the studio when Sioban found me—but now they
feel brighter, easier. I start small, just my foot against the floor and
my hands up, but soon let go. I'm dancing, in Felicia's living room
high above the Hudson. There's something okay about this moment.
Dancing in this luxury apartment. The air circulation system humming. I'm not sure if it's the sweet sadness for what is lost, or for my
own self, for Maurice, for the girl that I was and had abandoned.
But at this moment it doesn't matter.

I wake in the middle of the night, my heart pounding. At first, I don't
know where I am. I look around the room. I am lying in Felicia's
guest room, staring at the ceiling. I am trying to grasp simple facts of
memory, of the past and the present. Kevin who I just met in his
tower of gold and glass. This boy—this man—needed me enough to
have found me. *He* sought *me* out. I am his birth mother. I was *raped*
by a man three times my age. I got pregnant. I hurt him but I did not
kill him. These are the facts, how slippery they feel, and how much I
have resisted them.

I bring my hand up to the weak light from the window—thin
fingers grown thicker with age, no-nonsense, the pale freckled skin

that I've looked at for so long, now new to me. I feel tender toward it. I run one hand over the other, tracing veins, wrinkles, freckles. A life—one life. What will I do with the rest of it? I've squandered much of it by waiting, by giving in to my own fear of myself and what I could have done. But did *not* do. I hear my own notes from the modernism lecture in my head: *the grotesque, ugly, brutal, and the strong, Nijinsky wielded like a weapon.*

Is it too late for me?

Not to destroy the past, but to open up through thickets of inertia, new landscapes of future possibility.

I insisted to Sioban that she can be a scientist *and* a dancer. What possibilities are there for myself that I have not allowed? Can I become a mother this late in the game? What ways are there of moving beyond anger and sadness that I have yet to discover? Can I stop sabotaging my own ambitions?

Mira's mother lives in a colorful, peeling Victorian house that she shares with three other roommates. The overall impression is of macramé everywhere, shoes left in a pile by the door. Her mother's roommates, Edana, Brian, and Ralph, pursue various life changes— Ralph is becoming a priest, Brian is becoming gay, and Edana is becoming single after the breakup of a long marriage. The common area is draped in hanging plants, woven rugs, and stacked with magazines. But the kitchen is the real control room. In the kitchen, there are an array of various tins, jars, containers of messy, organic substances that had to be cared for in certain ways—reconstituted or blended or hydrated or ground with an ancient stone pestle. They are kudzu, protein mix, nutritional yeast, flaxseeds. In her mother's bedroom are her paintings and drawings, tacked up over mirrors, laid over bureaus and dressers, bound in portfolios piled underneath the bed and stacked in the closets. Mira sleeps in a room at the end of the second floor that is barely big enough for a bed, but she likes its smallness and its lack of furniture.

Her mother takes Mira to the Castro Theatre, where she sits in gold-painted balconies to watch black-and-white movies. Her mother takes her out to eat, places where they sit on the floor. They walk up to Dolores Park and watch the dog owners exercise their pets in the brave, golden light. They continue walking up into the hills, where it smells of sawdust and eucalyptus. Mira marvels at the plants: the trees whose flowers look like party favors, the palms whose spider-leg fronds walk along the sky crazily whenever a breeze comes. The jade's thick leathery leaves that burst into the air. Her mother tells her about "the California Dream," which is all about, her mother says—her face hawk-like, insistent—*freedom*.

At the end of a week, Mira doesn't want to leave. Her mother is very quiet and her freckles stick out as she says, "This is a big decision." She tells Mira that she's been taking time off work and can't do that again. "You'd have to take care of yourself a lot," she says. Mira nods. "You'll need to talk to your father about this."

Mira calls her dad. She tells him she wants to stay with her mother. "Why?" he wants to know. "How long?"

"I just need to be with her for a bit."

"That woman—"

"I haven't seen her in a long time. She's my mother. I want to spend some time with her."

There's a pause and then he says, "Why?" Listening to his breathing, she imagines the brilliance of her princess life—her bed on the floor, her posters of dancer superheroes. She smiles, almost says, *yes, she'll come home*. Then she remembers her terrible body, its spreading flesh, how shocked Judy would be. Of all the people in the world, only her mother can see her like this.

"They put me on the weight list, Dad." The silence on the other end lasts a long time. Into that crackly space, she wishes she could cry, but suddenly no tears are there. "Hang on," says her father. Her dad has gone to get Judy, she knows. How can dads be so powerful and so clueless?

Judy comes on. "Honey, your father told me. Mira, listen. I have a friend—she's a dietician. She can make a diet for you that's just perfect."

Judy's pragmatism makes Mira pause. Maybe this is something Judy can fix with her friends, her lists—her devices? But she knows that she's too far gone. This is what happens to girls who grow breasts and hips, who get too tall. There is no diet that can really change those things. She's seen girls try. The giant worry-stone hip bones, the collarbones like lamb shanks. Thinness does not make you smaller, it just makes you thinner.

"We can label all of your food. Ramona's daughter was horribly overweight and that's what they did—started labeling her food—and no one else could touch it and she was just feeling jealous it turned out. And it worked, she dropped twenty pounds. You just need a few pounds, right? Then, you'll be back on top—"

Mira feels it inside her, a broken, human thing. "I don't think so, Judy."

There's a silence. Then another silence. "And what about ballet?"

The thing that had always kept her going was projecting herself into the future. It was a bright and simple place: dancing onstage, beautiful, before adoring eyes. *His* eyes. But that future is gone. She feels a swell of vertigo. This city of windswept hilltops and eucalyptus and orange is as far as she can imagine from that future. "I'll quit," she says.

"Oh, dear. No, you don't." Then Judy is quiet for a long time. Then the phone rustles, and she breathes out a big sigh. "I'm putting your father back on—we love you."

Now her father is back on the phone. He asks to talk to her mother, and her mother takes the phone into her bedroom and she talks in a low, murmuring voice that reminds Mira of the days when they all lived in a house together. Before her dad hangs up, he says to Mira, "I guess—you can stay with your mother for a while. We'll be here when you're ready to come back. When you're ready."

Mira moves into the room at the end of the hall. Because she fits in well, her mother is only asked to pay a bit more in rent. Her dad sends the money. Mira's old life of grosgrain ribbons, hairnets, and Fiorucci sweaters is replaced by a small room, a window without shades, oversize shirts and sweaters strewn about, black eyeliner, antacids by her bedside. She takes in a desk off the street—someone had primed but not painted it. To go with it, a wooden thrift-store chair with a tie-on patchwork cushion that Edana, who sells things in flea markets, donates to her.

Her mother isn't home much, between her job at the lawyer's office and evenings at her studio. But Mira quickly feels comfortable in the house. She makes cookies with Brian, pasta with Ralph, and vegetable stews with Edana.

Mira spends most of July lying on the grass in a nearby park, letting the sun bake her. She likes to watch the stray cats wander by. They stare at her without expression and then move on. Or she sits by the window in her room, staring outside at the crazy blue sky. She's able to just sit now for hours. Just sit and stare, letting her eyes take in what she sees. Like a cat, she can just let her eyes move, take things in, let them come to her. They come to her in fits and starts—Ralph's Gregorian chant tapes, Brian's 1950s ballad singing, Edana's conversations with her girlfriends from what she calls her "other life," before she was married. People starting over. Lives after lives. Second, third lives. This city is filled with them.

Maybe this is what freedom feels like—the freedom *not* to move, to just sit, to just *be*.

One afternoon in the beginning of August, her mother comes and stands at the door, clears her throat. "We need to talk. I need to ask you something." She's holding keys on a chain, as if she were about to run out. She jangles the keys. "Okay. Do you have something you want to tell me?"

Mira looks at the peeling ceiling.

"Have you had your period?"

Mira shakes her head. Her mother asked her the same question a few times before during their infrequent phone calls, in the too-open air of Judy's kitchen, and she had shaken her head, the same as now, and said "no" with a secret proud smile on her face that she was glad her mother couldn't see.

"Do your friends have their periods?"

"Most of the girls I dance with don't." *Danced* with, not *dance* with. "*Danced*." The exercise keeps it away. That was what they all said to their parents, who believed them. But they also know that the less you eat, the more likely it is that your period will stay away. Even the girls who had had their periods pretended they didn't. They hid their tampons and wouldn't be caught dead with a bulging sanitary napkin. No ballet girl wanted her period. They wanted suffering, but not *that* kind.

"Really?" her mother says.

Mira nods.

"Never?" her mother says.

Mira doesn't answer. Her mother squints her eyes and looks at the ceiling, where Mira had just been staring. "Well," she says, but doesn't finish her thought.

It turns out that her mother has already made an appointment in a beige building with a big crowded waiting room lined with posters depicting medical procedures. Her mother waits, while Mira is led to an examining room. Here a doctor with glasses asks Mira to pee in a cup and listens to her belly. Then he asks her a lot of questions like "Who do you live with?" and "Has anyone touched you?" Finally, he sits on a chair across from her and holds his own hands. "Do you know you are pregnant?" he says.

People say they realize things in a flash, a bright bulb going off. Not Mira. She knows this doctor is right because she feels a dull thud in her chest. Her heart slows to a lizard's crawl.

"With a baby?"

The doctor smiles. "Yes, a baby. About four months."

"But I've never had my period."

He nods. "It's not impossible for a girl to ovulate before her first period. That's when the egg goes into the uterus. It's been known to happen—more frequently than you would imagine."

Egg, uterus. All of this she thought was simply about Pavlova's shoe, her desire, his desire, her need, his needs. That stupid brief, terrible thing he did—they did—made a baby. What has she done? It's unfathomable.

He moves a little closer. "Whose is it? I can keep a secret." But she won't say anything to the doctor. There are no words yet for what has happened. She is too close to the volcano, she must be still.

He continues: she can *press charges,* he says. She can *make whoever it is pay.* "Does anyone know about this?" he asks.

She shakes her head.

"This is *not your* fault," he says. "I know you're scared."

She's not scared, though. Not like he thinks. He can never understand her world. She's alone now: they were lying on the floor—and now she has a cat body with a baby inside.

"I can't remember," she says.

He sighs. He tells Mira to wait while he calls her mother into his office and they talk privately.

Back home, Mira and her mother sit across from each other on her mother's bed. "How did this happen?" her mother says.

Mira puts her head in her hands, but no tears come. "Are you going to tell Dad?"

Her mother looks at her for a long time. "Was it a boy at school?"

She thinks: it could have been Oliver, if everything were different. It could have been. "Not from my school," she says. She thinks about the other girls and things they did. Things she could have done if Maurice hadn't always been there. "I just met him once. We rented a room at a hotel. They invited some boys over. I never saw him again."

"What was his name?"

She shakes her head.

"Did he force you?"

If she says yes, they will look for him, for someone, to blame. She remembers some things—her own wild laughter, the Monopoly game, Maurice's pale face. If there are people to blame, she is surely one of them.

"No," she says, sweating. "Please don't tell Dad?" She can't cry now, when it would help. "Please don't make me go back."

Her mother sits down on the bed. "I have to think about this."

Several days later, Mira's baking cookies with Brian when her mother comes into the kitchen. She takes Mira into the living room, which is empty. Mira now has her mother's full attention. Her laser-like eyes are focused on Mira more than Mira can ever remember. Brian is humming in the kitchen. The streetlights are flowing in the windows. Her mother touches dried flowers in a vase on the table, then pulls her hand away quickly.

"My whole life I've been keeping secrets. You know that, right? That's why you came to me, right?" her mother says. "*I* left everything behind. It was the right thing for me. I was maybe too young when I had you or maybe—I don't know." She flushes, but it's a soft kind, not a blaze.

Mira stares at her mother. She's wearing a bandanna, like in the old days.

"You should know this—having you was the greatest moment of my life. It may be hard to believe but—it changed everything. A new life does that." It takes Mira a moment to realize that her mother is crying. Not the kind of crying people do on TV, loud and desperate, but a delicate kind of crying. It's like something is trying to get inside her mother and the tears are being pushed out.

"But you *left*. Then why did you leave?"

Her mother holds Mira's gaze. "I left to—I had to—find myself."

Mira thinks about this. Can you really lose yourself? And if you do—how do you find yourself again? Has she lost herself too? Is that what has happened to her? She surprises herself by not being angry. She says, "Did you? Find yourself?"

"Well—we all have many parts to ourselves it turns out. But I—I did find something—so, yes, I think I did. I mean, I have." Her mother does not wipe away the tears, which have spilled onto her eyelashes and beneath her eyes. "But I have caused you suffering. I see that. You have paid for my lack of self-knowledge." Her mother stares at her for a long time. Then she finally wipes away her tears with the back of her hand. "Oh, Mira," she says. "I am sorry this happened to you. I am sorry I left—and—"

Mira nods. She understands that her mother does not know what she should do. She could get rid of the baby or she could have it. Either way, what she understands is that it—this—has happened and can't be undone. Her life will never go back to the way it was.

"Do you know what an abortion is?" says her mother.

Mira nods.

"In some ways that is easier. In other ways, harder. But you can never be rid of a child." Her mother wipes her wet eyes again. "Whatever you decide, I can give you this," her mother says. "You can start again. I can give you that. I had that. And I can give you that."

It's a decision free of effort. Like deciding she wanted to be a dancer with Maurice standing before her, asking her, telling her she had to decide. A decision made possible by someone telling you have to choose. It must be yes or no, not both, not neither. And for this reason she trusts her decision completely. "I'll have it. The baby."

Her mother looks straight at Mira. "Okay. You'll have the child." She touches Mira's shoulder. "Give it to a worthy couple. Then move on. Start over."

Mira gives her mother her cat eye stare. Mira's hands are covered with dough. She nods, starts to sob, really sob, heavy tears. "Please don't tell Dad."

Her mother's eyes are lit with a too-bright light like they used to have in her studio, but her mouth, around it, is tired. She is quiet for a long time. "I won't ask who? why? when? where? ever again. I won't scream. I won't tell. I'm not a Betty Crocker mom."

Then her mother does the most incredible thing. She gives Mira a hug. It's not a simple hug, it's complex and in stages. She presses Mira's back with both hands and then clasps Mira to her chest.

She's never really sure if her mother kept her word. After that, her mom and her dad have murmuring conversations at night, but her dad stays away. Once she overhears her mother's voice rise, and she says "on *your* watch," before her voice lowers again.

As the months move on, through the fall, Mira walks the five sunny, then rainy, blocks to Mission High School. It's a huge public school. She is one of hundreds moving through this crumbling stone building while tired teachers look on. She listens to the teachers who speak half in Spanish and throw erasers at the kids—the ones in bandannas and with mustaches. No after-school drama clubs, no cabs whose waiting drivers ferry students to and from ballet class. But it's easy to survive here compared to SAB and Professional Children's School. Here, invisibility is an asset. She's in the back of class hunched over the desk to hide her growing belly.

She is too fat for ballet now. Her arms stay skinny but her breasts and stomach grow. Her body, which has always behaved so well compared to other girls' bodies, has completely stopped doing so. She eats and eats. This is a new kind of hunger, and one she can't defeat. She buys oversize shirts with company logos on the front and jeans she can leave unbuttoned. She buys Maybelline eyeliner—black—and draws lines above and below her eyes like she sees the girls on the streets do.

Her body should be locked up. It should be devoured. How unappreciated it is. How much she had given it! When she looks in the mirror, she sees something besides herself—she sees a girl who does not correspond to her idea of how she should be. Gradually she is coming into a new shape, hip bones, breasts, fat. Yes, it is *fat* that is between her and herself now.

Her mother takes her to thrift stores and buys maternity clothes with Kmart tags still scraping her thighs and underarms, seams so stiff they crack. Mira buys everything in black and too big and carries a notebook in front of her belly, so people will just think she's a PIB.

One day, a Chicano girl comes up to her. "What's your name?"

"Kate," she says. It's the first name that comes to mind. No longer a singular sensation, but one of a thousand.

"Who you live with?"

"My mother."

"You have a father?"

Mira shakes her head. "He's dead." This too comes out easily.

She nods. "Who's the daddy?"

Another thud in her heart spreads its dullness through her body. "He's dead, too."

The girl whistles, low.

Chinese slippers beneath her desk, an advent calendar, a metronome, a bottle of valerian to sleep at night. She sleeps and sleeps. The red kimono her mother lends her when she grows big. The orange plastic watering can on the bay window, a chart on the wall with a marker attached, names of her new housemates, next to their chores. Soon she is exempt from these. She sits at her desk and stares out the window, does worksheets in her math and vocabulary workbooks.

She can feel the thing—the baby. They say it is a baby; she's still not so sure. She knows only that it turns and pokes and kicks. It is not round and soft like babies are supposed to be but hard, all angles, ribs, elbows, knees, ankles, a bunch of sticks prodding her in the middle of the night.

Even at her desk at school. She jumps up, toppling her chair with a clatter. The thing—the baby, whatever it is—had poked at her *down there.* She runs out into the long hall to the bathroom. She shuts the stall door. In the barren cigarette-smelling bathroom, tearless cries heave her body, cries that she couldn't let her dad or Mr. B or Maurice or even her mother ever see. Suddenly, she can't get air; she gasps and heaves, the air fades to gray, static. The clang, clang of the bell. Screams of other kids. The water runs, a squeaky faucet.

She wakes in the bedraggled nurse's station—the endless thrum of footsteps and shouting in the hallways outside. "You fainted," says the nurse. She imagines the Russian lady who *talked to her,* standing over her, saying, "It's not a question of fat—" But it *is.* It is a question of fat.

She is really fat now. She is too embarrassed to be seen. She cuts school, lies in Dolores Park on the grass, the beards of the palm trees above her sway in the wind. The sky is a beaten-into-submission blue, clouds banished.

She begins to sleep in her mother's bed. Her mother takes her bed.

One night in January 1981, Mira wakes up with vise-like pains squeezing at her sides. She feels like her belly is a cement mixer. Pain runs up and down her back. The sheets beneath her are soaking wet.

"Mom," she calls. "Mom!" Her mother comes in. She is pale. She is already dressed.

"We're going to get through this," her mother says.

Her mother tells Mira to sit on the stoop while she pulls the car from the lot. Mira is surprised to hear someone groaning. She realizes it is her. Her belly is hard as a basketball. The car pulls up with a squeak and Mira crawls into the backseat. At the hospital, a nurse brings her ice chips and tells her to sit on the floor and make like she is taking a shit. "Use those muscles," the nurse says. Mira can't get it right—her dancer's muscles keep pulling up instead of pushing down. Her mother bites her lip and sits with her and counts and marks things on a paper and tells her to breathe. The nurse goes away and comes back and gives Mira a pill, and then the pain isn't so bad. She passes out and the next thing she knows is that she is in bed and something—something hot and wet—is coming out of her. She thinks at that moment—weirdly—that Maurice is coming out of her and he'd been in there the whole time, and she begins to cry. And then she hears another cry and she realizes that it *is* Maurice and that he *has* been in there the whole time and that she has finally gotten him out and she cries with the relief of it but then a minute later she thinks no! He's had something planted in me that can never be removed—claimed me in a way no one can ever touch—and this thing can always emerge whenever he wants—

Then she feels an unbearable pain, like a sun burning through her, and she screams.

The baby is small and very red, tiny and wrinkled and ugly.
She doesn't want to hold him. A nurse brings her applesauce and crackers and pulls down the shades, and she sleeps for a long time.

She remembers the other time, in the hospital, when she leaped, when she trusted too much. She remembers the girl with the gap-toothed smile, whose heart wasn't strong enough. Who is there to blame now? That what she and Maurice have done should have such consequences—hospital, nurse, a baby! When she was a child, she felt not like a child. Now she knows she is not a child and she feels more like a child than she ever has, like someone looking around at the dead bodies after a massacre, saying, "Did I do that? With my own two hands?" The reality of her own power to harm herself, to change things, to make things, descends on her. She hears a nurse's squeaky shoes outside the room. She will be leaving—going home tomorrow—but she must stay this night to make sure there are no complications.

The nurse pokes her head in, walks to her bed. She is carrying something. "Do you want to see him?" From the bundle in her arms comes a tiny noise, a baby sound, a gurgle, something human, something in-human. She turns her head away. This then was Kevin.

She begins to cry for the thousandth time. Something has been taken from her, something that protected her from other people's feelings about her. Some piece of her taken, along with the baby. The hole gapes, raw, and in it she can feel what other people feel about her. Before it was just Maurice and Mr. B—now it's everybody. It's not the child, who never belonged to her, but something else. She thinks of Maurice. She misses him. She misses her ballet body, how it made her feel strong.

The next morning, while her mother is out getting coffee, a lady wearing a blue suit and high heels comes to visit. She carries a folder with Mira's name on it. The lady says she has some papers for Mira to sign. The lady smells of shampoo. She thanks her for having the child. For giving joy to a childless couple. *Right on,* she says.

The lady hands her a folder and tells her to sign where she points. Her nails are long and pink and perfect. She has a file with Mira's name on it! It is that moment when Mira realizes she hates her name. This Mira who became Mirabelle, who became Maurice's Bella. Mira: too many sounds, too hopeful. Is it hope that gets you in trouble?

Mira begins to read the papers in her file. "Oh," says the lady, "you don't need to read it, honey. You just need to sign it." Mira glares at her.

She pages through the documents anyway. Attached to one of the forms is a photo of an old sad-faced couple. The address catches her eye—an address in Berkeley. The woman has brown bobbed hair and is smiling in front of a tree. The man has gray-blond hair and his arm around her. She is not pretty, not hopeful. When Mira looks up, she sees the blond lady averting her eyes and fiddling with the hem of her skirt.

Mira takes the pen and signs the papers. She signs over the too-small baby that she never holds. She signs over her mom's and her dad's privileges of ever knowing the child. She signs over Maurice, Mr. B, Tumkovsky, Danilova. What she is left with is unclear. Her signature is a girl's careful loops, a round circle hanging over the stalk of the *i.* How she would give anything to be the fat girl at SAB and not a girl with a saggy belly in a hospital room signing some papers held by a lady in a blue suit. Afterward, she is an empty pitcher. She might eventually be filled with anything—she doesn't care.

But then she changes her mind. She *does* care. She wants to be seen—one last time. She wants someone to know. That's why she does it—why she writes Maurice's name down next to hers on the line that reads: *father*.

CHAPTER 42

In the fall, when school starts again, Mira works like she never has before. In dog-eared workbooks, with sharpened no. 2 pencils, nudged into her desk, the smell of sesame noodles hanging in the air, pencil shavings collecting under her chair, she attends to her homework. She opens the math textbook, the history textbook, the science textbook, English. Because her body doesn't move like it did, she watches thoughts pile on top of one another, like rubber tires in a junkyard. They collect. For so long she was a limb of someone else's mind—following marching orders as they came out of Tumkovsky's mouth, looking for the light of response in Maurice's eyes (but is he dead?), waiting for Mr. B to come into the classroom and tilt his turtle head at her and say, *She's mine.*

San Francisco Superior Courthouse. Lives altered in the blink of an eye, the flick of a finger. In a dusty room with peeling-plaster walls, in front of a stern woman with close-cropped hair, Mira signs form after form. When she's done, she'll no longer have the name of a flower, the name of a bell. As if cauterizing a wound, she will cut the limb off: the hopeful girl, the yearning girl, the girl enthralled to beauty will become someone else. Beauty leads to a pain she has only begun to figure out how to survive. She signs over her too-hopeful name and gets a new one.

Kate Randell.

Kate, commonplace enough (yet she has never had a friend named Kate). Not too pretty, a name that does not ask you to watch it.

Randell, her mother's maiden name, the name she never really knew, the name of a blinding-white Connecticut house her mother left behind when she married her dad, a name her mother took back when she got to California and now owns again, along with her giant shell earrings.

A half hour later, she holds a photocopied piece of paper with her name on it. *This is me now. This is my new name.*

She takes her mother's hand and they walk to her rusty Peugeot. They walk right by the hippies selling dream catchers and don't even stop.

I open my eyes to the light pouring in. The sun stretches all across the bed, and I feel it making a design on my face. Felicia must have gotten in late—her door is closed. Alain's bag and coat are draped over the couch. I shower, dress, and head out, glad not to have to see them. I'm happy I don't have to try to put yesterday into words. Last night, trying it with my mother was strange enough.

Out on the street, it's still early for a Saturday in Manhattan. On Felicia's block, the new trees are sprouting hard-shelled buds that I feel a tender pity for—what will happen to them if this warm spell ends?

As I make my way to the West Side subway, I pass construction site after construction site. Up Seventh now to Columbus Circle. Bangs and slaps of boards on concrete. Piles of sandbags. This is New York, this struggling into activity. There is an old-fashioned eagerness to it all, a twentieth-century enterprise, a thing making itself.

I'm relieved to descend into the subway. New York subways: I've forgotten that particular smell of dirt and ammonia. It's an ancient industrial smell, so different from the mildew and food smell of the BART. The tracks start to rumble and the tunnel wind picks up. That old rising excitement, the quiver of air in front of me, and then the breakneck thunder of the train that shudders by inches from my face. Inside, the trains have the same submarine feel as when I was a kid. Metal, scouring fluorescent light, intimate anonymity. We barrel through the tunnels to Brooklyn. The knowledge of tons of water overhead and the sweat and the missing limbs of those who blasted tunnels in rock a hundred years ago.

Effortful, cheerful public service posters occupy the ad spaces. How hard the MTA is working to make things better! The Second Avenue line is on target! More Express buses! When I was a kid, these spaces were filled with ads for the lottery and skinny cigarettes, and they featured lots of girls in halter tops.

I watch a woman wearing high suede boots playing a game on her phone. The high-pitched sounds of fake gunfire reverberate over the clatter of the train and the station announcements. There is something primitive about this city, something honest and rapacious that hasn't changed.

I get out of the subway at the first stop in Brooklyn. It's the one nearest to my parents' old house. I pass through a park that used to be deserted. Now it's covered in AstroTurf and babies. Another blinding sky, this one blue, is pinned over the new MetroTech buildings. I pass several bars and upscale restaurants. All of this is new. Unlike Park Avenue, it's really changed here.

As I head toward the river, I remember how my life here was one of pure sensation, of cold winds from the East River in the winter, of heat coming from the sidewalks in summer. I remember a certain leaf that squishes underfoot and turns to a yellow pulp. We called them "stink bombs" and threw them at each other—though not me—I was too quiet and serious for that. But is that true? I don't know if I remember myself right at this age. It's a slippery part of my past, even more slippery than all that happened with Maurice. This is a different kind of loss of memory.

The houses are better kept up than I remember. Bricks repointed, shutters painted. Some houses even have metal plaques bearing nineteenth-century dates. House proud.

Now I'm on the block where we lived before my mother got California religion and moved out west and I moved in with Dad. Here it is—the house where we had all lived in my earliest memories. My father, slim and without glasses, planed and scraped the walls, he-roic to himself. He was younger than I am now. My mother in her bold colors and paisleys and kerchiefs.

I stand outside, looking. I find myself really looking, allowing myself, my eyes, to take in, to collect.

The house. In my memory, it's a dreary place locked under a gun-metal sky, in a state of incomplete transformation. But now the out-side is well cared for and cheery. The sidewalk in front of it is ironed flat. The weathervane on the roof is replaced with a satellite dish. The door has been painted a subdued gray-blue, a Martha Stewart folded-linens color. Outside, in the little yard—I see now it *was* a yard—someone has planted a magnolia tree. The magnolia is just starting its bloom, some early buds have even dropped a few petals onto a kid's Radio Flyer bike leaning against the house.

A warmth under my armpits spreads though my body. Something shifts, like the floor settling, and I clasp my hands together.

I take the well-swept stairs slowly, one at a time. In the planters on the top landing sprout begonias. On either side of the door are two Victorian-style gaslights that border on kitsch. The makeshift world my mother sought here is clearly gone.

I ring the doorbell. I've dressed carefully today in a tight-fitting black jacket, black pedal pushers, a red scarf, and Louboutin flats. Something jangles inside and the door opens as if someone were just waiting behind it. The woman who faces me is young, her skin a bright nut color, her hair curly, her eyes almond. A newer denizen of yuppie hood? She wears tight jeans and a Patagonia fleece vest over a T-shirt.

Behind her, the hallway spreads into shiny flooring and blank, freshly painted walls, and, beyond, into an expansive living room scattered with a few toys.

I tell her I used to live in this house many years ago, when I was a girl. "I'm in town for a conference and was just walking by," I say. She gives me a once-over and smiles. "Where do you live now?" she says. I hear an accent, a flat cheeriness and also a bit of a drawl.

"Ohio," I say.

"I'm from Columbus!" she says. She sticks out her hand. "Victoria."

"Kate," I say.

The door opens wider.

She is smiling in such a pleasant way that I'm taken off guard. I'm not sure what I expected, but not this—unfettered kindness. "Would you like for me to show you around?" says Victoria. "I have a few minutes until I need to pick up my son."

Is it really that easy to step back into your past? I thought I wanted this, but now I'm not sure. Part of me wants to grab her by the shoulders and shake her: *You must be more discerning. You must be careful! This city can burn you up. Don't trust it too much!*

But I don't. I can't. I'm caught in the grip of something stranger than I can say. What, I couldn't tell you. Only this: this strange, warm March week in New York when I have met my son. Kevin's face—his elfin face, precise energy, his emotional openness to me.

I follow her. I'm shocked when she leads me into the main room. It's totally unrecognizable. The parlor—as my parents liked to call it—is now a white rectangular box, all Bauhaus. It extends into an open kitchen. The whole back wall is windows. A couch and a few chairs float on a sea of oiled wool. A blank sail of walls. A few children's toys scattered about. "Sorry it's such a mess," Victoria says. A *mess?* I think about my parents with the endless work, never done, the splintering boards, mordant peeling plaster, their shipwreck of a house, their Victorian nightmare. It's impossible to imagine this is the same place.

Now she is leading me to the kitchen, which is all bamboo and metal. It reminds me of Felicia's, with one difference, this one is being used. I put my hand on the counter, a sheet of metal—at once industrial and kind of delicate—where there is a plastic cutting board, covered with onions being chopped. Everything is floating in a pool of strewn light. This diffuse light coats everything, just like at SAB. This entire city is being rebuilt out of glass.

Victoria stands by the counter. She's saying, "We really love these old Victorians but they can be so claustrophobic. We wanted the light and air. We were so happy to see this one. The owners before us did a gut renovation."

She picks up a workout bottle of water with lemon peels floating in it. She nods, gestures to the backyard. I can't really see out the back window into the yard because of all the light pouring in. "The people we bought it from put in a koi pond. I have to learn how to take care of it. I have to restock it this summer. It's not winterized or something. You have to actually move the fish." She looks at me earnestly. "Do they have that here? Fish storage for the winter?"

I laugh. "When we lived here the yard was just an old patch of grass," I say. "I lived here from when I was eight to about eleven. Only three years or so, before my parents split. It seems like a lifetime ago."

Is she lost in all this newness, like we were lost in the oldness?

Then, before I know what I'm doing, I'm heading upstairs. I see the same blankness and careful curating in every room I pass. Then I'm on the third floor, heading down the hallway. I'm standing at the door of my old room. It's now a workout room of some kind. There's a pile of sneakers in one corner and an elliptical machine in the other corner. And on the far wall, a large wall mirror. Against the other wall rests a Japanese screen leaning against the wall printed with words in a calligraphic font, *You Can Do It!*

I hear her coming up the stairs behind me. Her voice, with its polite twang, now agitated. "Excuse me. Excuse me," she's saying. I look around, at the Japanese screen, the workout machine, the mirror, the shoes. I remember Gary climbing up to *me,* my princess self waiting on the top, like it was a castle tower, waiting for my prince. He reaching *that same landing* that night the building lost power and he kissed me. I can see myself in the mirror across the room, trumpeting my fancy shoes. I want to take something. Maybe there is something in all this newness for me.

I turn around—she's coming down the hallway. She's clutching her water bottle. Her brow is furrowed. "Please, I have to go get my son. I can't leave with you in the house."

Victoria is younger than I will ever be again. She is rich, I am probably jobless. She is new, I am old. She has everything, I nothing. But there is something clean and new in my body that doesn't hate her.

There is nothing here for me. Nothing at all.

"We used to have a room full of junk here," I say. "There's no junk anymore."

I brush past Victoria. I walk the stairs like I'm descending from a high tower. I can hear her right behind me.

I was a fool to think it was the house. It was never the house, it was me, it was the city, wrapped in striving. It was my parents, it was Maurice, Mr. B, Tumkovsky, Danilova, the Russians coming from their distant land remaking us in the image of what they left. We were all caught in a vortex, the air on fire, the sirens ripping, and we danced so we didn't get burned. But everyone gets burned. Life burns.

I speed through the foyer, desperate to be back on the street, then jog down the stoop. I want to go to the water, to look at Manhattan. As I step onto the sidewalk, magnolia-strewn—as if the tree has pushed deeper into bloom in just the time I have been in the house— another memory returns. This one is different. It predates the selves of my wood-and-enamel box.

I remember. A concrete school yard. A half-inflated red ball burning toward the stone wall behind me, the splat of rubber on the wall, the thud of the ball on the ground. The gym teacher, a nervous man with a mouth twitch that showed his metal caps, yells, "Dodge!" The girls with braids squeal. The boys in T-shirts and Keds hurl spit. I'm back behind them all, not trying to win, but just ready, ready to move.

I stand backstage waiting. The lights in the auditorium dim. A hush falls over the audience. The series organizer takes the stage to introduce me—the final presenter in the New York Library for the Performing Arts spring lecture series, *Women in Dance Through the Ages: Goddesses, Sylphs, and Superheroes.*

The room is filled, I'm pleased to see. "For today's lecture," the organizer, George, says, "We are honored to have a special guest, one who straddles two worlds. Kate Randell trained as a dancer at the School of American Ballet in the late 1970s and early 1980s in the final era of the great George Balanchine's reign. Randell went on to get her PhD in dance history and performance theory from UC at Berkeley. As a feminist scholar, she has written about Balanchine aesthetics. Her book *Corporeality Subverted: The (Dis)embodied Feminine in the Aesthetic of George Balanchine, 1958–1982,* is published by Yale University Press. We are fortunate to have her as a scholar in residence at the New York Library for the Performing Arts this year."

A healthy burst of applause. "Thank you," I say and step to the lectern. The back of the room rises into dimness, but I can see the faces in front.

It's been a good year since I left Ohio. I have a nice apartment on the East Side. I have a few friends here, too—I've never needed many. Felicia, Alain, and Kevin, sort of. The beginning of something. Kevin and I have seen each other a half dozen times since I moved here. We seem to enjoy each other's company, which is a strange thing to say of one's son. But there it is.

An essay on Nijinska, "Modernism's Midwife," will be coming out in a few months. I seem to have found something in the administrative part of my residency, and there's talk of hiring me as a program director next year. Bernie was kind enough to give me a good recommendation (since this position includes no teaching). I'm starting to be in demand as a speaker. The extra income from the speaker's fees is what has allowed me to buy the shoes I'm wearing tonight, a gorgeous pair of red Manolo Blahniks. I have even been choreographing original work again, for the first time in years. I'm working on a group piece. I've found three young dancers and am renting a studio in Bushwick for our rehearsals.

Sioban withdrew her complaint before it was heard for review. I'll never know exactly why, but I do know that she started seeing a counselor at student services. We met once to discuss her "No Credit" in my class. She sat across from me and swiveled her body this way and that. She looked at me with her intense face, as if she were searching for something. I tried to hold my ground. She gave me a grimace that I realized was meant to be a smile. "I have abandonment issues," she said. She gathered her hair into a tighter ponytail. She had her sober scientist-student face on, pale except for her excitable acne scars. "But you *left,* and I didn't *die.*" She makes her grimace-smile again. "That's progress."

Yes, I thought, *you didn't die.* I wanted to say *thank you* to her but I couldn't. It was impossible. Still, I thanked her in my mind. I feel gratitude toward her. I will never forget the press of her long body into mine, and the taste of her, and how our moment together strangely spurred in me some tenderness for myself that I haven't lost.

I know why now. Why she, of all my students. It was the simplicity of her beautiful unencumbered form bringing me back to the time when the body—my body—was elemental. The world was elemental, too. I moved through it like each step mattered. And maybe because it did to *him.* To one man. Maurice. That was the gift he gave me.

Now at the lectern, I pick up my clicker and begin my talk: "We all know by now how the Balanchine myth begins—in 1946, Lincoln Kirstein freed George Balanchine from his duties as a choreographer of circus elephants and placed him in charge of the first great American ballet company. This became the New York City Ballet." A few knowing exclamations, and I say, "I see I'm among friends here. Balanchine has become a legend for modernizing ballet for America. Except for trotting out the party dresses for the annual *Nutcracker* bonanza (which could fund an entire NYC Ballet season), he eschewed the old stories and dramas. No *Giselle*. No *Swan Lake*. He is credited with inventing the 'Balanchine look'—the *pinhead* ballerina—hipless girls with long, lean limbs, and skin, as he once famously said, 'the color of a peeled apple.' In the Balanchine universe, the ballerina did not think. She became a vessel for his genius. Thus, the master chose his dancers young, driven only by an animal instinct to dance. She appears onstage in a simple unitard, perhaps a few feathers in her hair. She is no princess, no swan lady, she is simply female; she dances. 'Ballet is woman,' Balanchine opined. She is a chord on his piano, a drumstick to his drum. Balanchine looked for girls whose servitude to Terpsichore, goddess of dance, made her worthy of worship. But where to find her? And what did she look like? What did that mean for ballet in America?"

I click through my images of Balanchine history—the early years: Tanaquil Le Clercq in *Stars and Stripes*. When I reach the 1950s and Maria Tallchief, I pause. Look around the room. The faces are interested. I move on to more examples from the middle period of the 1960s, Balanchine's minimalist leotard-and-tights stage, severe lines and classical myths, his Martha Graham moment. I click to a screen of Suzanne Farrell and Peter Martins, at their most Olympian, in *Agon*. A few gasps at the extraordinary bodies on view. "But what of the Balanchine body?" I say. "Much has been made of it, but it bears reexamining from a feminist perspective. In Balanchine's choreography, no longer was the woman pirouetted on the arm of the prince. She stepped forward on her own by embodying her own physical power. It was no longer sublimated." I switch to the famous photo of Allegra Kent leaping with abandon in *Seven Deadly Sins*.

"Kirstein wrote, 'American young girls were not sylphides; they were basketball champions and queens of the tennis court, whose proper domain was athletics. They were long-legged, long-necked, slim-hipped, and capable of endless acrobatic virtuosity. The drum majorettes, the cheerleader of the high-school football team of the thirties filled Balanchine's eye. . . . The pathos and suavity of the dying swan, the purity and regal behavior of the elder ballerina, were to be replaced by a raciness and alert celerity which claimed as its own the gaiety of sport and the skills of the champion athlete.'"

I click and the final image comes up—a sixteen-year-old Darci Kistler in class leaping, her colt's legs flying apart, her wholesome face gleaming. I like to leave this one up on the screen. While I finish out my presentation, I let them drink in her bright exertion. Do they notice her half-lidded eyes, her slack cheeks—the shock that comes with seeing someone so far off the ground looking like they are asleep? She looks as if she were sleepwalking.

I'm nearing the home stretch. This kind of lecturing is not really like teaching—it's more like the performances of the old days—the warm lights, and the knowing darkness and intimacies of anonymous faces in the audience.

The applause splits the silence—it feels real, enthusiastic.

Next is the Q&A. They raise the lights, and a microphone is brought into the aisle. The curator of the Balanchine archives asks a question about the images, a graduate student asks me to clarify a point from my book, someone asks a question about dance notation systems that has nothing to do with my talk and doesn't seem to really have a question in it. Just when I am wondering if anyone really was listening at all, a wisp of a girl steps up to the microphone. She wears her hair long, her feet are splayed duck-like, and she is dressed in cutoff jean shorts and a T-shirt over tights and espadrilles. She's clearly a bunhead, and I'm amazed that she is here, at my lecture. She has a soft voice. *What do you remember about*—I have to strain to hear her halting words—*being a student at SAB when*—here she fades out again—*Mr. B was still alive.* She says this like a statement, not a question.

It all comes back to me then: this feeling of flying through the air, Mr. B saying: "Don't think—do!" And the Tchaikovsky music behind us as we flew across the floor, the long narrow lockers and the averted stares of the other girls, the skylights, the cracked and broken pointe shoes, the blisters and calluses, the scent of Mr. B's ballerinas in the elevator, the feeling of becoming something irrefutable, becoming beautiful, defying life.

I smile. "It was a long time ago, another world. But you're a bunhead—right—I mean, a dancer?" Laughter from the good-size crowd that remains.

"As a student at SAB, I learned from Mr. B, as we called him, the great power of my body, but I did not have the ability to understand that power. I loved going to class because I loved to feel what my body was capable of doing. It amazed me. But when it was over—in my case, I had to leave the school for external circumstances—it was gone. Maybe I wrote my book to get it back."

"So you don't hate him—Mr. B?" I'm shocked that she would ask this of an academic. The bizarre simplicity of it.

As a child, I had too much power, a strange power, the power of the object. It is passive, but it is total. When I hear the gorgeous notes of a child pianist or the lyrical call of a child violinist, I think, *poor child;* I think, *lucky child.* Now that I am a grown person—a *grown-up*—I see what we desire from them. I think of Maurice saying, "You were bright, you shone." It's like pebbles of fire. They eat it and they burn.

So you don't hate him?

But that is what some of us want and must have: to burn, to burn up, *to expire in flame.* I see an image of the earliest ballerinas who donned their shin-length tulle tutus to evoke the spirits of the other-world at the all-too-common risk of catching fire in the gas lamps at the edge of the stage. Their offering was to make themselves combustible. And many of them died. Maurice was the first to tell me that. But it was later confirmed in the headlines I found in microfiche while researching an article on the earliest ballerinas: *Another ballerina goes up in flames, suffers third-degree burns.*

Yes, I loved him as only a girl could love him with stars in her eyes, with dreams in her head. And he gave me ashes.

But first he showed me the fire. And for a moment it burned. And I stood in it, it was all around me.

I hear myself saying, "No, I don't hate Mr. B."

I look at this young girl and I feel like I'm seeing myself thirty years ago. Her hair is pulled back, her eyes are hooded, her cheeks without blemish, her body articulated and slight. She has the sinewy ethereal quality of a serious dancer. I know how hard she has worked to obtain it. Now I'm up here on this podium, shifting in my red high heels and black suit. What do we have in common? That girl is still in me. She is *back* in me. And as I open my mouth I find that I can't say what I've planned. This year away from academia, getting to know my son, has been like a long sleep that has left me refreshed. I feel like I have finally woken up.

What of that time in my life? It is finally past. The guilt is past. And the straining after beauty. But do I regret it? I find, with surprise, that I can't.

I give her a gift I never thought I could. I say, "I loved him as only a girl could love him. With stars in her eyes, with dreams in her head," I say.

I smile and I mean it. I close my laptop and pack up my things.

ACKNOWLEDGMENTS

I owe a great debt to many people for bringing this novel to fruition and helping to bring it into the world. Gratitude to my terrific agent, PJ Mark, for his sustaining vision and perceptive advice, and my brilliant editor, Terry Karten, for her confidence in me as a writer and uncompromising belief in this novel's potential. I am fortunate to have found them both. They have made this book more than I ever thought it could be. Thanks also to Shelly Perron for her keen eye and attention to the logic of my fictional worlds. I am also grateful to my many readers of the various drafts: Jacob Molyneux, whose perceptive readings gave this book a focus, and Jean Kwok, without whom it's safe to say this book would not have happened, and to my mother, Nancy Wilson, whose steadfast encouragement and keen literary sensibility have made all the difference. Marya Spence, who pulled it from the slush pile, and Tori Marlan, Joy Katz, Zoe Zolbrod, Eliza Amon, Samantha McFerrin, Natasha Chuk, Travis Holland and the Knight-Wallace Fellows writers workshop, Len Neufeld, and Randee Falk for all their insights and generous gifts of time. And to Jill Dearman, a great coach. To my wonderful husband, Josh Neufeld, my first reader, and with me every step of the way, thank you.

Special thanks to my advisers and interpreters of the dance world, whose insights (especially into SAB) helped give this book a depth and richness that augmented my own dance experience: Jennifer

Scanlon, Maydelle Liss, Karina Beznicki, Carolyn Hall, and Laura Flowers. For a window into academia and dance, I am grateful to UCLA professor Lionel Popkin and University of Michigan professor Beth Genne.

For granting me time for writing, I am deeply grateful to the Patricia Rowe Willrich Fellowship at Stanford University, the Provincetown Fine Arts Work Center Fellowship, Byrdcliffe Art Colony, and The Corporation of Yaddo.

I am also grateful to my teachers and mentors, from whom I've learned so much and whose words have resonated through the years: Tobias Wolff, John L'Heureux, Elizabeth Tallent, Gilbert Sorrentino, Daniel Orozco, Jaimy Gordon, Roger Skillings, the Stegner Fellows, Amy Davis, and Charles and Julia Eisendrath.

Though this book is fiction and I myself lived—and danced—as a child in the late 1970s and 1980s, the following books especially helped me fill out my understanding and gave me historical context: *Balanchine: A Biography* by Bernard Taper; *Balletomania: Then and Now* by Arnold Haskell; *Winter Season: A Dancer's Journal* by Toni Bentley; *Apollo's Angels: A History of Ballet* by Jennifer Homans; *Victorian Ballet-girl: The Tragic Story of Clara Webster* by Ivor Guest; *But First a School: The First Fifty Years of the School of American Ballet* by Jennifer Dunning; *Dance: A Short History of Classic Theatrical Dancing* by Lincoln Kirstein; *Once a Dancer: An Autobiography* by Allegra Kent; and the absolutely terrific documentary *Ballets Russes*. As well, repeated visits to the dance collection at the New York Public Library for the Performing Arts provided invaluable insights. I am indebted to all of the dance scholars, reviewers, and dance lovers who have transmitted their curiosity and passion through words, have written about dance, a most ephemeral art, and in doing so have helped me understand just a little bit more about the fascinating history that I brushed against as a child. My deep gratitude to them all.

I stole liberally from my childhood in creating Mira's fictional world. I am so grateful for the love and support of my whole family, and especially my own wonderful parents, Nancy and Robert Wilson, for giving me a childhood of abiding love and security, so different from Mira's. Thank you to Martha Rosler for inspiration. Sandhya Nankani for teaching me the ways of a detective. And Warren Wilson for saving those files. Also: Jill Verrillo, Julia Targ, Patricia Flynn, Joan Arnold, Sarah Dohrmann, Susan Karwoska, Katherine Burger, Cheryl Lu-Lien Tan, Ashley van der Grinten, and Creative Conversations. And my wonderful daughter, Phoebe, for patiently understanding my long attention to this book.

P.S.

About the author

2 Meet Sari Wilson

About the book

5 Sari Wilson on the Physicality of Dance, the "Normal World" v. the Ballet World, and More

Insights,
Interviews
& More . . .

Read on

14 Have You Read?

Recommended Material for Those Interested in Ballet

Meet Sari Wilson

© Elena Seibert

SARI WILSON grew up in a Victorian brownstone in Brooklyn Heights, New York City. When her parents bought the house, it had a coal-burning stove and a dirt floor. Her family would spend the following two decades renovating the house. Wilson was a childhood dancer, studying ballet seriously from age eight to fifteen. She began at Neubert Ballet Theater, a once-storied Carnegie Hall studio, and performed with Neubert Children's Ballet. Wilson went on to study at Harkness Ballet and won a scholarship to Eliot Feld's New Ballet School. After Wilson left the ballet world, she studied and performed modern dance with Stephan Koplowitz and at Oberlin College, where she majored in history and minored in dance.

During college, surgery for a dance-related injury effectively ended her dream of dancing professionally.

As Wilson wrote in an essay for *Catapult*:

> *The news was devastating for me. Dancing had been my creative life. I was more at home at the dance studio than anywhere else. I had more leotards and tights than actual clothes. For a dancer, as we all know, the body is everything: the instrument, the vehicle. The body transcribes, translates. Mine had betrayed me. Muscles are one thing, but bones are the very nature of the thing. I had lost a mode of expression, an identity, a sense of power. I had lost something like a language.*

After her recovery and a mind-expanding year abroad, Wilson began writing creatively. She graduated and spent a few years working in magazine journalism and a few more traveling in Southeast Asia and living abroad. Back in the States, now living in Chicago, Wilson worked in journalism and spent all her spare time writing short stories and taking writing classes. She won a Wallace Stegner Fellow at Stanford, where she held the Patricia Rowe Willrich Fellowship. Wilson was also awarded an emerging writers fellowship in fiction from the Fine Arts Work Center in Provincetown, Massachusetts. These fellowships, three years in all, allowed her to immerse herself in the craft of writing and begin the story that would become *Girl Through Glass*. After moving back to Brooklyn, ▶

3

Meet Sari Wilson *(continued)*

Wilson has held various editor jobs for more than a decade while developing her fiction. She was supported in the writing of *Girl Through Glass* by residencies at Byrdcliffe Arts Colony and from the Corporation of Yaddo.

Wilson's short fiction has appeared in literary journals such as *Agni, The Oxford American,* and *Slice,* and has been nominated for a Pushcart Prize. She is the coeditor of *Flashed: Sudden Stories in Comics and Prose*, an anthology of flash fiction. Wilson lives in Brooklyn, a few miles from where she grew up, with her husband, the nonfiction cartoonist Josh Neufeld, and their daughter.

Author, age 10. Photo by Robert Wilson.

Sari Wilson on the Physicality of Dance, the "Normal World" v. the Ballet World, and More

Originally published in Slice magazine in a somewhat different format. Interview by Elizabeth Blachman. Reprinted by permission.

BLACHMAN: *In some ways writing and dance seem to be antithetical—dance is ephemeral and resists capture, and writing arrests images and makes them concrete and tangible. But in your book you have wonderful passages like, "the stretch in her legs, the rising feeling under the breastbone, the white space of flame in her head." How did you find a way to put the physicality of dance on the page?*

WILSON: This was really my goal when I started this novel. I wanted to merge my two loves—dance and writing—to see if movement could have a written language. I felt good when I would stumble on a phrase that for me described that very evanescent feeling of movement in the body—for example, when Mira is doing her barre and she says she is learning how "to walk in that special dancer way—like a bright, fearful bird." This felt right and true. Dance was a part of my life I cordoned off from other aspects of my life—my "school life," my social life. It was a ▶

Sari Wilson on the Physicality of Dance, the "Normal World" v. the Ballet World, and More (*continued*)

kinesthetic reality, and it had its own vocabulary, in sequenced movements. When I left the world of dance, I mourned the loss of that space and that language, that relationship to art and self-expression. When I finally began to write about it, it seemed like I could get a little of it back. I agree that dance resists capture, but for me the effort to bridge the divide was ultimately very rewarding.

BLACHMAN: *How much of the dance world you have built for Mira is similar to the dance world in which you grew up?*

WILSON: I grew up in Brooklyn in the 1970s and 1980s, like Mira, and I studied at a studio in Carnegie Hall called Neubert Ballet Institute, a sweet, storied place (there's a Facebook group for dancers who trained there!), and part of the novel is drawn a lot from that experience. It was run by a kind, magical woman named Christine Neubert who brought the storytelling part of ballet alive for her students. At the time, Carnegie Hall was a unique place, filled with live/work spaces for artists, many of them European expats and eccentrics—it was a kind of down-at-the-heels bohemia that was filled with mystery and joy.

Then, I moved on to Harkness Ballet and was on scholarship at the Feld Ballet, but those parts of it aren't really in the novel. Mira, unlike me, goes to the famous School of American Ballet where the great Russians held sway. George Balanchine was like a god in those days—his aesthetics dominated the dance world and conditioned all of our dreams and desires. So I had Mira go there, to the center of the ballet world at that time. The interviews and the research I did to build this part of the dance world really transformed the way I saw my past and the whole dance world of that time. So Mira's world is really my world, the dance world I grew up in, but she moves differently in it and goes places I never went.

BLACHMAN: *I love how you capture the violence, decay, and gritty underbelly that are part of ballet. The destruction and the beauty live side by side. It's perhaps the part of ballet that Mira is resisting when she says that Degas's* Little Dancer *is not beautiful. Did you encounter resistance or surprise from readers or anyone else who wanted to ignore that aspect of ballet and focus only on its beauty?*

WILSON: Yes, Mira is too invested in the beautiful aspects of ballet, and there is a strain in that. That's why *Little Dancer* disturbs her. Degas was interested in exposing both the grittiness and even the exploitation of the ballet dancers of ▶

Sari Wilson on the Physicality of Dance, the "Normal World" v. the Ballet World, and More *(continued)*

his era (most of them were very poor—prostitution and ballet dancing overlapped). Mira is looking for ballet to protect her from the insecurities and cruelties of her world, as an escape into beauty and perfection. She can't see, doesn't want to see, is threatened by, a more complex historical picture.

As for readers, people actually seem enthralled with the undertow of the ballet world; they can't seem to get enough of it. I really wanted to honor the lives of dancers in this novel. I wanted to portray a complex picture, the passions and joys, as well as the hardships and challenges. And in fact, dancers—and more broadly people in the performing world—have been my most passionate readers. They see their experience, both passions and sufferings, reflected in the novel.

BLACHMAN: *Would you talk about how you did the research for* Girl Through Glass? *Are there things that you learned as you researched that made you look at the dance world in an unexpected way?*

WILSON: I spent some years unpacking my memories and weaving them into a fictional world that was consistent with my memories of the ballet world and the lost world of New York City in the 1970s. At a certain point I became constrained by my own memories, so I started interviewing women I danced with, some of whom had gone on to become professional dancers. I wanted a range of experiences and perspectives on the dance world. Then I realized I needed a greater historical knowledge of ballet, and I started reading and studying. I spent many days in the library, and at one point ended up auditing a college seminar on Balanchine. It was so exciting to be discovering the intellectual side of something I knew only experientially. I became particularly interested in the stories of the Russian expatriates who dominated the dance scene at the time. What that older generation had survived—war, revolution, exile, extreme poverty— really changed my sense of things. I couldn't imagine those realities, yet they were real to these powerful figures who shaped our dance world. All this research gave my childhood memories the feeling of a kind of brush with powerful historical forces that spoke to another land and time.

BLACHMAN: *Would you talk about why you chose to include the character of Maurice in the story?*

WILSON: Maurice emerged out of my writing—like a storybook character— both magical and creepy. I understood that there needed to be an adult from the ballet world who Mira could see—and who could see her, and her passion, in ▶

ways she doesn't even know she wants to be seen. And Maurice carries both threat and the promise of grace. He's an amalgamation of a lot of things. He is based partly on the character of Drosselmeyer in *The Nutcracker*, who offers Marie both growth and power—but there's something dangerous associated with this growth. Their relationship explores how the rules in the "normal world" don't really apply in the ballet world. As a child dancer, I had a split consciousness. The rules of the "normal world" were concerned with equality and fairness. The rules of the ballet world were harsher, and privileged single-mindedness and competitiveness, and demanded a total commitment to art-making on the part of all—adults and children.

Maurice also grew out of my historical research. I stumbled upon accounts of "balletomanes"—mostly men—who were ballet fanatics. In at least one famous instance, they made soup out of their favorite ballerina's pointe shoes and then drank it! They usually pledged their allegiance to a specific ballerina and were given bits of tulle, something from a costume, in return. This obsessiveness captured my imagination, and I wanted to explore this type of fan.

BLACHMAN: *There are so many images in your novel about eyes: the power of* *the dancer and the watcher. As the prepubescent Mira lies to her parents to dance for the much older man in his apartment every Friday night, does she have any power, or does he have it all?*

WILSON: Those images emerged organically too. As I tried to understand Mira, I realized Mira's deepest need is to be *seen*. Not loved, *seen*. And as a dancer, she needs a watcher to share—to witness—her ecstatic moments of dance. When I realized how Mira's desire to be seen affects her choices, the narrative started coming into focus—sometimes in disturbing ways. But being a performer is not like being a writer—the audience for a dancer is alive, present, can be sensed and responded to in real time. Performing is an exchange, a dialogue in time and in space through movement, sight, and sound.

Of course, I also thought about the "male gaze," and I was aware, especially with the history of ballet, of this necessary interpretation. At the same time I was really interested in a broad, layered exploration of that desire—to see and be seen.

I do think Mira has power in their relationship. It was very important to me that Mira be an actor in her own life. She is physically strong, whereas he is hampered. She chooses him, or believes she does. Remember, she follows him the first time they officially meet. ▶

Sari Wilson on the Physicality of Dance, the "Normal World" v. the Ballet World, and More (*continued*)

I remember reading *Lolita* when I was in my twenties and hurling it across the room. It angered me so much. I hated that we were in the mind of this older man obsessed with a young girl; I wanted to be in *her* point of view, I wanted to see him through *her* eyes. I took that as a challenge in this novel: could I write from a girl's point of view who sees herself, who feels herself— perhaps misguidedly—as powerful?

They each are damaged and needy and searching for some kind of healing. So in that way they come together in their mutual need.

BLACHMAN: *There's something so powerful in your construction of the two timelines in your novel and the way they seem to converge upon each other—with Mira in the past sailing toward the present and Kate in the present tumbling back toward her past. How did you construct the two timelines? Did you always plan to write the novel forward and backward at the same time?*

WILSON: I wrote the Mira storyline first but the novel didn't feel done. Then, after my daughter was born, I started getting this other voice—a much older woman's voice. I spent some more years writing the Kate storyline. As I wrote Kate's story, I interwove it with Mira's. This was when the book began to finally take shape—Kate's storyline allowed room for an adult perspective on the past. And somehow it helped me edit and find clarity in all of the pages I had for Mira. And then I spent some more time ordering and reordering the interweaving of the storylines, which involved making *many* charts with *lots* of columns. I was trying to understand how the two storylines worked together psychologically; I wanted to make *Girl Through Glass* a compelling read and also a psychological journey through time and trauma and healing.

I think we are all haunted by our pasts. They continue to shape us in conscious (and unconscious) ways. And it's not until Kate is called back to face her past, to look at it through the eyes of an adult, that she can be free to begin reinventing herself—not moving on, but moving forward. ❧

Ballet Girls, 1978. Photo by Robert Wilson

Have You Read?
Recommended Material for Those Interested in Ballet

READING

Apollo's Angels: A History of Ballet
BY JENNIFER HOMANS

Balletomania: Then and Now
BY ARNOLD HASKELL

Balanchine: A Biography
BY BERNARD TAPER

Winter Season: A Dancer's Journal
BY TONI BENTLEY

Once a Dancer: An Autobiography
BY ALLEGRA KENT

Holding On to the Air: An Autobiography
BY SUZANNE FARRELL

VIEWING

Ballet Russes,
DIRECTED BY DANIEL GELLER
AND DAYNA GOLDFINE

Afternoon of a Faun: Tanaquil le Clerc,
DIRECTED BY NANCY BUIRSKI